MEL SMITH

NAM

The Story of a Generation

A NOVEL

FSP
FIRST STEPS
PUBLISHING

NAM, *The Story of a Generation*
a novel by Mel Smith

Copyright ©2017 Mel Smith

First Edition ©2017

Published by
First Steps Publishing
105 Westwind Street, PO Box 571
Gleneden Beach, Oregon 97388-0571
541-961-7641

Library of Congress Control Number: 2017949341

Cover Design by Suzanne Fyhrie Parrott
Formatted for Publication by First Steps Publishing

ISBN - 978-1-937333-31-7 (hbk)
ISBN - 978-1-937333-40-9 (pbk)
ISBN - 978-1-937333-41-6 (epub)

10 9 8 7 6 5 4 3 2 1

Printed in the
United States

For my children,
their generation,
and all the generations to follow

Contents

1998

The aluminum grandstand felt as though the fires of Hell burned below. Adding to the misery of those watching the game was a hot, pervasive wind blowing from the south. We sat and sweat and swore in the shade. Shade...a visualization of cooling relief that held none on a day set up better for sno-cones and splashing in fountains than watching baseball. It was a day for handheld fans and white hankies, but this was 1998, and such practical novelties had been abandoned by our generation. We were the Baby Boomers, and we were cool. Way too cool. So we cursed and wiped our brows on shirt sleeves and sweat like pigs.

Flags flitted over a field of green grass confined by traditional, measured white chalk lines. The players were all in clean, bright uniforms with batting gloves stuffed in back pockets. They played with new balls, aluminum bats, and gorgeous gloves that cost a hundred dollars. They wore body armor at the plate and stepped out between pitches, just like the pros. Our generation had fostered this. It was the very picture of everything we had wanted as kids.

Next to me was a sad, shriveled example of my generation named Joe Wills. The once strapping, toe-headed six-foot-four army sergeant had diminished over the years. Skin hung in a prunish, liver-spotted pile and he repeatedly coughed while smoke from his cigarette curled around his pock-marked face.

Beside him, I looked like a young man, though he was just a couple years older. Evidently, healthy living and good genes paid dividends. I hadn't shrunk from my six-foot height, and though wrinkles were starting to show, I certainly exhibited no aging spots and just a speck of gray in my sandy brown hair. Not that it mattered to Joe.

"You know...it could all happen again," Joe said.

"What?" I responded, noticing his eyes hadn't left me though his son stood at the plate looking to hit for the cycle. Joe wasn't into the game at the moment.

"Nam," Joe said, taking a drag on his cigarette. "It could all happen again."

His gaze drifted back to the diamond, but those cloudy-blue, unfocused eyes looked beyond the field as smoke swirled his face from the ever-present coffin nail.

I groped for understanding.

"You mean...uh, something *like* Nam? Another war like Vietnam? In our time?"

"Yeah. That's exactly what I mean."

"Huh...no, I don't think so," I said immediately. "I think Desert Storm proved that the politicians and the military got the message. Quick in and out with lots of force. That's the way to fight now."

"Yeah? What about Somalia...Bosnia...troops committed haphazardly halfway around the world with little regard or understanding for what's going on there?"

"Well, that's hardly Nam, Joe. I mean... for one thing, there was broad international support and good cause for each. It was the right thing to do."

"You think so, Mark?"

"Yeah, that's what I think."

The conversation had come in a rush, and now Joe was mute once again. I turned my gaze to the field just as Joe's son slammed another pitch to the wall. I jumped up with the other fans to cheer him as he sped to second. He'd done it; hit for the cycle. We applauded, and Joe again tipped his hat to his fawning fans.

As we sat, Joe spoke again.

"Those conflicts are just a warm up," he said. "Just the beginning. Like a wounded giant who's healed...flexing his muscles and testing himself. Politicians never learn, Cam. Some cowboy like Johnson will come along one day and totally disregard the hard-learned lessons of Nam...all the bloodletting...for the thrill of seeing his army roll into combat to settle some misbegotten notion. A whole new generation of kids, just like my son there, could find themselves in the same shit...fighting a useless, endless conflict for all the wrong reasons in a country that doesn't want us there. The politicians who never fought never get it. Yes, indeed, it could all happen again, my friend."

August 16, 1948

Red River Delta, Vietnam

The humid, cool air caressed his skin in the quiet cover of night; his eyes resting while wide open. The occasional muted call of the delta birds was soft and calming. As long as he could remember, Le Van Dat had risen early to have this all to himself. He would miss many things about his home, but few as much as the comfort of predawn in the delta.

The wrenching sadness of leaving the only home he had ever known with the real prospect of never seeing it again was not nearly enough to keep him here. The place was fouled by the presence of their French occupiers, and Le Van Dat could not abide it one more day.

Soldiers seemed to fill the small hut, with many more outside. A French lieutenant, so young that acne still pocked his face, strolled between tiny rooms like an emperor with his arms clasped behind him. The Vietnamese couple and their four children huddled against a wall in the kitchen area. The lieutenant paused, looking them over with an indifferent air before noticing a shelf holding spices and herbs for cooking. Taking his knife out, he began poking around in the boxes. Tipping one off the shelf where it spilled onto the mats covering an earthen floor, he heard a sharp intake of surprise, maybe despair, from the peasant mother. He stuck the blade in another box and then, while looking purposely at her, tipped the box onto the floor. The woman quickly looked away.

Seeing this, the couple's second oldest son, Le Van Dat, was angered to a tipping point—such insolent disregard and waste! The French cared little for the Vietnamese beyond their servitude. It had always been and likely would always be their life in the rice paddies.

"Stop this! What are you doing?" Dat demanded in Vietnamese as his parents recoiled in shock at their son's outburst.

The lieutenant tilted his head, surprised. He turned to his Vietnamese corporal for translation.

The man smiled and then replied casually in French, "He commands you to stop...said it in a threatening way, too."

The lieutenant took the knife and swept the entire shelf's contents onto the floor, the tiny tins bouncing across the mats and ending up at the family's feet.

"Why?" Dat shouted, stepping forward. "What have we done to deserve this?"

The lieutenant tilted his head to his interpreter.

"He just called you an asshole," the corporal chuckled.

The lieutenant stepped forward, grabbed Dat's shirt, pulling him close while placing the bayonet under his chin.

"I should shove this into your brain, you little shit. Sergeant, bind this man. We'll take him back to base for questioning."

"Lieutenant, Lieutenant...," the aged sergeant sighed, "just... well, look at him. He's a little shit...blowing off steam, for chrissake."

"He's probably Viet Minh. They take 'em at any age."

"This kid's what? Twelve? C'mon, Lieutenant, the weekend's already started. Do we really need to deal with this?"

The lieutenant hesitated, twisting Dat's shirt in frustration and then pushing him away. Dat stumbled and landed at the feet of his frightened family. Undeterred, he quickly stood up, defiantly clenching his fists at his side while glaring at the officer.

"This is why we hate you," Dat spat. "You dishonor us every day. What right do you have to be here?"

"Corporal?" the lieutenant asked.

"Ohh...looks like he wants to fight you, Lieutenant."

Now the lieutenant laughed and flicked his hand at Dat's face, but Dat deftly dodged the blow.

"That's a good one," the lieutenant said, "you...fighting me. I should kick your ass."

The officer hesitated, then, "Okay, let's get out of here, Sergeant. The stink is starting to bother me."

Dat could speak French from the time he was seven but had played the ignorant peasant for his own purposes. The duplicity of the lieutenant's Vietnamese translator that day had angered him more than the arrogant Frenchman; a Vietnamese national working with his oppressors to abuse a countryman! It was intolerable, treasonous.

Dat carried on his shoulder a bag of bare essentials gathered silently in the dark as his family slept. The first hint of dawn faintly glowed on the horizon now; the muted promise of searing heat that would soon envelop the delta. He could just make out the shapes of the huts and knew the fourth on the right held Lee Nah and her family. A stab of guilt at the thought of her made him ashamed, and he looked away. He had known and loved her as long as he could remember. She was an extraordinary girl he had thought would make a good wife. Leaving her was most difficult; facing her would be impossible.

Standing just over five feet, Dat had garnered the attention of many of the village girls. Well-developed shoulders and legs, from years working in the fields, accentuated his slender frame. Yet, beneath his unruly black hair sat a pleasant, though unremarkable face. A local peasant that would otherwise go unnoticed if not for his brilliant, perfectly white teeth and effortless confidence—a combination of intelligence and purpose that caused local girls to swoon—all except Lee Nah.

A natural beauty, she exuded confidence beyond what was usual for the delta, and Dat found her spirit exhilarating. She exuded strength and purpose; a quality in a woman not appreciated by many. Yet, despite her appeal to Dat, he knew Lee Nah to be somewhat arrogant, believing her physical beauty would deter any other from capturing Dat's heart.

At the sound of padding feet in the stillness, he turned and looked up the path, startled to see the dim silhouette of a figure coming toward him. An encounter of any kind was not a part of the plot. A silent and unseen departure—a somewhat gallant disappearance with no witnesses—was what he had carefully planned. Now, someone would see him; tell the village they had been witness to Dat fleeing in the night. This was unacceptable. He slowly slipped back into the sheltering jungle that bordered the path and remained still.

As the figure came closer, he could make out the distinct shape of a woman carrying water on a yoke. Even in light reduced to shadows Dat recognized the graceful figure of Lee Nah as she walked past. His heart leapt, and he quickly covered his mouth to avoid calling out. As she silently vanished in the gloom, tears made their way down Dat's cheeks; it seemed God's last temptation. Embarrassed, he quickly brushed the tears from his face. He would not be deterred.

Dat was leaving the Delta to join his heroes, Ho and Giap, in the mountainous northern reaches of the Viet Bac where the Viet Minh had organized their rebellion. He was sixteen, and he could wait no longer. After a thousand years of humiliating occupation, the Vietnamese were fighting the French, just the latest of their centuries of tormentors.

Being second born, there was nothing for him to inherit, which meant he must find his own way. So, on that aspect, leaving his family was easy; he had brothers to fill his roll on the farm. His only obstacle was Lee Nah. He considered sharing his intentions and taking her with him; it could not happen. Her family needed her in the fields; her loss would be critical and, at any rate, there was no place in war for women!

Shouldering regret beyond his years, Dat stepped from the shadows and started up the path. He had a long way to travel this day.

August 16, 1948

Helena, Montana

Half a world away in Helena, Montana, Skip Cameron, a young carpenter wringing calloused hands, anxiously paced the waiting room of St. John's Hospital. Skip stopped at the window and looked down again at the darkened street with the one streetlight illuminating the yellow '42 Packard convertible beneath it. It was likely a doctor's car; maybe their own doctor. A pair of headlights brightened the street coming toward the hospital. The approaching car was weaving back and forth, nearly hitting a car on the far side before overcorrecting and slamming the yellow Packard. Skip looked on as the car continued down the street and disappeared around the corner. *This is not a good omen,* he thought.

A flash of lightning illuminated the sky silhouetting Mount Helena in the unsettled air. He turned and paced toward the gray-ish-green hallway with its one bright globe, sending his shadow back into the room as he walked alone.

His wife, Joan, had been in delivery for more than two hours. From the worried looks of the nurses he saw come and go, Skip sensed something was not right.

Joan was less than two years removed from her last visit to St. John's, a visit culminating in a stillborn death and immense heartbreak. Joan had been crushed, and they had not spoken of having more children before she became pregnant again. With it came a revival of hope for the couple. Joan had stopped smoking and all drinking, including her favorite Great Falls Select beer. She would take every precaution to see this child was born healthy.

Now, like a haunting reminder, Skip sensed another struggle taking place beyond the gray swinging doors and quietly prepared himself for the worst. He thought of praying to God, but he and Joan were nonbelievers. Still, Skip fired off a quick one, just in case. "God...," he said, his hand holding him from the wall as he bowed his head, "please...if you have any compassion."

As dawn crept in silently from the room's window, the swinging door banged open to allow Joan's doctor into the hallway. He stopped, searching the waiting room, and saw the man bent over in a chair, his head in his hands. "Skip!" he shouted as he removed a sweaty cap and mask. "Congratulations! You have another boy. Born at five-oh-three," the doctor said. "Mother and son are doing fine."

Skip grabbed his knees and let out the breath he seemed to have been holding all night.

"There, now. You okay?" the doctor said. "Touch and go for a while, all right. The delivery was difficult. We were lucky to save the little guy...had the umbilical cord wrapped around his neck...." The doctor demonstrated "...and came out blue as a blotter. Helped himself, though...had his hand up between the cord and his neck... can you believe it? Like he was fightin' for his life. I have a feelin' you've got one helluva little scrapper there.

"Your wife's just plumb wore out. She'll need time to recover... but she's happy, too."

"Thank God," Skip said. "They're both okay, though?"

"Like I said, it was a struggle. They'll be fine. You can see her soon. So, another boy, Skip...what're you gonna name the lad?"

"He's Mark. Marcus Joseph Cameron," the father said with much pride—and relief.

August 16, 1948

Fullerton, California

Late afternoon, on a busy construction site, a large bulldozer wrenched well-rooted orange trees from the grudging soil as an earth mover gobbled big scoops of rich soil to be deposited elsewhere in the doomed orchard. Nearby, a prewar, tin-can-of-a-trailer rested next to fuel pumps and spare machine parts. A second, unoccupied earth mover sat parked alongside the trailer, its engine idling. The open trailer house door, thrown wide to make way for a man in a hurry, swung in the dust and Santa Ana wind.

In the only bedroom at the back of the trailer, a young woman lay on a bed, moaned, and thrust her hips upward.

"Yeah, baby. That's right. Push now. Push, baby," George Johnson encouraged his wife, Clara.

"The baby's crowning," the midwife said.

"Holy mackerel, there he is," George yelled.

"We don't know it's a boy yet," the midwife cautioned, again.

"Don't you worry 'bout that. It's a boy," George said.

"I don't give a damn," Clara shouted. "Just get it the hell out of me."

The trailer began to shake, then jump, as a roaring earth mover passed within ten feet.

"Ohhhh," Clara moaned.

"Here we go. Here comes baby...it is a boy! Congratulations!" the midwife said.

"Hot dog! Told ya so!" George yelled, dancing a little jig and then kissing his wife, who had collapsed back on the bed.

Several minutes later, the baby was clean and wrapped in a blanket.

"Here is your baby, Mrs. Johnson," the midwife said, presenting the baby.

"Just a minute, honey," George said, intercepting the handoff. "Give me just a minute with him. I want to show him the course."

"George...for the love of God! Look at you...dirty shirt and pants...you've still got your hard hat on!"

Horror-stricken, the midwife nodded in complete agreement.

"Yeah, but my hands are clean. Be just a minute, baby," George said, running from the room with the man-child in his arms. The midwife crossed herself.

"That damn man and his golf course! Then again, it's why I married him. He does have a vision."

"Uh-huh," the midwife muttered under her breath. "Wait until the ladies hear about this one."

Outside, George walked into the field next to the trailer, holding his son tight to his chest. The Cat driver stops nearby.

"Is it a boy, George?" the driver yelled above the diesel engine.

"Of course it's a boy. Jeremiah Theodore," George yelled back. The baby began to cry.

"Well, whadyaknow! Way to go, George," the man shouted, clapping his hands.

George held the baby up in the hot wind and inspected him. He had George's dark eyes and complexion, a full head of his grandfather's ebony hair, and his mother's nose. George's face slowly broke into a deep, satisfied smile. He carefully turned the crying baby toward the field and cradled him against his chest.

"There it is, JT. Our future. Your future. Maybe it won't be August National, but it'll be a nice course, I promise. See those groves? We're gonna take 'em all out except those on 6, 10, and 15...we're gonna leave those holes lined with orange trees. You know, kinda keep the feel of what this place was. We'll call it the Orange Grove. You'll grow up hitting balls here, winning tournaments. This will be your home course...the one you tell everyone you learned the game on."

The boy screamed louder.

"What's wrong?" George said, turning the baby to face him. "Well, I'm sorry, but you can't play the course today. We've gotta finish her first. Now, back to your mama. I've got work to do," George said, turning for the trailer.

October 8, 1948

Cao Bang, Vietnam

As summer closed out in the mountainous valleys of the north, a complement of six new recruits and a strutting corporal made their way into the Viet Minh encampment southeast of Cao Bang. The recruits were farm boys from the delta who had never been in the mountains until then. They found the evening air cool and choked with the smoke of many fires. Around them, the bustling soldiers of Giap's Viet Minh better resembled a collection of guerrillas than an elite fighting force. It was an army of rebels without uniforms that carried mismatched weapons of many origins.

As the contingent approached the operations hut, a young sergeant stepped out to meet them. Just nineteen, he appeared only slightly older than the young recruits. But he was a distinguished veteran of the campaigns of '47, promoted in the field for his leadership and Communist zeal. The corporal and his recruits formed a line in front of him.

"I am Tran Van Minh," the sergeant announced. "You have been recruited to support the People's Army as porters. A great army cannot fight without the valued service of men such as you. Corporal Le will take you to the supply area, where you will be fed and given quarters." He dismissed them with a look and turned to leave.

One recruit quickly stepped forward. Clearing his throat, he called after the sergeant, "Tran Van Minh, sir. I have an honorable request to make of you."

Corporal Le, taken off guard, snarled his surprise. The sergeant spun on his heel, taking in the lone boy who was now standing a step in front of his comrades, head bowed.

"You will address me as Sergeant. What do you mean calling after me?! Did I not just dismiss you?"

"Sergeant...I must make a request. I joined the People's Army to fight for freedom. I wish to join my comrades in battle."

The recruit said this with a noticeable tremor in his voice, hardly believing the words were escaping his mouth. Like the fellows around him, Le Van Dat was a bit terrified of the sergeant and these ominous surroundings. But the tremendous disappointment he felt at being given duty as a lowly porter provided courage for him to speak up. He could not allow such a mundane diversion from his plan. He envisioned the noblest tribute of his life: fighting to right the terrible wrongs done to his ancestors. Serving as a porter would not suffice.

Tran Van Minh sized him up. It was very unusual for these young villagers to utter even a sound to a superior for weeks after arriving from their rice paddies.

"What is your name?" he asked.

"I am Le Van Dat, Sergeant."

"How old are you, Dat?"

"Soon to be seventeen, Sergeant."

"You are lucky I am an understanding man, Dat...or I would certainly beat you," Minh said with a menacing growl. "It is an *honor*," he intoned with patriotic gravity, "to serve the Communist cause under *any* circumstances. To fight...to be presented with a precious rifle, is something we will consider at another time. You are young...and we need porters now." Minh stepped a bit closer and glared at Dat. "Join the others. Again, you are dismissed!"

The sergeant did not move or turn away this time. But neither did the young recruit, who barely breathed. Instead, to Minh's amazement, he spoke up again.

"I do not make this request out of disrespect..."

Minh moved swiftly forward and hit Dat square in the face. "SILENCE!"

Dat hit the ground as Minh boiled. This young recruit, a child right out of the rice paddies, had the gall to show disrespect to a superior officer and he hadn't spent ten minutes in the compound! Minh had lost face. He could feel the eyes of his comrades upon him. Not far removed from the rice paddies himself, and lacking the wisdom of age and experience as a noncommissioned officer, Minh was unsure how to handle this situation.

The corporal, sensing his sergeant's dilemma, took swift action on his own. He ran up to Dat and swiftly kicked him in the ribs.

"How dare you?! We will have you shot for this!" the corporal screamed into Dat's face while crouching over him.

Inwardly, the sergeant breathed a sigh of relief.

"Easy, Corporal. No one is shooting anybody here...we need

porters too badly. Le Van Dat is, after all, a new recruit. He is ignorant and yet to be indoctrinated as a soldier, much less a Communist. We must try to understand his confusion...and his disappointment with the army. Dat!... Get to your feet," he said in a stern voice.

Dat, humiliated and dispirited, rose to stand meekly before the sergeant. All hope of fighting for his country was gone.

"I cannot believe your behavior here. Yes, I could have you shot for this! We are an army, and this is war. You will never disobey me or any superior again. Is this understood?"

"Yes...Sergeant," Dat said in a pitiful voice, barely audible.

Minh took pause to study the boy standing before him. He was not much younger than himself. The boy's speaking out showed his lack of military training...*and* immense courage for a young peasant. Such courage was something to be highly regarded and used.

"The People's Army needs porters, Dat. It takes four porters to keep each soldier in this army supplied, fed, and fighting. It is an important job. There are never enough," Minh said. He then added, "Do you feel being a porter is beneath you, is that it?"

Dat let a moment pass, thinking. He then solemnly responded, "No. Being a porter is an honorable position. I would not dishonor their important role of supplying the People's Army."

"Then...why do you show such disrespect for my orders? For this...important role?"

"No, no...I do not disrespect the order, Sergeant," Dat stammered. "It is only that I am not worthy of being a porter. I am filled with a great desire to be a soldier. It is my destiny to fight...and die, if necessary, for my country. Each must serve the People's Army in the best way possible. For me, that will be as a soldier. If I could be half as much use to the People's Army as a porter, I would not hesitate to follow your order...and I would not have spoken up."

The sergeant thought he had detected a note of sarcasm, but it was shrewdly delivered, and he was sure no one else had noticed. Not worthy, huh. It dawned on Minh that he was taking a liking to this brash young man; he showed courage, wisdom, a cool head under fire, and bravery—all good qualities in a soldier. But this created another dilemma for the young sergeant: how to reverse field and not lose face again?

"Hmmm...well, Dat, I think I understand now. Corporal!"

"Yes, Sergeant," the corporal said.

"Le Van Dat needs immediate education in the Communist and military order of doing things. I will deliver him personally to the political commissar. Take the others to the supply area as ordered."

"Yes, Sergeant." The corporal commanded the remaining five recruits to fall in line, and they ambled off. Dat stood rigid, facing the sergeant and fearing the worst.

"You should not have spoken as you did," Minh said, turning to Dat. "There would have been time to make a request once you had settled in. With a sergeant other than myself, this incident could have cost you dearly. Some have little patience with new recruits.

"I am granting your request to be a soldier in the People's Army. We can always use men with devotion and purpose."

Dat's heart and spirits soared. It showed in his face, and Minh could not help smiling.

"But military training and a rifle will have to wait," Minh said. Like an evangelist at a baptism, Minh could not let an opportunity escape without preaching the Communist creed. "It is much more important that you attend education and political classes immediately. You cannot become a soldier in the People's Army without understanding *Dau Tranh*, our struggle...why we fight together for the common man...and why you must be willing to sacrifice everything, life itself, for this cause. It is what joins us as free men and makes our task bearable."

The sermon delivered, Minh led him off. Dat would discover in the next several weeks what commitment, duty, and honor to the Communist Party meant.

July 1998

Helena, Montana

As I neared the crossroads of Hannaford and Townsend streets, an overwhelming sense of neighborhood, belonging, and home struck me. It was a path I'd traveled thousands of times in my life and, with each step the sensation grew. My fingers and toes tingled as I was swept up by something special and seemingly misplaced from many lives ago, yet as familiar as a hand sliding into a well-oiled, worn-out baseball glove.

Today, turning this corner, I was just a middle-aged salesman in a rental car. But I might just as well have been the ten-year-old on my bike, the teenager in the old Chevy, the college kid with his buddies. This was my street. My neighborhood. Home.

Two children on bicycles watched me slowly drive by. I was nothing more than a stranger to them, someone they were not allowed to talk to. I wondered, though, who had more ownership of this neighborhood.

The street had changed in the decades since my youth, though recognizable landmarks greeted me, as obvious as red flags in a wheat field: the now ancient tree I climbed as a boy, the sagging, tired old home of a friend, and a hundred other familiar reminders that winked at me, seeking recognition.

Working on my fiftieth year, I was in something of a midlife crisis and recalling a seemingly idyllic childhood that had taken place right here. I had been looking back to this childhood more than forward lately, feeling pursued and harangued by the growing pressures of my assumed responsibilities and chosen career. Things didn't seem to be getting better or easier with age, as I had imagined they would. All the same, things just seemed to be getting worse; the stress ascending, persistent and palpable.

I pulled up to the curb between the Anderson's new house and the folks' old place. I wondered if this side trip to the old neighborhood could help rekindle some of the zest and ambition for life that had consumed me as a kid; passions long extinguished by circumstances not of my choosing.

Eventually, I uncoiled my stiff, road-weary body from the confines of the car to rise and stand beside it. The folks' house looked much the same; a tired little bungalow of rose-colored brick. It had been eleven years since I had come home to bury Mom. I hadn't paid any attention to the house or the neighborhood then. Now, as I took it in, I realized the little house had lost its youth, as well. The place had never been entirely new or ever amounted to much, here on the poorer edge of town.

"What's he gawkin' at?" Mrs. Anderson said to her husband, Charlie, as she stared out her window toward the old Cameron home next door. "He's just standing there. Think he's from the city? Maybe he's the tax assessor. God, I hope he doesn't look at our place."

"Aw, baloney! Nobody comes door-to-door for anything anymore, Mim...'specially those damned lazy city employees," Mr. Anderson said, coming to the window.

Looking out, though, his own curiosity was lit. "Hmm. Somethin' familiar about him, don'tcha think? He's what... six feet, fair skin, sandy colored hair. I wonder."

The two stood at the window staring at the statue-like intruder. "He's sure interested in the old Cameron place. Maybe he's a realtor...heard it's for sale again. Wish my eyes were better," Charlie complained. "I'm gonna go out and say somethin' to 'em. Got nothin' else to do anyway," Charlie said, shuffling away.

Hearing the Andersons' door open, I threw a quick glance that direction. *Apparently, Old Charlie is wondering who's setting up shop on his front lawn.* I roused myself and walked his way, extending my left hand. Charlie took it as I saw recognition light up his face.

"Why, it's Mark Cameron! I thought it might be you. Didn't think I'd live to ever see you again."

I added Charlie's leathered face and missing teeth to the other familiar landmarks of our neighborhood.

"A few years ago I'd have said you were right, Mr. Anderson," I responded. "But I've got business in Billings...and since I was traveling close by, I couldn't pass up the opportunity for a look at the old neighborhood. How've you been?"

"Ain't worth a tinker's dam," Charlie spat out.

I laughed. "Sorry to hear about that tinker thing," I said.

"You here hopin' to see someone in particular? Jeez...there were a lot of kids around here in those days. Ya know, after the war and all. The big war, I mean. I think you hung out with Bud Brody, didn't you?"

"Yeah. Bud...Stan Wicks and Joe Wills, too, among others," I said, somewhat wistfully, the melancholy of the place washing over me. "We were a big buncha kids, all right."

"Well, you probably know both of Bud's parents're dead. Ol' Mabel passed away two years ago. Huh...seems like about everyone from those days is gone. Course, I mentioned Buddy 'cause he's back in town, ya know."

"What?" I said, shaken out of my stupor. "Buddy's back? He lives here? Since when?"

"Sure. Livin' someplace up by the Capitol," Charlie continued. "Been there since comin' back from Canada...oh, years ago now.

"Yup, just about everyone else is gone or dead...except of course for ol' Willy livin' on the corner."

Willy Wicks, the old buzzard. Sure, I knew where Willy was. Stan's father would spite us all by staying put and outliving everyone.

"Yeah," I said, absently. "The place isn't the same. Joe Wills disappeared after the war. I never saw or heard from him again."

"Joe Wills...yeah, big tow-haired kid," Charlie said. "I remember him...and, of course, Stan."

"Yeah, there was Stanley."

"Ahhh...," Charlie moaned. "It's been too many years, Mark. So, whatcha gonna do around here? Gonna visit Mr. Wicks? Look up Bud?"

"No, don't think so. I'm in the middle of a business trip...can't stay long. I just wanted to walk around the neighborhood again. That's all. These old buildings and stuff...it's all that remains of my childhood."

We were quiet then, both thinking younger thoughts.

"It's useless, Mark," Charlie said at last. "You won't find what you're lookin' for here. As far as our youth's concerned, this ain't nothin' but a boneyard."

I will be fifty this summer, a milestone as welcome as varicose veins and erectile dysfunction. I remember turning thirty. My friends and I had joked about it. I was far too busy with work to even notice forty. But fifty? No argument, I was a geezer! The big goals and dreams, unattained, had vanished. Life was sliding by, quicker now every day.

Young people look at an old face and can't imagine ever being that old. But at fifty, a person vividly remembers youth while knowing old age is on the step, knocking, and also that once, seemingly not so long ago, they were young too.

1953

Helena, Montana

Midafternoon on a sweet and mellow fall day. Mother had put me down for a nap, but I never napped. Knowing this, she always turned the radio on and left it low to keep me company. From where I lay on my side, I could see out the window of my parents' bedroom. Their new curtains were neat triangles of turquoise, yellow, and black on a field of white. Through the window, I could see Dad's old Chevy pickup sitting at the side of the driveway next to the high chicken-wire fence that surrounded Fred Field's house. The big fence corralled the three scary hunting dogs he kept in his yard.

An occasional breeze set the triangles dancing lightly on a rolling wave. Soon, Mother would allow me to get up and it would be time for my best friend to come home from school. I looked forward to that and to the day I could join him and my brother at Bryant grade school.

Mother hummed a familiar show tune as she dusted. In the quiet of the house it was a gentle sound, a comforting noise. A snuffle from below made me sneak to the edge of the bed and peer over at Blackie, an abused mutt my parents had rescued off the highway out by my grandparents' farm. He was the closest thing on earth to my guardian angel. He looked at me with pleading eyes, anxious to be out and bounding. Not yet; he laid his head on his paws and sighed.

Time moved in yawns and stretches, slowly reeling in the lazy afternoon. Somewhere a plane droned in the light blue sky, car tires crunched on a graveled street, a clock kept rhythm with the gently flowing curtains. Life for Mark Cameron on this afternoon was lingering and peaceful.

Fullerton, California

George Johnson, six foot-two inches tall, bronzed and handsome with wavy jet-black hair, carefully placed the dimpled ball on a high tee. He stepped back and looked down the driving range, imagining a ball hammered and flying straight and true as it split the vision neatly in half. His son, a smaller version of George, stood at his side with a cut-down driver gripped tightly in his hands, a smile lighting his eager face.

Behind them, wife and mother Clara couldn't keep the smile off her face; just look at the two of 'em. She was a standard California girl beauty with long legs and golden hair that tumbled about her shoulders. She held both hands on a bulging tummy.

"Okay now, Son. I've shown you how it's done. Time to give 'er a poke. Think you can hit that?"

"Sure, Daddy," JT said, stepping up to the ball like his father had shown him.

"Now, take your time, JT. You don't have to..."

But JT was already into a full backswing and took a mighty cut. His feet went out from under him, and he ended up sitting on the tee as the ball whistled away from him straight down the range, until hooking sharply and clattering off the greenkeeper's shed.

"Shit! I mean...phew! That was a hell of a...*heck* of a shot, Son! Fifty yards straight off the tee...then another fifty on the hook. A hundred-yard shot from a five-year-old boy! His first swing! Holy mackerel! Now, that's somethin' to remember."

JT smiled up at his dad. Hitting the ball and seeing it fly felt good.

"Now, George," Clara said. "Don't get overexcited. That's just one swing of the club...and it actually went maybe fifty yards."

"It's like I always said, Son...you're gonna be a champion," George said, ignoring his wife. "Go ahead and tee up another ball. Let 'er rip!"

"Oookayyy, Daddy," JT said, scrambling to his feet. "This is fun!"

George stepped back with his wife to watch JT, who whiffed on his second swing and nearly lost his feet again. Clara chuckled.

"Don't you do that," George said in a harsh whisper. "Don't ever make fun of him or act as if we doubt his ability. The seeds of doubt sow a loser. I mean, just look at 'em Clara. He's big for his age and already powerful."

"Oh, for chrissakes, George. He's only *five*!" Clara whispered back.

"In years, yes. But not in size. Our kids will be champions,"

George said, putting a hand on Clara's belly. "And we're not gonna hold 'em back by planting doubts...at any age!"

Clara placed her hand on George's and rubbed it affectionately. "I'm concerned, George. My father thinks he's gonna lose his farm and I know what the bank's sayin'. What're we gonna do?"

"That banker's an idiot!" George said in an angry whisper. "You hear me?! This city's growin' like crazy. The players will come. Your dad'll get his investment back and a bunch more. I'll make it work, damn it. I'll make jackasses outta the whole bunch before I'm through. You just watch!"

"Bull in a china closet. That's what my father says...and he's right. You give 'em hell, George Johnson."

"Now...*that's* my gal," George said, pecking his wife on the cheek. As he turned his attention back to JT, the boy hit a worm-burner that went twenty yards.

"Nice shot, Son!" George said. "Straight up the fairway. That's what we're aimin' for."

"Mr. Johnson."

"Yes?" George said, turning to a young employee approaching them.

"Mr. Kennison is on the phone. He's complainin' about his bill...says he was charged for drinks on the 12th he never ordered. I told him I'd have to talk to you."

"Damn! I can't believe he's doing that again. Cheap son of a... One more thing, Clara...the day will come when I give shyster lawyers like Pete Kennison the old heave-ho."

"An influential man like Peter Kennison?... Not likely George," Clara said. "We need men like him recommending the club to his friends and clients."

George turned, visibly seething and shoving his hands deep in his pockets. "Tell that...tell Mr. Kennison I'm so *sorry* about the mix-up. We'll...*of course*, take those drinks off his bill."

"Steady, boy," Clara said.

George turned his attention back to the driving range just as JT hit a ball that went straight up and about thirty yards.

"Another nice shot!" George yelled. "Straight up the fairway again!"

1956

Helena, Montana

Julie Wicks was my new infatuation. Dark-haired, cute as a button with a soft, feminine voice that drew you in...oh, what a gal! She was by far the prettiest girl in the neighborhood and had lit my sexual pilot light. While only slightly older than me, she seemed much older and always would.

"Would you like to come in for some Kool-Aid, Mark?" Julie said in that smooth voice dripping with honey. Yum.

I vigorously nodded as her younger brother, Stanley, rolled his eyes.

Julie went to the cupboard for paper cups and poured us four equal portions of orange Kool-Aid: one for herself, me of course, Stanley, and her pesky little sister, Katy who was three or four years old and just the biggest nuisance older siblings must endure.

"I got a record player for my birthday," Julie was saying, "and some forty-fives to play on it. It's in the living room. Would you like to listen? We can dance."

The player was a turquoise and white portable with the speaker on the side that she kneeled in front of while lovingly, cautiously, lifting the lid.

"What would you like to hear? I don't have many records yet, but I do have 'Don't Be Cruel' by Elvis. I just *love* Elvis, don't you?"

"Yeah...uh, go ahead and play it," I said, gulping Kool-Aid with my eyes riveted on her beautiful face and pouting lips. Zowie!

Stanley had drifted to the big living room window, neither interested in his sister nor her record player.

"Hey! Lookit this," he said. "There's TV trucks in front of your house an' everythin'."

"Jeez, I almost forgot," I said, running for the door.

We hurried across the dirt street with Katy toddling far behind. A swarm of workers was unloading antenna equipment from a trailer and our new TV from their panel truck. The four of us settled on the grass in the front yard to watch.

My father had arranged installation for Saturday so he could be home to supervise. He was everywhere at once. "Hey, watch that step.... Careful through the door.... Don't punch holes in my shingles.... Don't drill there!... And on he went like the impassioned ringmaster of this three-ring circus.

Better late than never, the World War II generation's day had finally arrived. My father liked to say he hadn't had two nickels to rub together growing up during the Depression. His wages and job had been frozen during the war, and there had been nothing to buy anyway. Now, with American industry turning out every kind of contrived appliance and convenience, each new purchase became something of a religious experience.

The crew assembled the tall pole on the ground, attached the antenna on top, and swung it up to an installation crew on the roof. When it was ready, four guys pulled on guide wires and the whole thing went up, high in the air. The antenna was imposing, but hardly out of place. The entire neighborhood was becoming dotted with these high-rise jungle gyms.

"In just a few minutes you can all follow me inside for a little TV watching," I crowed. "I am sure cartoons are about to start."

Now they were fishing the wire into the house through a hole drilled next to a window. We raced inside to see the hookup. Our new TV stood resplendent in the corner, an imposing piece of furniture trimmed in the latest "blond" oak veneer.

Soon it faded to life, slowly taking on more and more vivid shades of gray and white. The first thing we saw on our new TV was a Bufferin commercial. The little Bs were beating the little As to a two-dimensional brain. I had seen the ad before on other sets. Actually, I liked the local "live" commercials because you never knew what the manager of a hardware store might say.

Though we were primed for animation, there weren't any cartoons on, just a baseball game and a fishing show. We received only three channels and two of 'em didn't come in very good.

"C'mon," Stanley finally said, "this is boring. Let's see if the Brodys wanna play war."

Our games of army usually centered around the sheds, garages, and shacks that lay along the alley behind my best friend Buddy Brody's house. Bud was second oldest and an oddity in a family that would grow to seven kids. Good-looking, blond, athletic, and smart as a whip, Bud Brody stood out in the neighborhood and excelled in my class at school. By contrast, all the other Brody kids were homely, dim-witted, and less than gifted athletically, Bud's brother Bobby being the prime example. It was as if God had decided Bud alone would receive every talent his family possessed.

An enthusiastic reproduction of the Battle of the Bulge was later being carried out among the shacks when I literally ran into the new neighbor kid while making a flanking move on Stanley's plastic .50-caliber machine gun.

I went backpedaling from the impact and fell on my keister, my helmet sliding to cover my face. As I scrambled in the dirt pulling my helmet up, I was ready to spew the four or five cuss words I knew when I realized I didn't know the big blond-haired kid standing in front of me, smiling with hands on his hips. Standing next to him was a little fella, about five years old, with dark, wavy hair.

"Jeez. Watch where you're goin'," I said.

"I think you ran into me. Sorry anyway," he said with an easy smile.

"Chucka, chucka, chucka," went Buddy's brother. "You're dead, Mark." He noticed the two new kids.

"Hey...who're you guys?" he said.

"We just moved here. I'm Joe Wills. This is my brother, Paul," he said.

"Oh yeah, you moved into the old Nettleton place...on the corner," I said.

"Sure, I guess," Joe said. "We're just checkin' out the neighborhood. Heard you guys and thought we'd come look."

"I'm Mark," I said. "This is Bobby. C'mon, I'll introduce you to the other guys."

A truce was called and we all stood around talking. Joe was a funny guy with a friendly smile. I could feel a friendship growing. He was a couple years older than us, having turned ten in April, and tall for his age. His brother Paul, whose biggest feature was a head of curly black hair, the opposite of his big brother, never spoke a word, just looked kind of shy and stuck close to his brother.

"Hey, you wanna play army with us?" Bobby asked.

"Naw," Joe said. "I'm not interested in that. You guys play baseball?"

We looked at one another and shook our heads.

"Well, it's just the greatest game ever!" Joe exclaimed. "Babe Ruth, Ted Williams, Ty Cobb...you've heard of them."

We hadn't.

"But my favorite is 'Stan the Man,' Stan Musial of the St. Louis Cardinals. That's right, Stanley, you've got a world-class baseball name." Stanley beamed. "I saw him play last year when we went to visit my uncle in St. Louis. I got to see him hit a homer. Anyway, I'm on a team, the Reds. I'm a catcher. I might start next year. Say, if we got you guys playin', maybe you could join my team next year. It's a lot of fun."

I could see the other guys were getting as excited as I was.

"Look, you all have baseball gloves, right?"

We nodded affirmative, having gloves our fathers had given us but never used.

"Well then, why don't you go get 'em? We can have a game right here on this lot. This shed over here will be our backstop...and that's the outfield," he said, gesturing toward the next street. "We'll meet you back here in ten minutes and get started."

With that, he and Paul were gone, running down the alley. Like kids tardy from recess, we all suddenly realized we had to get going. There was baseball to play!

Baseball hadn't been played much in the neighborhood up to that time. My brother's friends all liked football and track. We'd neither been old enough nor had a leader like Joe to show us the game. Our fathers never spent much time with us, especially playing a game. But from the moment we met Joe Wills, baseball became our game of choice no matter the season.

Joe showed us everything: how to catch, throw, hit, field grounders, steal bases, and slide. He taught the subtleties, too, like how to fake a steal, annoying things to say to hitters and opposing pitchers, how to beat out a rundown, and a lot more.

A new friend had moved into the neighborhood, and things would never be the same.

Fullerton, California

JT stood patiently on the curb, junior briefcase held in both hands as he took a hard look up the street. His father was late, as usual. All his friends had been picked up and whisked away by waiting parents. He stood alone as a group of older kids approached, sizing him up. They appeared ready to pounce on him when a voice called from behind.

"Hi, Jeremy."

It was Darla Jean Kennison, a girl from his class.

"Waiting for someone?" she said, joining him.

"Yeah. My dad will be here any minute. Wait...is that him?"

The approaching boys looked up the street before swaggering by with a nasty look. Jay gave an inward sigh as they kept walking.

"I like your briefcase. It's very nice," Darla said.

"Yeah, yeah."

"Wanna play at recess some time?" she said.

"You crazy?" Jay said. "I don't play any *girl* games."

"We don't have to play girl games," she said, smiling.

At last, the Packard Caribbean convertible rounded the corner, sped to where they stood, and screeched to a halt.

"Hey, buckaroo!" George called. "Jump on in here. Miss, do you need a ride?"

"No, thanks," Darla Jean said. "I live on the next block."

"Okay then. Say, aren't you Pete Kennison's daughter? Make sure you say hi to your dad for me. I'm George. George Johnson from the golf club. Make sure you tell him."

Darla said nothing but smiled.

"You know, Dad," JT said, climbing into the car. "I feel real stupid standing here waiting for you. I'm always the last kid picked up."

George sighed and slumped back in his car seat, pushing his hat back as he did so.

"I'm sorry, Jay. It's like I told you before...business always comes first. I got here soon as I could. A man has responsibilities. I can't always just up and leave because *school's out.*

"You'll find out some day," George said. "The man of the house is the breadwinner. You think I enjoy this? If not for your mother's Women's League, she'd be the one picking you up. Picking up kids is the woman's job. If I could afford it, I'd get rid of Women's League."

"I know, Dad," Jay said, sulking.

"Well, then...stop giving me hell about it," George said, putting the car in gear and pulling away from the curb.

At the driving range, George set him up with a bucket of balls and stood back to observe. A couple of twelve-year-old girls were nearby, whispering and snickering as they looked in Jay's direction. JT backed off the ball and walked to his father.

"They're talkin' about me, Dad. I don't wanna hit in front of them. Let's come back later."

George Johnson observed the girls, gave them a smile and a little nod. One girl waved back. He led JT back to where the balls lay on the ground. Kneeling to JT's height, he picked up one of the balls.

"A golf ball's nothing more than tightly spun rubber with a dimpled plastic cover. It means everything to the game, but it doesn't do a damn thing by itself. It's the player that makes the game...and players who hit this little thing further and with better accuracy are its heroes. Nobody makes wisecracks or giggles when a great player steps up to hit a ball. You want the gallery with you? You want to shut up a couple young girls? Then you step up to the ball...concentrate, and hit a beautiful shot. See if I'm not right."

George stood and walked a few paces behind Jay, turned, and nodded encouragement to his son. Reluctantly, Jay made his address to the ball. He looked again at the girls, who continued their silliness. *Concentrate,* he told himself. Alignment, full backswing, lead with the hips, no peeking.

The ball left the tee in straight and glorious flight, a beautiful shot of about a hundred yards. When he looked at the girls, their gaze was downrange, their mouths open. He shifted his gaze to his father, who gave him a nod and a wink.

Phu Lang, North Vietnam

As Lieutenant Le Van Dat looked up the road, he was entertained by an ever-changing kaleidoscope of picks, shovels, and moving bodies ringed in the gold of a late afternoon sun. Workers and soldiers toiled on the road as far as he could see. A truck went here and there. He knew an old French road grader was somewhere around the bend, but people outnumbered machinery a thousand to one. The industrious nature of his countrymen never failed to inspire Dat. It had proved the difference at Dien Bien Phu, the thousands upon thousands of hands that moved the big guns, food, and material necessary to beat the French. They were indeed an impoverished nation, but better a poor nation than no nation. Some grumbling could be heard now and again among the peasants over Trong Chinh's Land Reform Program, but the national pride and spirit of these people could be seen in their labor, as they did whatever it took to improve what was now their country.

The victorious Viet Minh, one of the world's finest fighting forces, had been reduced to this: road and farm work. As a part of the Communist worker's paradise, the Viet Minh had been turned out to help rebuild the country after the war. His comrades now carried shovels and picks instead of rifles and submachine guns; drove wheelbarrows instead of trucks. From commanding troops in the field, Dat now supervised drainage ditch digging. He knew it was for the good of his country, but this is where he had begun life. If not for the commission granted Dat upon the recommendation of Captain Minh, he would be swinging a pick with the others. Like many of the soldiers in his company, fighting was what Dat had signed on for; commanding men in the heat of battle, risking all.

General Giap was said to be displeased over this use of his prized army, which, he believed, should be improving their fighting skills for the war to come. That was what galled Dat most. This was just a truce. The war was not over because Vietnam had not been liberated. The southern half of the country remained under the occupation of France and the United States, a situation unacceptable in the Communist North. Part two, or phase two, the next chapter, if you will, was soon to come. They were waiting for the other shoe to drop. Free elections were to be held in 1957, and the South was projected to vote to join the North. But America had stepped in for the French and Dat doubted they would allow a Communist takeover, even if it were democratically decreed.

Soon, Dat would be leaving for China. He was to be trained by the Chinese officer corps in the military arts and sciences, Communist philosophy, geography, map reading, mathematics, English language, and history. Even though it would be a marked improvement over his current status, Dat was apprehensive about returning to school. He had only received a primary education. But Minh and other officers who had gone before reinforced him, graciously saying they thought he would do well. Dat vowed to do his best. His new country deserved his finest effort and, as always, he would give it.

July 1998

Helena, Montana

I ended up a block away from my car, standing in what had been the center of our old sandlot baseball field. I found it interesting that two houses, neither exactly new, now occupied the space. How could so much time have passed? It's a question I ask daily.

A man putting gas in his lawn mower noticed my interest. "Hello," he said, giving me a "Can I help you?" sort of look.

Caught reminiscing without a license, I was a little embarrassed.

"Hello," I replied, amiably. "I used to live in this neighborhood...a long time ago. Your house is in center field. I'm afraid you'll have to move it."

The guy looked like one of those folks caught on *Candid Camera* in some bizarre stunt. A puzzled look said, "What the hell are you talking about?"

"Our ball field," I quickly added. "When I was a kid our ball field was right here. This was center field. Home plate was in the alley."

The guy continued staring at me a moment longer, then looked at his house and back to me. "Oh.... Well, how about that?" was delivered with as much enthusiasm as a guy getting a rectal exam.

Noticing his interest was lagging a tad behind mine, I quickly excused myself. "Well, I'll just be moving along...want to see the old 'hood before I leave. Uh, bye now."

'Hood? I *never* used that term. The man was busy pouring gas and had dismissed me, not bothering to respond or even look up as I left.

There was nothing familiar about this part of the neighborhood. The sheds, garages, and fields had been replaced with houses, trees, and driveways. "Where do these kids play ball?" I asked myself, failing to see a single empty lot. With a shrug, I hung a left at the Millers' old house and soon came to the Wickses' place. Old Willy's house looked like something out of a *House Beautiful* magazine, September 1948 edition. And the colors...yellow and pink?!

I walked quickly down the street, all the while watching the house with a wary eye. I didn't want Willy to see me and feel like he had to come out and say something, though if he did see me, he probably wouldn't anyway. Turning the corner, there was the home I grew up in. On second viewing it looked even sadder, as aged and wrinkled as myself.

1960

Near Dak Sut, South Vietnam

Captain Le Van Dat and his company had been walking through a steady downpour for eighteen days. His feet, in flimsy sandals, were numb from the cold and covered in scratches. His thin, soaked uniform clung to his legs. The poncho he wore was little protection from the cold, and occasionally his teeth chattered uncontrollably. It had stopped raining only briefly, now and again.

The entire company was suffering. The trip south along the Ho Chi Minh Trail was arduous and utterly exhausting. Many in Dat's company had fallen ill and been left along the trail to recuperate. Those who recovered would join up with other troops heading south. Many would die or never recover enough health to become effective soldiers.

Dat himself had endured a bout of dysentery that he was hoping was not the forebear of malaria, a common ailment among troops heading south. Dat had lost close to thirty pounds, as had most of his men. They were hardly a fighting force and would need time to recover from the trip before engaging the enemy.

Serving under Dat were two lieutenants, five sergeants, and a complement of ninety-five men. Since crossing into Laos near Lang Mo two weeks prior, they had been pushing south at a steady pace. Only late yesterday, by best guess, they had entered South Vietnam through the highlands.

Dat's command was a company of "Southerners"—a company, except for the officers, made up wholly of Vietnamese from the South who had fled to the North after the liberation from and departure of the French. With the Politburo's decision in late 1959 to repatriate the South through armed conflict, the Southerners had been conscripted into the service of freeing their fellow countrymen. Some had come willingly, some had not.

As for their nemesis, the Americans, whom he had not faced in battle, Dat held an active curiosity. He knew much of them, though he had never met one. At the military college he attended in 1958, Dat had learned the language and strange customs of Americans from his instructor, Pham Trong. Trong had lived in the town of

San Francisco before and during the Second World War. His American acquaintances had called him "Phil" for reasons Trong never completely comprehended. Trong enjoyed relating day-to-day life in the powerful and confusing country, a country where everyone had everything but was never satisfied, only wanting more.

Dat would very much like to meet an American. Not in combat, but to sit and talk about history, customs, food, warfare, and so much more. Dat knew Americans had once been revolutionary themselves. Now, they were a strong nation. He wondered if Vietnam could ever achieve what the Americans had accomplished. In two hundred years, who knew?

But there would be no "friendly conversations" with the Americans. They were allies of the South, and if Dat saw one in the field, he would kill him.

Helena, Montana

The sharp crack of horsehide on pine sent the ball toward shortstop. Stanley Wicks made a quick, cat-like move to his right but failed to get his glove down, the ball skittering into left field and bouncing on a couple rocks before being stopped by the left fielder. Head down and kicking dirt, Stan stepped back into his position. Any fielder in little league will miss his share of grounders, but Stanley was all-star material and had been missing too many of 'em.

My team, the Giants, was in an early summer preseason scrimmage against the Pirates, a good veteran team we had never beaten. We were a run up in the bottom of the last inning with two out. Stan had just let the tying run on base and, as the potential winning pitcher, I was a little miffed.

The next batter stepped in, and I recognized an easy one. The kid had struck out on a ball way out of the strike zone last time up. The best player on our team, Bud Brody, was catching and gave me a knowing nod as he settled in behind the plate.

"Easy out, Mark. Eeassy oouut. This guy can't hit his weight," Buddy said. Then, looking up at the kid, said, "What is your weight, squirt? About forty pounds?"

Blood rushed to the kid's face, now so angry that his nose flared like a bull's as he huffed and kicked dirt. Five pitches later he struck out again, then threw his bat in anger, causing his teammate on deck to jump out of the way.

As I walked to the bench, I heard our big-mouthed third baseman, Harry Rondo, giving Stan a bad time for missing the grounder. I was in no mood for Rondo's permanently bad attitude.

"Lay off, Harry. You aren't half the fielder Stan is."

"Shut up, Cameron. He's playing like shit."

I turned and grabbed a fistful of Harry's shirt. "Stop being such a jerk, Rondo."

"Me?! You're a fuckin' psycho, Cameron."

"You two save your energy for the next game," the coach said, as we stood nose to nose.

"Forget it, Mark," Stanley said, grabbing me by the sleeve. "He's right...I shoulda' had that ball."

"Work on it, Wicks. The season starts next week, and you aren't ready," Rondo said, walking away.

"I swear I'm gonna get that guy," I said. "He's never got anything nice to say about anyone."

"Forget it," Stanley said.

"Nice game, guys," coach Joe Dolan said. "Great to beat those Pirates, huh?"

Coach Dolan, a high school kid about sixteen or seventeen, was more admired, listened to, and revered than any of our fathers. He liked us and liked to coach. We loved the guy and would run through doors for him if he asked us to.

"Practice Monday, same time, same place. Don't you miss it." Kids started drifting away as the coach grabbed me by the shoulder and led me away from the team.

"What's with Stan, Mark?" Joey said. "He's never had this much trouble playing his position. I'm thinking of trying Randy at short."

"No, don't do that, Joey," I pleaded.

"I can't let Stan hurt the team, Mark. Randy's looking better right now."

"Jeez, Joey!" I stammered. "What're you talkin' about? You know how good Stan is. I don't know what's with him, but please, don't make a move yet. I'll work with him at home. He'll get better real soon. You know he will."

"Okay, okay. You're right. I'll try to be a little more patient. He was the best glove in the league last season," Joey said, somewhat wistfully. "I'd like to see *that* kid again."

While walking home, Stanley was quiet as Buddy and I glee-fully recounted our victory. We were excited for the season ahead. If we could beat the Pirates, we might beat anybody.

"Listen, Stan," I said, turning to him. "Let's play tonight. I'll hit you some grounders and you can work on your fielding."

"There's nothing wrong with my fielding!" Stanley said. Then louder, "I don't need to work on anything, and I don't need to walk home with you guys."

"But...jeez, Stan."

"Leave me alone," Stanley shouted, running away from us.

Bud and I exchanged looks.

"What's wrong with that guy?" Buddy said.

I could only offer a confused shrug.

Fullerton, California

"This is it! This is what I've waited for," George Johnson said, rising to his feet as the last putt dropped. "This guy's a gold mine! Wins the Masters. Wins the US Open. Loses the British Open by one lousy shot. Wow! He's gonna put a charge in people like we've never seen. It won't be long and we'll be limiting memberships and raising dues. I've got a feeling about the '60s and golf on TV. This is our decade...and it's about time, damn it! The course looks good; the population keeps growing...hot damn! We're gonna be rich!"

"That's nice, George," Clara said from the doorway.

"That young man right there, Arnold Palmer," George said to Jay, pointing at the TV screen, "that could be you. It's not hard to see. And, you know, Palmer grew up on a golf course, too."

"Yes...it could be Jay all right, if he can get through school," Clara added, giving George a knowing look.

"Oh...yeah, that's right," George said, deflating. He walked to the TV set and turned it off.

"What? Dad!" Jay said. "Turn it back on. I want to see the interview with Palmer."

"Yeah, well...we need to talk, son. I've been putting this off. See...we met with your teacher. Seems you're having a few prob-lems at school."

Jay crossed his arms and pouted. "That's not true. I understand everything. I'm doin' alright."

"No, you're not," Clara said. "You're not doing your homework. You're not studying for tests. You never seem to be paying attention. So, what's going on?"

Jay shook his head. "I don't know. I'm bored. I hate school. I mean, I'm gonna be a professional golfer. What do I need from school? I'll make a lot more money than some stupid seventh grade teacher."

Clara gave George a searing look.

"But, Son...," George added, hastily, "if you don't know history, math, English...you'll look and act stupid your whole life."

JT rolled his eyes.

"Okay, that's enough from you, young man!" Clara said. "You need to understand we're serious about this. Your teacher said you're in danger of flunking seventh grade. How would you like that? Seeing all your friends move on and leave you behind? You need to concentrate a lot more on school and a lot less on golf."

"Whoa, whoa, whoa," George said. "Let's not go overboard, honey. We've got the California Junior-Am in a month. There's time for golf *and* school."

"What about my friends?" Jay said. "When will I have time to play?"

"Play?! Good God Almighty! There's more to life than playing around with a buncha loser friends. This is your life, JT. You get one shot at it, and you'd better not miss the important stuff: school and golf...maybe not in that order."

"George Johnson!" Clara shouted.

"I hate you," JT said. "You're ruining my life!" He stormed from the room.

"Awww," George sighed when Jay had gone. "He doesn't know how good he's got it."

Clara gave him a look.

"What?" George said.

Helena, Montana

Baseball season was over—my team missing Helena's Little League World Series by one lousy game. With Labor Day approaching, a certain melancholy took over the kids in the neighborhood. Some looked forward to school...bored with the idleness of summer.

Others, like myself, reveled in that same idleness and bemoaned its passing. Our days were numbered, and we moved in slow, slouching shuffles like prisoners ready to be led back to their cells; summer's optimism replaced with the certainty of our fate, and fall.

So it was early one evening as I shuffled in sneakers worn out by the summer's activity over to Stan's house. I was going to see if he and his sisters were interested in some evening games. I took my time, kicking rocks and enjoying the warm evening air of an August day.

No one familiar with the Wickses ever entered their home through the front door. I plodded down the side of the house to their rear lean-to-like porch, silently opening the screen door and approaching the home's back door through a flood of light coming from the kitchen window. While passing by a window, I noticed the Wickses were having dinner. I hesitated for a moment, contemplating whether to go in or come back later. Through their open back door, which led into the porch, I could hear every word Mr. Wicks was yelling. Quietly opening the screen door, I slipped inside.

"Julie, you finish those vegetables or I'll give you what-for," he said. "I don't put food on your plate so we can just throw it away later."

I couldn't catch Julie's response, but it made Mr. Wicks mad.

"I'm tired of you damn kids always talkin' back to me," Willy said, threateningly.

I noticed Julie shrink. Everyone looked on edge. I thought this was something I shouldn't be watching and was about to turn away when I saw Willy pull back his hand to slap Julie. In a flash, Stan was out of his chair, placing himself in front of Julie.

"Don't you dare. You keep your hands to yourself," I heard Stan say.

The open hand became a fist and Mr. Wicks hit Stan square on the chin with a fury I had never witnessed. The impact sent Julie and Stan over backward where they sprawled on the floor. The silent witness of a vicious calamity, I was paralyzed with fear and couldn't move. Mr. Wicks pushed his chair back and stood.

"You're always askin' for it, aren't you?" I heard him say.

Julie scrambled to her feet and ran from the room. Mrs. Wicks grabbed youngest daughter Katy and fled as well. Now Willy hauled Stan up by the shirt and slapped him hard, back and forth. Then threw him away like a rag doll.

"You clean up this mess and do the dishes...then I want to talk to you in the livin' room. We'll have a conversation with Mr. Handy," Willy said, walking away.

I couldn't breathe. Shaking, I was just able to turn and move toward the patio's screen door, seeking an escape from this lunacy. But as I reached for the door, Stan came running from the kitchen...skidding to a stop when he saw me in the light. We stared hard at one another in a moment of silence. Then, Stan pushed past me and ran through the door. I followed him down the driveway to where he leaned on the family car. As I reached him I could see blood on his lip, a red welt on one side, and a blackening bruise on his chin. He was shivering in fright or anger, finding it hard to catch his breath. We said nothing for an immeasurable time. I was embarrassed, in shock unable to utter a single word.

Stan found his composure and spoke first.

"So, what're you doin' sneakin' around my house?!"

"I...well, I was coming..." I started, but nothing good would come to mind. My explanation seemed pitiful. I looked at my feet.

"I suppose now you're gonna blab this all over the neighborhood," he spat out. "Everybody's gonna have a good time with this one."

"Your dad hit you!" I blurted out in a savage hush. Four words that had meant something completely different just a few minutes prior now would never mean the same again. Parents hitting kids was supposed to be a swat on the rear...or, maybe an attention-getting slap on the back of the head.

"No shit," Stan responded.

"My dad has given me a spanking. Maybe twice, even. Took back his hand like he was going to punch me once...and maybe I even deserved that one. But your dad hit you...hard! Why?" I said, genuinely dumbfounded.

"You think I know?" Stan responded with a shrug. "It's the way he is, the way he's always been. He gets angry about something and pops me one. Guess it makes him feel good," he finished, choking back a sob.

"Who's Mr. Handy?" I asked.

"His two-foot razor strap. He lays it across my butt sometimes."

"Well don't go back in there! Don't let him beat you," I cried.

"Yeah...and go where?" Stan said in a surreal, calm voice. "Naw. He's blown his stack...so he's gonna be okay for a while. He only beats me when he blows a gasket. Once he settles down, he's okay. Really," Stan explained.

"Julie and Katy?" I asked, searching his face. "Does he..."

"Naw. I won't let him. He's gonna clobber me anyway...so I never let him touch them."

"How'd it start?" I asked.

"I don't know," Stan said, now agitated. "He used to hit Mom a lot. One day I just couldn't stand it anymore. So now he whups me. What're you askin' for? This is none of your damn business... and if I ever hear you tellin' anyone about it, I'll kick your ass!"

Just then the front door opened and Willy stuck his head out.

"Oh, it's you," Willy said, looking at me. "Thought I heard someone talkin' out here. Stanley's got supper to clean up. You go home now."

He gave me what I imagined was a nasty look, then slowly closed the door.

"See ya, Mark," Stan said sullenly, walking back to the house. "Go home...and forget about this."

I stood in the driveway for several minutes. Some untidy loose ends suddenly made sense. How easily we had been taken in with Stan's explanations of "accidents." He was often laughed at because of his clumsiness. He always had bruises or scrapes from "falling down" or "stepping on a rake." Of course, we'd never seen him involved in any of these mishaps. As athletic and agile as he was around us, we naively accepted he was somehow a stumbling klutz when he wasn't, simply because he said so. I could see now how well he'd duped us all.

I turned and walked across the street to my house. Would I tell my parents? No way. It was an evil I could not understand involving a grown-up, and I didn't like the look Willy had given me. Stan had asked me to forget about it, and although I never would, I wouldn't be saying anything to anybody.

My parents briefly looked up as I came in the front door. Dad was watching television. Mom was into the latest edition of the film fan magazine, *Photoplay*.

"Hey, Maverick," Dad said, using his favorite nickname. "I thought you were playing outside?"

"Yeah...well, they couldn't play."

"Oh, okay," Dad said, his attention already leaving me.

I fell ponderously into a chair, hanging my feet over the arm.

"Mark, I've told you not to do that," Mom said, not looking up.

"Sorry, Mom," I replied, putting my feet on the floor.

My parents weren't perfect. Dad wasn't smart or rich enough. Mom wasn't slim or pretty enough. At the moment, though, they looked awfully good to me.

I went to the couch where Mom was sitting, jumped in beside her, and snuggled in for a hug.

"What's this about?" she said, putting an arm around me.

"Nothin'," I responded.

1998

I pulled the rental car up in front of Helena Middle School, using the circular drive that must have recently been added. Otherwise, the place looked the same as when I attended as a seventh grader in 1961. It was old then, but, to me, it hadn't aged a bit.

For the second time in my life, I was in a new school: Helena Junior High School. I was now a seventh grader, the beginning of those miserable years of gawky growth and social dysfunction. The school, most of the kids, and all the teachers were new to me, and I felt the unease of the uninitiated.

Toward the end of lunch period on the third day of the fall session, all of us seventh graders gathered near the front doors waiting for the bell that would ring us in for the afternoon. There were little clutches of kids talking here and there with friends from their grade schools. Others, like myself, saw no one to talk to and became the silent watchers.

In front of me a tough kid, whom I would later learn was named Mick Northy, was giving a bespectacled, briefcase-totting little guy a hard time. This was bullying, and nothing set me off more. I had many fights at the old Bryant school defending smaller kids from creeps like this guy. I was the protector. Follow me, lads, I'll save you.

"Leave him alone," I said, getting Northy's attention.

Mick looked me over and evidently wasn't impressed with the skinny twerp challenging him.

"Mind your own business," he retorted, then knocked the kid's briefcase to the ground, all the while looking intently at me.

"You don't have to be such an asshole," I said.

Now Mick's menace left the kid, who quickly picked up his briefcase and hurried away, and centered on me.

"You should keep your mouth shut...and I don't like being called an asshole by some skinny little shit like you."

He pushed me in the chest, hard. I could tell he was strong... maybe a little taller...and, okay, somewhat heavier, too. I pushed his hand aside.

"Watch it," I said, with still a smidgen of bravado. "Dynamite comes in small packages."

"Huh?" Mick snorted. "You?!"

Okay, now I was feeling a little like Barney Fife facing the bully wanting to date Thelma Lou. I tried walking away. He kicked my leg, and I went down, skinning my hand. I immediately got to my feet, rushed him, and gave him a big shove of my own. I might as well have been pushing a boulder.

"You aren't serious?" he laughed. "You want your butt kicked? Apologize!"

I ignored him. The bell had rung and kids were moving into the building.

"Okay, tough little dynamite punk...I'll see you after school. Nobody screws with Mick Northy."

"Yeah, well...I'll be waiting," I said over my shoulder before hurrying off to class.

Afternoon class was a waste of time. While looking at my books, all I saw was that menacing glare of Mick Northy. I asked new kids in my class about him. Those who knew him pretty much said when the final bell of the day rang I should sprint out the back door and get lost.

As the day ended I looked around and didn't see him; his good fortune, I figured. I grabbed my books and headed for the back door. While walking down the path between the woodshop and the football field, I saw my oldest neighborhood friend, Bud Brody, leaning against the fence, waiting to walk home with me. I smiled and waved. He didn't smile back. Northy and his little sidekick, Pete Santos, who looked like a stumpy version of the *Little Rascals'* Alfalfa, stepped from behind the shop. I slowed my walk as Northy approached me.

"Hey, hotshot. Knew you'd try sneakin' outta this. You wanted a fight? Here I am."

"Yeah, well that was lunch period. Let's forget about it, huh?" I said. "It was no big deal."

He gave me that familiar shove in the chest. "It was a big deal to me! I've got a reputation to protect. Kids from my school know who I am. It's time everyone in this school learns you don't fuck with Mick Northy. So come on, little dynamite." He put his hand in my face and shoved.

Nobody does that to me! I blew my cork and moved to shove him back, but he was already sending a roundhouse right that caught me in the ear. I saw stars and then found myself looking up at him from the ground, not knowing how I got there. Before my senses returned, Mick kicked me as hard as he could in the rib cage. A blinding pain like nothing I'd experienced shot through me, and I screamed.

"Hey, that's dirty!" Bud Brody yelled. "No kicking."

"Stay outta this, kid," Northy said to Bud. "This is a fight between me and him."

"Yeah," said the stumpy Alfalfa Santos. "You shut up or we'll take care of you, too."

Bud shrank, leaning against the fence and looking my way with a "you're on your own" air. Too bad because I could have really used a little help just then. I struggled to my feet, pain rippling my side. Mick came at me again.

"No...look, I'm through," I said. "You win."

"Win?... What the fuck!" Northy said. "This isn't about winning...and I'll tell you when it's over."

He pushed me against the fence and kicked me in the groin. A new sickening pain shot through me. He grabbed a handful of my hair, pulling my face into his rising knee. That was it for me, but the beating went on for a while. Witnesses recalled several more kicks and a stomping to the head. I guess Mick told me it was over as he left. I didn't hear it.

I had been in many fights and schoolyard scraps growing up. I'd even fought Bud and other friends at times. There was always anger and energy, but no real malice. The most I'd ever gotten or given was a black eye or maybe a fat lip.

Northy just beat the crap out of me. He wanted to seriously hurt me, and he did. Maybe he wanted an excuse to get out of school, or maybe his old man was beating on him and he needed a way out. Whatever the reason, he was sent to reform school after that and we never saw him again. Nobody thanked me.

But the damage was done. I was no longer the protector of the meek; I *was* the meek. Every day through high school, freshman year of college, and into the service, I consistently shamed myself by melting away at the first sign of conflict. I was nothing more than a coward. Inside, it ground me up. There had been a time when this wasn't me; quite the opposite. But I lacked the courage, maybe the character, to save myself; to take a beating if I had to. Would a beating be worse than living with the person I had become? It didn't matter. Nothing I avoided seemed worth fighting for; worth messing up my clothes or bloodying my nose. Without being able to help myself, I was hoping for someone to save me.

Fullerton, California

JT sat on the diving board and looked over the little valley and the hills beyond. Their new home was on the edge of a ravine, one of the first homes built in the new subdivision. Popping up below him and spreading through the valley like some well-rooted vine of wood and brick were dozens of new houses in different stages of construction. It was a scene being played out in suburbs all over greater Los Angeles as more and more pilgrims sought the California climate and lifestyle.

The new home had been provided through the industry and hard work of George Johnson. Needing to make improvements to the course he had built that were beyond his reach, he sold a forty-nine percent interest in the course to local developers for $1.5 million. A new nine-hole par-3 was added, as was a new two-tiered driving range, a pool, tennis courts, a huge new clubhouse, and a hospitality room, plus dozens of acres for new home development. The investors insisted on a name change, thinking Orange Grove Course was far too pedestrian. So, the course was renamed Fullerton Park. Dues doubled, then tripled. They were talking with the PGA regarding tournament venues and were hopeful of landing a qualifying tourney. Life had gotten fat for the Johnsons.

The pool sat in the middle of the sandy dirt and weeds that was their backyard. Busy landscapers who were in high demand would be here tomorrow, or the next day. While he missed his old neighborhood and friends, Jay liked the new digs. He tilted his face to the sun and felt the rays searing his skin, turning it a deep brown that, with his ebony hair, made him look like one of the many Mexicans working the subdivision.

Sensing something to his right, he shifted his gaze. A tawny head darted below the ridge. Hello, what's this? He continued looking at the spot and, like a submarine periscope, the head rose again above the weedy chop. As their eyes met, the head again darted out of sight.

"I know you're there," JT said. "What do you want?"

There was only silence.

"Come on. I haven't got all day. Who are you?"

When the head rose a third time, he saw it was a girl with long, curly hair. She was smiling at him.

"Sorry," she said. "Didn't mean to intrude."

"Intrude?" JT said.

"Interrupt...without invitation. You seemed a prince...contemplating his world. I didn't want to startle you, invade your solitude, be a nuisance."

"What are you talking about?" JT said. "Me, a prince? That's a good one."

"Just an illusion. Sorry, my mother's a librarian," the girl said, walking through the weeds and onto the pool deck. "Her life's ambition is to teach me new words. Sometimes I forget myself and actually use them."

She was a sprite—thin, ghostly, and covered in freckles—with a sweet smile of straight, blinding white teeth. Her hair, though, was her most outrageous feature. Long, frizzy ringlets of reddish-brown hair fell in a giant heap upon her shoulders like a rusty mop, making her look even thinner.

"Where'd you come from?" Jay asked.

"We're building the house just there," she said, pointing to the house down the hill and north of his own. "It's almost finished. In fact, we're halfway moved in. I like your pool. We're not gonna have one. Can I swim here sometime?"

"What? Sure. Yeah, I guess," JT said. "But I'm not here much. I usually play golf all morning. Dad gives me lessons in the afternoon and I hit range balls."

"A real golf nut, huh? My dad plays golf, too. He's in real estate. Maybe you've seen his billboards.... Gabby Gaston? Mom works in the Fullerton library. What do your folks do?"

"My dad runs Orange Grove, er...I mean Fullerton Park," JT said. "Mom helps him."

"Well, that explains the golf," she said. "I'm Richelle Bouvier Gaston. I'll be going into eighth grade this year. And you?"

"Yeah, me too," JT said. "Uh, my name's Jeremiah Johnson, but..."

Richelle emitted a snicker.

"It was my grandfather's name! Everyone calls me JT or Jay. What do they call you, knucklehead?"

"Richelle, of course. It's a beautiful name."

"I don't think so," Jay said. "I've never heard anyone called Richelle. It must be French for Ricky, or somethin'."

"Ricky?! Seriously! Not a name to be calling a young lady."

"Young la.... Oh, so sorry. My apologies...Ricky!"

To her credit, Jay thought, Richelle only smiled in response.

"Fine," she said. "Shall I get my suit?"

"Suit yourself," Jay said, lying back on the board. "I'll be here."

When Jay had time to swim, Richelle invariably showed up, becoming a regular fixture by the pool. JT had never dreamed of having a girl as a friend, but since it was a new neighborhood and there seemed to be no boys about yet, it was better than nothing. She was, however, unlike any friend he had ever had.

"So, who's the Mexican señorita in your house?" Richelle asked one day.

"That's Rosita."

"So, what does she do? Is she an illegal?"

"Jeez, how should I know? She's just Rosita. She cooks, cleans, and stuff."

"Well, it doesn't really matter to me," Richelle said. "I mean if she *is* an illegal, then good for her. Makes no difference to me."

"Whaddya mean?"

"They do all the crummy jobs Americans won't do and make more money than they could hope to see back in Mexico. I know we're taking advantage and all, but it has to be a better life for them, too."

"I heard someone at the club say the Mexicans were takin' all the jobs from American workers," Jay said.

"Oh, please!" Richelle responded. "That's just some rich country club jerk who has no idea what illegals do or what these *American* jobs are worth. My father says all these Mexicans putting the landscaping in around here are probably illegals. Dad says, 'What American guy is gonna work that hard for a buck an hour?'"

Jay couldn't answer that question or many of the other that Richelle threw at him. He realized her knowledge and understanding of the world was far beyond him or any of his other friends. He found it amusing at times, infuriating at others.

"So...this Rosita...she's like a maid, then. Your parents can afford maids? That's pretty good for a golf course manager, isn't it?"

Jay steamed. "Ricky, sometimes!... Christ, you can be rude."

"What?"

"My dad doesn't just *manage* Fullerton Park; he *owns* most of it. He built it, you twit! But if you ever make a big deal out of that, I swear to God you'll never swim here again."

"Your dad *owns* Fullerton Park! My God, you're rich! You're Richey Rich, boy. Let's have caviar for lunch."

At which point she was tipped off the diving board.

Though Jay and Richelle became close friends, a time came when she stopped coming by as often, then hardly at all. Jay would sit on the diving board waiting to see her scrawny frame walking up the hill. Or, he would walk to the edge of the lawn to look down at her home, wondering what she was doing.

On one of the odd instances when JT had time to goof off with friends in downtown Fullerton, they ran into Richelle in the record department of the Woolworth store.

"Ricky!" Jay fairly shouted. "How's it goin'? I want you to meet the guys: Paul...Ray...and Wayne. They're all old friends of mine from my old neighborhood. This is Ricky, guys."

"Hey.... Hi.... Uh, nice to meet ya," the boys responded.

"We're just kickin' around downtown. You wanna hang out with us a while?" Jay said.

"Well...hello, boys. So nice to make your acquaintance. Sorry, though...while I'd love to 'hang out'...I'm afraid I must be going now. Toodaloo."

"Wow. What a snoot," Paul said.

"Yeah," JT could only agree. "She's...strange sometimes."

Jay decided, okay, he wouldn't see her anymore. But as time went by his agitation grew. She didn't come up to swim or call, and it was bugging him. He decided he would walk to her home and confront her. She answered the door.

"Oh, hello there," she said with a pleasant smile. "Please come in."

"What's with you?" Jay said, following her to the living room. "Where've you been...and why'd you act like a real prig at Woolworth's in front of my friends? That was just rude....and, and..."

"Ungracious?" she said, sitting on the sofa.

"Look," Jay said, "if you don't want to be friends anymore... well, fine! I could care less."

"I'd like to apologize for my behavior. That was rude. I can imagine what your friends must think of me. But you put me in an awkward position, Jay. You have to understand I'm not your *buddy*...or *pal*. I'm not like one of the guys...or a tom-girl who only wants boys for friends. I don't *hang out*. I am a young lady. Don't ever think you can treat me like just one of the guys...because if you don't realize who I am...*what* I am...then I don't want to be with you anymore. And one more thing...you can call me Ricky when we're alone, but don't ever introduce me as *Ricky* again. To everyone but you, I am Richelle. I would appreciate it if you'd remember that."

Jay didn't know what to think. Not a buddy? Isn't that what friends were? And what was wrong with hanging out?

"Girls!" he said at last, turning for the door. "Why do we bother?!"

After Jay left, Richelle sat on the couch, reflecting. That had been a risky confrontation because she liked Jay—a lot. No, more than a lot. She'd had an absolute mad crush on him from the moment she first laid eyes on him. But it might be a long time, if ever, before he understood her and what she wanted from their relationship.

1964

Hanoi, North Vietnam

The room was stifling; a sauna with windows. The large fans on the ceiling seemed to be doing little but sending waves of humidity at Le Van Dat, barely moving the heavy air. He shifted in the hard seat and placed his right hand underneath his left arm for support. It somewhat relieved the pain of a limb that ached constantly. He had come close to losing it and his life in the Cambodian jungle. Recovery had been complicated by infection and was long in coming. The arm had recently been pronounced "good as new" by an army physician of suspect skill. For the pain, Dat had been forced to find narcotics on a black market that officially didn't exist in Communist North Vietnam. The drugs somewhat numbed his senses but were necessary for dealing with the pain.

Dat was waiting in the outer corridor of the ministry building that held the offices of his old friend and one-time sergeant, General Tran Van Minh. Minh had summoned him from the sanitarium at Son Tay, where Dat had been recovering. It would be good to see his old commander again.

Sweating under his light dress uniform, he swore as he noticed his underarm sweat rings creeping slowly along the shirt fibers toward a meeting at the center of his dress blouse.

Dat guessed these quarters had once been a French administrative building of some sort, with long, marble halls and huge windows. A door opened at the far end of the large room, and a young lieutenant padded toward him, his footsteps echoing, growing louder with every step. He stopped to salute before Dat.

"Sir, the general says he would be honored by your presence at this time. This way, please," he said with a slight bow, turning to lead Dat down the long hall.

Dat slowly got to his feet and shuffled off after the lieutenant. Entering Minh's office, the heat was forgotten and his mood lifted at the sight of his beaming friend coming around the desk to greet him.

"Dat," he said with open arms, "it has been far too long. Wonderful to see you again. I understand we almost lost you." The two embraced warmly. Standing back, the general seemed to inspect him.

"Oh, your arm? How is it these days?"

"Passable. Getting better by the day...they tell me."

The general was still a very young man, just thirty-five years of age, but there were lines around the eyes and chin, a bit of weight to the belly, and a small shadow of gray at the temples.

"Thank you for the report of your harrowing escape at Duc Co. The arrival of American helicopters had us on the run for a while. We had to improvise a new strategy to fight them." Then, studying Dat, Minh added, "I hope I can speak freely...to such an old and valued comrade."

Dat softly chuckled. "Of course, Minh. Old friends, indeed. As has always been the case, what is said between us goes no further. I am most curious, though. You hear many things lounging in a hospital. The politicians tell us fabulous stories, but how is the war going...really?"

Minh smiled, walked behind his desk, and proffered an open box with cigarettes. "Smoke? These are Players."

"Yes, thank you. Excellent."

Minh gestured for Dat to take a seat across from his desk and then sat himself. Lighting up, both men took deep drags. Minh exhaled, looking at the ceiling. "I will be more honest with you than I am with my closest aides, even my wife, because you and I...we have history. And...I am tired of keeping it all inside. Suspicions. Alliances. In Hanoi you never know who is listening and with what agenda. But you, I trust."

Dat understood. "You are a gifted commander, General. Leave the politics to the politicians."

Minh steadied his gaze on Dat, lowered his voice. "Easier said than practiced in Hanoi, Dat. But you were interested in news of the war. To answer your question...the war is going well. In fact, as well as the politicians claim!" Minh exclaimed, more upbeat. "Momentum has swung our way once again. The incompetent South's government is coming apart, and we've captured vast areas. There is much in the wind, my friend. Significant new directions...and *you* will be involved."

"Me? How?"

"Listen, and I will explain. But first...a little formality is in order," Minh said with a sly smile, standing. Dat, of course, stood with him. "By direction of the chief of staff, General Van Thien Dung, and with the explicit approval of the Politburo," Minh pontificated, "I have the pleasure of bestowing upon you the new rank of major. Congratulations, Major Le Van."

Dat, surprised at this unexpected announcement, stuttered, withdrew his words, and beamed. The general was pleased.

"Yes, it is my *distinct* pleasure. I wanted to be the one to present you with your promotion. I have to say...to *my* benefit, I saw great things in you upon our first meeting in the mountains so many years ago. You were raw...but full of a confidence and purpose far beyond your years. To say you have done well is a gross understatement."

"Thank you for your kind words, General. But certainly not as well as yourself."

"Well, we both know your lack of dedication to communism has always held you back. With the right ideology and commitment, you could have been promoted to major years ago. Such a shame...a waste of talent," Minh said, shaking his head with genuine disappointment.

Dat nodded, looked his friend in the eye. "I would not deny that my Communist ideals...stray. It seems I am helpless to contain them. You spoke of being open with our thoughts. Then I will admit, only to you, Communist ideology and politics...do not interest me."

"Ha, this is exactly what I mean," Minh said with a frown. "Your confession means nothing. I have already seen it in your face. And your superiors, the commissars, know your innermost thoughts just by studying you, Dat. The open book, eh? Ah...it will be your downfall. I should have done a better job indoctrinating you in 1948.

"But enough of this old regret. Sit, and I will tell you how it is.

"So far, 1964 has been an excellent year. The coup in the South?... It has worked superbly for us. The Khanh government is a joke, failing. The Southern army is more demoralized than ever. We've tested the Americans with pointed attacks on them here and there...and they've done nothing. They will not get in deeper. We have had sweeping victories all year. The curtain is closing." Minh brought his hands together.

"But..." Dat started, then stopped. "I do not wish to be contradictory..."

"Oh, really!" Minh tossed in.

Dat laughed.

"You...*contradictory*?!" Minh expounded, hands wide with a look of shock on his face.

"But as you mentioned just minutes ago," Dat continued, "the Americans? Speculation and rumor say they have invested too much to give up. They will...boost their commitment."

"Where or how do you think that would be?" Minh said, leaning forward. "The only thing they haven't committed is troops, boots on the ground...and, the general staff believes they will never commit to sending their own to be killed here. Let's hope that never happens. Perhaps they learned their lesson in Korea."

"Yes," Dat said, "that would be quite surprising. I cannot disagree with the general staff. But as I have been told in the past, the Americans do not like losing, and they rarely give up. And, it is an election year in America. That could change things. It is impossible to know." He paused slightly and then said, "You mentioned some big surprises in store...involving me."

"Yes. This is where you come in, Dat. Your orders," Minh said, sliding a page toward Dat. "You will lead one of the brigades from the 95th regiment of the 325th into the South with none other than Nguyen Thi Thanh at the front."

"What?" Dat said. "Am I hearing you right? The 325th into the South?... With Thanh?"

"Yes. Thanh is to be the commander-in-chief of all the Southern forces. He will be going with you."

"Extraordinary news, Minh," Dat said, thinking. "We are not talking about 'Southerners' or about the Viet Cong, here. This is the 325th. Main line troops...the People's Army. This will be viewed as nothing less than an invasion of the South. And...the Americans!"

"All true," Minh said. "But it hardly matters. I think...we *all* think...it is what our Southern brothers are waiting for. We are coming to deliver them from Khanh and the Americans. When they see our forces in the field, they will know the end is here. Perhaps they did not get to vote for joining us in 1957, but now that will not matter. The capitalists and old French elite will scatter like rats from a sinking ship. Rejoice, my friend! By this time next year, we will both have important new positions in Saigon. Or, should I say...Ho Chi Minh City. It will be renamed at the end of the war to honor our uncle. How about *that* for news!

"You know, Dat, I was here in Hanoi at the end of World War II when Ho claimed independence for our country. I was just a boy. What a glorious day! Throngs of people, all joyous, waving red flags. Officers, diplomats, and dignitaries from around the world attended. Even the Americans were there for the celebration! And the French?... They had been gone for years, the duration of the war. We knew our liberation had come."

Minh looked hard at Dat. "You know the rest, of course, but you should have been there. Ho is the only reason we are a sovereign nation, and for that reason alone you should be a better Communist! We can only hope he lives out the war to its inevitable conclusion."

Dat nodded in seeming agreement. A thought had sprung in his mind and would not leave him. Finally, he said, "Now...the Americans and their allies are our enemies. I hope you are right about them, Minh. If they ever do bring in troops, it will change everything...and the war could expand beyond any nightmare we could dream."

"I know you do not trust the generals and politicians," Minh said. "But listen this time, Dat...and mark *my* words. The Americans will be gone before the end of the year."

Fullerton, California

"I'd like you to ask Darla Jean to dance."

"Ahh, Dad! Please, not her," JT said.

"C'mon now, Jay. You know this is important to me. One dance won't kill you, son."

Judge Peter Kennison and his wife stood on the edge of the dance floor looking for all the world like Thurston and Lovey Howell III from Gilligan's Island. The judge with his prominent nose in the air appeared to be looking down with indifference upon the minions surrounding him. He was impeccable in his white dinner jacket that was beginning to reveal his growing girth. His wife appeared confused, as she usually did, in a lilac moo moo with a flash of gold jewelry that would have dazzled Phyllis Diller. Her pile of hair looked suspiciously like a wig. Accompanying them was daughter Darla Jean, a pudgy nut job JT had been trying to avoid his entire life.

JT walked, head down, to where the three stood swaying to the five-piece band's rendition of Peggy Lee's "Fever," with local twelve-handicapper Bill Gosforth on the trumpet.

"Well, JT!" the judge boomed at the approaching young man. "You're looking fine tonight in your dinner jacket and all. There aren't enough young men like you dressing up anymore. They're all caught up in this surfin' crap...baggies, sandals, and a T-shirt. Christ, what's the world comin' to, eh?"

"Yeah, really, Judge. I was wonderin'...," JT started.

"I read that you were in the California amateur. That's high cotton for a youngster like you. We all expect you to win it one year."

"Uh, thanks...Your Honor. I was hopin'..."

"Heard about the Kellor kid from San Diego sneakin' in the back door and beating you, though. Guess you just had a bad tournament. Hell, it happens to all of us. Where'd you place?... Twentieth, was it?"

"Thirty-fourth," JT sighed.

"Damn," the judge said at length. "We were hopin' for a little better effort than that, Jay! Maybe you should be out on the puttin' green right now."

"*Peter!*" the judge's wife said.

"Hey...just kiddin'. *Just kiddin'.* Hell, you're a good little golfer, JT. Someday you'll make us proud...I'm sure."

"I was wonderin' if Darla Jean would like to dance," JT said quickly.

The judge looked at his daughter, who had her eyes closed and was swaying to the music, seemingly oblivious. The three of them stood looking at her, transfixed. She seemed in another world, far away.

"Darla Jean!" the judge said.

"Shit...what?" she said, surprised.

The judge and his wife grimaced. JT could hardly contain his smirk.

"What is it with you these days? Try to pay attention, girl. JT would like you to dance with him."

"Cool."

"I told you to stop using that damned beatnik lingo. Now, go ahead. Don't keep JT waiting."

Jay offered his arm, and the two walked to the middle of the dance floor as the band struck up "Louie, Louie." Darla Jean launched into a wild Watusi that drew more than a few odd looks. JT cringed at the exhibition and hung back from her as far as he could while doing the Twist. He would be counting the seconds until the song ended. Darla Jean, on the other hand, seemed to be having a wonderful time, even though he might as well have not been there.

There were fewer and fewer kids showing up for club functions these days. Jay felt his generation moving away from dinner jackets and club dancing. Having to dance with the judge's daughter was one more reason he wished he wasn't here. But Judge Kennison was a charter member of the club and head of the membership drive, an important man in the community, to the club and his father. So, Jay would dance the part of the good son in the monkey suit and ignore the judge's snide remarks.

The arrival of Richelle Gaston and her family caught his attention like unexpected fireworks on a clear night. He saw her standing in the light at the top of the stairs dressed in a beautiful green, full-length ballroom gown that was perfectly matched to her coloring. She looked like a lime popsicle among the many white and pastel dresses in the room. Her hair was pulled back and tied off in an explosive ponytail. Jay had to smile in admiration.

With his eyes and thoughts centered on Richelle, he barely noticed the song ending. Darla Jean, in fact, didn't seem to notice at all. Jay tapped the silently swaying debutante on the shoulder.

"Yeah?" she said, opening her eyes.

"Jeez, Darla Jean, the song's over," Jay said. "Thanks for the dance. C'mon, I'll walk you back to your parents."

"Let's dance some more, please!" she said, suddenly grabbing him by the arm and pulling him close.

"Uhh...sorry. I've gotta use the men's room. Maybe later."

"Well, then, take me over to the refreshments. I sure as hell don't wanna stand around with Mumsy and Duddy any longer."

With Darla Jean's hand locked firmly on Jay's arm, they walked to the refreshment table where the toothy Norma Ruddnik, club secretary and punch bowl operator, greeted them.

"Oh...don't you two look just darling together! Punch?"

"Thank you. That would be nice, Miss Ruddnik," Jay said.

Standing beside the table sipping punch, Jay was desperate to remove himself from the vice-like hold Darla Jean had on him. It felt as though his hand was going numb.

"Darla...I really..."

"Let's go outside," she said, interrupting him. "I have something I'd like to share with you. You'll like it," she finished in a conspiratorial whisper.

"Naw, look," he said, grabbing her hand and removing it as gently as possible. "I have to excuse myself and use the men's room. I'll see ya later...I'm sure."

Without looking back, he moved swiftly toward the men's room.

His father was inside, busy trying to rearrange thinning hair over a growing bald spot.

"Ah, Jay. Nice job with Darla Jean. I appreciate that," he said, frowning one last time at the disappointing hair and straightening his bow tie before turning to his son. "I know you don't care much for her, but you'll find there are many things in life you have to do that are unpleasant. The best advice I can give you is to just..."

"Soldier on," Jay finished in a martial voice. "Meet your responsibilities head on with a smile, get it over with, and move on."

Leaning on the counter with a smirk of his own, George let him finish—then changed the subject.

"How about that Richelle? Have you seen her? What a gown."

"Yeah," Jay said, brightening. "She looks great."

"Well then," George said, slapping his son on the back, "that's your next assignment."

Jay approached Richelle from behind as she stood alone by the dance floor.

"Hello," he said. "You look, uh, radiant tonight."

Richelle turned to him and smiled broadly.

"And aren't you just the handsome one?" she said.

Jay blushed. Richelle giggled.

"That's a very nice dress, Richelle," Jay said in response.

Richelle paused and smiled warmly before responding.

"Thank you."

"Well hello, young fella," Richelle's father said as he and his wife, Gladys, joined them. "Haven't seen you in a while, JT. Seems like a nice little get-together."

"Yes, sir, Gabby...er, sorry, Mr. Gaston. It just slipped."

"No sweat, Jay. I guess the advertising's working. Say, Gladys, isn't that Bill and Henrietta? I heard they were considering listing their house. Uh, excuse us, kids. We should say hello."

"Wonder why we're here?" Richelle said to Jay as her parents literally ran across the room.

"Seems to be what it's all about," Jay said. "Impressing one another. Making contacts. This whole thing is so phony."

"I haven't seen you much lately," Richelle said.

"Yeah...well, with golf and all," Jay said.

"How's the Rink?" Richelle asked.

"Just like any other school...except there's no school grounds, no sports, no band, no clubs, and almost no students."

Starting his freshman year, George and Clara had placed Jay in the Rink Academy, a private school. His mother had hoped the extra attention would help his grades, while at the same time the Rink's relaxed and very accommodating schedule meant Jay had all the time to practice golf, like his father wanted.

"There is one upside," Jay said. "I'm fifteenth in my class."

"That's great!" Richelle responded. "I guess it's been good for you."

"Sure, but then again there are only eighteen kids in my class."

They both laughed. The band struck up its lively rendition of the Beach Boys' current Top Forty hit, "Surfin' USA." Bill Gosforth was at the microphone singing the lead. Richelle and JT winced in unison.

"Okay," Jay said with a sigh. "I guess this is about as good as it's gonna get tonight, Richelle. Let's dance."

"Yup, let's rock and roll!"

On the floor, they joined the multitude of forty-plusers who were trying to jitterbug or do the Twist. Others jerked spasmodically to the beat or tried a quick two-step.

"I heard you were elected secretary of your student council," Jay said over the music. "You know, for sophomores that's always been a stepping-stone to student body president."

"A girl?! President? Not likely."

"Ya never know, Richelle. You could be the first."

"If I really wanted that...and I'm not sure I would. Hey, I've heard Tony Dow goes to Rink. Is that true?"

"Naw. I've never seen him. Anyway, isn't he really like twenty-five or somethin'?"

"How about you!" Richelle said, brightening. "I read the article in the *Times* about the California Amateur tournament. You must be proud. You did really well."

Since she had seen her very first sports article that mentioned JT, Richelle had been keeping a secret scrapbook of his accomplishments. Having every article and having read each many times, she knew Jay's accomplishments better than he did.

"Yeah, well I'd rather not talk about that stupid tournament," Jay said, still seething over the judge's inquisition.

It caught Richelle by surprise.

"What do you mean?" she asked. "I think playing...and placing so well in such a big tournament is a really good thing. I don't understand."

"You don't know, Richelle. It's not a good thing for me. Knowing there are thirty-three better amateur golfers than me in this state...including a kid from San Diego my age who I've beaten every time we've played. He was three strokes better. All that work on my game...for what?!"

"It's just one tournament, JT. Give yourself a break. I think you did really well."

"I really don't want to talk about this," Jay said.

The song ended with the band immediately launching into Mancini's "Moon River." Richelle assumed a dancing pose, arching her eyebrows. JT moved in, putting his arm around her waist as they proceeded into a slow two-step.

Having her in his arms smothered his irritation. She smelled terrific with just a hint of an intoxicating fragrance.

JT cursed himself. Why did Richelle get under his skin so? He liked her. He really did. Yet every time they talked, it seemed to end badly. Why couldn't they get along better?

Richelle sighed inwardly. Why did it seem everything she said to JT turned into a confrontation? As much as she loved Jay, it seemed impossible for them to have a normal, civilized conversation. Was it JT, or her, or were they both to blame? Perhaps they needed to grow up, but would JT ever mature into the man she wanted him to be? If he didn't, she knew she would still want him.

"You smell nice," Jay said, breaking the stream of thoughts.

"Thank you. I like your cologne. Jade East?"

"Yeah. So...your family's new club members, I see. Let me welcome you."

"Thanks. It seems your dad wanted Mom and Dad in the club. So, they worked out a good deal. My dad thinks a lot of your father."

"Oh... I get it."

"Get it? Get what?"

"Well, er...it's just, you know, real expensive to join Fullerton Park."

"What do you mean by that?"

"Nothin'."

"You don't think we belong in your club? Not richy rich enough for you?"

"No...oh, come on, Ricky. That's not what I meant. It's just..."

"Really. What did you mean?"

"Hey, look...let's forget about it."

They danced a moment longer, but just a moment. Then Richelle pushed him away, turned, and left the dance floor so quickly that Jay was left as if holding a ghost.

"Hey, kid," a man dancing nearby said. "Don't worry about it. It won't be the last time."

"Oh, stop," his partner said.

Why did I say that? Jay asked himself again. *Why do I say these things?*

He walked with seemingly every eye on him off the dance floor and through the sliding doors to the pool area. Except for eddies created by the inflow valves, the pool was a sheet of glowing, blue glass reflecting a quartering moon.

You're an idiot loser, he told himself. *With all the benefits thrown your way you can only place thirty-fourth?! I could beat grown men when I was eight years old. And women?... Well, you just thoroughly insulted the shit out of the one girl you ever really liked. Smooth move, Ex-Lax.*

On the far side of the pool was the lifeguard's chair. Behind it were the five campy cabanas put in for nostalgia's sake by his father.

They lay between the entrances for the large club dressing rooms for men and women. Each had a louvered door, giving the pool area an old-timey look like a scene out of Billy Wilder's comedy hit *Some Like It Hot.*

He walked around the pool, noticing one of the cabana doors slightly ajar. As he passed the open entry, he moved his hand toward the knob to give it a push shut. Instead, the door opened. He was grabbed firmly by the wrist and yanked inside the darkened room. Jay briefly wrestled with someone in the dark before recognizing Darla Jean in the dim light.

"What the hell?" Jay said.

"Relax," Darla Jean said, laughing. "I won't bite you...maybe."

Jay started to make his excuses and reached for the knob. Darla grabbed his arm. Again, Jay noticed how strong she seemed.

"No, don't open the door," Darla said. "Like I told you, I've got something I'd like to share. You like to share, don't you?"

"Sure," Jay said with more than a touch of sarcasm. "What're you up to, Darla?"

"Trust me, you'll like it," she said. Digging in her small purse, she produced a hand-rolled cigarette.

"Nah, thanks anyway," Jay said. "I don't smoke."

She giggled. "Yeah, I knew you wouldn't have a clue. It's Mary Jane, man. The real stuff—good stuff. I've got some hip friends in Encino..."

"Marijuana!" Jay cut in. "Whoa, Darla Jean. I mean...here? I smoked once, but I mean..."

"I'm shocked! Mister all-American tight-ass smokes reefer? Shocked!"

"Yeah, that's right," Jay said. "Some guys at a match play tournament had it. Whaddya mean tight-ass?"

"You get high, JT?"

"Well..."

"Not really, huh?"

"Look, I did it just once. It didn't work for me."

"Well, then. Let's see if we can get you stoned."

"You're crazy, Darla Jean. Here?! Fifty feet from the clubhouse? Your old man.... Judge Kennison for God's sake. My father? I don't think so," Jay said, reaching again for the door. Once more, the hand intercepted his.

"I saw you with Richelle," she said.

"So?"

"Didn't look like it went so well. You didn't look too happy walking over here, JT. Wouldn't it feel great to get stoned and just forget about your problems? Getting high is a great escape, man. Sometimes...reality really stinks. Know what I mean?"

"Yeah. Sometimes it stinks, all right."

With that she flicked a lighter, illuminating the cabana and throwing an eerie light on her face as she sucked on the reefer and drew deep breaths with accompanying pops and crackles from the weed's mixture. She closed the lighter and stood in the silhouette of the louvers, sucking in more air before exhaling in a burst.

"Ahhh, yesss. C'mon, your turn."

Jay backed off, but not much given the close confines. "Aw, I don't know..."

"Ah, fuck, JT..oops! I shouldn't say that," she giggled. "Forget about it, man. Smoke up. Let's get loose. This'll make everything better. You'll see."

Jay tentatively grabbed the reefer and put it to his lips. But after sucking in the harsh smoke, he coughed violently. Darla grabbed the joint out of his hands.

"There, there," Darla said, between hits on the joint. "There, there."

Jay puffed on the reefer again, with less coughing this time. Then again…and again. He was starting to get the hang of it.

"I still don't think I feel anything," he said, passing the joint.

"You will. Just relax and enjoy it, man," Darla said. She reached out and grabbed him around the neck. Pulling him to her, she kissed him passionately, working her tongue inside his mouth. Jay didn't resist. In fact, it felt good. While taking another drag on the rapidly disappearing joint, she moved her hand to his butt. Jay giggled.

"Whoa, now," he said. "That's a little fresh, Darla Jean."

As she passed the joint, Jay noticed that her eyes looked glassy and half open in a dreamlike stare. "There's one thing I just know you'd love to do high, Jay," she said.

Inside the clubhouse, Norma Ruddnik had just turned to open a cooler for more ice when she noticed smoke coming from the louvers in one of the cabanas.

"Fire," she said hesitantly. Then, "FIRE!" she screamed.

Inside the cabana, Jay and Darla heard the commotion and, through the louvers, saw the legs of George Johnson running to the cabana. Darla quickly swallowed the roach before the door was flung open. Jay's dad stood looking at them, shaken and surprised. Jay must have had the same look on his face. A small crowd, led by Judge Kennison, was making its way to the cabana.

Shifting his gaze downward, George said in a harsh whisper, "Zip it up, JT, for chrissake." Which Jay did just before Judge Kennison and several guests arrived on the scene.

"No problem," George said, good-naturedly to the crowd, giving them a shooing motion with his hands. "False alarm. It was just a cigarette. There's no fire. Back to the dance now. C'mon, let's have some fun."

People moved away, laughing, except Peter Kennison, who had an odd look on his face.

"Cigarette...my ass!" he hissed, looking at Jay and Darla, who were quite red-faced. "I'm a judge. I've taken my share of criminal awareness classes. That's the distinct odor of marijuana."

"Oh, now, Judge..." George stopped mid-sentence after seeing the look on his son's face. "What's the meaning of this?" George said to Jay.

Darla Jean broke from the cabana, moving quickly to her father. Looking into his face, she said, "I didn't want to, Daddy, really. JT said it would feel good and..."

"What?!" JT said.

"Is that right?" the judge said.

"No, that's not right," said Jay.

"Oh, I think I know what this is about," the judge stated in a cold, flat voice. "Cocky young athlete thinks he owns the world. Picks up drugs from his jock friends with the idea of corrupting innocent girls."

"That's outrageous!" Jay said. "She pulled *me* into the cabana..."

"Don't you yell at me, punk! I'll call the police and have you thrown in jail tonight. Think how that'll make your father look. And no more tournaments for you...what with a criminal record and all."

JT turned to his father. "Dad, you gotta believe me, I'd never..."

"This is an abomination...and I blame myself," the judge

continued. "I should have seen this coming from the likes of you. Smartass hotshot."

"Now you wait just a goddamn minute!" George said.

"If I were you I'd hold my tongue, George Johnson," the judge said. Then to his daughter, "Join your mother, girl. You don't need to hear any of this. We'll talk at home."

"Dad, you believe me, don't you?" JT appealed to his father. "She had this stuff in her purse."

"Now you stop this nonsense!" the judge fairly shouted. "As if my daughter would ever..."

Inside the clubhouse, a few people heard the commotion and drifted back to the patio door to listen.

"You're accusing my daughter of perpetrating this atrocity?! You're quite mad if you think anyone will believe that, young man."

"I think we should move this discussion to my office," George said, looking at the growing crowd.

"Oh, there won't be any further *discussion*, George," the judge said, warming up. "I won't be a part of a club that promotes the use of dope."

"Judge, really?!" George said.

"And the ruination of young ladies...while you protect this... this spoiled pothead! I'm resigning my membership, immediately. You'll have my letter in the morning...and don't be surprised if I pursue legal action in civil court. The idea!"

JT could take no more. The anxiety and frustration of the moment overwhelmed him. Seeking an escape, he broke and ran to the gate leading to the 10th hole.

"Sure, run away," the judge called after him. "But you can't run away from who you are, punk."

George sat on the sectional, massaging the taut muscles in his aching neck with his right hand. Clara paced and worried her handkerchief into little knots. Charlie sat in a corner on one of those forgotten chairs that are in every large room for balance and appearance only, rarely entertaining a seat.

"What the hell has gotten into that boy?" Clara was saying, over and over. "Where would he get marijuana? What would make him do such a thing? And...where the hell is he?"

They both turned at the sound of the sliding patio door. George rose from the couch as JT walked silently into the room. It wasn't the sulking, contrite entry of a wayfaring boy they had expected, though. Rather, Jay's posture was erect and his expression one of confidence and peace.

"Where have you been?" immediately jumped from Clara as she rushed to Jay and wrapped him in her arms. "You worried us silly, JT."

"Sorry, Mom," JT said, returning the embrace.

"You have some explaining to do, young man," George said, with a gravity that didn't hint of the relief he felt.

"Yeah, I do," Jay said. "We need to talk."

"It's been a difficult night, thanks to you and Miss Kennison. I for one would love nothing better than to go to bed right now... but that won't do now, will it? We need some answers. Sit down, son," George said.

JT left his mother's embrace and took a place on the couch with a composure that could be interpreted, in such circumstances, as impertinent. It made George boil.

"First...what in the hell were you thinking? Smoking marijuana during a club function?"

"Well...," JT began.

"You knew exactly what you were doing. This isn't like you, so please explain this to me."

"I kinda had to figure that out myself," JT responded.

George sat down next to his son.

"So, what?... It's all figured out now?"

"It doesn't help to be so sarcastic, dear," Clara said.

"I'm not happy," JT said.

"Good, we have that in common," George said.

"See, Dad...I'm not gonna do this anymore. I'm tired of tournaments, the practicing, the travel...it's all I've ever done. I'm finished. I'm not doing it anymore. And Rink isn't a school. I don't have any friends...the kind of friends you make at school. I'm leaving Rink and I'm going to enroll at Fullerton High."

"Ridiculous," George said.

"But JT...you know why I wanted you there.... It's your grades," Clara said.

"How did you get the idea that high school was all good times and fun? It's not. It's overrated. This is a short time in your life, and Rink allows you time for your game," George said. "It's what we..."

"You said it, Dad. It's a short time in my life. It's high school. I want to play other sports...like football. I love the game, and I'm big enough to play. And they have a golf team. So I'll do that too."

"You've got to be kidding. These are the *important* years..."

"I miss school," Jay said. "I don't have any friends at Rink or on the links. Fullerton High is just what I need.... I'm really excited about this decision. And, Mom, I won't let you down. My grades will improve—you'll see."

"Okay, okay. It's been a trying night...a strange night that's getting stranger. We need to get some rest and talk about this in the morning," George said, getting up.

"It won't change a thing, Dad. I'm so excited about this I'm vibrating. It's gonna be great for all of us. You'll see."

1965

Helena, Montana

Mom was preparing dinner while Dad and I watched the evening news. As usual, there was a report on a civil rights demonstration, this time in Kentucky. Then came a report from South Vietnam. The reporter was standing by a transport plane in Da Nang as soldiers marched off its ramp.

"...these two battalions of the Marine Expedition Brigade are the first significant ground forces ever committed to duty in South Vietnam by the US Government. A press release from General Westmoreland's headquarters states their only mission is the defense and protection of this air base at Da Nang, guarded until now by South Vietnam forces. In a recent evaluation of those defenses by Westmoreland's Deputy General John Throckmorton, security was deemed dangerously inadequate for the safety of the US servicemen who work here. General Westmoreland's staff stresses that the Marine deployment is strictly for defense of the base. I had an opportunity to speak with a few of the Marines..."

The video shifted to a young Marine with a crew cut, a big smile, and a T-shirt, standing confidently with his hands on his hips.

"So, how does it feel to be in Vietnam? Was this a surprise for you?" the reporter asked.

"Well, sure," said the Marine. "But I'm ready. We're all ready to do our duty here. Actually, we're itchin' to get into this thing."

"Why's that?" the reporter cut in.

"You know, bein' Americans, none of us like oppression. South Vietnam deserves to be free. The Viet Cong have had an easy time till now. But we're the real deal. We're gonna kick some Commie [*bleep*] very shortly."

The Marine grinned broader. The camera shifted back to the reporter.

"Brave? Without question...and ready to do their duty. These Marines bring a security and firepower that has been sorely lacking in the South's effort until now. No one seems to know just how long these Marines will be deployed in Vietnam..."

Some recent comments by Buddy came back to me. He said
Vietnam would be a big problem. I didn't think it would, but the
news story got me thinking: Marines in Da Nang? Could Bud be
right? I looked at Dad, who seemed somewhat disinterested.

"Whaddya think about Vietnam, Dad?"

"Hmm. Oh, uh...I dunno. Haven't paid a whole lot of attention. Just another situation the politicians are all riled up about."

"Well...there's been some talk about Vietnam at school. Ya
know, it's been in the news a lot more lately. The idea's been brought
up...sorta...that maybe...uh, we shouldn't get involved there."

Dad turned his attention to me in a way that indicated a closer
interest in what I was saying.

I quickly added, "I don't mean everyone, ya know. Everyone's
really behind our stopping communism and stuff."

"Shouldn't be there?" Dad said, warming up. "Well, who *should*
be there then?"

"Hey, I don't know. It's not *my* idea," I replied turning back to
the set. *Danger, Will Robinson!* my mind screamed. *Danger!*

"We're the only ones who're standin' between those countries
over there and the Communists, Mark. If not us, who? Truman
gave up China and it led to Communist Korea. We ended up fighting'
in' the Koreans *and* the damn red Chinese. We let the Commies
take Vietnam and the whole area goes after that. Don't they teach
that in school? Hell, if we'd only stopped Hitler sooner. I remember
before Pearl Harbor...no, nobody wanted to get involved. Keep the
US out of it! Well, that idea cost us dearly in the end, and nobody's
gonna forget that anytime soon. You gotta stop the problem at the
source or it will just keep growin'."

He took, if possible, an even more severe look at me. "Who's
sayin' these things at school? I'd like to know who their parents are.
Probably some of those liberals. Disgraceful! Situations like this are
when the president and servicemen need everyone's support," Dad
finished.

"Forget it, Dad. It's just a crazy idea from some nut. Nobody
else feels that way. And look at those guys! They're gonna kick some
butt. That's the US Marines there," I added with a savage grin.

"You're right about that," Dad agreed, sitting back in his chair.
"Those commie rats aren't gonna mess with that base now."

As Mom called us to supper, I was happy to be done with the

subject. I would have to stop listening to Buddy and his wacko ideas *and* wise up about what topics I brought up with my parents. My folks and others would start thinking I was un-American.

Joe Wills stuffed his shaving kit on top of his clothes and closed the lid, snapped the latches, and hauled the suitcase off his bed, placing it on the floor between us. He turned and gave me a smile.

"How about this, huh? I'm finally outta here. This time tomorrow I'll be in Fort Lewis."

"Wish I were goin' with you," I said.

"Your time'll come. Enjoy school."

Joe's mom showed up at the door. "Well, honey, you ready to go? Mark, you comin' with us?"

"No. I've got a couple lawns to mow. I just took a few minutes off to say bye."

"Okay, then. Joe, I'll see you in the car."

"Right, Mom," Joe said as his mother left the room. "Well, Cam, this is it, bud. I'll write you from boot camp and let you know what to expect."

"I already know what to expect. My brother was in the Navy."

"Yeah, but he was a swabbie. I'm goin' to a *real* boot camp."

"Huh! Just wait, Joe. You'll be jealous of Navy guys someday," I said.

With Joe having graduated and leaving for the Army, it reminded me of how short a time remained before I would be doing the same. Brother Jim had been bugging me to join the Naval Reserve, as he had. In a way, I was excited by the idea, somewhat catching Joe's and my brother's enthusiasm for service duty. Another part of me, though, deep inside—residing next to the coward I'd become—cringed at the very thought.

Ia Drang Valley, South Vietnam

Dat stood beside the trail watching men straggle by. After two and a half days of heavy fighting, they were retreating into Cambodia. His back and shoulder hurt, as did the burns on his legs and hands, but his wounds weren't nearly as severe as most. Many of the men filing past were in sad shape, their eyes sunken and fatigued. There were many wounded—some walking, some carried. Hundreds of dead had been carried out and buried, while hundreds more were left behind. This last bit was the exclamation point. You don't abandon six or seven hundred men dead on the battlefield unless you have certainly lost.

By any sane person's account of war, this had been a terrible defeat for the People's Army of Vietnam. Yet, Dat knew even now his superiors were telling the people of the North how this had been a great victory. It was necessary to do so. The boiler of war fever had to be regularly stoked to keep the people's will and spirits at a feverish pitch. The propaganda machine was large and extremely critical to the war effort, but never more important than now. They had been fighting twenty years and, Dat feared, might have to fight twenty more.

Dat himself felt there was a certain "victory" attained by his troops. Under tremendous pressure from ceaseless bombardment, the army had pressed the attack. They had proven themselves dedicated soldiers; had not run or put up only a token resistance. They had fought hard and had shown their good military training. The Americans had to be impressed. It had taken a tidal wave of ordnance to repel them. He thought a message had been sent. But, he wondered, would the egotistical Americans get it? Did they understand the People's Army now?

Their first conflict with the Americans showed just what kind of war this new war would be. The Americans never had more than a regiment on the battlefield. They were outnumbered eight or ten to one. Nevertheless, they had prevailed. Fighting them on a stationary front at battalion size would never produce a victory. Any ideas of an invasion of the South would have to be squelched. Invasion of the North by the Americans must now be a great concern.

As Dat turned to join his men on the trail, he reflected on his last meeting with his old comrade, General Minh. The general and all the politicians had read it wrong. The Americans would stay; would commit their youth to the fight. What his people had given and sacrificed would not be near enough. Somehow, they had to get better.

1967

Helena, Montana

I hated to see the holidays end. The start of classes was as welcome as Dad dragging me out of bed by the ankle on a chilly morning, which he sometimes did. Before me stretched month upon month of unbroken school weeks, the cold and dark Montana January adding to my misery. Arriving at school before sunrise, I would leave with the sun already behind the mountains and the mercury descending faster than a Mickey Mantle pop-up. Furnaces ran nonstop to keep up with the arctic fronts barreling down through Canada, and every venture outside required head-to-toe bundling. Such was our life in winter's coldest month.

Into this winged Joe Wills, fresh from Vietnam, in an old DC-10. In the year since he had gone to Nam, we'd corresponded a few times, and there was occasionally an article about him in the "Men Who Wear the Uniform" section of the local paper. Joe had received a Bronze Star and a Purple Heart.

The war was hardly a quiet little affair anymore. To us in Montana, the mood was one of hope, support for the troops, and confidence in the final outcome. The Hawks had plenty of supporters in the Treasure State. Still, there were protestors, too. They were in the minority, but I knew they existed and who they were.

While walking to my locker at lunchtime, I saw Stanley leaning against the wall reading the first edition of the 1967 school newspaper. He didn't look happy.

"What's up, Stan?" I said, throwing my locker open with a flourish and a vibrating clang.

"Have you seen the stuff our senior editor wrote in the paper?" Stan snarled, looking up at me. "What a crock! It's un-American to say the things he says about Vietnam. Somebody needs to shut this guy up!"

"C'mon, Stan.... It's just Buddy. Old news."

"Uh-uh. Not this. He goes too far this time. North Vietnam is just like all Communist countries. They lie and cheat and take away

the rights of their people. Buddy has no compassion for those people and what they're suffering. You don't agree with him, do you?"

"No, don't think so. My Naval Reserve commander would not
look too kindly on me protesting the war," I said, not actually an-
swering the question.

"Yeah, of course not. Sorry."

He wadded the paper up and threw it on the floor.

"Calm down, for crissakes. This is just Buddy, man. And...you
shouldn't litter the halls like that."

I looked up, and there she was. As chosen unanimously in my
biased, one-person opinion poll, the most beautiful girl in school,
Jan Fred, my girlfriend. Her long shapely legs and seductive looks
were probably a real turn-on for every guy she met. She gave us
that fabulous smile.

"Hi," she said. "Who ya havin' lunch with?"

"Buddy, I think. He's a little late. What're you off to?"

"Chemistry class, and I'm going to be late myself if I don't
scoot. How about Buddy's editorial?"

"Uh, Stan was just talking about it. I haven't read it."

"That Buddy's a nutcase! Where'd he get those ideas?"

"Well, I'll tell you it's nothing new. I first heard Bud talk out
against Vietnam two years ago. Imagine him having these ideas *two
years ago*! I don't know..."

"It's sure gonna be trouble for him. It's not what anybody I
know thinks. Cripes," she said, glancing at the clock in the hallway.
"I gotta run. See you after school?"

"I wouldn't miss it. Love ya."

"You, too. Later," she said while being swallowed up in the
lunch crowd traffic.

I couldn't get over how fortunate I was to have such a babe as
my girlfriend. I watched the last of her red mane bobbing down
the hall. Stan turned and looked at me.

"How?... You are one lucky guy, Mark."

I could only smile. She was the smartest, sexiest, most talented
girl I'd ever known. She was a majorette and a straight-A student. A
popular girl in her sophomore class, her friends called her "Fred the
Red" because of that wild burst of reddish orange hair I just loved.
Winning her affection was the most amazing accomplishment of
my entire life.

"Look," said Stanley, giving me a poke that broke my reverie. "Here comes the commie creep now."

Bud looked angry. Not acknowledging us, he opened his locker and literally his books into a bind-breaking heap at the foot of his locker. He grabbed the metal door and stood swearing silently. Then, looking at me, he said, "I've been fired!"

"What? From your Dairyland job?"

"No, no. Principal Harper fired me from the school paper. Fuck!"

I glanced at Stan and saw the smirk on his face.

"I think, uh...Harper's probably had it out for you since your column about his opening day speech last fall."

"No, he actually complimented me on it. Said it was a good parody. Creative and funny. Man...I had confidence the guy had my back. Well, I was wrong! He said he couldn't allow an article like my Vietnam piece in a student paper. Can you imagine? Shit! I mean...it's what democracy, freedom of the press, self-expression is all about, isn't it? He said, 'We might live in a democracy, but this high school isn't one. I control what goes on here and you're out.'"

"Damn right!" Stanley said. "It's time someone shut you up, Buddy!"

"Well...who's this, Mark? Joe McCarthy? Wake up and smell the napalm, Stanley."

Stan's face turned red. He reached for Buddy's shirt as Bud reached for his. I hurriedly stepped between them, the three of us now face to face.

"Gentlemen," I said. "Not here...C'mon."

"You right-wing asshole!" Buddy said. "I could kick your ass right here, right now...and you know it."

"Commie faggot!" Stan retorted. "Bring it on!"

"Stan, I believe you have class now. You'll be late. Buddy and I need to get goin'. We're late, too."

Stan turned and stalked off.

"Think about it, Stan," Buddy shouted after him. Stan raised his middle finger and kept walking.

We walked to my car for the short trip up to Scotty's Drive-In for lunch. Buddy wouldn't shut up.

"There are half a million US troops in Vietnam right now. Half a million! In 1965 there were 2,500 US casualties. Last year, the number was 33,000, man! But that's nothing! We're on a record pace. Last year's figures may double or even triple! They're killing off our generation, man. We're being fed into the killing machine."

"You can't control that from a high school paper, Buddy," I responded. "And you'd better cool it with this Vietnam stuff because nobody else in this school sees it your way. It's un-American. You're just pissing lots of people off. Some of 'em have brothers there. Remember Dick Meyer? He's there right now."

That really set him off. "Doesn't make it right!... And I've got lots of supporters."

"Yeah," I said. "Name one."

He plowed on. "I'm no Communist. Vietnam's a civil war. Two ideologies battling it out. What the hell are we doing there? It's like our own Civil War.... What if France had put their lot in with the Confederacy? Would that have been right?

"But here's the kicker. You'll like this one, Mark. There's no way in hell the US will ever win this thing."

"You're fuckin' looney, Buddy," I heatedly interjected. "The most powerful nation on earth! There's no way we're gonna lose in Nam. It's a matter of time."

"Time?! Time is on their side, Mark, and you don't have to look very far to understand that."

We climbed in my car. I started the car and slammed it into gear. Buddy looked at me, bemused, waiting for the question I didn't want to deliver. I knew I'd lose this argument. He had it all set up in his mind, and I was the hopeless idiot he had baited. Part of my frustration was being such a poor representative of my generation when it came to defending the American way of life. I refused to ask what he meant by his last comment, so he forged on.

"How do you think America won the Revolutionary War, huh?"

Crap. Here it came.

"We didn't have the manpower...the weaponry...the money... and yet, we were victorious! Was it all the battles we won? Hah, we didn't win shit. What we did was persevere. We stuck it out. It didn't matter that we were grossly overmatched by the world's finest military. Didn't matter they regularly kicked our butt and occupied every major city and port. We refused to go away. We refused to lose. Americans were passionate, fighting for a cause, and the Brits didn't understand that.

"Vietnam will be the same. The North won't give up and Johnson won't invade.... He's rightly afraid of starting World War III. Americans will get tired of the war, of all the casualties, the cost... and opinions, lots of opinions, will change. We're gonna lose it all right, but thousands of dead soldiers our age, maybe some good friends, won't be around at the end."

"But it's our duty, man!" I yelled in frustration. "I don't agree with you. Communist aggression has to be stopped. We have to draw the line. I'm sorry you don't get it, and I think it would be better for everyone if you quit bugging people."

We pulled into Scotty's and got out of the car, Bud coming around to face me.

"You see all these kids?" Bud said, looking at the lunch crowd. "They're lookin' for the glorious adventure. Lots of these guys think Nam is it. They wanna kick some commie butt. None of 'em agree with me now, and yet, one day they will. And one day, so will you," he said.

Bud walked into Scotty's with his hands in his pockets looking like he hadn't a care in the world. I noticed lots of guys throw nasty looks his way.

As always, Bud had made his points. These arguments over Vietnam made me squirm. I didn't have strong enough feelings about saving Vietnam from communism. I wasn't gung-ho like Stan, and Bud knew it. I'd been listening to him for two years and, frankly, a lot of what he said made sense.

In just admitting it, though, I felt like a traitor. What would my folks or my brother think? What about Joe Wills, or Stan? I was going to keep quiet about my lack of commitment, my uncertainty, and hope for the right kind of inspiration—the kind I would need if ever asked to pick up a gun.

It was ten below zero on Friday night when I fired up the old Chevy and headed out to meet Joe and a friend of his, Larry Carter. Larry was a Vietnam vet who had befriended Joe while he was in high school. Joe had invited me to Larry's apartment for a night of partying. I'd told Mom I was meeting a friend, going to a movie, staying overnight. She didn't offer much resistance. Now that I was a senior, she'd begun to give me more leeway and, of course, I took advantage on occasion.

Coming up the street, I saw Joe getting out of his mom's car. I swung the Chevy in behind and hopped out. We shook hands, briefly hugged, and slapped each other on the back.

"Great to see you, man!" I said.

"Yeah, same here. Come on, man, it's cold. Let's get inside."

The change in Joe was noticeable. He had filled out his six-foot-five frame. There was a maturity about the eyes, a serious slant to his mouth. Carter greeted us at the door and threw an arm around Joe. They hugged like brothers and leaned back to look at one another.

"You're a vet now, man. Got yourself the ribbons and everything, huh? It's good to see you back in one piece. Grab a seat. You too, Mark. I'll get a coupla beers."

Joe rubbed his hands and blew into them, trying to warm up. "It's cold, man. Real cold. Nam was cold sometimes, too. Not like this, though."

"Cold? Shoot, I've seen pictures of Nam on the news. It's a jungle," I said. "The Vietnamese walk around in this see-through stuff. So, what're you talkin' about?"

"Yeah, well that's in the delta...or in summer. Where I was... up in the DMZ...during monsoon I was as cold as I've ever been. Sittin' all night in a downpour with nothing but an unlined poncho to keep warm. Of course, the tension made it seem worse. And then the wind would blow. Yeah, it was damn cold!"

Carter returned with the beer. "Yeah, the fuckin' monsoon. The endless rain. Problem was always getting the right equipment out in the field. Am I right, Joe?"

"Fuckin' A. The quartermasters and mail guys had all the poncho liners. Used 'em to line their bunk spaces to keep warm while us grunts froze our ass off out there."

We raised our beers in a salute to Joe's survival and swallowed deep.

"Hey, I just got a new album by Jefferson Airplane. I'll put it on," Larry said.

"Jefferson Airplane? Never heard of 'em. Are they new?" Joe wanted to know.

"Yeah, they've got this song about Alice in Wonderland that's a big hit," I added. Larry snickered, Joe looked confused.

"So," Carter said, grabbing a seat on the sofa next to me as the music of Jefferson Airplane kicked on, "tell us about it, Joe. Things've changed quite a bit since I was in Nam, I'm sure."

"Better believe it, man. They changed a lot in the year I was there. Shit was flyin'. Things were gettin' hot about the time I left. We were killing more of them and they were killing more of us. Don't have to tell ya I'm glad to be home and thank God I'm through with Nam. I did my stretch."

"Yeah, but...you weren't scared, were you, Joe?" I said in more of a statement than a question. I knew Joe had been brave in Nam. He'd earned medals. He was a natural leader, a tough kid from a tough neighborhood who'd never backed down from anyone.

"Sorry, Mark...but, yeah...I was damned scared at times. It's a war. Real bullets...not that 'playin' army' stuff. Seein' a guy blown away...all the blood, fuck! It's amazing how much blood is in a body, man. There's nothin' you'll ever do to prepare you for that. It changes you," Joe said, hanging his head. Suddenly, he was deep in thought, moody. I looked at Carter. He just drank his beer and looked at the wall.

"Well, what was it like, Joe? I mean, you know...every day?" I asked, breaking the silence. I felt uncomfortable, but my curiosity was running wild.

Joe thought on this, took a long pull on his beer. Shook his head and looked at me...chuckling slightly when he did. "It's no John Wayne movie, Mark. When I first landed, that's the way it seemed; like a war movie. Barbed wire, towers, bunkers, machine guns...no mistakin' it was a fuckin' war zone, all right. I was nervous, maybe scared, right off the plane. I didn't have a weapon yet, and I felt naked.

"Day to day...I'd say 'miserable' describes it best. Fuckin' miserable place! And boring too. Time dragged on. Days would go by and nothin' would happen. Weeks were like months and, man, you wanted it the other way 'round. Then, in a moment about as short as a flashbulb, it got more exciting than you ever wanted.

"The first three months I was there it rained, every day. Every stinkin' day! You know what it's like to work, stand guard, eat, sleep, and shit in the rain and muck? To sit in a foxhole in a foot of water in the middle of the night? That's misery, man. Hell, I was wet at least from the knees down for months on end; couldn't get my feet dry. Socks were always wet and rotted right off your feet. I'm serious!"

I thought on this and didn't understand it. "Well, couldn't ya just get a pair of socks from a store?"

Joe and Larry laughed at this.

"Except for four or five occasions, I was at C-2 or A-4 the whole time. There was something that passed for a supply bunker there, but they never had important stuff like socks. They only had shit you didn't need. I had Mom send some socks, but the first ones were stolen out of the package before I even got it."

"What's C-2 and A-uh...?" I asked.

"C-2 and A-4...they were firebases. A kind of fortified position and gun emplacement out in the boonies. We worked on our APCs there—got a meal, ammo, refueled. During the monsoon, it was a dry place to roll out your sleeping bag. Kind of a safe place. Safer'n the boonies, anyway. The perimeter was barbed wire and personnel mines. No walls or anything like that."

I was starting to feel right uncomfortable. Everything I said seemed ignorant and naive. I didn't know the language, hadn't walked the walk. So, I decided to just shut up, stop sounding stupid, and let the vets talk.

"Who were your buds?" Larry asked.

"Best bunch of guys I'll ever know," Joe answered. "J. R. from Enid, Oklahoma, Spud from Boise, and Vince from San Luis Obispo. We were tight."

"Yeah, I know, man. There's nothin' like it," Larry said.

There were a few moments of quiet reflection. Joe was staring off into a corner, a smile creeping up his face.

"Yeah, tight," Joe repeated. "When you live through that shit with a bunch of guys, you get real close. It just happens. Man... thinkin' about it gives me the willies. I'll never forget the guys I served in Nam with."

Carter nodded in agreement, then said, "I've talked to a few old vets at the VA; they say you'll never be as tight with anyone again in your life...not your wife, family, old friends...nobody."

"There was one other guy, too...," Joe continued, as if he hadn't heard Larry. "Ray James. Raymond. We called him Ray J., or Sarge, of course. I guess I was tighter with him than anyone else." He paused, looked at Larry. "Which of course is a big fuckin' mistake. A guy shouldn't get too close to anyone. It's not healthy in a war. But I couldn't help it. Ray J. was like a brother to me. Course he was older...about twenty-five or -six. Married. Had a kid. And he was a big guy; bigger than me. He played football for Oregon State. You had to prove yourself to Ray J. He didn't like slackers or cowards. He was the type of guy you could count on in a firefight. Ya know...had his shit together. Ray wanted people around he could count on. He was intent on getting out of Nam in one piece."

"Sounds kinda old for a grunt in Nam," Larry said. "Was he career Army?"

"Hardly," Joe snorted. "Ray J. didn't believe in the war. He had a degree in philosophy...which, of course, made him a big fuckin' target when the bullshit started. He was a deep thinker, and he'd decided while in college the war was not worth dyin' for, so... he fought the draft. But he made the mistake of pissin' off a draft board bigwig during a hearing on his eligibility after he'd graduated from OSU. Ray J. said the guy was a Ducks fan, too. Ray'd already been drafted...by the San Francisco 49ers. He wanted to play pro ball. Instead, he went to graduate school to avoid the other draft. Said he thought they'd forgotten him a year later, so he cut a deal with the Niners, dropped out of school, and went to training camp. A week later, he got the letter...and ended up in Nam. He was not happy about it."

"You see that a lot? Guys who didn't want to be there?" Larry asked.

"Not early on when I was new myself. But later, yeah. When they started the buildup, they were drafting more guys and morale started going downhill. There were some very unhappy people there."

There was a pause in the conversation, then Larry said, "Well, guys...I'm hungry. Whaddya say we get on down to Gerties' and get us a Gertie Burger with fries?"

"Hot damn! Now you're talkin'," Joe said.

On the way to the drive-in, Joe was feeling cold again. "Miserable motherfucker...Vietnam. There was the cold and rain...but it was hot as hell in summer. Dry and dusty up by the DMZ. There were scorpions and poisonous snakes...and rats! I was tellin' you about my feet...how cold and wet they were. Well, one night we were sacked out at the firebase during the monsoon and a friend of mine had his toe chewed off by a rat."

"No way!" I said.

"His feet were so cold and wet they were numb. He said during the night he felt a kind of tingling in his foot. Woke up and there was nothing left of his little toe but the bone. He freaked! But, ya know, it was his ticket home. So, when he found out about that, it wasn't so bad."

Joe was eagerly anticipating his first Gertie Burger in some time. He started talking about how lousy the food was in Nam, which led to a new subject: C-rations.

"It all tasted like the cans it came in. Course, since it was left over from the Korean War it's not hard to understand," Joe said.

"The worst was the ham and lima beans, man," Larry said to me.

Joe burst out laughing. "Horrible shit! And how about the turkey loaf? Ahh, but everybody liked the beans and weenies, or pound cake and peaches. You had a tough time findin' those. Sometimes you had to trade something real good for beans and weenies. We'd heat 'em up with C-4 and have us a hot meal."

"Did you ever get a real meal?" I asked.

"Not often," Joe remarked. "Once in a while they'd fly one in... but it was rare."

Our food arrived. I always liked the Gertie Burger. It was an oversized patty on an oversized bun dripping with ol' Gertie Brown's special sauce. On this night it looked better than usual. Joe dug in and kept eating until it was gone—the sauce running down his arm, his face covered in it.

On the way back to the apartment, I was thinking how disappointed I was in Joe and Larry's recollection of Vietnam. The recruitment commercials on TV didn't mention scorpions, jungle rot, C-rations, or rats. I thought such hardships only related to World War II or maybe Korea. This was 1967!

"Sometimes they'd fly in Carling Black Label or Schlitz. We preferred soda pop, but the beer was better'n nothin'. You know, they had a contest once...that Carling Black Label came in second...," Joe started.

"Yeah, and horse piss finished first," Larry finished.

"Anyway," Joe continued. "We'd be driving along some back-country trail, bouncing along. There were always grenades rolling around on the floor of the APC, and when we had beers, they'd be rolling around with the grenades gettin' all mixed up. I've had this dream...still have it...where I'd reached down, grabbed a beer, and popped the top...tipped it back for a drink and discovered I'd pulled the pin on a grenade."

The night wore on. We drank several beers and were feeling loose when Larry brought out a bottle of tequila. I'd never had tequila; rarely had hard stuff at all. They showed me how to lick the salt, down the shot, and bite the lemon. It left a nice burn, and pretty soon I had a glow about me. Joe kept talking.

"You know," Joe said. "Those NVA are tough motherfuckers. Losing isn't an option. Charlie don't care if he dies if he can take a bunch of us with him. They've got sappers who run into command bunkers with satchels of explosive and blow themselves up...taking out your command center. How the fuck are we supposed to beat an enemy willing to do that?"

After four shots of tequila, I went back to beer. I had a pretty good recollection of the last time I had drunk hard liquor, and I knew I'd better cool it. Larry and Joe kept on drinking tequila. The evening got longer and the talk looser. Larry fell asleep on the couch. Joe and I drank, talked, and ate potato chips long into the night.

"Ah hell," Joe said. "The service is screwed up, Mark. I remember once complainin' to Ray J. about it...sayin' how disappointed I was with the whole fuckin' mess...how it was all such a big waste of time. Now, I thought I was preachin' to the choir 'cause 'ol Ray really disliked the Army bullshit. But he surprised me. He said someday I'd remember my time in Nam as my finest hour. Boy, did I hoot at that one. Like I said, he was a philosopher. He said it had nothin' ta do with the fuckin' Army. Said, you'll remember it as the time when you were pushed...pushed beyond your limits. You'll remember that despite the problems and the Army crap, you responded to the challenge, an' so did those aroun' you. You'll be proud that you did...an' you'll remember this time as a definin' moment in your life. Wow, Ray J. could really surprise you once in a while. I don' know yet if he was right...too soon to tell.

"But the bullshit! It's little things like no socks, but big things, too. Our intelligence stunk. They'd say a big NVA unit was somewhere, an' out we'd go into the boonies to get 'em. They were *never* there. Never. But...they knew where *we* were...exactly! We'd be out runnin' aroun' in our APCs an' tanks...lookin' for 'ol Charlie. Sooner or later, we'd get tired of lookin' and stop for lunch. Set up the perimeter, get all comfortable...jus' set down for chow and in would come the mortars right on top of us. Sons-a-bitches! I saw a lot of our guys die an' didn' see enough dead gooks to suit me."

"Didja kill anyone, Joe? What was it like?"

"Oh, yeah. I killed gooks...but not enough of 'em. An' I can tell ya it didn' bother me." He shook his head slowly to make the point. "In fact, after three, four months...I *liked* killin' em. It felt like I was in little league and I'd hit a home run. We'd whoop it up, slap hands. I remember once we ran down a coupla gooks in the boonies...surprised the shit outta 'em and actually had 'em on the run in front of the APC. I got on the fifty and fired a burst...blew this guy's arm clean fuckin' off, whoooeee!...that was neat. But we didn' see 'em often. There was only one time we nailed Charlie's ass the whole time I was there."

He thought about this, taking another pull on the tequila bottle. "Ya know, we'd go out in the boonies for days at a time. At night we'd find some high ground and dig in as best we could... set up claymores, trip flares, chain-link fence in fronta' the APC... maybe blast myself a foxhole with some C4 explosives and settle in for the night. We tried to do it before nightfall so we had a good look at the surrounding area, knew our defensive position, and set up our fields of fire.

"Well, this one night we didn' get set up during daylight. A tank threw a track and it took a long time to fix. Anyway, we drove to this place and set up in the dark. Course, after dark we didn't use flashlights or light fires or anythin'...didn' want Charlie to know our position, even though we always thought he did anyway. They had scouts, spies and shit...they knew every fuckin' thing we did.

"Wait, where the fuck *was* I?" he said, taking a pull on the bottle and rubbing his chin. "Yeah...yeah," he said, remembering. "So, we set up inna dark. I figure the gooks mus' nota seen us. Didn' know where we were. In fact, couldn'a knowed 'cause in the middle of the night a whole battalion of NVA was goin' right by our position an' tripped a flare. Suddenly..." Now animated, his eyes big, hands sweeping, a smile creeping up his face as he rose out of his chair with the memory: "It was as bright as daylight an' hundreds'a fuckin' gooks was right in front of us...like a dream, man. Bing, bam, boom...we opened up with everything an' they had nowhere to go. Shot the shit out of 'em. Shoulda seen the little bastards, Mark. They was runnin' 'roun like a Chinese fire drill. Oh, man..." He sat down again. "It was beautiful. Counted close to four hundred dead the next mornin'. We only lost two guys.

"But, I gotta tell ya, sometimes we'd go months and not see a dead gook. They were hard to find. Sir Charles always took their dead with 'em, I guess. An' yet, saw lotsa our guys die. I remember once...we were straight leggin' through the bush..."

"What?" I interrupted. "Straight leggin'?"

"Yeah, straight leggin'...you know, walkin'. We always had ta leave the APCs and get out in the boonies...beat the bush for those little bastards. Anyway, this one time...mortars came in an' blew the shit outta us when we were straight leggin' through an open field. Whenever the shellin' started I always looked for somethin' close to jump behind, right away. Ya had to get outta the way o' sharpnel, ya know? I saw some limbs from an ol' deadfall stickin' up through the grass, so I took off an' jumped behind it...only, there was already someone there. Damn near landed on 'em." He paused, took a long pull on the tequila. An agonized look crossed his face with the memory. I thought he might cry, but he went on, slowly, "There was someone there...," he groaned. "One of our guys...an FNG I didn' know. He was holdin' his chest, white as a ghost, an' lookin' scared. Shit, I knew it was bad. I pulled his arms apart an' he had a big hole in his chest. It made a sucking, gurgling sound when he took a breath," Joe said, now in a whisper. "He was dyin'. He knew it, too. He was real scared...but, ya know...tryin' to be brave. And those fuckin' mortars kept fallin'. I yelled and yelled for the medic. There was nothin' else I could do but hold'm ...an' that's what I did, man. I held'm until he died, but he didn' die alone." He paused, staring. Then: "When a guy dies, Mark, he gets a look in his eyes," and suddenly he chuckled...a dark, morbid chuckle. "Like...like a cartoon where the eyes go dim and then go out." The pain was back in his face. A tear rolled down his cheek. "When they die, you see life leave 'em through their eyes...they get a stare, with no soul behind it," he finished in a whisper. "Then... they're inna better place."

It was spooky, riveting. Joe was half a world away in a lonely field again. Involuntarily, his hands twisted the neck of the tequila bottle. We said nothing as seconds loudly ticked by on the kitchen clock. Finally, the vision left him and he looked at me, a sad expression frozen on his face, and took another pull on the bottle.

"It's all still fresh, ya know? It's right there in front of me still. I have trouble sleepin'...those guys, the dead...they're with me... always. I need some time, man. Jus' need some time."

"Was that as scared as you ever got?" I asked.

"What?" Joe said. "Fuck no. I wasn' scared then. It was...that was jus' an experience. A Vietnam experience. I saw a lot o' death inna year, Mark. I learned a lot. Survival means everything. "Ya know FNGs...tha's short for 'fuckin' new guys,' it's what we called, uh...fuckin' new guys. Anyway, they'd always ask what the fight was like. They were scared shitless at first. But after a while your instinct for survival kicks in...your trainin' kicks in...an' you start fightin' like hell. Tha's why guys get so tight, man. Survival. I didn' give a shit what the war was about when I was over there. I was tryin' to survive. So were the guys aroun' me. I wanted to leave Nam alive, man! We were only fightin' for ourselves and each other. I didn' want anyone dyin' on me."

"What'd you ask me?" he said, suddenly.

"What...?"

"Oh, yeah," he went on. "You wanted to know my scariest moment in Nam. Let me see..."

I didn't remember asking that but I let him go. He took another swig, and I honestly didn't think he'd remain upright long enough to tell me. Joe was hammered.

"Picture this, Cameron," he started, putting down the bottle and using his hands to illustrate. "Monsoon. We're dug in up on a hill, entrenched. We set up late...didn' get flares or claymores out. We're in our holes, an' it's my shift on watch. But, here's the thing... ya can't watch nothin', man. I mean, it's too dark to see diddly. There's no light. It's so fuckin' dark in monsoon it's dark inna middle o' the day. An' it's pourin' rain. It hits your helmet like so many drumsticks poundin' your ears. Ya can't see, ya can't hear a goddamned thing. Maybe once inna while you'd think you heard somethin'...so, you take off your helmet to hear better...only, ya still can't hear 'cause the rain's still poundin'. Meanwhile, all the mud and sweat is washin' outta your hair an' into your eyes an' ya can't see nothin' either. An' the rain goes down your poncho, makin' you even colder. Fuck, man...what a miserable son of a bitch!"

Suddenly Joe came alive. His head cleared and he became more animated. "But that's nothin'!... Ya hear?! Nothin'! It's the fear, man! The mind games. I mean, you ask yourself, 'Did I hear somethin'? Was...was that a twig snappin'?' Are you willin' to let it pass...even if it could mean everyone gets killed? Or, do you shoot a flare...give away your position and risk getting everyone really pissed at you if you're wrong?"

He sat down again. "Oh shit. Those black nights in the hole during monsoon. I put on ten years."

I shivered involuntarily. "Is that it?" I asked. "Being in the foxhole during monsoon...your scariest moment?"

"What? Fuck, Cameron. I'm gettin' to the scary part. Not there yet. I'm jus' 'splainin' every monsoon night inna boonies." He tipped the bottle, thought, put it down again. "So, tha's the scene, man. Dark, monsoon, can't see, can't hear. And there's no claymores or flares for an enemy to trip...so, ya gotta be careful, huh? Anyway, you know what lightnin' does on a black night? Like a strobe light? Well, I never saw lightnin' in Nam...the bright flashes. It was probly too cold. It jus' stayed dark, black...'cept this one night I'm tellin' ya about. 'Cause this night I'm on watch an' there was a flash in the sky...like lightnin'. Maybe it wasn' lightnin'. Maybe it was 'splosions somewhere, but there was a flash of light, lit up everythin' for jus' a moment...and right in front 'o me, right above my foxhole was a gook with a rifle. We saw each other, all right...looked right into one another's eyes...and then the flash was gone an' it was pitch dark again."

Joe paused, no doubt for effect.

"I can tell ya for a fact, there's moments that seem to last forever. I was sure I was reactin' so slowly I was gonna be dead the nex' instant. Seemed like it took me five minutes to pull up my M16 and start shootin'. As soon as I did the flashes totally blinded me... couldn' see a fuckin' thing. I emptied the entire clip. Had no idea if I hit 'em or not. Thought he might be out there smilin'...ready to pop me one. Guys in other holes opened up with machine guns, rifles, threw grenades. I'm jus' slumped back in my hole...sure I'm gonna be dead the next moment. Pretty soon, our lieutenant slides over to my foxhole and asks me what the hell I'm doin'. I say, there was a gook standin' right by my foxhole. We saw each other. Now everyone's awake and just pissed off. You just imagined it... you were asleep and dreamin'...how could you see'm in the dark? I said it was the lightnin'. Nobody else saw any lightnin'. Bullshit, I said...it happened! Now, the problem is do we fire off a flare and see what's out there? Give our position away? It's scary...not knowin'. Everybody's pissed at me, but I'm not backin' down. So, anyways... we finally shot a flare. About ten feet away was a kid, maybe sixteen, with an AK-47 beside him. Three slugs through his back. He was runnin' away when I got'm."

"Man! That's freaky," I said.

"Only time I ever saw lightnin' in the Nam.... Ya believe it? And that sucker was right by my hole. The thing I think about is, 'cept for that instant, in the dark and rain, he coulda walked right by and I'd never knowed...an' he wouldn' either."

"So tha's it. When that lightnin' flashed and he was right there... well, tha's what fright is, I guess," Joe finished.

I thought the moment would come during the night when Joe might tell us about the Bronze Star he'd been awarded, but it hadn't. My curiosity jumped in.

"Joe, I know you got the Bronze Star. How'd you do that?"

He nodded, looked down at the bottle, and in a barely audible whisper, "The wors' day of my life."

Joe was quiet again, contemplating the tequila. I heard a sob... then another. He let go of the bottle. His face crashed on top of his arms and he shook with sobs, pouring out a grief that caught me by surprise. It went on for some time, and I became uncomfortable in my chair. Finally, he got hold of himself and spoke with his head still down.

"Ray J. was a sergeant in the tank unit that sometimes went with us inta the bush," Joe said, raising his head to look at me. The anguish on his face was gruesome. He looked away, then down again, apparently unable to face me as he struggled for words.

"Uh...it was always so good to see'm up there, man. Comfortin'...like havin' a parent takin' cara you. He usually led the column 'cause he trusted himself to see danger 'fore anyone else...an' he was good at it, for sure. We were out on patrol this day...like any other, really. I was drivin' the APC myself 'cause my driver was sick and laid out inna back. I was right behin' Ray J. and he was standin' up in the turret. Funny...we'd stop once inna while so's he could check somethin' out...an' every time we started again he'd wave his hand in a circle an' shout 'forward, ho,' like he was Ward Bond on *Wagon Train* or sumpin'. He knew I gotta kick outta that." Joe laughed. Then he became emotional again.

"The las' time we stopped, Ray had the binoculars up checkin' somthin' he musta seen in a thicket to our left...when an RPG was launched right out of 'em. I saw the whole thing...real close. Those damn RPGs...slow enough to see...fas' enough you don' have a chance. An RPG like this one hits somethin' an' there's a big-ass 'splosion tha' kills people right now. But tha's only part of it. There's a secondary 'splosion too...and that pushes a bore spinnin' into the metal and it throws hot shrapnel everywhere inside your unit... it jus' destroys everythin'. It's one 'o the things tha' scared the shit outta us over there."

Joe pushed himself up, took another slug from the bottle, and shook his head again. I wasn't sure if he'd finish, but he labored on.

"Charlie opened up on us then. We were covered from all sides...hot shit, man. Ray was slumped over in the turret and smoke was pourin' outta it. I kinda lost it then. It was stupid, but I jumped outta my APC an' up on Ray's tank. I remember grabbin' Ray under the arms...an' I pulled hard 'cause, like I said, he was a really big guy an' I thought it would take a lot ta drag his ass outta there."

Tears were streaming down Joe's face now; his mouth quivering.

"Only...only, he came out so easy. Light...as a feather. See, there was nothin' left of'm from the waist down. I was holdin' on ta half of'm...tha's all that was left. The shrapnel just tore'm apart. Already dead. Ol' Ray J. didn' get outta Nam in one piece after all."

"Holy shit!" I said, under my breath.

"The days tha' followed," he continued. "Well, they're a bit hazy. I gotta Bronze Star, okay. Ya know, bravery under fire an' all that. They don' recognize insanity under fire. They don' see the difference an' is all good for them. Be a fuckin' hero.

"Ray J. He was a neat guy...an' tell me if you heard this one already...he only had a month ta go when he got it. Don' know, Marky...but it sorta seems you're gonna get it right away...or jus' before ya set to leave."

I'd never imagined anything so frightening or gruesome in my life. I pictured Joe holding the bleeding torso of his good friend and a chill went through my body.

"War...s'really hell on earth," Joe said. "It has a whole new meanin' to ya now...doesn' it?"

I don't know what I'd expected to hear this night. Something gallant, even chivalrous...carried forth by rugged, handsome men performing Herculean tasks while not suffering a scratch. I hadn't been ready for the gritty reality.

"Outside our comp'ny...I never tol' anyone 'bout this. 'Prised I tol' you. Maybe I'm drunk or sompin'...'cause I can talk 'bout it. Nope...'can talk 'bout that."

Joe suddenly got up, tipping the chair over. He mumbled something about being tired, staggered to Larry's old recliner, and fell in it. I sat at the table a while looking at Joe, knowing I wouldn't soon see the same fun-loving guy I'd known my entire life. I got up and moved around the table, picking up the chair Joe'd knocked over. He was asleep. I ratcheted the footrest up and threw a blanket over him...and Larry. I turned out the lights and crawled up on Larry's bed, pulling my jacket over me. It was three-thirty in the morning, and I was tired as well as drunk, but I didn't sleep right away. Joe's matter-of-fact bombshells had my mind reeling. Thank God I hadn't joined the Army! I would be in the Navy on one of those sleek destroyers cutting through the clean blue ocean. I would never have to worry about getting my ass shot off...or, foxholes filled with water and scorpions. I would have a clean, dry bunk to sleep in every night, hot meals every day. And, who knew?... I didn't think I'd even go to Vietnam.

While Joe Wills was sending my mind reeling with his war stories, Stanley and old Willy were having a major blowout at the Wicks residence. Sometime during the night, Stan ran away. He didn't come back the next day or any days after that. Stanley was gone.

Katy started showing up for a ride every school morning. I enjoyed it in many ways. She was a San Francisco Giants fan; I liked the Dodgers. She liked the politically dead Nixon; I was a true-blue Democrat. Every morning's ride to school was a lively debate with a lot of finger pointing and laughter.

Ten minutes to eight on a Friday morning came a knock on our front door.

"Mom, it's Katy. Bye."

As I opened the door, though, she jumped me. "He called. He called. Stan's okay...he called from California. Oh, I just couldn't be happier! He joined the Marines!"

"What?!..." Mom came running to the door.

"The Marines!" Mom said. "Can he do that? He's not old enough."

"I dunno, Mrs. Cameron. He said he's in the Marines all right."

"How'd he sound?" I said. "Was he okay? How'd he get to California?"

"Panhandling for change, eating at the Salvation Army. He got there hitchhiking and riding trains."

"In the dead of winter!" Mom exclaimed. "God love him. He joined the Marines."

"But...he's okay," Katy said. "He's okay...that's all I needed."

"Yeah," I said, "and now Uncle Sam can take care of him. It might be the best thing that could have happened."

Some kids, anxious to move on, look forward to graduating from high school. Others, such as me, aren't ready for the transition. I didn't want to leave Jan; didn't want to assume the responsibilities I knew awaited. High school had been fun. Ready or not, though, graduation day arrived. There was a giddy, childlike euphoria among the graduates as we lined up in caps and gowns. Kids I'd hardly known were suddenly talking to me as if I were an old friend, and I was doing the same. I chanced to see Bud Brody and felt I had to talk to him. We'd hardly said a word to one another for months. After he'd been dismissed from the school paper, Buddy seemed to just give up on high school.

"Congratulations, Bud," I said, socking him playfully in the arm. "You goin' to the All-Night Party after graduation?"

He turned my way, "Uh...no, I've got other plans."

"So, what've you been up to?"

"The same...workin' and stuff."

There was an uncomfortable silence that passed between us, with both of us looking around and trying to find common ground to build a conversation on. It was strange that I could suddenly find nothing to say to my oldest friend. Finally, Buddy broke the silence.

"So, what're you gonna do now, Mark?... I mean, after graduation."

"I'm enrolled at Montana State. I'm gonna try majoring in art. It's the only interesting thing I could think of."

"Why Montana State? Isn't the U of M the liberal arts school?"

"Well, MSU has a better football team."

"Huh?... Well, there ya go! So, you're holding off on active duty in the Navy?"

"Yeah, for a while."

"That's good. Stay in school and outta Nam as long as you can."

"How about you? What're you doin'?"

"I'm goin' to San Francisco...the Bay area."

"Really, what're you gonna do there?"

"It's where it's happenin', man. Some friends of mine in Haight-Ashbury invited me down...said I could crash at their place. There's a groovy pop festival at Monterey comin' up. I wanna be there."

"So, you're not going to college? I thought you were interested in journalism?"

"Yeah, well...I don't have the money and my folks don't really care. Don't expect me to join the service like you and Stan, though. If they draft me, they'll have fun tryin' to catch me...'cause I'm not goin'."

I guess that about summed it up. Two old friends headed in opposite directions. We stood momentarily looking at one another.

"Well, good luck then, Buddy. Have fun in San Francisco."

"Yeah, good luck in school."

I stood a moment, hoping to find a better exit, but Buddy had dismissed me. There was nothing to do but walk away.

The All-Night Party had lived up to its expectations. We danced until three in the morning, had a buffet breakfast, then Jan and I left the party before sunrise. Dawn of my first day as a high school graduate found Jan and I parked on a hillside in the valley, making out.

With record speed I had unhooked her bra and was feeling those perfect breasts in my hand. It was very disappointing to reach for her crotch and find the girdle waiting there. Damn! There's just no way to defeat this modern-day chastity belt.

They say redheads are passionate, and I knew for a fact Jan enjoyed our making out and my clever hands, but going all the way was an impossible idea for her. Jan's father was a deacon in the Plymouth Congregational Church. Her religion, her pride, the moral standards of her family and friends all played a part in the taming of Jan Fred.

In the clinch, however, Jan couldn't deny the reckless passion that lay just below her moral façade. At times she was barely in control, her lust driving her to the brink of submission. It was a bitter reality that she always pulled back at the last moment.

Sure enough, she put her hands out and grabbed me gently by the upper arms...holding me at arm's length.

"It's time I got home. Mom and Dad will be waiting."

"Not yet...they're sleeping...they need their rest," I said, making a lunge. She laughed and held me firm. Frustration settled on me as I knew it was over. Letting out a silent, exasperated breath, I slumped back in the seat. Now she cuddled me, throwing an arm around my waist.

"I'm going to miss you," she said. "Try to stay out of trouble, okay?"

It caught me by surprise.

"What? What do you mean trouble?... At school? It's an agricultural school; a cow town for chrissakes."

"What I've seen of cowboys, they can be pretty wild. You don't know. Lots of college kids drink and party. Some do drugs."

"I won't do drugs. You're kiddin', right?" I said, pointedly leaving drinking out of the conversation.

"Be careful," she said. "It could happen to you."

Xuan Loc, South Vietnam

Le Van Dat sat, seething, on an old wooden chair near the sidewalk that ran by the café. Around him on the avenue, rampant capitalism, brought to the South by their wealthy American occupiers, moved in mighty waves of greed.

Loud-talking teenagers at the table next to him ordered Cokes and hamburgers. It was that easy. It made him sick! At home, the populace had willingly sacrificed every day for more than twenty years. Their hard labor brought enough to survive and sometimes not even that. These soft Southerners were at war but knew nothing of sacrifice! Without America, there would be no South Vietnam. The South had no soul, no purpose other than Americanized greed. This is why we will win, Dat thought, and our victory will be that much sweeter.

He looked like any other peasant from the country, but Colonel Le Van Dat was the North Vietnamese Army's new sector commander for the National Liberation Front (NLF). He reflected that it was a good thing his commander, Tran Van Minh, wasn't here to see him wandering among the soldiers and townspeople. Minh most certainly would not approve. Full colonels were not encouraged to go masquerading as peasants. Dat reasoned that in his new position, and with the major offensive they had planned, it was an absolute necessity to know the people they were working so hard to liberate. After all, how these people would react to the new offensive would be a key to victory. And, so, on occasion, he took a peasant's identity; not that it was hard. It didn't seem that long since he had left the delta. For his peasant role, he had learned customs, dialect, local history, and more so that he could be readily accepted as a local and taken into the Southerner's confidence.

As Dat walked the street among the Southerners that his forces were fighting so hard to liberate, the joke was not lost on him. He had understood for many years that the Southerners were not being held captive by the Americans; neither were they oppressed or eager for a Northern victory as his countrymen were constantly told by Hanoi's robust propaganda machine. No, these Vietnamese were content with what they had: a big sugar daddy.

Dat found a location near an intersection and squatted Vietnamese-style by the curb, observing the people and traffic. An American MP pulled up near him and parked his Jeep in the intersection, cutting off traffic from opposing streets as a convoy rumbled toward them. He waved the convoy on while keeping an eye out for probing bicycle or civilian traffic that might get in the way. Dat looked closely at the soldier. The MP was clean-cut and rugged in his crisp, starched uniform. The American soldier was an imposing figure.

The trucks, packed with American soldiers, continued by in an endless stream. Perhaps more than any Northern soldier, Dat knew they would never beat the American army in the field.

An attractive, young Vietnamese woman in a simple white dress purposely walked up and, standing beside Dat, impatiently watched the convoy. About Dat's height, the woman had a beautiful face and figure, yet there was no sense of pretense or airs in her demeanor. She scowled, glancing at her watch several times. Dat decided this would be a somewhat safe opportunity for him to practice the Southern dialect he had worked so hard to develop.

"So many trucks and men...I wonder where they are going," Dat said rising, directing the comment toward the woman.

"Oh, who knows!" the woman responded. "It is such a nuisance."

"Are you late for something?" Dat asked.

"Yes, I am meeting my cousin for lunch...just across the road... if I can get there."

"Are you from Xuan Loc?" Dat asked.

"No, I am from Cholon. I visit my cousin once a month or so. Sometimes she visits me in the city. I prefer her to visit me there." She looked Dat over. "Are you from here?"

"No. I am not from here, either. Uh...the countryside, to the north," Dat responded.

"Do you farm?"

"Yes. My family...we are rice farmers," Dat responded. It was more or less correct. "Cholon?... Are you Chinese, then?"

"That is my heritage. However, I am fifth-generation Vietnamese. You would hardly know it, though. My family follows and honors the old traditions," the woman said. Then, "For a rice farmer, you are most curious."

"Please," Dat said. "Pardon me if I have made you feel uncomfortable. Curiosity is an affliction of mine."

"An honorable affliction...to be sure. I am Luang Nu Chi," she added, extending her hand, waiting for a reply.

Dat took her hand. "I am Le Van Dat...a pleasure to meet you."

The woman smiled. "You are so unlike a rice farmer. Oh," she said, embarrassed, looking down. "I am sorry. Please...I do not mean to insult you."

Inside, Dat panicked. He had found himself enchanted with the young woman, and in his spellbound state had fallen completely out of character. He would have to scramble now.

"Er...yes. No need to apologize. I have always been 'different' from others in my community. I enjoyed school. My father had to insist I leave to work the farm. It was a...problem. I enjoy learning, and when I meet someone, I ask too many questions. Did you attend school long?"

"Yes. In fact, I am still in college."

"College. My, you are lucky...and unusual."

"It is very important to my family. Father wants me to be a financier and work for our government, like he does. Though I find working numbers easy enough, it is not my passion."

"So...do you have a passion?"

"Well, I love to design...clothes mostly."

"You are something of an artist, then. Financier...I did not know that was an occupation for a woman," Dat replied.

"I know. Father was doomed to have only girls. As oldest, I play the part of a boy in our home."

They both laughed.

"Well," Dat said. "You certainly could have fooled me. You are a charming young lady."

What am I doing, Dat thought immediately. *Am I flirting?*

"Thank you. Older men...oh, Nu Chi, you idiot!" she said, her face turning red.

Dat laughed heartily.

Nu Chi continued. "I am sorry, Le Van Dat. It seems I am destined to insult you. What I meant was...I find mature men to be more honest and open...though not as liberal as you seem. I hope that does not insult you...again! It is a pleasure to be treated with such kindness."

As the last of the trucks rolled by they stood, uncomfortable now, looking at one another. In her shy smile Dat thought he caught a bit of a flirt. The MP walked to his Jeep, patting a few children on the head as he did so. Noticing Dat, he nodded his way as he climbed into the vehicle and roared off after the convoy.

"Well," Nu Chi finally said. "I suppose I should be going... I am dreadfully late. It was a pleasure...perhaps I will see you here again, Le Van Dat?"

"Perhaps," Dat added. "It was my pleasure also, Nu Chi. Enjoy your afternoon."

Dat watched Nu Chi cross the street. She looked back once, smiling and waving, then disappeared into the crowd.

Incredible young woman, Dat thought. *So smart and outgoing and a college student to boot; highly unusual for a Vietnamese woman. And she was so personable; chatting away with a complete stranger. She would be a good catch for the right man. If things were different...*

Dat walked slowly down the broad street, a new ache in his heart. He rarely had contact with available young women outside his own cadre. Nu Chi was an enchantress who had taken him completely off guard. Had she been an ARVN operative, he would easily have been caught.

He naturally thought of his long-lost love, the woman he still cherished in his memory, Lee Nah. Lee Nah, of course, was the youngest member of the Politburo and one of its very few women. Amazing the events that transpire in a lifetime.

Lee Nah was the hero of Dien Bien Phu, the pivotal 1953 victory in the first Indochina War. Though Dat was at Dien Bien Phu the day the French dropped into the area, it was long before Lee Nah arrived. Dat's company had escaped along the river before the siege began.

Lee Nah's actions in the now-famous battle were the stuff of legend. A lowly porter, she picked up a machine gun and fought off French troops when those around her had been killed or wounded. Wounded herself, she helped rescue several men from the battlefield while under fire and was credited with saving many lives.

Her heroism and good looks were just the kind of inspirational story Communist propagandists loved. There were rallies and parades in which Lee Nah was praised and glorified. Her story was made into a movie with Lee Nah herself in the starring role. The Matriarch of the Politburo, Gao Jinh, became her champion and skillfully maneuvered her political advance. Lee Nah operated at a level far removed from Dat now.

The night of their separation was now nearly twenty years in the past, and they had not seen one another since. Dat often found himself wondering how Lee Nah had ended up with the army at Dien Bien Phu. Had she chased after him? Joined the Viet Minh searching for Dat? He might never know. It was at times like this that these aged feelings for her caused a deep aching. After all, he was just thirty-six years of age and still entertained thoughts of marriage and family.

Perhaps it was not too late. While Dat had vowed never to become involved with a woman while the war continued, big, ambitious plans were being made here and in the North—an outlandish offensive that could end the war. The upcoming offensive, called the General Offensive, General Uprising, would be a massive, well-coordinated attack using all available Viet Cong forces. The Southern populace, it was reasoned, given the opportunity for freedom from the American military and their own Mandarin elite, would rise up and fight alongside the Viet Cong.

Victory would largely swing on the reaction and support of the people in these streets. Would they play their role when the opportunity presented itself? From what Dat saw on this day, the outcome was predictable. While the Communist propaganda machine painted their "brothers in the South" as little more than hostages, reality was quite different. The Southerners Dat saw seemed like hardcore Capitalists and were doing quite well. The coming disaster was all too clear. Expending every unit of the Viet Cong would result in the guerrilla force's total destruction. All Dat could hope for was a miracle.

Monterey, California
June 16, 1967

Like any traffic jam in California, the cars were packed bumper to bumper. The only difference with this jam was all the cars were parked to the side of the road. JT, riding shotgun in Rad Huddle's VW Beetle, craned his neck, looking for any break in the long metal barricade. Huddle and JT's friendship went back to sophomore year when he became Jay's first acquaintance as he'd entered Fullerton High, though they shared little but friendship. Compared to JT, who sported jet black hair, a toned physique, and chiseled, nearly perfect face, Rad wasn't athletic. In fact, he could be described as small and pale with weedy straw colored hair. His only distinguishing facial feature was a wisp of a mustache that looked like it would someday be washed away during a drink of milk.

They were getting close to the fairgrounds, a virtual certainty that no parking space of any kind existed. But just as Rad was set to turn the bug around, JT spotted a break in the line.

"There!" he said, pointing. "God is good."

"Where?" Rad said. "That hillside? Jeez, it meets the road at about a ninety-degree angle. How'm I gonna park on that?"

"What're you talkin' about?" Jay said. "It's not that steep! They say bugs can go anywhere. Well...now's your chance, man."

"Naw, no way. I saw a space back a ways I can point this thing into. It won't hang out far."

Rad turned the Beetle around, and they backtracked a quarter mile to where Rad lodged the bug between two cars, likely making them immovable. They got out of the bug by crawling through the windows. As they were hiking to the fairgrounds, a van sped by them and abruptly stopped at the impossible parking spot Rad had passed on. The backup lights came on, and the van backed quickly into the space, the rear end bouncing and tires spinning as it climbed higher. When finally stopped, the van pointed downhill like a Norwegian on a ski jump.

"For chrissakes...look at that! A van took our spot!" Jay said, punching a slack-jawed Rad in the arm. "Ya gotta have balls like that guy if you want the last parking spot."

However, balls weren't involved. With a little trouble, the two laughing female occupants climbed out of the van and started down the road. Jay turned to Rad to heap more scorn on him, but his friend was looking elsewhere.

On one of the retreating van's occupants, Jay caught a flash of a freckled arm and a bounding mop of hair.

"I'll be damned," he said, stopping in the middle of the road. "Those are coupla Fullerton High girls, Rad. Definitely Richelle Gaston and, I believe...Sarah Tierney."

"Tierney...the valedictorian?"

"Yup, the only four-point-oh in the class. Jeez, I wasn't sure what we'd run into here, but I didn't think it'd be those two."

"Yeah, well, it's a free country. Hey, let's cut across the football field," Rad said.

"Don't ya wanna talk to 'em, Rad?"

"No...they're not friends of ours. C'mon."

"Uh-uh. I think I'd like to talk to Richelle. It's been a long time."

"What the...," Rad said, eyes wide. "You've gotta be kiddin'."

"C'mon. It won't kill you."

"Oh, man. Shit, JT, they're a part of the establishment. Richelle was class president. I wanna meet some hippie chicks and party."

"If they're a part of the establishment, then what the hell are they doin' here? Jeez, Rad...don't be such a prude. Time to get over high school, man."

Rad sputtered, spun a 360 on his heel, and said, "Ooooookay. Shit!"

They set out after the pair, who were now a considerable distance away and, seemingly, in a hurry. Jay picked up the pace, then broke into a jog. Before they could catch up, though, the girls were gobbled up by the crowd.

The crowd. So, *these* were Northern California's love children. Though JT was no stranger to large, rambling crowds, he hadn't experienced anything like this since his first trip to a carnival. All around him was the wildest, weirdest collection of people, sights, smells, and sounds he had ever encountered. A girl with vacant eyes dressed in what appeared to be an old band uniform was placing a flower in each head of hair she passed. A multicolored bus, with hippies hanging off it and blaring music, drove slowly around the grounds. Big balloons floated overhead, and everywhere there was the beat of the thing: cymbals, drums, bells...in constant rhythm. The scent of many types of incense melded in vaporous, heady rhapsody. All in all, it was a stunning setting for all the senses.

While Rad looked at crystals in one of the many booths set up to profit off this kind of crowd, JT surveyed the crowd, hoping to see Richelle again. A man wearing a shaggy vest and Lennon glasses walked by, blowing bubbles. One bubble tracked Jay like radar and burst surprisingly on his nose. He was wiping off the suds when she approached from behind.

"I guess bubbles just like you."

He turned to face a smiling Richelle.

"Small world, JT."

Jay smiled, too. It had been a long time since they had said a word to one another, though they had seen each other often enough in school.

"Hey, Richelle," he said. "You look great."

Then, silence enveloped them and they stood grinning at each other like embarrassed kids at recess. Sarah Tierney stepped around Richelle and extended her hand.

"You're the football player, right?" Sarah said.

"Oh," Richelle finally said as JT took the proffered hand. "Sorry...JT, this is my friend Sarah Tierney. Sarah...Jeremiah Johnson."

Rad had approached them unnoticed. He coughed slightly, and they all turned to him as he reddened with the sudden attention.

"Ladies," Jay said, "this is Rad Huddle. We've been friends since sophomore art class. Rad's the best artist in Fullerton. Hell, maybe LA."

"Really?!" Richelle said. "Sarah's something of an artist, too. She writes poetry...been published."

"Richelle, please!" Sarah said. "Nobody cares about poetry anymore. So, what're you guys..."

"I care...about poetry," Rad interrupted. "That's really neat, Sarah."

They beamed at one another.

"Thanks," Sarah said, twirling her hair with a finger. "Rad, isn't it? Uh, you guys with anyone? Maybe we could sit together, ya know?"

The Association were only two songs into their festival opening set when the girl on JTs left nudged him and offered him a joint.

"Wanna hit? Pass it on, man."

Jay grabbed the joint and looked hesitantly at Richelle, who seemed engrossed in the performance. JT wasn't one to let a joint go by without toking on it, and his hesitation was only momentary. While holding the smoke in, he noticed Richelle was now looking squarely at him and the joint in his hand. Then, to his amazement, she plucked the thing from his fingers and took a big hit before passing it to Sarah, who did likewise, and Rad, and so on down the line.

"Hey, man," Sarah said, exhaling, "keep 'em comin'."

"Don't look at me," JT responded. "The guy next to you is the one holdin'." Rad grinned and pulled a doobie out of his shirt pocket.

"You're blowin' my mind, Richelle. I thought I knew you," JT said. "Or, I knew the old you."

"As Dylan says, 'the times they are a changin'," Richelle said.

"Who really knows anyone anymore? But we have the power to change that, don't we?"

"We do," Jay responded.

By the time Lou Rawls was done with his lounge act, the Fullerton foursome were feeling very mellow. JT and Richelle were standing and stretching their legs while Rad and Sarah had their heads together.

"It's kinda hard for me to get a grasp here," Rad said. "After all, you were the valedictorian. I mean..."

"You expected mousy? Maybe obsessed? Hard-ass? Bookworm?... No. Okay, I am a bookworm. But, man, there's so much more to life. Graduating like freed me up!"

"But that crowd you hung out with."

"Part of graduating and letting go, Huddle. Richelle and I have had long talks about it. We've liberated ourselves from that small high school world...and those prigs we hung out with...Ewww!"

"Weren't they your friends?"

"They didn't stand up to inspection. There was never enough rock 'n' roll, ya know?"

"So, now what're you gonna do, JT?" Richelle asked.

"I'm enrolled at Fullerton State. On a scholarship, I'll have you know."

"Football?" Richelle asked.

"Hey, maybe I'm on an academic scholarship."

Richelle cocked her head.

"Okay, you know me. But not football, golf."

"Well, I didn't think it was academic, but you're hardly stupid, JT."

"Yeah," Jay said, "tell some of your friends that."

Immediately Jay thought, *Oh no, here we go again.*

"That was another time, Jay. I'm sorry about that."

As a sophomore transferring in to Fullerton High School, Jay had been treated badly by a lot of kids and cliques. One of the most unpleasant surprises had been how hostile Richelle's scholarly friends had treated him. It seemed Richelle did little to help him out. It had been a big disappointment during a tough time.

"Yeah, well, that's past, isn't it? Where are *you* movin' on to Richelle?"

"I have some choices...narrowed it down to Stanford or UCLA."

Jay had his arms around Richelle as they listened to the mellow sounds of Simon and Garfunkel's *The Sound of Silence*. He snuck a peek at her and saw her eyes were closed and lips pursed. She sighed and snuggled a little deeper into his embrace. Jay gently leaned over and brushed his lips on her cheek. She turned in a way that spoke not so much of surprise as longing, and kissed him on the lips without hesitation.

Though it was late and they were all tired, the crowd's energy seemed unabated. They hung out on the football field nearby that had been set up for campers. They smoked more dope, sang songs with a mellow crowd, and danced into the night. By the time the girls were ready to leave, the four had become arm-in-arm.

When they found the guys had no money and nowhere to sleep, Sarah offered her van. The girls were lucky enough, perhaps insightful enough, to have a motel room. In exchange, Rad offered his VW for their transportation.

But Jay and Rad partied on. Toward dawn, the two hiked down the road, moved Sarah's van to an open spot on the road, and crashed on the mattress in the back as the sun rose on day two of the First Annual Monterey International Pop Music Festival.

The guys arrived late, getting to the festival as Canned Heat was finishing its set. Moving through the crowd toward the stage, they didn't find the girls as another San Francisco band, Big Brother and The Holding Company, cranked it up. Immediately they felt something electric fill the air. The lead singer for Big Brother made every other act of the night before look lame and out of date. Janis Joplin screamed, cried, moaned, shimmied, kicked, and stomped the stage, putting her emphatic, undeniable stamp on the evolution of rock music. Mesmerized, the guys could only stand and watch as Joplin sung her guts out. By the time she finished "Ball & Chain," she was a Monterey legend.

Before Country Joe came on, they headed back to the meeting spot and were there when the girls arrived.

"Sorry," Richelle said, "we got hung up downtown."

"Too bad. You missed Big Brother."

"Who?" Sarah asked.

"They're just a Bay Area band," Rad answered. "But something tells me we'll be hearing more from them."

By late afternoon they'd had enough for the day. Jay and Richelle left Sarah and Rad with a big group outside the grounds, where they sang and chanted to several sets of drums while passing a pipe.

"Can you believe those two?" Richelle said. "They're inseparable. This is so good for Sarah."

"Rad, too. But really, I'm more interested in us," Jay said.

"Yes," Richelle said, leaning into Jay.

Later, while sitting near the rocky shore, they kissed again—this time a long, passionate kiss from which the two came gasping. Their expressions were not unlike children looking upon Santa Claus for the first time: wonder and amazement. It occurred, simultaneously, that this might be love. Jay wanted to put words to what he felt but was interrupted by Richelle, who placed both hands on his face and drew him forward for another kiss. When it finally ended, she put her head under his chin and hugged him as if her life depended on it.

"I'm sorry, Richelle," JT said. "Sorry for all the stupid things I've ever said to you. It seemed I could never get it right."

She pulled back and smiled. "And I'm sorry for being so intolerant. I never gave you a chance."

Though the Beatles had recently introduced the sitar into their music, it was an odd, Eastern presentation that, after an hour of Ravi Shankar on Sunday afternoon, prompted the four to move on.

They made their way to Denny's and had the kind of dinner you'd expect from two love-struck couples. They were euphoric, happy, silly, and seemingly unaware of any other's existence, so they missed the nasty looks thrown their way by locals upset with this invasion of their comfortable community by hordes of weird kids.

They all agreed that the festival had been a mind-opener. The counterculture that had been talked about, but never experienced by the four in LA, was all around them here. It was the first popular public forum where long hair, drug use, alternative lifestyles, and protest were openly displayed and flaunted. Many festival-goers whom they'd met had accused the government of conspiracy and manipulation. The Vietnam War was routinely and generally criticized. The four Southern California kids hadn't seen much of this in Fullerton, but here the war was being viciously attacked.

"This one guy last night went on and on about Vietnam," Sarah said. "He actually called President Johnson and Secretary McNamara war criminals. He said they were lying to Americans about what was happening there...how it was being fought."

"Who knows?" Richelle threw in. "I mean...what do any of us know about Vietnam? Why are we fighting and what are the issues? There are so many unknowns. Will it be like Korea? I don't know if it means anything...or will ever be remembered once it's over."

"You damn kids!"

It came from the table next to their booth. An elderly man was rising from his chair despite his wife pulling on his arm.

"All you need to know, miss, is that our country needs you. You don't ask why...it's the way it's always been. I was too old to serve in World War II, though I volunteered to go. It was tough on those guys. War isn't *cool*. There's always a good reason we go to war, and I for one expect you boys to go without questioning the people who know better!"

"Harold, let's go," his wife said, still pulling on his arm.

"Don't be the first generation of Americans to chicken out when your country needs you. You suck it up and go do your duty, boys.

"Aw, ya make me sick, the whole buncha ya...and all those other idiots out at the fairgrounds. I know a man on the city council. This'll be the last festival ever held here," he said as he let his wife drag him toward the door.

An embarrassed silence filled the void. Now, they noticed the unfriendly looks.

"Jeez," Rad said, quietly. "It's not like you're being unpatriotic, Richelle. You just asked some questions...good questions, I think. Is that so wrong? Is it wrong for us to question why we fight? JT and I could end up over there. I for one would like to know what it's about. How about you, JT?"

The three looked at Jay. In return, he looked at each of them and then around the room, where most of the patrons had gone back to eating their meals.

"My father was a Seabee in World War II," he started. "He was in or around a lot of battles. Names most people know: Guadalcanal, Tarawa, Okinawa. It's not like he ever sat me down and said, 'Hey, this is where I was and what I did.' No, I kinda pieced it together over the years. He doesn't talk about it, but sometimes from a look he gets, or something he says, you get the idea that remembering hurts. Those aren't good memories for him. Dad doesn't want me joining the service."

He paused. "But...if I were in a position where I had to make a choice...yeah, I'd go regardless of what it's about. I wouldn't dishonor my father...or, guys like the old fellow who just yelled at us. In a way, he's right. We should listen to the people who know. They must have a good reason to send us halfway around the world to fight somebody in a jungle. Right now, I have to believe that. I *want* to believe that."

Arguably, Sunday night at Monterey was the finest evening of rock music ever performed on one stage. Among others were Janis Joplin with Big Brother, Buffalo Springfield, the Who, the Grateful Dead, the Jimi Hendrix Experience, Scott McKenzie singing his anthem, and The Mamas & The Papas in one of their last performances. Of interest was the second band to play that evening. It would be referred to as the Band With No Name. On this night of unparalleled rock performance, a group of musicians never heard of and never recognized played among the greats. Who were they and what happened to them? Why were they chosen to play on the festival's climatic night?

Monterey is remembered for the times and the place; for the big names that rose out of it to become rock's biggest stars in the music genre's finest year. The same month, *Sgt. Pepper's Lonely Hearts Club Band* was released, and the Doors' "Light My Fire" and Procol Harum's "Whiter Shade of Pale" hit the charts.

Those filing out of the fairgrounds following the final act knew Monterey had been more than just a rock festival. They'd had a good look at who they were becoming. The generation had started to push out on the walls of civility, opening new doors, testing society and themselves. Dissent was on the rise, but not yet fully realized or popularly accepted. The hair was getting longer, the clothes a little wilder, the lifestyle a little crazier. Monterey created momentum for the peace movement, the dissemination of social unrest, and widespread drug use. There was a storm of mythic proportions brewing; it was a generation on the brink of cultural interruptus. But like the beautiful calm before it, 1967 would be a mostly tranquil year of political and social naiveté for American kids. One successful, peaceful music festival, though, was the spark that lit the fire.

Rad and Sarah stood before them on the football field while all around there was a swirl of people on the move. Rad's arm hung on her shoulders; her arms were around his waist. They couldn't keep the smiles off their faces.

"Huddle here wants me to drive back to Fullerton with him," Sarah was saying. "Would that be okay? We're gonna take his Beetle. You guys wouldn't mind taking the van back, would you?"

JT and Richelle had been about to make the same suggestion. They feigned surprise and nodded like twin bobblehead dolls.

"Great," Sarah said. "I'll pick up the van tomorrow...or sometime. You guys drive careful now...no distractions."

Instead of heading for the 101, JT decided he'd try old Highway 1 that ran along the coast. At night, he reasoned, nobody would be on it. Everyone else must have thought the same thing. They were past Big Sur before the mass thinned out to where they were doing better than forty miles per hour.

JT and Richelle were separated by three feet of engine housing that stood between them. While leaning against it, Richelle was thinking the VW would have been a much cozier ride.

The night was dark, with the only light coming from the cars behind them and the dash. Looking at Jay, she could not deny there was a physical attraction to the man. She loved his beautiful black hair and classic movie star good looks with a strong chin and nose. He wasn't wearing a shirt in the warmth of the summer night, and the muscles of his shoulders and arms stood out. Put a thin mustache on him and he could pass for a young Errol Flynn.

"JT," Richelle said, "where do we go from here? Was this just a wonderful summer event?... And now it's back to business as usual? I don't want that. I want to be with you...from now on. I want to be your girl."

"Jeez, Richelle. The way you say that...it's like you think I'd just play games with you."

"You dated a lot of pretty girls at Fullerton High...cheerleaders, majorettes. A girl has to be careful around a guy like you."

JT scoffed. "Richelle...I've liked you a long, long time. I just never...well, you know, felt like I was worthy, I guess. You're so smart...and I haven't exactly been Mr. Smooth Operator with you in the past. Cheerleaders are easy; they just want to be with the hunky jock guy. It's so shallow. But someone like you...well, a guy's gotta be on his toes."

Now Richelle scoffed. "Oh my God! That's so silly...and so correct. You know...there was a time when I thought I might flunk a few classes for that reason. I thought guys...you.. might find it easier to approach me if I wasn't so smart. I guess it's a woman's thing."

"Yeah, well, it was intimidating is what it was."

"How do you feel now?"

"It's not the same. Things are different. You said high school was over. I feel right now like it definitely is."

"I don't want it to end, JT. I've never felt this way about anyone else."

"God...what you're doin' to me here, Richelle? You're all I want. If that's being 'my girl,' then that's what I want." He had a terrible desire to kiss her.

"Damn," Jay said. "I've got to pull off this road somewhere before we end up taking a quick ride to the surf."

The next bend they came to had a very small space just off the edge of the road and was hard against a drop-off that went ninety feet to the rocky surf. Jay pulled into it, bouncing to a stop. He put the gearshift in Park and turned off the engine. A steady stream of cars continued passing within feet of the van, but the two were hardly conscious of traffic. They leaned across the motor cover, faces within inches of one another.

"I don't know what this is, Richelle. Maybe something...something I've wanted a long, long time. I honestly felt you and I would never get together. I'd resigned myself to that. But, oh, I wanted it...and it felt so...unattainable. Now...here *you* are saying it's what you want...and *you* don't want it to end. If I'm dreaming, this is one hell of a dream, because you are all I want in this world."

"I think I just decided to go to UCLA."

Their first kiss had been filled with surprise and discovery. The second, a confirmation of their longing for one another. This kiss was all fiery passion and lustful desire. Somehow, in a tangle of arms, knees, and elbows, they managed their way into the back of the van, coupling as if they were modeled from the same lump of clay. Cars continued past without end, just feet away. They didn't know they were there.

Two months later, friends and family were astonished to learn that Rad and Sarah had married in a quickie Tijuana wedding. Jay and Richelle were witnesses.

Helena, Montana

According to my folks, high school was going to be the finest time of my life, but my parents had never been to college. If high school was an Impala Super Sport, college was a Corvette. To my delight, I discovered that being responsible for myself also meant I could be irresponsible for myself. For the first time, I felt the exhilaration of real freedom. I was free to come and go and do whatever I chose. No one would be waiting for me at two in the morning. The only hitch, of course, was school itself. We were expected to study, attend classes, take tests, and be, well, students. I figured I would have to get to that, in time.

Every few weeks, if there wasn't a football game, I would go home for the weekend. It was during one of these visits home that Bud Brody found us at the RB Drive-In. Jan and I were having fries and Cokes and he just walked up to the car like the ghost of Jacob Marley paying a little visit.

I hadn't seen him since graduation night. His hair was long and lay on his shoulders. He wore a flowered shirt open at the neck to reveal a beaded necklace. His pants were flared at the bottom and looked like they were cut from someone's old striped living room drapes. All and all, a strange apparition. As he approached, Jan said a silent and uncomplimentary 'ewww.' I rolled down the window.

"Hey, Cameronmyman! What's happenin', dude? Long time no see."

He had a strange odor to him. I couldn't tell if he smelled dirty or of something else. It was a sweet, smoky smell.

"I never thought I'd see you back here so soon," I said, shaking his hand in the strange grip he offered. "What're you up to?"

"Long mind-blowin' story, man. Okay if I sit a while with you?" he said, moving around to the passenger's side before I could respond.

"Is he going to sit in here...with us?" Jan whispered. "I don't like the looks of him. And...he smells!"

There was nothing else to do. Bud opened the door and climbed in beside Jan. She put on a phony smile for him. He barely acknowledged her.

"Phew...what a trip seeing you again, man."

The odor filled the car. I saw Jan wrinkle her nose and give me a conspiratorial glance that said *I don't like this.*

"Yeah, well, I'm just home for the weekend. So...did you go to San Francisco, or what?" I asked.

"Oh, sure. It was a fuckin' trip, man. Wish you'd been there. We'd a loosened you up a notch or two," he said. Then looking pointedly at a shocked Jan, added, "...and it looks like you could use it."

"Hey, Bud," I said, glancing at Jan. "Ease up on the language. There's a lady present. Okay?"

"Uh...hey, that's cool. Sorry."

"Yeah...well, what brought you home?"

"Heather and I had to bug out, man. The heat was on."

"Heather?"

"I met her in the Haight. She's got like a grocery bag full of pot and her old man's rich...which is really good 'cause I ain't got no money, honey."

Now Jan was just openly stunned. She turned to look at me as if to say, *Should I throw him out, or will you?* Buddy was giggling again.

"So, is Heather around here somewhere?" I asked.

"Yeah...I left her at Itchycoo Park with her guitar. She was trippin' on acid and didn't wanna go anywhere. So, I walked down here. Smoked a reefer on the way...and look who I found! Say, I'm kinda dry, Jan...got cotton-mouth. Can I have a drinka your pop?" he asked, while grabbing Jan's soda off the dashboard and taking several big gulps.

"Get him out of here!" Jan hissed.

"Well, Buddy. Uh, me and Jan have to get going. We're gonna be late for the matinee at the Marlow..."

"Yeah! What's showin'? Maybe I'll come along."

"Come on, Bud. It's a date," I said, nodding to Jan.

He looked at me with watery eyes, then laughed out loud. "Hah!...of course it is. Shit, I'm sorry. But, hey, how about driving me back to the park first?"

"Sure, no problem," I said with a shrug. Jan, wearing a tight-lipped frown, crossed her arms and then pressed into the seat cushion, as we pulled into the street, driving toward Hill Park.

"We're livin' in the micro-bus," Buddy said. "It's groovy. We stay high and...uh, sleep there, all the time, too. Say I can sell you some pot if you're lookin' to score. Sellin' lids for just ten bucks... and it's good shit, man. Here," he said, pulling out a hand-rolled cigarette and offering it to me, "we can smoke this an' you'll see."

Jan gasped. "I don't believe this!"

"You mean...you haven't turned on yet? Wow...you're like the only two straight people I know. Hey, I smoked a joint with Jerry Garcia. Yeah, right in his living room in the Haight. Can you dig it, man? I mean, they played at Monterey!"

"Jerry Garcia?" I asked.

"Yeah. You know...of the Dead. The Grateful Dead."

"The... Grateful Dead? Jeez, what a name. Is that a rock band?" I asked.

"Fuckin' A.... Oh, sorry. Of course they're a rock band. What planet you livin' on?"

Thankfully, we were at the park. Another half block and I'm sure Jan would have opened the door and rolled him out. I spied a VW van and figured it had to be his. There was, in fact, a girl with a guitar up in the park. I pulled up to the curb.

"Well, here you go, Buddy. Take care of yourself."

"Hey, why don't you stay a while, Marky. We can all go in the van and have a toke or two, huh? You'd like it, I guarantee," he said. Then noticing Jan's expression, added, "You could stay in the car, Jan."

"We won't be doing that," Jan fairly shouted, now very upset. "We have to go. Bye, Buddy."

"Oh," Bud said. He opened the door and climbed out. He paused by the door, turning serious. "I'm not sure how long I'll be around, Mark. See, I've got the Selective Service on my butt. I sorta forgot to tell them I was going to California. They sent the police to my folks' house...Dad told 'em where I was. One day I looked out the window of our place in the Haight and there were two big Marine cops asking for me. We decided to hit the road. I'm not sure what'll happen next. Anyway...I'll catch ya again another time.

Remember, if you wanna turn on, I have some great stuff. Uh, bye, Red. Er...good seein' you again."

As we pulled away from the curb, I got an earful.

"My God!! I wouldn't believe it if I hadn't seen it myself. What happened to him? The language...offering *us* dope...evading the draft! And he was high! Oh, I don't want you to ever see him again and I wish you'd gotten rid of him at the drive-in!"

"What could I do? Buddy's my oldest friend."

"Some friend," Jan said, sulking.

Our neighbors in the dorm were a bodacious bunch from Great Falls...three guys who came to college with an agenda that somewhat differed from the administration's. While they liked to party and get wild, they were also smart, adventurous, and bold. Perhaps Tim and I shouldn't have been surprised when one day before Christmas break one of the group suggested we all try smoking pot.

Rather than just another way of breaking the law, it was proposed as a scientific experiment. Rick, our impudent and respected leader, wanted to know what the buzz was all about...why lots of kids were trying it...why the authorities were so upset. He'd read what he could find on marijuana and told us it definitely wasn't addictive.

"Hell, cigarettes are more addictive than heroin, and they're legal," he'd said in defense of the idea.

As part of a group experiment, it didn't sound that bad. I was curious to know what pot was all about. It was everything else that came with it that made me nervous. If caught, I would end up with a criminal record, lose Jan, and lose the respect of my family and friends at home. This weighed heavily on my decision to leave it alone. Roommate Tim and I decided that, for once, we wouldn't go along with the gang.

However, it did show just how much I'd changed since entering college. Smoking grass, and a lot of things I would never have tried before, didn't seem that outrageous, and I realized I might change my mind someday.

With one brief encounter, the day came sooner than I expected. Tim and I came home for Christmas break and happened to run into Steve Summers, an old high school classmate and mutual friend who was attending the University of Montana.

Jumping into Tim's car, he asked if we'd tried grass yet. Surprised, we looked at one another and said no. He proceeded to tell us in very descriptive phrases, and with the enthusiasm of a carney salesman, what a kick it was to get high. His excitement was infectious; his stories amusing, wild.

"You're never out of control...even when you're *really* stoned... and you wake up the next day without a hangover," he said. I liked the sound of that.

One short ride in the car that lasted maybe fifteen minutes made Tim and I converts. We had to try it. It was during this same weekend that I received a call from Joe Brody, Buddy's father.

"Mark, have you seen Buddy?" he said.

"Not lately, Mr. Brody. I did see him at Hill Park a few weeks ago...but I've been away at school and haven't seen him since."

"Any idea where he might be?"

"No...well, maybe in his van. That's where he said he was living. Has he been home?"

"No," Mr. Brody answered. "He's called a couple times...said he wouldn't come here. I suppose you know about the Selective Service trying to reach him. I can't understand that boy. He's in trouble! The police were back...they think he's around. If you know anything, I'd like to hear it."

"Sorry, Mr. Brody," I replied honestly. "I don't know anything more than what I've told you. I don't know where he is."

Just after Christmas break, Mom told me the neighborhood was all abuzz about Buddy moving to Canada to avoid the draft. "Imagine the shame," she said. I wasn't happy to hear about it, either. I planned on buying some grass from Buddy if I ran into him again.

1968

Westwood, California

The scene is a room in one of the many high-rise dormitories on the UCLA campus; it is similar to other dorm rooms in the building. The walls are covered with psychedelic posters announcing peace rallies, concerts, swap meets, and love-ins. A leather headband hangs from a desk lamp next to a string of love beads. The ceiling is a cloud made of tie-dyed sheets intermittently attached to the drop ceiling with paper clips. The light from several flickering candles and a green lava lamp illuminated the room. Incense burns in an ashtray. On a floor mostly covered by an India-print rug are piles of clothes: sandals, bell-bottom jeans with wide leather belts, tie-dyed waffle shirts, Jockey briefs. Entwined on the twin bed are a young man and woman perspiring from recent, impassioned love-making.

One glimpse and the dormitory manager in her apartment several floors below would have a heart attack. This is women's housing with strict rules on male visitation enforced with locked doors and by resident assistants on every floor. But desire fueled by love and the ingenuity of youth has easily defeated the barriers of civil society, as it often does.

Jay leans over and lightly kisses Richelle's neck. He knows this turns her on, and she moans softly as his kisses move toward her ear. He runs his hand the length of her side to rest on her thigh, which is thrown across his legs. Goose bumps on her arm betray the thrill of the touch. The nipple of her right breast hardens against his chest. In response, she lightly squeezes the skin just inches from his penis, where her hand lies. Jay feels a stirring inside.

"Umm...you are insatiable," Richelle says. "I need a few minutes."

"Sorry," JT responds.

"Actually, just a few moments," Richelle says, kissing him.

"It's okay," Jay responds. "We need to talk anyway."

"Oh? Is it about us? Is it good news?"

Jay rolls off his side and gets comfortable on his back. "Yeah... it's about us. Things have changed, Richelle."

The tone in JT's voice sends a different kind of shiver through her.

"I, uh...hell, school didn't go well. You know that. The scholarship...the golf team...college...it's all gone. It's over."

Richelle didn't respond immediately. After all, this was not unexpected news. She knew college wasn't going well for Jay. In fact, it never really got started. Winter quarter grades had just come out and she had been expecting the news.

"You sound like it's the end of the world, JT. All you need is a break from school, that's all. Time to think. I'm sure your dad will put the time to good use. You can work harder on your game... maybe try qualifying school. You're playing well."

"Yeah, it's kinda funny, huh? Everything's going to hell but my game."

"...and me?"

"No.... I mean...well, us *and* my game are going real well."

"So, work real *hard*...on the things that are going well," she answered, kissing him on the cheek.

"Yeah...well, there's more. I got my draft notice, too."

"What?!" Richelle immediately rose on her side to face Jay. "You have a school deferment."

"Not since I flunked out."

"Come on!" she stammered. "It takes government bureaucracy a little longer than that to respond! You're kidding me...aren't you?"

"No, I'm not. I was just a little surprised myself."

"Well," Richelle said, thinking. "You can appeal, of course. Reapply for student status. Lots of kids do that."

"I joined the Navy," Jay said.

"What?!" Richelle screamed in his face. "Why? We should have..."

"No, calm down, Richelle. Calm down. Look...here's the deal. I got my grades Tuesday. The draft notice arrived Thursday. It's a done deal. If I had screwed around any longer I might've ended up in the Army. I had to do something."

Richelle's mouth moved without words escaping. Her brain was attempting to catch up to this surprise.

"Dad and I agreed the appeals process was a big gamble. He's real good friends with the commander of Fullerton's Naval Reserve Center. I think they were war buddies or something. Anyway, I think the commander pushed through my enlistment over quite a few guys on the waiting list."

"But...you've told me more than once your dad knows people on the draft board, too. That you'd never get drafted. You told me that!"

"Yeah...but those guys never got to say a word. The head of the draft board sent out the notice himself. There was no meeting or anything. Probably broke a few rules."

"He singled you out?! Why would he do that?"

"Because we know him, Richelle...and he sure knows us. Peter Kennison?... Judge Peter Kennison...head of the draft board. Damn, the guy sure knows how to carry a grudge. Dad and I figure he must've been watching my grades the whole time. He knew it was coming."

"One man. One man can do that? It's not fair. It's not right! You should say something...do something. One man...even *that* prick...can't ruin someone's life for personal reasons. Don't you see that?"

"C'mon, Richelle. Calm down. What was I gonna do? What could anyone do? He's got enough clout to carry it off...and don't forget the power of the government behind him. That's just the way it works, darlin'. Here, I thought I had a couple aces up my sleeve. Ends up I didn't have shit. So, I joined the Navy. All in all, I think joinin' the Naval Reserve was the best thing I could do. Better to not screw around with the judge."

"So...your Naval Reserve commitment...that's like meetings and stuff, right? You can go to school, too."

"Yeah...if I want to."

"Well, you want to, right? I mean..." Here, a dread-filled Richelle thought of Jay heading off to the service. "You're going to stay around, aren't you?"

Jay didn't say anything. He avoided her eyes.

"JT Johnson...you look at me and say you aren't going anywhere anytime soon!"

"I can't," JT said. "I can't say that, Richelle. Hell, there's no reason to put it off. What am I going to do? Go back to school? It's not for me. The sooner I get in and get this over with the sooner I can get back here to you, to my golf game, my future. It's two years...and they say after you do your active service, you don't have to attend meetings ever again. It's like getting drafted...only I get to go in the Navy and serve on a ship."

Now, Richelle's eyes brimmed with tears. A sob burst out and tears streamed down her flush cheeks.

"No, don't cry. It's not worth crying over. C'mon now. I have other news."

"Shit," Richelle said. "I don't want any more news. Your news isn't worth a damn."

"Really," JT said, a mischievous grin filling his face. He leaned over and, out of a pocket in his jeans, produced a small, green velvet box. He placed it in Richelle's hands where it balanced on her fingers. Slowly, she opened the box and took in a quick breath. Sparkling in the flickering candlelight was a diamond ring.

"Marry me, Richelle," JT said. "Take pity on me, darlin'. I just love you to death."

Saigon, South Vietnam
January 31, 1968

Street lights flashed by as the old rusted taxi sped down the wide avenue toward the US Embassy. Remarkably, in a city of over a million people, there was little traffic on the street this night. The South had imposed a Tet ceasefire and sent most of their soldiers home on leave. So, those who could were there, sleeping off the celebration of the New Year. It was unthinkable that anything would happen during the most important holiday for all Vietnamese. The National Liberation Front was counting on it.

Now, just after two-thirty in the morning of January 31, Le Van Dat sat in the back seat of the old wreck, the NLF's chosen transportation on this night, pinned between comrades, rocket launchers, machine guns, and explosives. The men around him were little more than fidgeting kids. He felt like an uncomfortable grandfather on a family outing.

"Remember your goal," Dat said, above the grinding of the engine, "no matter what should happen. You are to occupy the US Embassy and hold it until reinforcements arrive."

No one would look at him. Dat could see they were on edge. Too much so, he thought.

"Be confident!" he said boldly. "This will *not* be a tough fight! You have surprise on your side, superior numbers, and weaponry. Just get inside and hold it. Thousands of your comrades are striking Saigon tonight. We will own the city by this time tomorrow."

They nodded, quickly looking at Dat, then away.

"You must be ready to die. What greater fate than dying for your people's liberation? Tomorrow you will all be hailed as great heroes by your countrymen...the handful of men who took and captured the embassy of the United States and changed the course of the Vietnam War."

He could see the glory come to their faces; this is what he wanted.

"You are a very lucky few to be given such an honor. Fight to live up to your countrymen's expectations."

It had been seven long months in coming. Despite the constant pressure their forces had endured, the men were ready. Morale was high; fanatically so. The work of hundreds of thousands was about to be realized.

Thirty-five battalions were to strike Saigon from the north, south, and west. General Minh had overall command; his headquarters located with the 267th and 269th at the Vinatexco Mill west of Tan Son Nhut airport. Dat's old friend and comrade would personally oversee the attack on Saigon's airport. Though their attacking force on the outskirts of the city was immense, Saigon was one of the most fortified cities in the world. Any possibility of reinforcements reaching these units before they were routed was highly unlikely. These young idealists were being sacrificed in the name of favorable press. He was, he reflected, riding with ghosts.

On this night Dat's command was limited to the elite members of Saigon's C-10 sapper battalion. Some ambitious objectives were being placed on the all-Saigonese team's shoulders. Among other jobs, the battalion would be attacking the National Radio Station, Naval Headquarters, the Presidential Palace, and the US Embassy. Ambitious, audacious, and achievable. The installations, while holding great esteem and prestige, would be lightly guarded during Tet. Dat had confidence that all their missions would be successes. Looking at his watch, he realized the Presidential Palace raid was already underway. Unfortunate, he knew, that President Thieu was not in residence this night.

They were nearing the embassy. Ahead, Dat could see the gate was wide open. That was a surprise! Who would leave the gates to the US Embassy wide open? He nearly leaned over to tell the driver to pull right up to the entrance so they could shoot the guards where they stood. It was at such times you had to be bold; inventive. But Dat thought better of it. These were not seasoned warriors.

As the old taxi swung onto the street paralleling the embassy, the outside passengers could not restrain themselves and opened fire on the surprised gate sentries, who now ran to close and lock the gates.

The car stopped and the sappers piled out, running to the wall to set charges.

The explosion blew a three-foot hole in the embassy wall and they immediately poured inside. Dat could hear automatic gunfire. Then it was quiet. The guard on top of the embassy opened fire with what, strangely, sounded like a handgun. The sappers returned his fire. Now there was a big explosion...the main embassy doors. Things were going well. Before they got too hot, Dat wanted to be somewhere else.

"Let's go. Back to the Presidential Palace. I want to see how we are doing there," Dat said to the driver. The car sputtered and pulled away.

The Presidential Palace was just three blocks from the US Embassy. The driver could not get close. American and ARVN Military Police were already there, the streets blocked off. Dat got out of the car and walked to the edge of a building half a block from the Palace.

Looking up the street he could see that his force had evidently not penetrated the palace and had been pushed across the street. They were now surrounded and in a firefight with the Palace guards and American MPs. He turned and walked briskly back to the car.

"Call C-10 at Naval Headquarters," Dat said, entering the taxi. "Let's hope things are better there." The driver worked the portable radio and soon had a harried commander on the line.

"What is your situation, Captain?"

"Not good, sir. ARVN is putting up a tough fight. We have not been able to secure the boats to bring our reinforcements across from the other side of the river."

Dat swore under his breath. The Naval Headquarters plan was too complicated. They had not counted on ARVN providing much resistance, especially with a weakened holiday roster. The Naval Headquarters should have proved an easy target.

"What is your disposition? Will you achieve your objectives soon?" Dat asked.

"A matter of time, Colonel. When I get my reinforcements across, the fight will be over."

"This is vital, Captain. Vital!" Dat said, "You cannot let a bunch of cadets stall this attack. Move forward!" Dat handed the phone back to the driver. "Tune in the National Radio Station. Let's see if our comrades are on the air."

The driver played the dials, but could not find the station. "There's nothing being broadcast at that frequency, Colonel."

Dat said nothing. As he had long suspected, the Great Offensive was too big. Too much was being counted on from far too little. The holiday forces were not going to roll over. Now despondent, Dat said, "Get General Minh on the radio."

The hopes the North held for the operation's ambitious goals were not being met. So far, they had caused nothing but a nuisance. The driver handed Dat the radio phone.

"They are getting the general," he said. Soon the smooth voice of Minh came on the line.

"This is Minh. How are things your way, Dat?"

"General, I am afraid we are not having much success here. They must have killed the power to the radio station. ARVN at both the Palace and Naval Headquarters have put up a good fight. Our situation in both locations is critical. I am now at the Palace, and I will move up the street to the US Embassy again."

There was silence from Minh. "Damn," he finally said. "We needed swift victories. It is Tet after all!"

"Things began well at the embassy," Dat said. I am going there now. I will call you with another report."

"Fine," Minh said, disappointment in his tone. "Don't despair, Colonel. Your attacks will make headlines around the world. It is all that was expected...really. We are having some early success here. We have penetrated their defenses and are rushing the airport."

"General," Dat said. "If things do not go well I will head for Cholon and meet you back at the tunnels."

"You have a duty, Colonel...to see this through. I expect you on the front lines of this until the end."

"The end will come when hope dies, Colonel. We must both live to fight another day."

"Baah," Minh responded. The line went dead.

Dat handed the driver the phone. "Back to the embassy," he said, then slumped in the back seat as the driver maneuvered the car through side streets toward the embassy. As they got close, they could see the road blocked ahead by US Army MPs.

"Can you get close in...down an alley, perhaps?" Dat asked the driver.

"Yes, I think so," he said, turning left into a tight alley and then hanging an impossible right on a very tight corner. Entering an alley not much wider than the car, they crept toward the embassy, stopping at an intersection with nothing more than a walking lane left and right.

"Follow me, Colonel," the driver said, squeezing out of his door.

Turning left, they ran down a dark, refuse-strewn path that intersected another small alley. Stopping just short of its entrance, the driver pointed at a large building half a block away.

"That hotel is across the street from the US Embassy. There is a back door."

While approaching the hotel, Dat saw the back door was open. Tentatively, he stuck his head in, scanning the lobby. The place was dark and deserted. Through big windows pocked with bullet holes, he could see the brightly lit embassy and hear gunfire. Now, he hurried across the lobby and up the stairs. He paused at the top, looking left and right. There was nobody in residence. Doors were flung open, clothes scattered on the floor. Patrons had evidently left in a hurry. Walking three doors down to his left, he entered a room that gave him a good look at the embassy. The window had two bullet holes in it. He ran to it and crouched down for a look. It was like having a good seat at a soccer match, everything laid before him. He could see over the wall and pinpointed two locations where the sappers were firing at the Americans. American MPs were at the wall in force, returning fire.

"Raise your hands where I can see them," came a voice from behind Dat. "Then stand. Slowly. No sudden moves or I will kill you where you are."

Dat felt his hair stand on end. Slowly he raised his hands and got to his feet.

"Turn slowly...slowly now."

Dat turned to face an ARVN soldier with his rifle pointed at Dat's chest. The soldier was very young, perhaps eighteen or nineteen.

"What are you doing here?" the soldier asked.

"I am a guest of the hotel...watching the soldiers in the street." The soldier didn't move.

"Everyone else fled. I stayed behind. That is all."

"I do not think so," the soldier said. "You are lying. All the guests have left...for good reason. Why would you stay?"

"I am just interested. You must believe me. You would not shoot a civilian."

"You are no civilian. You are with them," the soldier said, indicating the embassy.

Dat noticed a tremor in the boy's voice and watched as the young man's hands continuously gripped and released his weapon. He was nervous and perhaps a little scared by Dat.

"We are going downstairs," the soldier said. "You first—be very careful. The safety is on automatic. One wrong move and you will be all over the room."

The soldier stepped to the side into the room, his eyes riveted on Dat, who moved slowly across the floor toward the door. The soldier fell in behind him. As Dat reached the doorway, he paused and looked down the hall. At the far end, another soldier was just leaving the hall and entering a room. Dat suddenly jumped backward a step forcing the soldier behind him to hastily retreat several steps.

"What the hell are you doing? You are lucky I did not pull..."

With a bigger space now between them, Dat moved quickly out the doorway and to his right, disappearing from the soldier's sight.

"What..." The soldier ran forward. Dat had turned quickly outside the door and met him at the doorway, grabbing the barrel and stock of the rifle and jamming it into the soldier's midsection as hard as he could. Air rushed out of the man's lungs and he slumped back into the room. Dat immediately brought his right foot hard up into the man's crotch. Enough air for only a small groan left the man. As he slumped to the floor Dat twisted the rifle out of his hands and hit him with the stock as he went down. All this took place within four seconds; there was hardly a sound.

Dat ventured a slow look out the door and down the hall. The other soldier was again in the hallway, but then entered another room. Quickly, Dat set the rifle by the door and made for the stairs. He glanced down the hall as he turned and hurried down the staircase.

"Where do you think you are going?" The words stopped him dead.

A sergeant said, holding a rifle on Dat. They stood looking at each other.

"I am a hotel guest," Dat said. "The soldier...he told me to get out. I'm getting out."

The sergeant looked dubious. "What are you doing here?"

"I am just a visitor...for Tet. I was asleep in my bed when all this..."

"Yeah, yeah. Why didn't you leave with the others?"

"I was curious. In our village..."

"Enough! Please, just get out and try not to get shot in the process," the sergeant said, jabbing his thumb toward the back door.

As he came out the door, Dat saw that two Jeeps filled with soldiers had arrived in the alley. He steeled his mind and reminded himself that he was just a citizen leaving a dangerous area. He was unarmed and looked harmless; nothing to panic about. *Just walk fast and don't look back.*

It was then Dat saw his driver, hands secured behind him, lying on the hood of his old taxi with an armed MP covering him. The radio lay on the hood next to him. One soldier was yelling at the man while another hit him with his fist. The driver silently watched as Dat helplessly moved on.

Dat headed down the alley, picking up his pace once the ARVN soldiers were behind him. After several minutes of running, the alley terminated at a broad avenue. Across the street, he spied a bicycle locked to a tree. His transportation to Cholon.

Suddenly, a Jeep rounded the corner. Dat stepped back into the alley and slid behind a garbage can just as the vehicle turned into the backstreet. Dat caught his breath as the Jeep hit the can in front of him, sending it crashing and rolling down the alley.

Exposed, Dat recognized the ARVN sergeant from the hotel lobby in the front seat but neither the soldier nor the driver looked back.

Watching the retreating vehicle, Dat rose quickly and ran across the street. The bicycle lock looked old, so Dat grabbed the bike and yanked hard several times. The lock burst. He jumped on and rode due west, exiting into the first alley he found.

General Le Chi Cuong was shouting orders and sending message runners between talking on the radio with field commanders. The sun was up in Cholon and the heat was on. They were in operational headquarters at the Phu Tho racetrack. Dat stood by, patiently waiting for the general's attention. Finally, he turned to Dat in exasperation.

"The surprise is over, Colonel," he said. "ARVN is rolling tanks down the avenues toward us. I expect helicopter gunships will follow. The good ground we took last night could disappear just as quickly."

"With your permission, General, I would like to make a suggestion. Let us not forget who we are, and where we are. Normal fronts, or lines, do not exist here. We are among the people. We *are* the people. I suggest we simply do not give ARVN or the Americans a clear target."

"And how will we do that?" General Le Chi shouted. "Are you suggesting we should slink away into the shadows? Not fight? We are here to liberate Saigon."

"We *will* fight...but a frontal attack would be suicide," Dat said. "We are outgunned and pinned to the area. But our options are not suicide or cowardice. There is a middle ground here.

"During the day let's stack our weapons in safe houses and blend in with the populace. Every evening, when things become more veiled, we will be in excellent position to retake the city. It will be hard, if not impossible, for our enemies to know who or where we are. If things go well, our enemies will have to destroy the city before they will be rid of us," Dat finished.

The general stroked his sparse beard while looking intently at Dat. "Yes...I like the idea, Colonel. You know I am a political man, myself. Your military experience gives you an advantage. Fine, that will be your assignment, then. I want you to take charge in the streets and of the military defense of Cholon. See that my political cadres are not interfered with and organize this deception you talk of.... I believe it could work for a time."

Dat immediately went to the radio and ordered a pullback. He met with company commanders and outlined his plan. They selected strategic safe havens and worked out an operational plan for retaking the offensive every evening. The commanders received his ideas enthusiastically, not desiring deadly, straight-on confrontations in daylight. Troops followed the deception plan to perfection, evaporating before their enemies every morning.

It was evening of the second day of the offensive when he saw her again, Luang Nu Chi, the young lady he had met in Xuan Loc. Dat was in a home near the front on the east end of Cholon that served as his command center. Political displays and rallies of all kinds were taking place in the street outside: flag burnings; public demonstrations against the South; condemnations and executions of ARVN soldiers, suspected collaborators, sympathizers, and officials of the government. He happened to be looking out the window when Nu Chi and several others were led past, being roughly escorted by political activists.

Dat jumped to his feet and strode to the door. Upon opening it, he searched for and found the officer of the detail. He beckoned him over with a gesture. The man hurriedly complied. Nu Chi was now just five meters away. An older man, perhaps her father, was bound and being pulled by a rope that had been placed around his neck. The officer stopped and saluted Dat.

"Lieutenant, what is the purpose of bringing this man bound into the street?" Dat asked.

The officer smiled. "He is a criminal, sir. The man is a well-placed money changer for the despised traitor government of the South."

Dat looked at the group. Cowering next to Nu Chi was an older woman, undoubtedly her mother, and two younger girls—all being treated roughly. The crowd poked them with sticks while they paraded the old man around in a circle like an animal.

Dat looked at the lieutenant. He indicated the man should come closer. When he did, Dat grabbed him by the shoulder.

"This man is not to be harmed, Lieutenant. You understand?" Dat hissed.

"Yes, sir!" the officer responded, the smile quickly disappearing.

"I cannot tell you why, but he is a favorable citizen... I know this family."

"You *know* them?! I do not understand?" the officer stammered, visibly upset. "The commissar said..."

"I will have words with the commissar about this. Do not worry; you have done your job well. However, we must find a way out of this demonstration and be careful not to indicate favoritism upon the Luang family. There are, of course, many Southern spies among us. If they thought he and his family were friendly to our cause, they would have to answer to the Thieu regime when we have gone. You understand?"

"Yes, sir. I believe I do."

"You will have to proceed carefully," Dat said, pausing to think it through. "Announce that new allegations are being considered and no further action will be taken at this time...that we are placing him under house arrest. Yes...that will have to do. Untie him and have your squad escort the man and his family back to their home. Instruct Mr. Luang that he is not to leave his home for the duration, but that the rest of his family is free to come and go as they please. Post a twenty-four-hour guard of two men outside their home. It will appear we are keeping him from escaping...but this is for their protection, Lieutenant. It would be most disagreeable if something happened to the Luang family...you understand?"

"It will be exactly as you wish, Colonel."

"One last thing...ask the young girl...that one with the pink ribbon in her hair...if she would please stay behind to talk with me. You will escort her here."

"Yes, sir."

The lieutenant left and Dat stepped inside, closing the door. He quickly called his staff together and told them he wished to be left alone a few minutes, then he walked to the window and watched as the officer made his proclamation to the crowd. The father shook his head despondently as the women consoled themselves. The angry mob was indignant, shouting obscenities.

"We need no more evidence," one man said. "Let's kill him now!"

But the lieutenant ignored this outburst and instructed the man be untied. While this was being done, the lieutenant went to Nu Chi. As he talked, Nu Chi looked searchingly at Dat's headquarters. She turned and spoke with her family. A sharp exchange and protests from her father ensued and he was hit hard in the back by a soldier. The lieutenant grabbed Nu Chi firmly and led her away. As she was brought forward, Dat moved to the center of the room and waited. The door opened and she was led inside.

"Thank you, Lieutenant. Please remain outside so that you might escort the young lady home. And...do not let anyone else through this door, understand?"

"Yes, sir," the officer said, closing the door.

Though she would not look at him, Dat saw a sad sort of resentment in her expression. She said nothing and kept her chin down, her hands twisting together in knots.

"I am sorry for the inconvenience," Dat said. "It is a war, and some bad things are happening. Please, do not think of us as barbarians. Most of us come from good families. Perhaps someday, when we have time, we can discuss what has happened here."

With this, Nu Chi looked up with a perplexed expression.

"I say this because now that we have met, quite by accident, two times, it might be perceived as no accident at all. Perhaps it is destiny. Do you believe in destiny?"

She scrutinized Dat. "I *have* met you," she said, her expression changing to one of confusion. "The rice farmer...in Xuan Loc?"

"Yes," Dat said, pleased that she would remember the brief encounter. "I was the rice farmer you talked to on the street that day."

"It was all a show then? You are one of them?" she said with a rolling disdain. "Evidently a well-placed officer.... I am confused."

"I apologize for the ruse. I wanted to understand the people of the South. You cannot know a people unless you mingle with them, talk with them. I very much enjoyed talking to you."

Nu Chi nodded in apparent understanding. "Just an actor. What will you do with me then? You know who my father is...and you know I am following in his footsteps. Will we be murdered?"

Dat knew this was coming, knew his position would be difficult to explain. He walked closer to her, looking intently into her face.

"Understand, Nu Chi, that I had nothing to do with this demonstration in the street. Luckily, I recognized you when you and your family passed by my window. No more harm will come to you...I have made sure of that. Your family will not be bothered again. I have placed a guard around your home for that purpose. The locals, your neighbors, unless you tell them otherwise, will think your father is under arrest."

"Why do you do this? Do you expect a *favor* from me? Do you expect me to become a Communist like you...a spy? I will not!"

Her eyes flashed with hatred and contempt. Instead of being insulted, Dat found her spirit embracing and full of courage. She was far different than most women he had ever met. Here was someone who would make the man she loved stronger...or completely dominate him.

"Of course not," Dat said. "I myself am not a Communist."

"That is not possible! You are lying. You cannot be an officer for the North without being a good Communist. I may be young, but I know that much."

"Not so. You are wrong," Dat responded, levelly.

This seemed to upset Nu Chi's flow of thought. She stammered, looked unsure, set her mouth in tight defiance, and said nothing in response.

"Not everything I said in the street that day was a lie. My family does have a rice farm...in the Red River Delta. I joined the People's Army in 1948 when I was just sixteen. I was not moved by the Communists to join...but by a resolve to see the foreigners expelled and our country achieve freedom and independence. Generations of my family have been exploited. My uncle was literally worked to death on a French plantation. My cousin died in a Japanese jail...tortured for days on end. I want the foreigners out. Comrade Minh tried mightily to bend my mind to the Communist philosophy, but it did not take. I can never be a Communist, but I tolerate them because they fight for independence. I am fighting for the Vietnamese...I like to think *all* Vietnamese."

Nu Chi looked very uncomfortable. "Why are you saying such things? Is this common knowledge? Are you trying to trick me?"

"No, of course not. Within the first minute of our conversation in Xuan Loc, I felt I wanted to know you better. I imagine everyone who comes into your presence feels the same. You will not betray me. It would not be like you to do so. However, I am not sure it would make much difference at any rate. Our political commissars consider me a suspicious scoundrel. I have been promoted partly because I have survived all these years and partly because I am a good officer, something the politicians can do little about. I am a colonel in the People's Army despite my lack of Communist zeal... which is no easy task, I assure you."

"Why did you have me brought here? It seems you have taken a huge risk saving us. It would have been better for you to let us die. I must ask you again...what do you want from me?"

"Nothing. I expect nothing of you, Nu Chi. I just find it interesting that our paths have crossed twice in such a short time. I know what kind of person you are when your guard is down... when you are not facing a colonel from the North. I like that person. I could not see you or your family harmed.... I had to save you from the political cadre."

"You do not approve of who I am...you consider me the enemy," Dat said. "I would like you to reconsider. I am not in the street persecuting people...because it is my belief that such barbarism, such brutal idealism will not change anything. I am a soldier and follow Confucius' teachings. I believe that virtuous behavior has a greater effect on society than any laws or punishment—for the same reason I am fighting a foreign government and the corrupt Mandarin system that must be defeated if Vietnam is ever to be one nation and, hopefully, perceived as an exemplary one. But all political systems are corrupt and war is sometimes cruel. I do not condone what is being done in the streets."

"But, you can look the other way! My father, too, is a virtuous man, a loving father, a good husband and provider. Your Communists would have no problem murdering him."

"I *must* look the other way! You are correct...the Communists would have no problem killing your father. The political radicals have their own twisted agenda. It bothers me. It has always bothered me. But as you were unable to control it in the street, neither am I. I can save you and your family with a little lie to a junior officer, but right now a political commissar is outside in the street wondering why your family was not persecuted...and what I am doing in here with you. I have seriously overstepped my authority, and I will have to answer to that man.

"Good people on both sides are being killed, Nu Chi. In the last twenty years, I have lost more friends than I can remember... most in horrible, gruesome deaths. They were men and women with loved ones...who will never see them again. The South has no monopoly on tragic losses. Believe me when I say the North is paying a bigger price for our freedom."

Dat was relieved to see the hatred had finally left Nu Chi's face. In its place was what he thought might be compassion or, perhaps, just sad resolve. He could not tell.

"So, then," Nu Chi said quietly. "What now?"

"I am going to say goodbye to you, again. I am going to wish you and your family well and hope nothing further happens to you during this war. If there were no war, I would certainly pursue a relationship with you...because I find you captivating...enchanting."

"Enchanting?! Me?" Nu Chi said with the slimmest of smiles. "No man has ever referred to me as enchanting. Tempestuous, bold, argumentative, and many other uncomplimentary things... but never enchanting. Men do not pursue me."

"Ah, they are the fools! You are not just any other woman, Nu Chi, and, if you ever had the chance to know me, I believe you would find I am unusual also. We shall see. I asked you when you came in if you believed in destiny. Do you?"

"Perhaps I do."

"Good. We have met twice now. If anything further is meant by these encounters, we will meet yet again. Maybe many more times and, I hope, under better circumstances. As for the near future, your government or the Americans will soon push us out of here and I will vanish with my forces...but, I look forward to our next meeting."

"I have one more question, Colonel," Nu Chi said. "I have forgotten your name. What is it?"

Dat smiled awkwardly, in embarrassment. "I am so sorry. I was caught up in the moment...I should have reintroduced myself. I am Le Van Dat."

"Yes...Dat," she said. "Well, I am not sure I believe in destiny to the same degree as you, but as you have said...we shall see. I am more concerned with surviving this crisis with my family...and how I will explain all this to them. How it came to pass that I know, and that we were saved by, a North Vietnamese colonel."

"It should make an interesting story for your children, someday," Dat said with a smile.

At first, ARVN forces filtered deep into the city looking for the guerrillas. Soon they discovered that this left them vulnerable to snipers and was a virtual trap; it became hard or impossible to extract forces as evening fell. Days went by and the growing frustration of the South Vietnamese government began to show. After announcing to the populace that they should abandon Cholon, the South began wholesale shelling and strafing of large sections of the city.

Dat made sure the Luang family was safely evacuated.

On February 10, the Americans sent in the US Army 199th Light Infantry to finish the job. They surrounded Viet Cong headquarters at the Phu Tho racetrack but found it empty when they attacked. Once again, the Viet Cong had vanished.

Dat and a considerable number of guerrillas made their escape to the extensive tunnel complex at Cu Chi. It was there Dat learned the toll for the Tet campaign: thirty-five thousand men lost through death or capture, about half the Viet Cong forces in the South. Militarily, it had been the disaster Dat saw coming. But the Great Offensive had surprised their foes and the Viet Cong had put up stiff resistance in Pleiku, Cholon, and other sites. Hue was still being contested. As Dat expected, there had been no General Uprising. ARVN had fought fiercely against them, which was very much a surprise.

The political consequences of their bold, suicidal attack were yet to be known. Certainly, they had thrown a fright into the government of the South—and the Americans. There would be new military uncertainty and sagging morale among their enemies, and that would be a valuable asset.

It was during Dat's briefing that he learned Minh had been seriously wounded at the Vinatexco mill when they were trapped by ARVN and American forces in a counter-assault. Minh was not expected to live. Dat pondered the possibility of his death and realized, with a start, that Minh was his only close friend in the People's Army. If he died, Dat would be quite alone in a political and military system he often felt at odds with.

More incredulous news was delivered the same day. After his Cholon defense held off superior forces for almost two weeks, Dat received a field promotion to the rank of general. A glowing recommendation from General Cuong combined with the death of other high-ranking officers created a new, critical demand for experienced leaders in the South. Dat was immediately promoted. Inconceivably, he had risen to the rank of general...this despite a fresh complaint of anti-Communist meddling filed by a political commissar.

Tragedy, defeat, and fulfillment mingled in a crushing cocktail of emotion that created a deep depression. As Dat sat brooding in a dark corner of the tunnel works, Dat reflected that it was unlikely he would be alive to see the end of the war. He had been lucky to escape a close call in Saigon...the bombing in the Ia Drang...the helicopter attack at Duc Co. Fortune undoubtedly smiled upon him; disaster was long overdue. For twenty years he had been expecting death. As it took many of those around him, he had prepared himself for the same fate. Now, however, Dat recognized that something fundamental had changed. He was no longer pre- pared to die. In fact, he very much wanted to live...to see Nu Chi once again. The young woman increasingly filled his thoughts and fantasies. Knowing this, he felt his demise even more certain, for he had always advised his men that fighting not to die was a sure way of ending up dead.

Helena, Montana

Finals were over and school was out on the 1st of June. My folks were on vacation and talked me into going camping for a few days. It was not one of my favorite activities, but I felt I owed them the time. As I was helping load the camper, Katy Wicks showed up.

"Hi," she said with a brilliant smile. "Home for the summer?"

"Well, for a little while," I replied. "I guess you haven't heard...I'm going active in the Navy this summer."

"Oh, no!" she said.

"Yeah. I'm not happy about it. I realized this past year just how much...I really don't like the idea of serving in the military. I guess I joined up because it was expected. My cousins were in the Navy... my brother, too, but I don't like the regimented bullshit and, right now, the political climate. I don't think military life and I are going to mix. I feel like I'm leaving to serve out a prison sentence."

"Gee, I'm sorry, Mark. I guess I won't see you around much then, huh?"

"Um...I'll be here another month or so. Say...if my brother's right, I'll be heading for Treasure Island for processing. It's in San Francisco Bay. I'll get to see Stanley."

She didn't look excited.

"I guess you didn't hear that news, either. Stan's shipping out for Vietnam. He made enough noise...they were just too happy to send him."

"Crap," I said. We stayed silent a while, both bummed out.

"What about your girlfriend?"

"Jan has been offered a student exchange posting in France. She'll be gone for a year...so, I guess the timing's good."

"You'll probably go to Vietnam, too," Katy said. "How do you feel about that?"

"Buddy was right all along, Katy," I said, looking at my sneakers. "I finally accepted it this year. I mean, what are we doing there? It's an ill-conceived, politically motivated, poorly organized, hopeless fight with no possibility of victory and no end in sight...the worst kind of senseless slaughter.

"The hard-liners say we're all being duped by a liberal, anti-Vietnam press. But ask yourself...when did patriotism, love for one's country, doing one's duty become a blind obligation? The military and government's responsibility to us is to make sure our causes are just and worthy. Vietnam's not...they've violated our trust."

That sounded good, practiced. Katy wasn't ready for the Vietnam debate I'd honed in many midnight bull sessions. She jumped at changing the subject.

"You still a McCarthy supporter?" she asked.

"I still like him, but..."

"Okay, no! Let me guess...Kennedy?"

I smiled.

"I like him, too," she said. "What a hip guy. Can you imagine him as president?"

"It's not just that hip look...the image thing," I said. "The guy really cares. You can see it when he's in a rally, or riding in a parade. He loves people, all kinds...kids, workers, old folks...he connects. I like what he's saying about Nam. If he gets in office, I think he'll just pull the plug on the war. Right now you can probably guess how much I'd like that."

"So, is he gonna win?"

"Can't miss," I said confidently. "Look at the momentum he's gained in just a few weeks. I saw him on the news last night. He's in California for the primary Tuesday...people are going nuts, screaming his name and reaching out to him. They all want a piece of Bobby. He'll win California...then at the convention in Chicago. By election day the whole country will be with him. Nixon doesn't stand a chance." Then I added, "Speaking of which, what about Nixon, Kate?"

She gave me a droll little smile. "I *still* like him. He seems so... presidential. He's no Bobby Kennedy, though. Bobby's cool."

I smiled. The guy could probably have any woman he wanted.

"Imagine Nixon losing to another Kennedy," I said. "He'll play that disappearing act again...and, hopefully, this time he'll stay away."

"That's not nice. Dick Nixon's a good man—you'll see. So, how long before you're out of the service?"

"Two years active. That's the deal. Two years."

Man, I hated talking about it. Two years seemed like an eternity. Yet, Joe Wills had been in almost three already. Knowing that didn't make me feel any better, though.

"I wish you weren't leaving."

"You know, Kate, the war just started heating up about the time I turned eighteen...draft age. Sixty-six was a lousy year to turn eighteen."

We were in the old camper on Canyon Ferry Lake that Wednesday morning in June. Being the middle of the week, the lake was calm, the campground quiet. Mom was getting ready to bake Pillsbury cinnamon rolls from a refrigerated tube. I was drinking coffee with Dad and reading *MAD*. Mom flipped on the radio and we heard the news.... Bobby Kennedy had been shot at the Ambassador Hotel in Los Angeles after winning the California primary the night before. He was not expected to live.

We sat in numbed silence as the announcer droned. It was a shocking, surreal moment. I felt like the world had become a cruel, mean place of successive disappointment. I was dumbfounded; couldn't find the words to react, the actions to respond. I wondered how in God's great plan such a thing could happen...again?! I realized tears were flowing down my face. Angry? I was *damn* angry...and frustrated, disappointed, disillusioned, bitter. The world had gone brutally insane. Would there be no end to the carnage? Who would be next? Who was left? was a better question. Another promising leader murdered...and now, it seemed, we were fresh out of inspirational heroes. Martin Luther King, Bobby Kennedy, the Vietnam War, protests, demonstrations, race riots, bickering between generations...it was the spring of insanity. I wondered, too, how much more of this the country could take? America was being torn apart, and the one man I saw as our savior, who more than anyone wanted to fix it, was gone.

I hadn't heard from Joe Wills in a while. I hadn't seen his mother recently, either, so news of Joe was sketchy. I did know he was still in North Carolina, but little else. During the first week of July I received a letter from him, the first in a long time. I tore it open by the mailbox and read...

> *Hey Mark,*
> *Long time no see. I guess we both just kind of ended up doing our own thing in different places. It's easy to lose touch. I'm writing because I heard from Mom you're going active in the Navy this summer.*
> *Got some news of my own. I'm going back to Nam. When my unit got the word I went up to the top-kick and said I wasn't going...didn't have to go because I've already been there. He thought that was real funny. He said nobody is guaranteed just one trip to Nam. The whole outfit is shipping out in September. All I can say is...FUCK THIS!*
> *I'll be home in August for a month. From what I've heard, you'll be gone by then. It's too bad I won't see you. Well, "good luck," guy. I hope things go well. I hope you don't end up in that shit hole with me.*
> *Write if you can. I'd like to hear from you. And, don't tell Mom I'm going back overseas. She doesn't know yet and I want to tell her myself.*
> *Regards, Joe*

Treasure Island, San Francisco Bay

As my brother had instructed, I grabbed a cab to take me to Treasure Island. While crossing the Bay Bridge, the cabby pointed at the square patch of lights in the middle of the inky blackness that was the harbor.

"That's it, Son...Treasure Island. Your home away from home, eh?"

I was finally able to drag my sorry rear end into the barracks around 2 a.m., guided by the on-duty watch messenger and his flashlight.

"Here's an empty rack," he whispered. "Just drop your bag here. You can get a locker in the morning, which..." He pulled up his sleeve to look at his watch. "...is about four hours from now. Better sleep fast."

I'd slept maybe two hours the night before and was exhausted. I immediately fell into a deep sleep.

I was pushing a wheelbarrow down a steep incline toward a ledge. My intent was to deposit my load over the edge of the precipice. I struggled mightily to keep from slipping on the wet grass and rock...knowing if I did so I would go over the edge with my load. I was surprised to notice Jan was in the wheelbarrow.

What are you doing here? I asked.

You put me here yourself, she responded with a smile. Where are we going? she said, enthusiastically.

Get out!... I shouted.

Will it be fun? she said, with a radiant smile.

Get out! Get out!

But now, I was in the wheelbarrow and Jan was pushing.

This WILL be fun! she said, looking ever so lovely, as I went over the ledge, falling, falling.

"Reveille, reveille! All hands heave forth and thrice up. The smoking lamp is lit in all berthing spaces. Now, reveille!"

I awoke with a start. The lights were on and guys started piling out of racks. Exhausted, I couldn't keep my eyes open. My legs felt numb.

"What the hell was that dream about?" I asked myself, but I knew. Jan and I hadn't exactly been connecting the last month of my stay in Helena. I worried about our relationship.

"Come on, out of those racks. Move it!" said a first class working his way down the main aisle. He walked up to my bunk and shook it. My eyes snapped open.

"You're the new guy. Find yourself an empty locker and stow this gear. Report to me in the office up front before muster. My name's Porter. On the double, sailor."

Crap. "You're in the Navy now," I swore under my breath. I struggled to get out of the top bunk, catching one foot momentarily on the blanket, landing cross-legged, and falling on my butt. There was derisive laughter all around. I looked up to see my bunkmate sitting on the lower rack.

"Hey," he said.

"Uh...hey, yourself," I returned.

"Didn' hear ya come in las' night," he said in a heavy southern drawl. "Name's Jimmie Bob...Jimmie Bob Enright."

"Mark Cameron."

"Accent like that...yur a Yankee. Where ya from, Mark?"

"Helena, Montana. What accent? I don't have an accent."

"Sure ya do. I'm from Lake Charles, Loosiana. We better get goin'...the head's down that way," he said, and left me with a grin. Nice enough guy, I thought.

By the time I got out of the bathroom it was almost time for muster. I threw on dungarees, my light Navy jacket, and hurried to the front office. The first class was just grabbing his clipboard.

"Well, you're too damn late now, mister. You're Cameron, right? Get on out there and stand on square number 64," he said, scrawling on the clipboard. "That's your number for muster every morning. If you're not standing on 64 you are AWOL. Got it? See me after muster and we'll get ya squared away."

I headed out the door just before him and located 64 with little trouble. I thought we might have to stand at attention, but everyone seemed pretty relaxed. There was a cold, stiff breeze coming across the bay. I pulled my light jacket closer. There were boisterous catcalls from across the street, and I turned to look at the men lining up there for muster. They looked older. Their dungarees were faded and, to a man, they had a distinct, slouching appearance. Some of them had full beards. I saw one guy look our way. He cupped his hands and yelled.

"Two days, Polliwogs. That's what I got left. Two fuckin' days an' a wake-up. How about you? Hee, hee."

I looked at the fellow next to me. Number 65.

"What's with those guys?" I asked.

He gave me a wry smile. "They're short-timers. This whole street is transient barracks. All of us on this side are going in. Those guys..." He gestured. "...are getting out. They rag our ass every morning. My name's Johnson...Jeremiah Johnson," he said, extending his hand. "But everybody calls me JT. I'm from Fullerton."

"Cameron. Mark Cameron," I said, taking his hand. "I'm from Helena, Montana. You been here long?"

"Let's see...three days, this morning. Er, two days and a wake-up."

"Is it always this cold?" I said, shivering now.

"Yeah, summer in San Francisco. Who was it said the coldest winter they ever spent was a summer in San Francisco? We don't get this bullshit weather in Fullerton."

"Where's Fullerton?"

"Greater LA. You really are from Montana."

It didn't take me long to get the hang of things. There wasn't much to our daily routine: reveille, muster, muster for work details, work detail, chow, lights out, etc. Right away, I knew the work details would be the worst part of Treasure Island. The guys in the transient barracks got all the lousy jobs. On my third day at Treasure Island, I was sitting on my bunk after evening chow when Jimmie Bob walked up to me and dropped a letter in my lap.

"Ya weren't at mail call, so I took yur letter fur you. Ya should always go to mail call...don' wanna miss those letters."

Even before I saw her cursive styling, I knew it was from Jan. I hadn't gone to mail call because I thought there was no way a letter would reach California from Montana this fast. I popped it open and read.

July 15, 1968
Mark,

It is late, past midnight. You have been gone a few hours and I cannot sleep for thinking of you...and the recent warmth of your arms around me. There were so many things you did that attracted me to you. It is all swirling in my head.

I know we should have talked before you left, but I couldn't face you and tell you we need to go our separate ways.

I didn't have the courage. I hope you aren't hurt too bad, but if you look at what's in our future, there is no future...at least for us.

You'll be gone most of two years and by the time you get back I'll be off to college—in Oklahoma, not Bozeman. It's unfair to both of us to try and continue a long-distance relationship that holds no promise.

So, this is goodbye. There won't be any more letters. Please don't write me. It would just be too hard for both of us. I wish the timing were different, but there could never be a good time to end something that has been so special. I will never forget you and I will always measure others against the best of you, the times when you were so good.

I hope the Lord sees fit to protect you and guide you. Take care of yourself! There are many people, myself included, who want to see you safely home. I will pray for your safe return and that you have a good life.

God's Speed,
Jan

I slumped back onto my bed. Okay, maybe I should have seen that coming. Jan hadn't been herself with me in some time. She was there, but not really there. I took her for granted.

We had drifted apart since I'd entered college, no doubt about that. And I had cheated on her a couple times at school; okay more than a couple. High school was over for me and so was my high school romance. Wow, she was something, though.

The timing sucked, big-time. Could she have picked a worse time to send me a Dear John? I would have to deal with everything new and sucky being thrown my way...now with added heartbreak. Fuck!

The next morning, JT tried to strike up a conversation during muster. I ignored him. Then I got pissed at the short-timers across the road and yelled at them to go fuck themselves. It drew more than a few curious looks.

"Something's bugging you, man," JT said. "Maybe you should come with me today."

"And where would that be?"

"I haven't told anyone because I'm afraid of ruining it...but I've got the best work detail on the base."

"Really?"

"The mattress warehouse, man."

"There's a *mattress* warehouse here? You're kiddin'!"

"Yeah...well, it's not much of a warehouse, really. But it's great duty, man. The other guy working with me, Worthy, he's got his orders, so Sanchez's gonna need another man."

"Anything would be better'n moppin' another floor."

After muster, JT did a good job of selling the first class on the idea and I was cleared to go to the mattress warehouse.

I liked Sanchez immediately. He was a portly Mexican lifer who treated everyone like they were his best friend. We took a huge stack of thin Navy mattresses to a barracks on the north side of the island and spent all morning hauling beds in and out of the place. It was hard work. We finished at lunchtime and Sanchez drove us to a base mess.

After chow, we took a few older mattresses outside the warehouse and lined them up against railings. Sanchez told us to start putting them back in the building at four o'clock...then he took off. The three of us, JT, Worthy, and I, ended up in the warehouse lounging on mattresses. Worthy fell asleep right away while JT and I talked.

"So, what kind of duty you hopin' for?" he asked.

"I'm not very particular. I just wanna do my time and get the hell out."

"Yeah, me too. I didn't even consider a training school. Do you know about the lists?"

"Lists?"

"The list of postings, man. It's what we're all here waitin' for. They put 'em on the barracks wall twice a week. There'll be one there tonight when we get back. Usually, there's twenty or thirty names on it. The posting only lists the name of your ship, or maybe *Coronado*. You can go to the base library and look up any ship you're assigned to...they have pictures, the ship's history, all kinds of info."

"*Coronado*? What's *Coronado*?"

"You don't wanna go there, man. Riverine school. The brown water Navy."

"Brown water Navy?"

"Man...how long have you been in the reserves? The brown water Navy patrols the rivers in Vietnam. It might be river patrol boats, you know, PBRs...swift boats, some other kind of gunboat, or an LST. *Coronado* is in San Diego Bay. That's where they train you for duty on the boats. So if you get *Coronado* on the list...it's gunboats and off to Nam straight away, Jack."

"This doesn't sound good."

"You got that right. Those guys get their ass shot off. I hear it's pretty hazardous."

"So...how many guys get *Coronado*?"

"Quite a few outta here. Nobody in these transient barracks has any Navy schooling...you notice that? They either skipped schools like you and me, flunked out of 'em, or didn't qualify. So, yeah, there's quite a few get *Coronado* on the list."

Crap. I hadn't even known about the brown water Navy before that instant. My brother's suggestion about extending for schooling suddenly sounded like a good idea.

"So, Mark," JT said, changing his tone somewhat. "You looked pretty bummed out at muster this morning. What's up? Care to talk about it?"

I was relieved he had asked. I felt like unloading on someone. So, I filled him in on my love life starting with my senior year in high school and leaving out few details. When I finished, he shook his head, slowly.

"Sorry about your old lady, man...bad timing. But ya know, it doesn't sound like she was right for you anyway. Too religious. Put it behind you, dude. Move on."

"That won't be easy, JT. I really loved her. How about you?... You have a girlfriend?"

"More than that, man. I have a fiancée."

"Congratulations," I said cheerfully, but inside it hurt. "When are you gettin' married?"

"When she heard I'd joined the Navy, Richelle wanted to run off to Tijuana like our friends did. But, I know inside she really wants a big church wedding. We decided to wait and see what kind of orders I get. If I get something on the coast, we'll probably get hitched right away."

"And if it's *Coronado*?"

"I don't know, dude. I've got some thoughts. We'll have to see," he said, reflectively. "What kinda music do you like?"

"What? Oh, uh...the Beatles. Stones. The Monkees..."

"The Monkees? Are you serious?"

"Yeah, I like 'em. The Doors, the Who. Most rock and roll."

"You ever hear of Janis Joplin? Or Jimi Hendrix?" JT asked.

"No."

"I saw 'em at the Monterey Pop Festival last summer. They're hot in California. Most of the country hasn't heard of 'em yet. How about The Mamas and The Papas?"

"Yeah, I like them."

"Guys in Montana smoke pot? How about you?"

Whoa, I didn't see that one coming. After a pregnant pause in which we sized each other up, I decided JT was probably cool.

"You wouldn't be a narc or somethin', would ya?" I said.

"Me?! Hah, that's a good one. So, are you a head or not?"

"Yeah, I've turned on," I replied at last.

"Excellent," he said, reaching into his pocket, "'cause I got a doobie and it seems like a good time about now. Let's go up in the loft and fire this thing up."

It was good stuff. We sprawled on old mattresses feeling very mellow.

"We need a night out, man," JT said. "Whaddya say we catch the bus into the city tonight?"

"Okay," I said. "It's too bad we weren't both here a month ago. I had an old friend living out by Hunter's Point. But he's gone... volunteered for Nam and shipped out."

"Really? Is he fucking nuts?"

"No. Just patriotic...and a little confused, I suppose."

When we returned to the barracks at the end of the day, there was a crowd around the bulletin board. "The list is up," JT said. "Let's take a look."

After a minute or two we'd worked our way to the front and I looked at the list. One sheet of double-spaced names with serial numbers down the left side. Across from each name was anything from USS *Blue* to USS *Canberra* to *Coronado*. I saw my bunkmate's name, Jimmie Bob Enright, on the list. He was being sent to the USS *Taylor* (DD-468). I noticed that the few seaman apprentices on the list were being sent to ships and I mentioned it to JT.

"Hmmm. I have no idea who generates the lists...how it's done. Someone out there is playing God."

"Yeah, well, I don't particularly like the fact all these seamen are going to *Coronado*... know what I mean?"

The mattress warehouse job was just as JT had said it would be. The workload was easy. We didn't sweep or mop any floors, and there was plenty of time for sleeping or shooting the bull.

A couple days into it, JT let me know what was on his mind. He'd been talking to the old salts and instructors and said he knew just what we should do.

"Volunteer for PBRs."

"Are you out of your fucking mind!" I laughed. "I can't think of anything more dangerous."

"Whoa, whoa, whoa...just listen. You saw the list. All the seamen were sent to Coronado. With no schooling, no rank, no training of any kind...we'll end up on some stinking old World War II LST anchored in a river in Nam. We'll spend our days chipping paint, pulling watches, KP, sweeping, swabbing, and filling out work parties. That's when we're not manning some machine gun fighting off the VC...who consider LSTs as just really big, really good targets. Once in a while, they actually attach a mine to one and sink it. I know you think of the service as prison. Well, that kind of duty in Nam is worse than prison. That's like being in prison *and* fighting for your life."

Okay, that was a persuasive argument, but any kind of big steel structure sounded safer than PBRs and I said so.

"Let me tell you a thing or two I've found out. PBRs are just kick-ass, man. They're fast, loaded with armament, run in pairs, and have helicopter support, too. They bring a lot to bear. There's nothing on the river to compete with 'em. Cam, it's the Navy's version of a hot rod.

"But safe? No, it's not safe. I know that, but a PBR is a helluva lot better than sitting on some stationary LST piece of crap waiting for a VC diver to blow you out of the fucking water. And on a PBR, you're on the river, Mark...catching the breeze like Ventura Boulevard with the top down. All you have to do is pull a patrol once a day and then hit your air-conditioned rack. Easy, smeasy, Japanesee."

"Whoa. I haven't had to listen to a lot of Navy bullshit, yet... but, boy, I sure know it when I hear it. Easy, smeasy my ass. Fuckin' PBRs are a floating target with not much to protect ya when the bullets fly. There'll be nothing easy about it."

"Like I *said*," JT continued as if explaining it to a child. "It's *not* safe. What *will* be safe? Huh? Will any duty in Nam be *safe?* Consider the options, man. The list for us isn't out yet, but we're goin' to Nam...that's a fact, Jack. We don't have the luxury of asking for a nice air-conditioned billet out of the way somewhere. It ain't gonna happen. We've got the best of some lousy choices. So I'm gettin' out in front of it. I'm goin' PBRs 'cause I'd rather live life crusin' the river than die slowly...chipping paint on some fucking rust-bucket to nowhere."

JT was on message and upset that I didn't seem to be grasping the situation. Well, I understood all right. Sitting on what amounted to an anchored barge in the middle of a dangerous river was far from what I'd expected to do in the Navy, though I really had no expectations. The one thing you could say about an LST, though, was that they were big steel ships; something of substance that would better protect me, providing we didn't get mined...or take a few rockets. Part of my problem with PBRs was I couldn't envision myself as the gunslinger type...riding around shootin' em up at the OK Canal.

"I dunno, Jay," I said. "About the only time in my life I fired a gun was at basic training in San Diego. One day...about twenty shots. I think I hit the target maybe once. I just can't see me doing this."

"That doesn't mean a damn thing. We'll be going to training at Mare Island. You'll get the hang of it."

Here, JT paused to think. "The time will come when it'll be all the excitement we can handle, then some. But I'm used to bein' out there...doin' things, man. LST duty for me would be death! I choose to fight, to be active in this war. If I die, it'll be with guns blazin' and I'll take a few of those bastards with me. Think about this, Mark. Can you really see yourself sittin' on a river workin' your ass off for nothin'? You gotta join me, man. You'll always regret it if you don't."

I felt sick to my stomach.

"How the hell did I get here?" I said, more to myself than Jay. "One minute I was just a school kid. Now I'm going to war?! What kinda fucked..."

"You're not alone. My old man's a millionaire. What the fuck am *I* doing here, man?"

"I don't think I have what it takes, Jay. I'm not brave. Shit, I've spent the last several years avoiding every conflict, every challenge put to me. And character? What character? I cheated on the woman I most loved and thought I would marry someday. I don't believe in this fucking war and really haven't for years. I'm scared, I admit."

"Don't undersell yourself, Mark. I don't know you real well yet. But you're no flake...or a pussy. I can see that. I think you'll find something out about yourself that'll surprise you. But first, you gotta change that attitude. It doesn't help. Go in tough, man. Survive!"

"No...growing up I was a different person," I said. "I was a cocky kid from the wrong side of town. Ah, shit."

I am still undecided about God, religion in general, the Bible, the Torah, the Quran...all that stuff. But I have a sense now, in middle age, that there is a power of good and another of evil. Either can line up circumstances that guide you to their end. At times they will use people you know in their plan. JT was one of those messengers. Was he a messenger of good...or evil? In hindsight, I think he was both.

It was the toughest decision I've made in my life. The next morning, I volunteered, with JT, for PBR duty in Vietnam. The guys who served on PBRs were all volunteers who wanted to serve in some naval capacity where they could make a real contribution to the war. Those weren't my reasons for volunteering. My reasons were strictly personal. Since seventh grade, I had become increasingly disturbed about the many shortcomings in my personal makeup. I felt desperate to change all that. I wanted to be more than just an actor playing a part. I wanted to find some kind of honor or purpose I hoped was inside. Who I was at the moment ran opposite to everything I embraced and aspired to. It was time I faced my demons. One way or the other, I was going to find out what I was made of.

As I volunteered, the conflict within nearly tore me apart. My inner senses and emotions were screaming so loud I could hardly hear what was being said. Through the din, I went ahead with signing on...then ran to the head and puked my guts out. It was the most difficult thing I've ever done and, to this day, I cannot believe I found the courage to do it.

1998

The thought of going off to war didn't just frighten me; there was the issue of my self-respect. I knew I'd be scared, but how would I react to the fright of being in battle? Would I roll up in a ball? Freeze and do nothing? Cry and humiliate myself? It weighed on me, and I think all men before they enter battle.

I'm not embarrassed now by how I felt. In fact, I don't mind telling people of my feelings when I made that decision. I know, in hindsight, that sometimes being scared is as natural as breathing.

We had been training for just a couple weeks when JT invited me home to Fullerton.

"It's a birthday party, man. You gotta be there. Richelle is putting it on for me at my parents' house. My parents will be sailing with some friends around Catalina, so we'll have the joint to ourselves. Knowing my brother and some of that crowd, it could get wild."

"Your birthday, huh. How old?"

"Twenty."

"Yeah?! I'll be twenty this month, too."

"So, you're a Leo? I guess that figures. When's your birthday? We can make it a double celebration."

"The sixteenth."

"What?! C'mon, man. You're pulling my chain...big-time."

"Hey, sorry. That's my birthday. I was born August 16, 1948."

"NO FUCKING WAY!" Jay yelled, very excited now.

"What'd I say?"

"That's *my* fucking birthday, man. The sixteenth! You sure you're not just messin' with me here? Let me see your ID card."

I didn't know what to say, so I just smiled. It was enough that I had found someone in the service I felt tight with, but having the same birthday cemented what was quickly becoming an extraordinary friendship.

At four o'clock in the afternoon, Friday, August 9, the boats returned to the training center. As we approached the dock, there was a young woman dressed totally in white, shorts and halter top, standing on the pier waiting for us. Four boatloads of riverines whooped it up when they saw her. Jay leaned over and yelled above the diesels, "You're about to meet my fiancée."

The first thing I remember about Richelle was her hair. At a time when long, straight hair, preferably blond, was the style every young lady in America wanted, Richelle had short, bushy curls of rust brown. It framed a face that was cute, not beautiful. But she was *so* cute, she *was* beautiful. I think it was her smile. When she smiled, her upper lip curled over white teeth in a way that made you blush; it was so sexy and cool.

Jay embraced her and they kissed, which set off the riverines again, and they both laughed.

"How the hell did you get out on the docks?" Jay asked.

"Long story," she said. "I ran into the base commander. What a nice man."

"Oh, man. I can't wait to hear this one," Jay said, laughing. He grabbed me around the neck with an arm and brought me closer. "Richelle, this is the guy I have to share my birthday with. Say hello, Mark."

"Hello," I said from under Jay's armpit.

"So, you're his new friend. Jay's said a lot about you."

JT let go of me, and I stood looking at her, feeling somewhat envious. It was then that she stepped forward, put a hand on my shoulder, and kissed me on the cheek. "Thank you...for being a friend," she said. The event was carried off with class and a dignity you don't find in young women. I've never forgotten that moment, that kiss.

"How soon can we go?" Richelle said.

"We're done," JT answered. "Soon as we get changed."

"Well, then, get after it," she said.

Walking to the parking lot in our tropical whites, Jay asked, "Where's your car?"

"Right there," Richelle said, pointing at a little black MGB roadster with red vinyl interior. Jay did a double take.

"Since when?"

"Since I got all As my freshman year at UCLA," Richelle said. "Had my parents understood just how many nights I stayed up late with you, it would have been a Cadillac."

She threw me the keys.

"You know how to drive a five-speed, Mark?"

"Yeah, but...," I started.

"Then you're driving."

My brother's '59 Chevy was a standard "on the column" shift, but I'd only driven it about five times—my entire experience driving with a clutch. Looking at that incredibly cool MG, though, I wasn't about to refuse an offer to drive it. There were very few sports cars in Montana. In fact, that was the first time I had ever been in one. After a jerky start, and an apology, I got a little better at shifting. By the time we reached the freeway, I was in a comfort zone.

I had seen houses like Jay's parents' home in the *Home Beautiful* magazines my mom liked, but I'd never been close to one before. The landscaping was impeccable, with bushes trimmed so sharply that not a leaf was out of place.

We literally ran into Jay's parents coming out the front door. JT introduced me. They were a handsome couple, and rich. Somehow you can always tell when people have money. It's the hair, the way their clothes look, a flash of gold, perfect teeth, shoes. But they were nice to me, apologizing for not being home and playing host to JT's new friend. Then off they went in a new Jag.

The home was huge, low, and rambling. From the top of the canyon, large windows looked into the ravine and valley below. An oversized deck ran out to the pool and Jacuzzi. The putting green sat on the south side of the deck running its length. I turned to tell JT how impressed I was with his home, but he and Richelle had already disappeared and I was totally alone. So, for the moment, I sat in a cushy chaise lounge and imagined it was all mine.

JT pulled Richelle close in the bedroom, running his hands inside her shorts and along the smooth curve of her buttocks.

"I missed you," Jay said. "I think of you every second."

"I miss you, too," Richelle answered. "I just want to be with you always."

"The most we'll have is maybe thirty days before I ship out," JT said. "I'm just starting to get the picture now of how much I've screwed up everything."

"No...let's just enjoy this moment...tonight. Let's make it count."

"Yeah," JT agreed. "Let's make this weekend count."

Richelle had invited one of her girlfriends to the party for me, a blind date. Though Richelle meant well and the girl was very pretty, she didn't want to be with a serviceman. Everyone at the party, excepting Jay and I, had at least shoulder-length hair. So, the girl and I spent long stretches in uncomfortable silence until she eventually drifted off to spend the evening with some kids she knew.

Lots of people showed up for Jay's party: jocks, eclectics, poets, artists, cool people, brainy people. It was a California party. Jay's brother, Charlie, invited some wild kids who did their best to knock all the water out of the pool. Everybody drank too much, smoked too much, imbibed too much. After midnight all the girls in the Jacuzzi were topless. By Montana standards the party was off the charts; the wildest I would ever attend.

Four in the morning found JT and I alone lying on chaise lounges at the edge of the ravine looking over the lights in the valley. It was cool and quiet. We were tired and still slightly stoned and drunk.

"When I was sixteen," Jay said, "I brought a bucket of balls home from the range. I set up a tee on the edge of the putting green and started hitting balls out into the ravine."

I looked over the edge at houses that spread out for maybe a half mile.

"Hitting 'em...where?" I asked.

"There were fewer houses then...that was the thing. I had to hit every ball at least four hundred feet to clear the newest houses being built. A whole bucket. It was a challenge I set up for myself... like the time I made the twenty-footer blindfolded on this green. I bet Charlie ten bucks I could do it. To this day he thinks I cheated." He laughed at the thought.

"So," I said. "Did you cheat?"

Jay just smiled.

"A bucket of balls. How many is that?"

"Probably fifty," Jay said. "I used dad's big new driver...the one he forbade me to use. One miss...a topper, shank, anything...and I'd have hit a house, gone through a window. It was a test of will, concentration. Anyway, I zipped 'em out there...one after another. As the balls disappeared I started to get tired. So, I concentrated more and they kept goin'. The last few balls were the biggest challenge. The second to last just missed hitting a house. The last one... was the one."

"The one that finally hit something?" I said.

"No," Jay went on. "That ball cleared everything, too. It was the club that didn't. It flew out of my hands, cartwheeling away. So down the ravine I went to get it. Took a while...but I finally found it stuck in the middle of a thick new rose garden...like a spear. I had a hell of a time getting to it...and then this little yipper dog comes roarin' out into the whole thing, nipping at my legs. I started to run and the rose thorns just tore the shit outta me. I was whacking at the bushes and the dog with the club...and the next thing I know some old lady is screamin' at me. Long story short... she called the cops. I was arrested, and Dad had to come and get me. Funny thing is when he found out what I had done...hitting all those balls over the houses...he got excited and forgot all about everything else."

I chuckled, but it was more of a tired wheeze. I was seriously on the nod. Jay continued.

"Maybe Dad should have just kicked my butt. At some point everyone deserves to get their ass kicked for screwing up. At some point you have to stop being a jerk, a jock, a spoiled kid. I'm actually looking forward to Nam. Maybe I'll grow up. One thing's for sure, dude...it'll be a hell of an adventure. Richelle and I are getting married in a few hours."

"Huh?" I said, suddenly coming awake again. I looked hard at Jay. "You guys messin' with me?"

"We're driving to Tijuana at sunrise with you, Sarah, and Rad. We've decided it's the best thing for us."

"But...the big wedding Richelle wanted?... And your parents will kill you."

Jay rolled his head sideways and looked at me. "It's like World War II or somethin'...you know? Young soldier is home...about to be shipped out. The lovers do something wild and crazy because... the time just isn't there for them. No...not enough time. Richelle and I want to spend what we have...together. We know we won't regret it."

"Jeez, JT. Have you really thought this through? This is a really big step you're takin'."

"Oh yeah. I love her, man. I think I've loved her my whole life...long before I knew I did. She feels the same way. We're not waitin'."

I always laugh at the memory of what followed. Between that talk on the pool deck and the serenade sung by Rad, Sarah, and myself under the newlyweds' second floor room at the San Diego Holiday Inn, there was Richelle talking the California Highway Patrol out of giving us a ticket for driving too slow, the Mexican kid who wanted to sell his sister to JT, the Justice of the Peace who was too drunk to perform the service, the complete strip search at the border, and, finally, running out of gas a block from the hotel. But we got the deed done. In the end, they definitely made the right decision.

Firing the weapons had been hard for me to get a handle on. The damn bucking of the guns made it near impossible to hit anything. All of my classmates except Jay told me they didn't want to be on my boat. But I figured if I got in close enough that it was dangerous, I wasn't going to miss much with a .50-cal. The incredible racket the guns generated left my ears singing soprano. It's no surprise I have hearing problems today.

As we got closer to finishing school and shipping out, JT fixated on the idea of getting PBR tattoos...*esprit de corps*, a badge of brotherhood, and all that. I told him he was nuts.

"If God had intended us to have drawings on our skin he'd made us all cartoonists. Remember, these things don't rub off like the kiddie decals you get inside a bubble gum wrapper. And, what about your wife?... Your parents? Or, your golf career after the service? You may not want this tattoo all your life," I said, sounding remarkably mature.

I think, now, that it was the thrill of doing something so outrageously outside the norm in his life, like PBRs, that drove JT to do it. I couldn't sway him. He found a design he liked in downtown Oakland and had it drilled into his upper right arm. He nagged me mercilessly about following him to the needle. "We'll be soul mates for life," he'd said. I again reiterated that nothing imaginable could ever move me to get myself painted, and I was right.

Thirty years later, driving across the Townsend flats, I touch my own upper right arm. Under the sleeve of my dress shirt, I know there is a PBR tattoo...the same as JT's.

In fall 1968, Jay and I shipped out for Nam. As I suspected at the time, it would be the end of wide-eyed innocence. I was stepping into a world I could not have envisioned...then or now. The ordeal left me knowing with certainty that somewhere, in every instant, one human being is killing another in a violent act. Yet, the rest of the world goes about its business without noticing or perhaps caring. But for time, place, and opportunity...we are all victims, we are all killers, or we are both.

1968

In Country

On October 14, Mark Cameron was in seat 24C on a Braniff Airlines 707 as it touched down at Tan Son Nhut airfield in Saigon. After a quick taxi to the terminal, the jet jerked to a stop; perhaps a nervous rookie hitting the brakes too hard. The pilot switched off climate controls as a hundred servicemen, waking body parts, struggled as one to get out of their seats. The door was opened, and it immediately started to warm up as bodies, packed armpit to elbow, surged en masse toward the door.

By the time I reached the stair ramp, I was sweating hard. The heat and humidity hit me like a hot towel in a steamer. I gauged the temperature close to ninety with likewise humidity.

We shuffled like cattle toward the processing center. By the time I reached the terminal my hands were slick and my brow dripping while sweat rings spread like a Montana prairie fire from my armpits. I heard a commotion, the catcalls, before I saw the chain-link fence with the crowd of grunts behind it. Outgoing veterans of all services were exiting Vietnam, their tours done. They were leaving on the same jet we had landed in. Their comments directed toward us were merciless.

"Welcome to the Nam, suckers."

"Make sure you keep one hand on your balls at all times if you wanna leave here a man," another said.

"Oh...you in deep shit now, honkies," a black guy bellowed, laughing.

I was with JT; we both had orders to River Division 536, a PBR base on the Bassac. After hours of processing, we were told a bus would pick us up for transport to Binh Thuy. Our new acquaintance, a first class named Paul Cutler, turned to us with a frown.

"Oh, I've been here before," he said in his Arkansas twang. "They'll put us on some hot, stinkin' bus like a buncha pigs from back home. If the VC don't shoot the shit outta us, we'll die'a heat stroke. What we need is to find us an officer with a big Suburban who'll give us a lift. Wait here."

Cutler, who we were already calling Cutty, had befriended us during our layover in the Philippines. Drinking coffee in an over-crowded café at Clark Air Force Base, we'd discovered we all had the same orders to the 536th. After that, he'd entertained us with service stories going back almost twenty years. He was a boatswain mate first class and Korean War veteran...one of those crusty old salts who know their way around any military situation. He was back within fifteen minutes.

"Found a lieuy goin' to Vinh Long in an air-conditioned rig. Just him and a driver...there's plenty of room. We can find another ride from there to Binh Thuy—let's go."

As we drove through the Vietnamese countryside, I stared in childlike wonder at rice fields where people labored without a hint of modern machinery. For the first time, I saw a people who could truly be called peasants, living in crude huts made of mud or bamboo and palms. Farm machinery here seemed to be a water buffalo, a hoe, and a couple kids. The smells of rot and refuse occasionally wafted through the vehicle. Maybe I should have been scared, being in the Nam, but I was mesmerized by a world unlike anything I'd ever seen.

In Vinh Long, Cutty found an Air Force corporal from Binh Thuy who was picking up helicopter parts and insisted on giving us a ride. As we piled into the Jeep, now overfilled with sea bags, parts, and bodies, he handed Cutty an M16.

"Keep the safety off and the selector switched to full automatic. The gooks are known to set up ambushes on this road," he said. "You guys, too. I want your weapons pointed to each side. Don't be afraid to pull the trigger. Remember where the fuck you are, huh? I had to make this trip by myself this morning, and I'm glad to have your firepower going back."

I thought the corporal was a little over the top, but who was I to say anything? We had been issued weapons in Saigon. While JT and I had received M16s, Cutty had talked his way into a hard-to-find .45.

The road to Binh Thuy made the two-lane gravel road we'd just traveled look like an LA freeway. The Jeep bounced and careened down an overgrown, rutted, bombed-out trail of slick red clay at breakneck speed. I tried desperately to stay in the saddle while hanging on to the M16 with my right hand. We swerved hard to miss a bomb crater. One instant I was in danger of being thrown across the Jeep, the next, as the driver swerved hard the other way, I was hanging on to the seat for dear life as roadside palms whipped my face and arms.

"Fuck," I finally yelled in frustration. "You're gonna kill us before the VC do."

The driver threw a glance at me. "I guaran-fuckin-tee you that would be better, pal. VC are tough motherfuckers."

I couldn't believe that this pathetic excuse for a road led anywhere substantial, but forty minutes later we pulled into Binh Thuy, a city larger than my hometown but built to a shed-like height without a single two-story building in sight. Putting our feet gratefully on solid ground, we gave the corporal a reserved "thanks" and walked toward the river.

As we got closer, the river opened up before us and I got my first look at the Bassac. Brown with silt, the river was a virtual highway of commerce. Sampans and junks by the dozens moved up and down the river in front of us. We found a couple shore patrol who told us a landing craft from the YRBM-21, the base for the 536th, came up the river at irregular intervals and would dock at the pier. We would have to wait and keep our eyes open.

Cutty nudged us and pointed to a nearby establishment that had *Madame Cho's* prominently painted on the front.

"Looks like the local watering hole," Cutty said. "Let's get a beer while we're waiting."

As we were to discover, Madame Cho's was the place in Binh Thuy where you could get anything you wanted. It was a combination bar, whorehouse, laundry, and money-changing tailor shop run by the tough, wrinkled Madame Cho. A couple soldiers hung out at the bar with two girls hanging all over them. A few pretty, scantily-dressed young girls, who I assumed to be hookers, leaned on the bar and looked us over. I recognized Mick Jagger on the jukebox singing a song I didn't know. Seeing new meat, the madame immediately approached us.

"Ohh, welcome, welcome. New sailorman always good to see in Madame Cho's. I have just the thing you need after long, dangerous ride," she said, motioning to a couple girls beside the bar who smiled and walked our way.

"Ohh, mama. That is sooo what I need, but I ain't got the

time," Cutty said. "What we'd like is three ice-cold beers...something American if you've got it. We'll be outside."

"Oh, you sure you want no nooky, nooky? Could be quick."

"Give it up, mama," Cutty replied. "We gotta catch the launch next time it pulls in. We'll be on the patio. A nice cold beer each, please."

"Okay, but you be sorry, sailorman."

We moved outside to a table on the "patio," which was nothing more than dingy, rusting tables under a canopy of palms with a good view of the river. A minute later a young man arrived with three bottles of iced Schlitz.

"Hello, Navy man. I am Phan Van Khoa. All my sailor friends call me Fannie...fly boys and grunts, too," he said with a laugh. "Beer always icy cold at Madame Cho's. Extra cold if you ask for Fannie. That dollar fifty, please."

"Four bits a bottle! Jesus H. Christ, man...that's fuckin' robbery," Cutty complained. "I'm bettin' you got those beers for fifteen cents apiece on the black market."

"Oh, Madame Cho never tell good business secret. Dollar fifty good price. You no find beer this cold anywhere else on Bassac," Fannie shot back with a wide grin.

"Trouble is, you're probably right...and that would include real Navy establishments," Cutty said, handing him a dollar fifty in MPC, the money chits used as currency by the military in Vietnam.

"Thank you much. If you need anything else in Binh Thuy, ask Fannie. I get sailorman anything," he said with an exaggerated wink, then left us.

"The little shit," Cutty said, after "Fannie" had left. "Guys like him and Madame Cho operate everywhere American servicemen go in this world. Mark, JT...watch out for him...and the good Madame...they're friendly enough when you've got money in your hand, but let your guard down an' they can clip you in a dozen ways."

We sat in the sweltering shade and gratefully drank our icy beers as delta life passed by our table. The heat and humidity made it hard to breathe. Even sitting in the shade with a cold brew in my hand, I watched as my fatigue blouse finished soaking with sweat. *How do these people work in this?* I asked myself. I kept one hand resting on the M16 that leaned against my knee. Cutty had warned us that fighting could break out at anytime, anywhere. Regardless, the hot afternoon, lack of sleep, and cold beer left us drowsy.

I looked at JT, who was seriously on the nod, and that's where I was headed, too.

Cutty nudged me awake. "Here comes the boat. Grab your shit, gentlemen."

About fifty yards down the river a large Navy launch was making its way toward the pier. A sailor manned an M60 as the coxswain deftly steered the craft toward the landing, reversing engines in a roar as the boat lightly tapped the pier. Immediately, half a dozen guys jumped off and pushed their way past us into Madame Cho's.

"You three the only guys getting on?" the coxswain asked. When he got the affirmative, he said, "Jump on then, and let's get the hell outta here."

I was the last one aboard, but before my feet even left the pier the boat roared into reverse, backing quickly into the river and knocking me on my butt.

"Sorry," the coxswain yelled. "This ain't no PBR and I'm not gonna stick around waiting for a rocket or a satchel charge."

The boat moved downstream at full speed, about twelve knots, weaving in and out of river traffic. The sailor manning the machine gun wore a helmet and flak jacket, training his weapon on the southern bank as the craft bore hard down the middle of the river. We passed every kind of watercraft: large junks, medium and small sampans, water taxis, and a Navy minesweeper.

"You ever get shot at?" Cutty asked the coxswain.

"All the time," he said. "Snipers. We don't really control the south side of the river, so it almost always comes from there. Lucky for us, though, their aim's pretty bad. Still, you never know. Somebody gets lucky."

Maybe ten minutes later, stuck out in the middle of a wide part in the river a mile away, we saw the YRBM-21. It was nothing more than an anchored floating barge with smaller barges and docking facilities sprouting off in all directions. The YRBM stood for yard, repair, berth, and mess...we would always call it the Yerby Mike. It would be the only home I would know in Nam.

Once aboard, we took a break in a wonderfully air-conditioned passageway before finding the commanding officer's quarters, where we presented our orders to the lieutenant. The three of us stood at attention while he scanned our orders. Leaning back in his chair, he gave us a quick, cursory inspection.

"Glad to see you guys. As it turns out, we've got a little special action going on this afternoon. We can use the extra guns. Seaman Bossard, our yeoman, will show you to your quarters. Then find Chief DeYoung—he's the senior patrol officer of the 536th and a good man. He'll assign you to boats. That's all for now. Dismissed."

Walking down the corridor, Cutty let out an expletive. "Damn! The first fuckin' minute we're here we're goin' on patrol? I'm hungry. I was counting on a good meal and some rack time!"

My reaction to the news was surprisingly benign. I had thought about battle action for several weeks. It meant finally facing the music; a time and place I knew would eventually arrive. I found myself relieved it would come immediately, before I had a chance to think on it too much.

We met Chief DeYoung coming out the door of the mess with a sticky bun in his hand. In unison, our mouths watered at the sight of the glazed delight. Cutty couldn't help himself.

"Beggin' your pardon, Chief, but we haven't had much to eat today."

The chief grabbed a half tray of sticky buns, and we ate them while following him out to the boats.

"We're goin' out to shit island to give the VC a little taste of American justice," the chief said.

"Shit Island?" I said before I could stop myself.

"Yeah, Dung Island. It's at the mouth of the Bassac. Anyway, the assholes tried to mortar a couple of our boats again this morning. We're goin' in with the Seawolves to land some SEALS and flush 'em out. Everybody's been prepped. You guys just follow orders from your boat captains. See that fat guy there?" he said, pointing at a very large, slightly overweight guy with a crew cut. "First Class Hook. Get a steel pot and a flak jacket from him. Meet me at the 6715 boat and I'll assign you."

I was directed to join the crew of the 6709, captained by a first class named Sutey. Boat crews were stacking ammo around guns and securing gear. As we walked by we got a curious look from each. I stood on the dock at the 6709 boat, looking her over.

"Is there a Sutey on board?" I yelled from the pier.

"That's me," a short, balding guy said as he stepped out of the wheelhouse conning station.

"Seaman Cameron, Sutey. Chief DeYoung assigned me to your boat for this patrol."

"You new to the Nam, Cameron?"

"Got off the plane this mornin'."

"Fuckin' great. Well, come aboard."

Ten boats of the 536th made their way at top speed down the Bassac. Our boat carried one of the YRBM's officers, an Ensign Dewey, a forward gunner named Sanchez, and a rear gunner, a black kid they just called Streak. Though we were all in battle gear and ready for some heavy shit, none of the veterans on the boat looked stressed. Streak leaned on the railing at the back of the boat, one hand on the .50-cal. Ensign Dewey was on the radio. Sanchez stood up in the forward gun tub, taking the cool breeze off the river.

I was manning the M60. It had a belt slapped in and a full ready tray. All I'd have to do was switch off the safety and pull the trigger. I felt that no matter what happened I would be able to accomplish those tasks. Though my hands shook slightly and my stomach tossed the sticky buns around a bit, I thought I was doing quite well.

Dung Island came into view, large and in the middle of the Bassac. We veered to port and continued at full speed. Sanchez and Streak got in behind their guns. Ensign Dewey cracked an M79 grenade launcher and loaded a round. Showtime.

Four Seawolves swept in across our bow at about a hundred feet and opened up with rockets and machine guns. It was not like a training exercise. There was a distinctly different feel about this. The rockets exploded in terrifying unison. Trees, palms, and dirt flew in all directions behind the smoke trails of the rockets. Shells from the machine guns splintered wood, the red tracer rounds skipping and ricocheting off into the air. The calamity of this destruction filled the area with smoke, dust, and debris. I felt a little more confident of our situation, wondering how any living thing could survive such pounding.

"Okay, stand by," Sutey commanded. "We're goin' in. Cameron...you just watch Streak. Fire anywhere he fires. Got it?"

"No problem," I said, hugging the M60.

The boat turned sharply as all ten boats simultaneously headed toward the island. We were a cover boat; we would stay a little off shore giving support fire while five other boats landed SEALS.

As we got closer, skimming the light chop at twenty-nine knots, my nerves started getting the better of me. I tried to swallow, but my throat was like sandpaper. I realized my hand was shaking hard and I grabbed the gun tighter. Breath came in shallow gulps. Then guns everywhere erupted; the noise from Streak's .50-cal was painful and deafening. Streak had swung his gun forward and was firing bursts. My eyes followed his tracers to a spot where, for the first time, I saw enemy tracer rounds coming toward us. They splashed in the water in a line far to starboard and ahead of us. The tracers, going and coming, as if I were a spectator at a Roman candle duel, mesmerized me. I wondered how so many of the enemy had survived the pounding by the Seawolves.

"Cameron!" Sutey screamed, getting my attention. "Use that fucking weapon or I'll stick it up your ass!"

I sighted in, aiming at a grove of nipa palms where I could see tracer rounds, thumbed off the safety, and opened up. The gun jumped and rattled its distinctive M60 chatter. I saw my rounds land far in front of my target, in the water. I adjusted and saw the rounds go up the beach and into the trees. I thought I heard rounds hitting our boat, somewhere. Suddenly, there were tracer rounds coming at us from many locations. I tried to shift as rapidly and surely as possible, one to the other. Now I could see movement... behind a palm there, a mound of dirt to the right, that tree to the left, the palms again. Fucking gooks were everywhere!

A hard slap to the back of my head sent my helmet over my eyes. I let go of the gun and looked with surprise at the ensign, who gave me a disgusted look and walked away. I glanced around and saw everyone else looking at me. Then I heard laughter and catcalls from other boats and from Streak. The firing had stopped. Everything was quiet. I had been the only person shooting anything. Engagement with the enemy had ceased. The daisy-chained, four hundred-round magazine at my feet was almost empty.

"Fuckin' A, man. I think you killed every livin' thing within a square mile," Streak laughed.

I felt the blood rise to my face. Embarrassed, I was ashamed to look at the smoking gun. I slowly sat down on the engine cover. What had happened to me?

When we got back to the Yerby Mike, Sutey sat down with me on the edge of the boat. "You totally freaked there, man," he said. "You were gone. I've seen it happen before. First-combat jitters...or maybe you're just not cut out for this. You gotta keep your head, sailor. Your crew needs you alert, sharp. You can't lose your cool like that. I'll hafta report this to the chief and we'll watch you close next time out. Just remember your training—that's what it's all about over here. But look, it coulda been worse. You coulda froze and not done a damn thing. Remember, that M60 fires ten rounds a second. Shoot in bursts. It'll be enough to get the job done...honest."

That night JT and I sat in the mess deck talking before hitting our racks. I was still upset.

"I can't explain it, Jay. I swear, I saw gooks everywhere, man. I didn't close my eyes. I saw them."

"Just broke your cherry, Cam...that's all. Forget about it. Tomorrow's another day...you have action under your belt now. You'll be all right."

"Easy for you to say, man. You didn't screw up. I could still end up on some LST. It definitely wasn't like going up the slough at Mare Island."

"Naw. Look, the next hundred times we're out, it'll just be two boat patrols. You'll get another chance," he said. Then he added, "I wasn't exactly John Wayne, either. But when you kept shooting... well, it was kinda funny...'specially when that officer conked you one," he laughed. "The guys on my boat...they said it wasn't that unusual. Everyone's a little nervous their first time on the Bassac."

Later, reflecting on the day while lying in my rack, I realized how fortunate I was to have a friend like Jay. His loyalty and blind trust lent confidence at a time when I really needed it. In the morning, 6 a.m. to be exact, I was to report to Ensign Dewey for permanent placement with a crew, my own boat. I hoped they either hadn't heard about my episode or would be as forgiving as my friend.

"Hell, you're that guy that fucked up yesterday. Gunny, why do we always get the shit end of the stick?"

"Shut up, Bubba," Gunny said. "You'll be all right, kid. Better bc or you'll answer to me. What's your rating?"

"Don't have one," I said. "I went to college and didn't attend enough meetings to strike for anything."

"You mean to tell me you're a reservist?!" Gunny said.

"Well...yeah."

"How the fuck did you get on PBRs? You gotta volunteer! Reservists don't volunteer for this kinda duty. What the hell's the matter with you, boy?"

My first meeting with my new crewmates didn't seem to be going well. A gunners mate first class named Miller, who everyone called Gunny, captained the 6770 boat. He was maybe five foot six, crewcut with a pot belly. Most often he had some kinda cigar looking crag stuck in his yellowing teeth.

The second class boatswain's mate Smith, or Smitty, was a quiet guy with a steely stare who, as yet, hadn't said a word. The other seaman on board was boatswain's mate Bubba Binks, a hayseed from Georgia. He was maybe six-foot-two and 180 pounds with dark curly hair and light, freckled skin that was permanently sunburned. Immediately, I knew I wouldn't like him.

"You and Bubba stow this ammo," Miller said, returning to the wheelhouse.

There were several cans of .50-cal and M60 ammo stacked on the pier. Bubba looked at me with hands on his hips. I jumped onto the pier and handed him a heavy box of .50s. At first, he didn't move. He stood looking at me, slowly shaking his head. The box was getting heavier.

"Take it," I said. He reached out and took the can, sliding it across the deck with a slinging motion.

"You're a Yankee, aren't ya?"

"Yup," I said, handing him another box.

"Where ya from?"

"Helena, Montana."

"Montana? You aren't a Yankee. You're just a hick from the sticks. Montana...I think I heard of it. Where the hell is it?"

"Out west...up by Canada. It's the fourth largest state in the union."

"Big fuckin' deal," he said. "It can't be that special if I don't even know where it's at."

I had a feeling there was a lot Bubba didn't know.

"Well, at least you're not a nigger...that's somethin'."

I looked around. There were black guys all around us. I couldn't be sure if any had heard his comment.

"Hey, man," I said, in something of a whisper. "You'd better be careful what you say."

"Yeah, why?" he said in a loud voice. "You think I care what a buncha niggers think about me? You probably never even seen a nigger before you joined the Navy. I was raised around 'em. Unlike Montana, we got histry in Jawjah. We know how to handle our 'race relations.' Up north...all you know is kiss their ass and give 'em welfare. What a fuckin' joke."

"You got any niggers...any niggers at all up there by the North Pole?" he said.

I didn't answer. While growing up there had indeed been very few blacks in my hometown; he was right about that. But I knew all about prejudice, for which Bubba seemed the poster child. In just five minutes I already disliked him more than anyone I had ever known.

"Fuckin' hick!" Bubba finished.

Our patrols on the Bassac went as Jay had predicted. We roamed the river stopping sampans, checking their *Can Couics*, or identification cards. The Vietnamese we stopped on the river were often friendly. They knew the routine and cooperated, seemingly happy to have us there.

Patrols were tedious and long, lasting fourteen hours. They were also wet. The monsoon was on in the delta and would continue, according to Gunny, until maybe November. My Navy-issue poncho did little to keep me dry, and I wrote home asking Mom to send me some proper rain gear.

Often snipers targeted us. They usually fired from two hundred to three hundred meters. Their aim was terrible, and we applauded if they managed to come close to the boat. We were quick to return their fire and, in the process, I got better at firing the guns and began taking snipers for granted. Strange as it seemed, it actually became a welcome break from the hot, boring tedium of our search and seizure operations.

Had the routine remained so "normal," my Vietnam experiences would have been quite different. A few weeks into patrols, though, I got a taste of just how dangerous our mission was on the river. The call from the TOC came in the heat of the afternoon, a time when we tended to doze at our stations.

"White Night Black...this is Flashlight. We just received transmission from an ARVN squad heading toward the river at Suicide Bend two klicks south of your position...they are under fire from Victor Charlie and request extraction. Over."

White Night Black was Chief Bill Johnson's call sign. We were his cover boat, White Night Indigo. Gunny pushed the throttle to the wall and cranked the boat one-eighty, as did the 6771 boat, and headed toward Suicide Bend...so named because it had long been a bastion of Viet Cong activity. To get too close was suicide. The place had been bombed and shelled so often it looked like the surface of the moon. It was likely the VC remained in the area simply to show us they couldn't be intimidated.

"Flashlight, this is White Night Black. Copy your last transmission. We are underway and five minutes from rendezvous. What is ARVN's exact position? Over," came Johnson's reply.

"White Night Black...ARVN is on the west bank of Runnin' Scared approximately one klick upstream. Seawolves have been apprised and will rendezvous your position. Over."

"Wouldn't ya know it. The one place I don't ever wanna see again," Gunny said aloud.

Smitty was standing a few feet away and pulled the rain cover off the M60.

"Hey, Smitty," I said. "What's Runnin' Scared?"

"An old French canal that cuts right through Suicide Bend. It has some French name I forget. Everyone calls it Runnin' Scared 'cause that's what you do when you go up it. Get ready for some heavy shit, Cameron," he said while pulling on his flak jacket.

I pulled my own on, slapped on my helmet, then reached for more ammo for the .50-cal. I was the rear gunner on the PBR, a position I really didn't like. Unlike Bubba, who sat up front in the protection of the gun tub with the twin .50s, I stood on the rear deck with only a splinter shield between me and whatever came from the direction I was shooting. If fire came from both sides, one side of me would be totally uncovered. As the junior seaman, though, that was the position I earned. JT was rear gunner on his boat, too.

"White Night Indigo...this is White Night Black. Goin' up the canal. Close to twenty, Gunny. Over."

As we approached the canal and got closer into shore, I trained my .50 on the starboard shoreline with the safety off. I expected fire immediately. We followed the 6771 at full speed into the canal, a body of water maybe fifty meters wide in its widest spot. It was my first trip up a canal and I didn't like the close proximity to the shoreline. Luckily, though, the tide was high and slack and we were at the same level as the canal bank. They wouldn't be shooting down on us.

"Yeah, keep your .50 starboard, Cameron. Bubba's port...I'm playin' both sides," Smitty said.

I quickly scanned the sky for the Seawolves. They were nowhere in sight.

I heard the guns open up on Johnson's boat before I saw the tracers. It looked to be just a few snipers getting off some quick shots as we flew by. Their aim was so bad I thought they must have been firing blind out of their spider holes. I fired several quick bursts at tracer locations as we passed. A minute later the boat abruptly slowed, throwing me off-balance and forward, swinging my .50 backward as I hung on. Evidently, Gunny had hit reverse, throwing the redirection sleeve over the Jacuzzi jet and sending the 96,000 gallons per minute water stream immediately in the opposite direction. When necessary, PBRs could stop on a dime.

The boat hit the bank with a jarring thump. The sound of grenades and semiautomatic fire filled the air. From the other bank, maybe fifty meters away, an AK-47 opened up on us; the stream of tracers hit short, but were aimed directly at me. I sighted the .50 and rattled off a long burst in his direction. I noticed several other AKs now opening up...maybe half a dozen in all. A clatter caught my attention, and I stole a glance amidships where a couple ARVN had jumped on the boat. They were lying on the deck, firing their M16s. A bullet hit my splinter shield, sending shrapnel flying. It focused my attention back to the other shore. I sighted and fired bursts. My tracers were finding their mark. A few AKs stopped firing. But now there were more, many more shots being fired from the east bank and the west bank behind me. I could hear bullets hitting and rattling around the boat. The Seawolves still weren't around and the fight was getting intense. Gunny was firing the M79 as fast as he could load it. I saw a rocket headed my way. In a split second, I recognized what it was and then it was by me, missing my position by less than six feet. There was nothing I could have done to duck or get out of the way—slow enough to see, too fast to do anything about.

I fired a long burst in the general area the rocket had come from. Smitty was now firing with me toward the east bank. Then the east bank just erupted in explosions. The Seawolves had arrived and were strafing the shoreline with a deadly barrage of rockets and machine gun fire. A couple ARVN helped a wounded comrade on board, and as soon as they were off the bank, Gunny threw the boat in reverse, full throttle, while cranking the wheel. I was just releasing a burst, and the motion swept me off my feet. The next instant I was looking skyward from the deck with my thumb jammed on the butterfly trigger, tracers from my .50 cutting through one of the Seawolf choppers as I looked on like a shocked spectator. Immediately, the chopper started smoking, wheeled right, went low, and ran from the battle.

I regained my feet on the turning boat as we headed back down the canal toward the Bassac. Behind me, Chief Johnson's boat was on our tail. I kept my gun sighted on the east bank and continued to fire. Quickly, we were out of the battle and again flying at top speed down the canal toward the Bassac. I swiveled my .50 forward, port side, just as the snipers started firing at us again. Two minutes later we were on the river heading for a deserted island where a medivac chopper would pick up the wounded. Hundreds of shell casings rolled and clattered side to side on deck. I could feel the heat from the barrel of my .50. Noticing the ready tray was empty, I quickly opened another ammo can and loaded my weapon. The chopper was landing as we off-loaded our wounded ARVN. Another two minutes and we were back on the Bassac cruising half-throttle now toward Binh Thuy, where we'd drop the remaining ARVN soldiers.

Suddenly, I was tired. I got a drink from the cooler and sat on the engine cover, setting my helmet on my knees. I was soaked through with sweat and shaking. I thought about the big exchange of gunfire, rockets, grenades...and nobody got as much as a scratch. I looked up...Smitty was watching me.

"You okay, Cam?"

"Yeah, fine."

"You did all right, kid. You hung in there like a veteran."

I smiled. It was the first nice thing anyone other than JT had said to me since I'd joined the river rats. I slipped out of my flak jacket, and the cool breeze hit my soaked T-shirt. It felt good, and for the first time in my life, I felt like a real man.

"Cameron," Gunny yelled from the wheelhouse, the radio mic in his hand. "You know anything about shooting down one of our choppers?" My smile disappeared.

Fortunately, the pilot had made it back to his base and no one was hurt. I fully expected to be court-martialed. Instead, I got my ass royally chewed by the CO and extra duty from Gunny. They took into account the circumstances and my time in service. It was let known, though, that any reoccurrence of such an incident would not be tolerated. Gunny took me aside after the CO butt-chew.

"This is the second time you've fucked up, Cameron. This type of thing doesn't look good for me or the boat. I'm warnin' you... you better be A-number-one on top of things from now on. Get your shit together."

Part of my extra duty was sanding and painting the boat hull while they pulled her for maintenance. While I was at it, Smitty showed up and sat down beside me.

"Don't worry about this, Cam," he said. "Shit like this happens in every war. Grenades go off prematurely. A soldier stands up and gets shot from behind by a buddy. Jets strafe friendly troops. War is barely controllable homicidal lunacy. Shit happens. Gunny knows it. So does the CO. Nobody ever means for stuff like this to happen...it just does. Like I said on the river, you acted like a real sailor in a hot situation. For one, I'm not afraid to ride with you ever again. You're okay, kid."

That good feelin' had just returned when Binks showed up.

"Tch, tch. You are one major fuck-up, Montana. It isn't bad enough we've got Charlie to deal with...we got guys like you, too. Just try not to aim your .50 in my direction, okay."

"Fuck you, Bubba," I said without looking up.

"You're dangerous, Cameron. I don't like havin' you on my boat. I'd even prefer a nigger to you, pig shit. It'd be nice if Charlie'd take cara you for us."

I jumped to my feet to face him. He had a lazy, smart-ass grin on his face. I wanted to punch him and was angry with myself for just standing there, staring. Bubba didn't budge, as if he was reading my mind. He knew I wouldn't do anything and stood inches away with his bad breath washing over me.

"Don' ever think about taking me on, Cameron...or I'll show you some south'n justice," Bubba continued. "When I punish someone...it goes on and on. It never stops. So, you listen to what I have to say. You nod yessah, like a good boy, and do what I tell you. Got it? Now, get back to your chores, boy."

With that, he turned casually away. Deep inside me something sprang forward; something I wasn't in control of and hadn't felt in a long time. When he turned, I wound up and kicked him as hard as I could square in the ass, almost knocking him over. Guys on other boats whooped and hollered. Before he could turn and right himself I rushed him, driving into his midsection. We both went off the dock and into the water. When I came to the surface, lots of guys were already standing at the edge of the dock. As they were pulling me out I turned to see Bubba was being helped as well. As soon as they let go of me, I turned and jumped across the dock opening and onto Bubba, hitting him behind the head with my clasped hands. His head hit the edge of the dock and we both went under again. When we surfaced, I had my hands around his throat. His forehead was gashed and bleeding. Now lots of hands reached into the water and pulled us up. This time when I was hauled up three guys kept hold of me. BM1 Cutler was in the middle, separating Binks and me.

"Okay, enough of this shit," Cutty said. "You two have had your swim and now you're cooled off, right? Get back to work and we'll just keep this between us, okay? Let's shake hands now..."

But as soon as they relaxed their grip on me, I broke free and slammed the palm of my hand to Bubba's face. Four guys wrestled me away again.

"You prick, Binks. Let me go!" I screamed.

Cutty grabbed the front of my shirt and pulled me close.

"Officer's comin'.... Shut the fuck up and I'll get you outta this. You don't need more trouble."

Somehow, Bubba disappeared in the departing crowd as Ensign Dewey approached the mob. I stood dripping wet.

"What's going on here, Cameron? You're not allowed in the water. It's not safe," Dewey said.

"Sorry, sir," Cutty said. "I accidentally knocked him in and the boys were giving him a razzing, that's all. Everything's fine now."

"Be careful, Boats," Dewey said to Cameron. "We don't want anyone in this water. It's full of germs."

With that he walked on. I breathed a sigh of relief as Cutty turned to me, smiling.

"Jumpin' Jehosaphat! You're quite a fighter when you're riled. I'll tell ya I was glad to see it an' I know I'm not alone. That Binks is nothin' but white trash. I don't think he'll bother you much anymore."

I saw Binks a half hour later walking by the boat. He had a big bandage on his forehead. I had to grab the railing of the 6770 to keep from jumping him again. While I stared with disgust and loathing, he quickly glanced once at me and kept going with his head down. He rarely said anything in my direction from that day on.

It felt good. First the compliments from Smitty, and then I took care of Binks. I realized I hadn't felt this way since I was a kid; full of spunk and vinegar. I was through putting up with characters like Bubba. I knew that meant I'd occasionally get my butt kicked. But now it didn't matter. I felt like a warrior—a feeling I'd been searching for a long time. There was no way I would ever let this go again.

1968

Bassac River, South Vietnam

JT and I were at a table sucking on lukewarm beers on the beer barge that was permanently tied to the Yerby Mike. Hendrix was being played through the sound system. JT was sharpening his knife on a stone while I cleaned my M16. We were both a little stoned.

Our Navy buddy Fannie from Madame Cho's had delivered a nickel bag of good Cambodian weed, and we imbibed a little now and then when we were off duty.

"Say, heard you took a run up the Boogie Man again," I said.

"Yeah...third time since we got here, same time of day. That fucking Cowles...," Jay said. "He's too predictable. You think Charlie doesn't notice? One of these times he's gonna get our ass kicked...big-time."

"It's nothin' but macho bullshit," I agreed. "Some of these boat jocks wanna prove they're tough mothers. They flaunt their ego without thinking about anyone else. It's criminal, man."

"True that. I'll tell ya, though, I think we made the right decision...volunteering for the boats."

"Well...it's better'n a lotta things...I guess. I mean, given our options an' all," I replied.

"I do like the action, just like I thought I would," JT continued, not noticing my hesitation. "It really jacks ya up—know what I mean? Outside of golf, I never had much responsibility growing up...or excitement, for that matter. Nobody really depended on me. I spent all my time playin' golf and screwin' women. Other than marryin' the woman of my dreams, this is the most worthwhile thing I've ever done.

"And the guys...you, Stoney, Mick, Spud.... It's kinda like a big, tight family. Brothers, ya know?" he said. "Most of the time growin' up I didn't have what you'd call buddies. I like it. It's cool, man."

We heard the explosion and then felt the impact. Everyone on the barge jumped and turned to the sound. On shore, perhaps six hundred meters away, a huge fireball was rising over an area where ARVN had a compound.

"Holy shit!" JT yelled.

"Let's go topside for a look," I said.

We ran to the top of the Yerby Mike where lots of guys were gathering. Victor Charlie was hitting the ARVN compound hard. Another, bigger explosion went off, sending flaming fifty-gallon drums and all manner of things flying.

"Oh, man. That's fuckin' cool," JT said.

Now red and green tracers were flying throughout the ARVN compound. Four PBRs roared away from the Yerby Mike and were soon in the battle.

"It's Olson and Steinborn. Kick their ass, guys," JT yelled. The rest of us took up the call, becoming a cheering section.

"Shoot 'em up. Shoot 'em up. Go team, go!" JT laughed.

From the PBRs we could see round after round of grenades and mortars flying. The Seawolves arrived with rockets and machine gun fire, adding to the melee. Multiple explosions tore the surrounding jungle apart. Quickly, the fight was over.

"Whooo," Jay said. "That was a show. Wish I were there."

And he meant it.

I believe it was a Tuesday in November. Smitty and I joked and grab-assed as the boat slid through the river breeze on a beautiful, dry morning. Smitty said the monsoon was about done. We were hoping for a quiet patrol. Gunny pounded the radar and cursed.

"This damn Raytheon isn't working again. Looks like no radar for this patrol."

"White Night Indigo, this is White Night Black," came over the radio. *"Got a big sampan hightailin' it on our starboard quarter about half a klick. You see that, Gunny?"* Chief Johnson called.

"Yeah, I see 'em," Gunny replied into the mic.

"Let's ride!" Johnson came back.

Gunny threw the throttle to the chocks and the engines roared. I leaned over the edge and looked. I could see the motorized sampan making tracks ahead. At top speed we would catch him in no time. He had to know this. The Vietnamese suddenly pulled the tiller sideways and the sampan threw a big wake as it moved starboard and into a canal.

"Fuck," Gunny said. "He's up the canal now."

It was decision time. Following a sampan up a canal was always asking for it. The VC were known to lay traps just like this. Then again, maybe the sampan driver was desperate and the canal happened to be there. We were close to the canal, close to the sampan. He wouldn't make it far. It must have been what Chief Johnson was thinking.

"White Night Indigo, this is White Night Black. We're gonna go up the canal and get that little sucker. He won't make it two hundred meters, " Johnson said.

I was already into my flak jacket. I strapped my steel pot down tight as we took the corner into the canal at full speed. I checked the .50's breech...ready to go. The ready tray was full. Smitty was on the M60. I could hear Chief Johnson relaying our position and requesting immediate Seawolf cover.

Johnson's forward gunner laid down a line of tracers that ran up the side of the sampan. The Vietnamese at the tiller just ducked lower and kept the throttle open.

"They'll hafta throw a grappling hook on her" was the last thing Smitty said.

Abruptly, the sampan slowed...seemed to have been thrown in reverse. Both PBRs slowed accordingly. The sampan driver dove overboard just as the first rocket hit Johnson's boat point blank. The explosion was forward, near the wheelhouse. I whipped my .50 to the location of the rocket's launch, but before I could fire a round the canal around us exploded with AKs, rockets, and recoilless rifles. An RPG hit us nearly head-on, knocking me momentarily to one knee as I hung desperately onto the .50. It appeared the whole front of our boat was blown off. I saw Bubba and the gun tub somersault into the air. The next explosion was too near to see.

I remember floating. I was a bit of paper tumbling on the wind, nearly weightless. Then I hit a palm, rolled off, and was falling through bamboo before landing in a belly flop in water maybe a foot deep. I lay stunned, immersed in the water. Lying there, I tried to figure out who I was...where I was. I finally pushed myself up with my arms...staring at the water just inches from my face. I looked left into bamboo and palms. *Where am I?* I asked myself. I smelled smoke...could see smoke drifting around me. My ears rang and blood dripped into the water...from where? *Is this a dream?* I asked myself. I looked right and caught sight of a burning boat, totally engulfed. I stared for some time before trying to stand. I immediately lost my balance and fell sideways into the grass at the bank's edge. *What am I doing here?* I kept asking myself. I felt like I was really stoned. My mind kept skipping like a damaged record. I had trouble focusing and rubbed my eyes. I did finally realize the smoke was rising from me...my flak jacket was smoldering. I shook my head again and things cleared...a little. Again, I failed to stand...falling backward into the water this time. I lay there looking at a cloudless blue sky. At last, one of my senses was aroused... anxiety. Something was not right and now I could detect voices.... Vietnamese voices. Impatient voices. I rolled to my belly in the shallow water and my predicament hit me. I looked again to the burning boat. My boat. The voices were there, again...closer now. No doubt, VC. I slowly slid backward, trying to immerse myself in the reeds...trying to get lower in the water.

Two Vietnamese clad in black pajama clothing burst through the brush and immediately saw me in the water. There was nowhere to go and I had nothing to fight with. Chattering excitedly they ran into the water, grabbed me under the arms, and hauled me to my feet. My knees buckled, they lost their grip, and I belly flopped into the water again. They hauled me up, kicking me in the shins and calves...jabbering all the while.

We set off at a good pace through the jungle, a slow run. I was trying to keep up, staggered now and then, and was momentarily dragged. More VC joined us. It seemed to me we were running blindly through tall swamp grass and palms. Then again, they never slowed, directing me with hard jerks. Soon we were running down a path. My head was clearing fast now as the blood pumped.

I heard helicopters, but the moment I tried to look skyward I was shoved hard into tall brush, a Vietnamese landing firmly on top of me, shoving my face into the soft turf. The sound of the chopper quickly went away. I was grabbed by several hands and jerked to my feet. Again, we were running quickly down the path. We went through a low cut-away arch in the jungle and into a compound that opened up to reveal several grass huts, livestock, women, and kids...cleverly hidden under a high canopy of trees.

Out of breath I slumped and grabbed my knees as we stopped. Immediately I was kicked and shoved forward, where I landed on my face. Again, I was grabbed by several hands and pulled up on my knees. They forced my arms behind me, tying my hands and wrapping rope around my upper arms...cinching them tight. I almost cried out with the pain, but decided not to give the assholes the satisfaction.

Looking up, I found I was staring into the face of Phan Van Khoa...better known to his Navy pals as Fannie from Madame Cho's. Still very foggy in the brains department, I was confused.

"What the fuck are you doing here?" I asked.

This seemed to infuriate him. He screamed something in Vietnamese and then swung the butt end of his AK, hitting me behind the ear.

It was the last thing I remembered before being slapped to semi-consciousness. Water was thrown in my face, some of it finding its way down my nose. I sputtered and coughed. I was lying on the dirt floor of a hut with no less than three rifle barrels inches from my face. The room swam, the images skewing and dark. I momentarily lost consciousness. Grabbed by the hair, my head was pulled up and I was slapped hard. It brought me around and I found I was again staring into the face of the now-menacing Fannie.

"I'll have a Schlitz," I mumbled. "Be sure it's Fannie cold."

His face contorted in rage. He reached back to let me have it again but was sharply rebuked by an older man who was standing at the back of the room. Fannie jumped backward. Everyone around me came to stiff attention.

Slapping him again would do nothing. The man was barely conscious. Couldn't these idiots see that? Daily now, Dat was losing his patience with the Viet Cong. Most of these soldiers were nothing but undisciplined, weekend warriors...playing soldier for a day or two, then back to their families and jobs. They liked to play tough guy, as long as it was just for a few days.

During his career, Dat had seen many atrocities committed by Vietnamese on both sides of the conflict. He often wondered if it was the work of humanity reduced to its lowest level or some element of their own Asian culture. He believed the former, that all men placed in war are capable of committing unspeakable acts. It seemed to be more prevalent, however, in the some-time soldiers caught up in a situation where they could step outside society's rules. Professional soldiers were trained and disciplined. In a bizarre way, the professional had more respect for an enemy soldier than did fellow citizens or undisciplined ragtags like this bunch.

"Who is this man?" Dat asked the young revolutionary who had wanted to strike the prisoner.

"Montana. That is what we call him where I work, General. He is a PBR sailor," Phan Van Khoa said, standing stiffly at attention.

"So...you know him, this...Montana?" Dat said. He sat down, thinking. *The state of Montana? He is named after a state?* Those around him looked on, puzzled by the name.

"Bring him here. Sit him in front of me," Dat commanded.

They grabbed the man and dragged him across the floor, Khoa slapping the man behind the head as he left his side. Dat looked at the young American reflectively, smiling.

"How do you do? I am General Le Van Dat of the People's Army.... I think you call us the NVA, or the regular army. I apologize for your rough treatment. It is hard to control the emotions of the some-time soldier, you understand?"

Holy shit! This guy speaks better English than I do, Mark thought. *Best be careful what I say.*

"War is hell," Mark replied.

"Would you like something? A drink of water perhaps?" Dat asked.

"Yes," Mark responded. "I'd like that."

"Water, please," Dat commanded. Mark was brought a plastic container of water, which was tipped up for him. The pour was too quick; water rushed down the wrong way and he coughed violently.

"Easy," Dat said. "Not so fast."

The water was tipped slightly this time, and Mark drank deeply. As he finished, the two of them were left looking at each other.

"Is your name Montana...like the state?" Dat said.

"No. I'm from Montana," Mark said, hesitantly. Then, remembering his brief military training in such matters, he gave the obligatory "Mark Lyle Cameron, Seaman, United States Navy... uh, reserve, B89-52-61. Will I be treated in accordance with the agreements...uh, conditions...of the, uh, Geneva Convention? It was Geneva, wasn't it?"

Dat smiled. "Yes, I think it was. War is anything but conventional, though, wouldn't you agree? We don't concern ourselves with convention here in the delta. Besides, I don't believe this is a declared war, now is it? You will shortly, very shortly I should think, be sent on to another facility for, uh, deprogramming. Though, I am sure you will not have much to reveal...Seaman Cameron."

"Your English is good."

"Thank you. Seems I have a gift. I am very interested in your country...and Americans. When I can I listen to American Armed Services radio. I have picked up a lot of, uh...lingo, though I do not care for your music. When I heard of your capture, I asked to talk with you. I rarely have an opportunity to speak English with someone who speaks it well. Tell me about yourself," Dat finished.

Mark had to think. Was this a ploy to get information? Loosen him up and get him to reveal something important?

"I don't think I have to answer your questions. The Geneva...," Mark started.

"Oh, please," Dat interrupted. "I am not interrogating you. I just want to talk. As I said, we will be leaving soon...you sooner than us. I just want to talk. If you do not want to talk, then I will send you on to interrogation straight away. There, you will no doubt do a lot of talking. They are very persuasive."

Mark didn't want anything to do with interrogation. Images of Nazi Gestapo filled his head. Get talking, he decided. Keep things moving...maybe give the Navy time to find us.

"Sorry," Mark said, nervously. "I'm...a little uncomfortable."

"Of course, the ropes," Dat said.

Speaking to the men in the room, he ordered the ropes loosened. It hadn't been what Mark meant by uncomfortable, but the results were terrific. His arms had gone numb from lack of circulation.

"There, that should be better. Now, tell me about Montana?" Dat said. "Are you a farmer?"

"No...my dad's a carpenter. He builds cabinets for houses."

"Cabinets?" Dat asked, unfamiliar with the term.

"Yeah, kitchen cabinets. You know, cabinets."

Dat was confused. Cabinets? He'd never heard the term. It didn't matter.

"Well, tell me more."

"Uh, my mom works in a clothing store, J. C. Penney. I never had much of a job myself. I was a student before joining the Navy."

"What is Montana like?"

"It's, well...up by Canada. About six hundred miles across or so. Big mountains in the west, plains in the eastern part. It's agricultural...we grow wheat mostly, I think. For flour, you know? There's some logging and mining too."

"Logging?" Dat said. "I am familiar with that term.... Now I have a question for you. Something of a political question, if you do not mind. No military secrets, Seaman Cameron...just curiosity. The American soldier...why are you fighting here? What would make a man travel around the world to fight a war? I know your government's position—that is not the answer I am seeking. I am asking you...personally...why are *you* here?"

"Uh...it's expected of me, I guess. It's what everyone expects."

"Everyone?" Dat said. "Who is everyone?"

"My family. My country. My friends. It's about honor...and freedom and independence, I suppose."

"Your friends," Dat said. "They must be here too, then."

"A couple are...but my friend Bud Brody wouldn't serve. He's in Canada."

"A war protestor," Dat said, in a noncommittal way.

"Yeah."

Dat looked at Mark with a sour expression.

"Perhaps you should have been more like your friend Bud," Dat responded. "I am fighting because of centuries of subjugation. My people have always been oppressed...to the time before Genghis Khan. Personally...my family has suffered under colonial rule. The fight is right here...," he said, pausing for effect, "...in *my* country. *I* am fighting for freedom...like your revolutionaries, you understand? I am willing to die...or, sit in the stinking jungle with a bunch of...undisciplined children...to see this happen. It is a cause for which I have fought for over twenty years. And, you...and your military...you are occupying *my* country. Both of us cannot be fighting for freedom! One of us is wrong...would you agree?"

This was an argument Mark had never had with anyone. He wasn't prepared...had never really spent any time or thought deeply about exactly *why* he was serving or what it was like being on the other side. But, he had a suspicion the old guy was right.

"I'm just a seaman, General. I do what I'm told."

"You have no resolve then? You were nearly killed this afternoon. Now, you are our prisoner. This is going to get very ugly for you, Seaman Cameron...and you cannot even put together a good excuse for being here? Remarkable!" The words were delivered without prejudice.

Mark didn't know what to say. It was hard to think straight. He had a splitting headache, and now this asshole was putting him through a pretty grueling test of his will and fortitude.

"The Americans seem willing to waste a lot of young lives in Vietnam and you cannot tell me why. It is sheep to the slaughter, eh?"

This pissed Mark off.

"Oh, I just remembered, General. I'm here to kill fucking dinks like you and this asshole from Madame Cho's. That's why..."

Mark was halted by a hard slap from the asshole that left his ear ringing.

"Look, General," Mark continued, "you're asking the wrong guy. I don't understand the politics of what we're doing here. Wouldn't you like to know something else...maybe something about our lifestyle...sports, fashion, music maybe?"

Dat sighed. "Yes, I would. Unfortunately, there is not time. I have never had the opportunity to speak at length with any American. In fact, this is as much as I have ever spoken to one. However, we must all go now. You will be taken to another facility a few kilometers from here. I would say good luck, but I do not believe you will have any. You should not have gotten yourself into this war, Seaman Cameron. It will not turn out well for you. Goodbye."

The old guy rose and left.

"Wait, hey wait. There's time..."

I was immediately swarmed by several men...who carried, pushed, and kicked me out of the compound and back onto the trail. I had to concentrate and work hard to keep my feet.

Again, I was running down a trail with half a dozen VC. They were paranoid now, continually looking skyward and all around us. After we'd traveled maybe a quarter mile, the pace slowed to a quick walk. The ground now was less swampy with a few small rises, which I struggled to ascend because my hands were tied behind me.

After half an hour, we came to a bank with a sharp six- or

seven-foot rise. There was no way I would climb this without help. We paused at the bottom as my captors argued in Vietnamese. Three VC climbed the bank, then those below pushed me up. I was grabbed and pulled...pushed from below. It was a struggle. I was trying hard to get a foothold, my feet spinning. When I finally caught my footing, I shot forward and we all lost our balance. I landed with a face plant as the four of us toppled to the ground. I looked up and found myself staring into the face of a black man, clearly visible through parting leaves in the undergrowth. He put his finger to his mouth: *shhhh.*

Three pissed VC scrambled to their feet and hauled me to mine. While they were distracted, helping their comrades up the rise, I stole another glance into the bush. The black guy signaled me to drop to the ground. As I jerked from the grasp of one of my captors and belly-flopped into the bush, the jungle around me opened up with M16s. I kept my face firmly planted in the turf.

When the melee was over, I was grabbed again by the flak jacket and hauled up...this time by a bunch of Army Rangers.

"What the fuck are you doing out for a walk with these guys? Didn't your mama ever tell you not to hang out with trash?" a black sergeant said with a smile.

"Man...am I *glad* to see you guys!" I said. My knees grew weak with relief and I started to collapse. A couple Rangers caught me.

"Now, there's an understatement," the sergeant said with a belly laugh.

I was flown by chopper to Army headquarters, where a captain debriefed me. My report of the conversation with an NVA general raised some eyebrows and more than a little skepticism, producing many more questions. Of course, by the time the Army swept into the area, Victor Charlie had evaporated...not leaving even livestock to be interrogated. Eventually, I was treated at the base hospital for a concussion, some lacerations, and burns.

I ended up back on the Yerby Mike and, after another debriefing, this one by the CO, I headed exhausted and drugged for some much-needed rack time. JT was off-duty and jumped from his rack in our berthing space to envelop me in a big hug. Others in the area crowded around. It seemed I was a celebrity. They slapped me on the back and applauded.

"Man, you look like shit...but it is sooo good to see you alive.

I thought you bought it. We all did. It's a fuckin' miracle!" JT said. His eyes welled and his voice quivered a bit.

"Yeah...I think you're right. I was pretty lucky today."

I pushed through the crowd to my rack. I was deathly tired and not in the mood for conversation. They peppered me with questions. As I related the affair, mouths dropped and heads shook. Unraveling my story, I could see them living their own worst nightmare in my experience.

"I guess I shoulda been a little more frightened, but I was in a fog most of the time. The explosion really fucked me up. It was kinda unreal...like a dream. Seeing Fannie there was a trip. The condition I was in...it really confused me. I thought I was seeing things."

"Wait a minute!" JT said. "Fannie?!... Our Fannie from Madame's?"

"You guys didn't hear this? Yeah, Fannie was VC. A lot of this..." I indicated the bandages and bruises. "...was done by that little shit. I wasn't sorry to see him lying in the bush with six or seven M16 exit wounds."

"So...he's dead. That's just too fuckin' bizarre!" JT said. "I don't think I've ever met a bigger capitalist in my entire life. He'd screw his mother for a buck."

"I'll never trust another gook in my life," I said.

"They gonna give you a medal?" some guy asked.

"Yeah, the CO said a Purple Heart. Nothin' else, though. Guess they don't give out medals for gettin' your ass captured."

This was as much as they got out of me. I fell asleep during a question and JT shooed them all away.

I was given a couple days off patrols to mend and get my shit together. The full impact of the ambush soon hit home. Every member of the two boats died except me. They never found Binks' body. It was probably swept down the canal and into the river. I had some survivor's remorse, but this was war. I had to get over it and concentrate on doing my job.

They closed Madame Cho's for her association with known Viet Cong. However, the Madame had greased more than a few palms in her day and was back in business within twenty-four hours.

Meanwhile, I started looking for a pistol. I liked the punch of a .45, but like a gunslinger, I wanted something quicker, something

I could use in an instant without thumbing a safety. JT found it amusing.

"It's like the Old West and you're Wyatt Earp or somethin'. What's this all about?"

"Getting captured by the enemy screws with your head, man. I was lying in that water.... I knew they were coming for me and there was nothing I could do. I didn't have a weapon. Well, next time I'll be ready."

"Maybe you should wait a while. You know, get your mind through this."

"No way. I know now there's no such thing as being over-armed. I've already got a line on a .38 that a guy wants to unload before he ships out."

It cost a week's wages, but I thought worth every penny. The pistol was a large revolver with a long barrel. I let the belt and holster slouch on my waist so the handle was just above my wrist. I oiled the inside of the holster so the gun would slide easily. I got a leather thong and tied the holster to my leg. I practiced drawing the pistol quickly, playing an imaginary game where several VC jumped me and I would blow them away. Guys on the boats started calling me Kid Cameron. It didn't faze me. You couldn't be bad enough in this neighborhood.

The Mekong River Delta, South Vietnam

Comrade General Minh,
*   I am very relieved to hear of your continuing recovery. We feared the worst, so you can imagine our joy at this most excellent news. You are an inspiration! I hope my letter finds you in good spirits and continued improving health.*

Minh had been near death when carried out of Saigon on a litter and under fire from the Americans. He had briefly been kept in the "hospital" in the Cu Chi tunnel complex. Dat had seen him there, unconscious and clinging to life. They had amputated a shattered left leg before loading him into an ambulance for transportation to the Cambodian border. The ambulance was ARVN, and Minh had the papers of an important ARVN general. If stopped, the documents would state he was wounded and being transported to his estate near Tay Ninh for recovery. Near the border, he was carried by foot to COSVN headquarters in Cambodia, driven to Phnom Penh, and flown to Hanoi. Dat had taken great pains under difficult circumstances to keep abreast of Minh's slow, steady recovery.

Getting news was tricky. It often took months to get a letter from the North. In the last message Dat had received, Minh had been moved to the same Hanoi sanitarium Dat had been taken to when he had shattered his arm in the Duc Co attack.

> *I am sure you have heard of our recent difficulties. At this writing, though, many things are improving and we are hopeful the war will be finished with the year.*

It was as confident and positive as Dat could be, given the circumstances. The year 1968 had been the most disappointing one of the war for the old veteran. The Viet Cong forces under General Le Van Dat were barely more than a ragtag bunch of kids. The solid leadership and seasoned veterans of the old Viet Cong had been all but wiped out in the General Offensive, General Uprising.

Morale was a serious problem, and defections had remained steady throughout the year. The Americans' Vietnamization and pacification programs seemed to have a new life, and the enemy had made significant inroads into Communist-held territories. Supply routes had been disrupted, and Dat's forces had had to live and fight under the worst of circumstances.

Recently, though, things had improved. At the end of October, under intense political pressure, Lyndon Johnson had ordered a halt to the "ineffective" bombing of the North. This made access to the South easier, and their supplies of food, weapons, and materials had increased significantly. The North used the Americans' desire to extricate themselves from the endless morass of Vietnam to their advantage.

> *Our new strategy in the field has brought renewed vigor and morale to our forces. Truong Chinh's policies, as you well know, follow the strategy I myself have been advancing since the Ia Drang. It is unfortunate it took the carnage of the General Offensive to bring it about.*

Chinh's new strategy was actually an old one: protracted war. No more frontal assaults or massed force attacks. Guerrilla warfare was back in vogue, with a twist. The twist was the inclusion of sappers—young, pathetic Communist idealists, filled with party zeal and opium, who would strap explosives to their backs and find the nearest American or ARVN command post in which to immolate themselves.

Dat knew the real reason behind Chinh's "new" protracted war strategy. They were barely able to keep a recognizable force in the field. Massed attacks were no longer a viable tactic for the Viet Cong. Being a pesky nuisance was all that could be hoped. Any further full-scale operations resulting in their own large losses would have a disastrous, perhaps fatal, effect on the Viet Cong. Protracted war would both preserve the forces they had and help to rebuild confidences destroyed the previous year.

The new front that has opened in America is most encouraging. I can almost hear you say, 'I told you so.' Let me be the first to kowtow and applaud the politicians. I did not believe anything positive or constructive could have resulted from the General Offensive. In the end, it may well prove the difference.

Dich van, or action among the enemy, was paying huge dividends for the North. The organization and influence of antiwar sentiment in the United States had profoundly increased during 1968, applying pressure on America's politicians. Revolutionary war uses every path, person, and advantage for victory. As a warrior, Dat was inclined to see only the military front, but it was now easy to see that *dich van* could be a key strategy in winning the war. The welcomed bombing halt was a clear result of this new weapon.

Hailed a military hero, Tran Van Minh was elected to the Politburo while still recovering from his wounds. His military career, or at least his career in the field, was over, but as a politician, he would prove a valuable asset for the nation and Dat.

Our coming endeavor may very well add to the gains we have made on this new front. I realize now it is just a matter of time before the American youth movement forces the US's hand. Our intelligence is excellent. Daily, we are striving to discover new facets in our relationship with native "Southerners" that we can exploit.

As a greeting for the newly elected American president, an offensive was to be launched on February 22. The attacks would concentrate only on American units and installations. While there was no chance of victory or significant gains, Dat anticipated the new offensive would help boost morale and further *dich van*. It would be their largest assaults since the General Offensive of January 31.

Under the guise of intelligence gathering for the coming offensive, Dat had requested information on Nu Chi, preposterously alluding to her as a possible recruit. Reports on her arrived weekly but never came close to sating his real interest.

In the depression that had followed the Great Offensive, Dat had decided he would force thoughts of the young woman out of his mind. It was sheer fantasy, he reasoned, to continue longing after a vision as reachable as an untethered kite fleeing in a typhoon. But to his surprise, Dat discovered his feelings in this matter controlled him, not the opposite.

Nu Chi was working in the Finance Ministry with her father. Every day the two went to work together, and every night they returned as they had gone. She rarely socialized, seemed devoted to her family, and was often seen reading alone at a sidewalk café.

Oh, the agony! It was as though the woman lounged purposely, remaining unattached, waiting for his return. Dat vowed to see her again at the first opportunity.

Take care, Minh. Your many friends wish to see your complete recovery. When next we meet, I will revel in your good health and toast you with cognac until the bottle runs empty. Salute!
Your Friend and Comrade,
Le Van Dat

1968

Bassac River, South Vietnam

At the end of my time off, I was assigned to the 6758 boat. Eddy "Boats" Duba, the captain, was another salty boatswain's mate somewhat in the mold of Cutty, but thinner and in much better shape. He was friendly and surprised me by offering his condolences for my lost crew members. He seemed genuine. We jumped aboard and then he called to the two black guys who were messing with the diesels.

"Lenny, Bird...come here a minute. I want you to meet our new gunner."

Lenny Murfitt was a serious-looking, muscled dude. He was a gunner's mate second class, married with two small children and in his second hitch in the Navy, first stretch in Nam.

"Glad to meet ya," he said. "Sorry about your crew. We can all learn something by it, huh?"

Seaman Tyrone Sparrow was a thin wisp of a black dude, maybe six-foot-one and one hundred thirty five pounds. He said he was from Detroit.

"Hey...but I ain't from no ghetto, man. See, I'm middle class. I've never been to the ghetto. I got five brothers and sisters and we're all goin' to college. And that raggedy-ass black music all these niggers listen to, forget that shit! I was raised on Etta James, the Duke, Cab Calloway...I like blues, jazz, that big band sound. You can stuff that rock and roll shit, man."

Lenny and Boats called him Bird.

"Bird's okay, man. I can dig it. Bird was a fabulous sax player, and it is an honor to carry the name."

"I don't think that's what they mean...," I started.

Tyrone jumped me. "I know what the fuck they mean. You think I'm stupid? I'm goin' to college, motherfucker. I'm smart. I've got a future. Call me Bird and think whatever the hell you want. I'm thinkin' sax player...you good with that?"

We were minutes from leaving on our first patrol, and I wanted to check out the .50-cal. I grabbed the gun and looked in the breech. Bird was suddenly in my face.

"What the fuck you doin' with my weapon, man?"

"I, uh...*your* weapon?"

"That's a fact, Jack. You're in the tub, man...up front with those twin .50s. This is my position."

"You're the senior seaman here...I thought you'd have the front. I think most crews..."

"I don't give a shit about that. This is my place and you're sure as hell not movin' me. My choice!"

"Don't mind Bird," Boats threw in. "He's superstitious."

"How many times I gotta say...it's not superstition. I just got a better grasp on karma and the supernatural aura that envelops things...and people. Common folk, like all you, only wish they had the power, baby."

They both laughed.

"Welcome to the 6758, Mark. The only boat in Nam with its own aura," Lenny threw in.

I sure didn't mind being up front. Bird said the bow scared him; that he knew nothing good would come from his being there. He never set foot forward of the wheelhouse. My first impression of Bird was middling. Regardless of his defense or how he railed on me, I had the impression he was constantly laughing at himself. He was a character unlike any I'd ever met.

The first day out on patrol, early evening, we were tied to the 6759, our cover boat, drifting on the river so crews could have some "dinner." I pulled out C-rations and found the selection was not good. I was about to open lima beans when I heard a gag.

"Oh, man," Bird said. "You aren't really gonna eat that shit?"

"Yup. I think I'm hungry enough," I said, looking at the disgusting can.

"C'mere," he said. He took a sack out of his diddy-bag and opened it up to reveal two extra-thick ham sandwiches.

"How the...," I started.

"It's my aura," he said. Then laughing, added, "One of the stewards on the Yerby Mike has a mother in the Philippines who's a fortune teller. We understand one another and he does me a few favors."

I looked at my can of lima beans and my stomach turned.

"Sit down, Camaroon. You ain't eatin' none of that shit. I know you'd like prairie dog or whatever the hell it is they eat in Montana, but one of these will have to do. I'm buyin' dinner tonight."

Sitting, eating, Bird rambled on about Detroit, his family, and his weird "gifts."

"I look at people and I see things others don't. For instance, when I first saw you, there was something about you...a good feelin'."

I snickered.

"Don't worry, I know you ain't no fuckin' angel or somethin', but whatever it is...is with you. A coupla predictions, Camaroon...I don't think you're gonna die in Nam. And...when you first came on this boat I felt a sense of calm, like you were a good omen. Helps me get over the fact you're such a hick."

"How about you, Bird? What kinda predictions have you got for yourself?"

His mood darkened, visibly.

"Don't see nothin' good for me, Montana. There isn't a place on this boat that's comfortable. Those .50s up front, I know for a fact if I were there, I'd die there. The rest...I'm unsure about. The boat's not right with me...and it's funny, I don't get that feeling on other PBRs. Just this one. It might turn out bad. What the fuck."

I didn't have the same impression of the 6758. I felt a lot more comfortable on this boat. I liked the crew; even the wacky Bird. When I finally felt more comfortable with him, I told him I thought all his aura and glows talk was bullshit. In return, Bird thought I was the biggest hick in Nam and made incessant wisecracks about cows, sheep, and the Montana sex life. We were merciless with each other. Nothing was off-limits, and we spent hours showering each other with the worst, most degrading insults we could think of, often ending up laughing each other sick. We drove Boats and Lenny crazy. Though I wouldn't admit it, I loved Bird's observations of life that flowed in a never-ending stream of chatter.

∧∧∧

"Hey man, what's with these Vietnamese? Ever notice how they all look like kids or cadavers? They're all twelve or a 102. Where are they keepin' all their middle-age gooks, man? It's a *Twilight Zone* kinda thing. And the women! Some of these young Vietnamese women are gorgeous, knockouts! But have you ever seen one old mama-san who doesn't look like a prune? When they go bad, they go *bad!*

∧∧∧

"Yeah, I like your sidearm, Cam. You know what it is though, doncha? You're goin' back to your roots. You're a distant relative of Liver Eatin' Johnson or some long-dead relative who was a no-account Montana gunslinger. Probably got his self lynched. Your past has come home to roost, baby.

∧∧∧

"The thing with farts is, nobody can see 'em. They're the invisible menace. But what if they came out blue? That'd be a different story now, wouldn't it? No more sneakin' one off in an elevator or at the basketball game. No sir...and old folks homes would just be one big blue cloud."

The day before Christmas we were on the Bassac laying off one of the many canals that tied into the river. Four PBRs and the two Seawolves were engaging VC up the waterway. From where we drifted we could see the Seawolves circling, firing rockets and strafing, maybe half a klick away. I was standing in the gun tub, my charred flak jacket close by. Hook had wanted to replace the jacket, but I wouldn't part with it. You needed every lucky charm you could find in Nam.

Bird was standing by the wheelhouse. When I looked at him, he wore a sullen expression.

"What's the scoop, dupe?" I said to him.

"Look at the 6650 boat over there," he said, pointing out another PBR near our position. "They're flying the stars and bars, flag of the good 'ol South."

I looked at the boat. A small Confederate flag was hung under the Stars and Stripes. I didn't know what to think about these flags. I saw them here and there in Nam. I'd never given them much thought; a relic of the Old South.

"You don't get it, do you? What a fuckin' hick."

I was confused. "Get what?"

"That fuckin' flag, man! It stands for black slavery, discrimination, segregation. Here I am fighting for my country and I gotta look at shit like that. I'll tell ya somethin' I think about every time I see one of those...why am I fightin' dinks who never did anything to me? I should be fightin' guys that fly that piece of shit. They actually represent somethin' that pisses me off."

I'd never really thought about that. Being who I was and where I'd come from, the Confederate flag only stood for a war that happened more than a hundred years ago. Now, I would look at it differently.

The radio was full of chatter between those engaged in the battle, providing us with a lively play-by-play of the action as we watched.

> "*Seawolf 33, this is Razor Strap Zulu...that rocket came from our ten o'clock.... You see it?... Over.*"
> "*Roger that. We're on it.*"
> "*Razor Strap Zulu, this is Checker Board Pete.... I have wounded. Repeat, wounded. My rear gunner's down. How long we stayin' in this fight, Sully?... Over.*"
> "*May Day. May Day. This is Seawolf 33. We're hit... somethin' not good. Not good a tall. I'm headin' for the river. Keep an eye on me.*"

We could see him from our position. He wheeled and headed right for us, smoke pouring out the starboard side.

"I saw him take that one," Bird said.

The Seawolf was losing altitude quickly as he approached the river.

"Get to your stations...we might have to save these guys," Boats said.

The Seawolf pilot had his chopper at about two or three hundred feet off the deck as he made the Bassac. Then, there was an explosion, pieces flew, the engine died, and the chopper dipped into a nosedive, going down fast and heading right for us. It looked like he would crash hard, might even hit us, but at the last minute I saw the pilot pull back on the stick and the chopper hovered slightly before it crashed into the water right next to us. The chopper went under, popped to the surface, listed to port, and started to sink like lead weight.

Boats cranked the wheel hard and we came about. The gunner was in the water, but as we pulled up to the chopper I could see that the copilot and pilot looked unconscious, still strapped in. I dropped my sidearm to the deck, put one foot on the edge of the PBR, and leapt onto the chopper as our boat pulled alongside.

It was easy getting to the copilot. I snapped his harness off and rolled him upright in the door, and it seemed as if a hundred hands grabbed him as he was swept up and away, onto the boat. When I turned back to the pilot, he was under water and the chopper was going down.

I dove inside, into the murky brown Bassac. There was no seeing through the silt. It was all feel. I had to find the harness release, work it off him, and pull him out. If his foot was caught, or he was snagged on something...that was it. I would have to let him go.

As I got the harness undone and worked his shoulders free I noticed the water getting much darker and colder around us. We were sinking fast.

The pilot floated free and easy, banging into a few things as I pulled him up through the door. Outside the chopper, I looked upward. The light was dim; it seemed we were pretty deep. This would be the tough part. I kicked hard and pulled at the water with one hand while holding onto the pilot. I strained to see the surface, but it was impossible to make out. As we steadily rose, my lungs started to burn and a slight panic enveloped me. I kicked that much harder. Quickly now I was running out of oxygen, my lungs suddenly screaming. I thought I couldn't take another kick, but made several more. Then, the agony was too much. The light in the water was brighter now, but I could no longer hold back. I threw my mouth open, sucking in air, as I broke the surface.

Some of the Bassac came in too, and I coughed violently... spewing water. I gasped several times, then remembered the poor pilot and drug his head above water. I felt exhilarated to be alive, but I was exhausted. Not a good swimmer, I wouldn't stay on the surface long holding the pilot.

The boat was about twenty yards away. I'd been carried downstream by the current and was on the starboard side of the PBR. Everyone on the boat was port, looking into the water where we'd gone under.

"Help," I said. It was feeble and seemed to drain me. The pilot and I went under again. I kicked to the surface, but now I was in real trouble. It came to me, after all this, what a waste it would be if the pilot and I both drowned. I needed one last big effort. One push beyond anything I'd ever given. From deep inside I sucked the strength and air to save myself. My chest heaved with the effort, then...

"BIRD!" I screamed and immediately sunk like a rock.

No, damn it! Come on! I was able to kick hard once more and just got my mouth above the surface for another breath. Now, I was truly done. The pilot and I started sinking. I didn't make an attempt to kick back to the surface. There was nothing left and that was okay. I'd given everything I had. My mom would have been proud.

But it wasn't my destiny to die in the river, as Bird would say later. Hands grabbed me under the armpits, and I was pulled upward. As we broke the surface I sucked air—giddy, ecstatic to be alive! I was hauled on to the back of the PBR and laid out, so exhausted I couldn't move. I lay face down on the engine cover. My lungs felt like two big sponges, and I coughed repeatedly, gurgling and dredging up river water. Lenny jumped on me and started giving resuscitation, pushing on my back and raising my arms. I felt like an old handle pump being worked. Every time he raised my arms, water came up and I gagged. My mind screamed for him to stop, but I had no voice to say it.

Then there was the soggy, dripping Bird, a big help. "Ya know, Cam," he said, as I lay on the deck wheezing, "the pilot had a life vest on. If you'd just pulled the handle it would have inflated and you coulda' riddin' him to the surface...and I wouldn't have had to jump into that crap."

"Nobody tells me this shit," I said, eventually.

1969

The Bassac River, South Vietnam

After my underwater ballet, I came down with some nasty viral infections and ended up in the Saigon hospital. I held a feeble hope they'd send me home, but after a week I was back on the Yerby Mike.

It was good being back on the river, though. My early fears of not cutting it had long left me. In fact, having survived firefights, capture, and drowning, I felt the confidence and surety of the warrior. I had been tested in the firestorm and felt I had passed.

I also realized, like a cancer, my dislike for the Vietnamese continued to grow. It was damned uncomfortable the way the villagers and sampan jockeys constantly watched us as we patrolled. We knew many of the dinks were Viet Cong or VC collaborators looking for a weakness or pattern they could exploit. We were in a country whose population, by and large, considered us the enemy. It was safer to not trust any of them.

In a ceremony on the Yerby Mike, I was awarded the Bronze Star for pulling the pilot out of his chopper submarine. It was the proudest day of my life. I felt brave and bulletproof; my old doubts were long gone. Unfortunately, life, and certainly war, doesn't abide such arrogance and I was about to be slapped a good one.

Mail call.

JT had five letters from Richelle; all thick and nicely scented.

"Richelle has her ticket for Hong Kong. I get to see her in, what?... Two weeks, five days, and, uh, a little over three hours," JT said.

"Not looking forward to it, I guess," I said.

I had three letters: one from my parents, something official-looking from the Navy, and a letter from Stan Wicks. Stan the Man was with the Marines somewhere up by the DMZ and had been in the country longer than me. I decided to open that one first.

Mark -

Just got your letter. We're at our firebase for the day, so I thought I'd drop you a line.

Glad to hear you're feeling better. Hero, huh? I'm not surprised—proud to know you.

Okay, I've got something incredible to tell you. You'll never believe who I saw the other day. We were in a convoy on Highway 1, traveling between Gio Linh and Dong Ha, when we met an armored division coming the other way. They pulled to the side of the road and let us by. Same old shit, guys were yelling stuff back and forth with the Army grunts. I stood up in the back of the truck to get a better look at these fellas. I caught sight of a tall, blond haired sergeant talking with a couple officers. I couldn't help but see a resemblance to Joe Wills. As we poked on by I thought that it just might be him, so I yelled his name real loud. Guess what? It was him. He turned and looked—didn't see me at first, but I started yelling and waving my arms. Finally, he saw me. He waved once and yelled back. Isn't that the damndest thing? It's a small world.

We're tight up on the DMZ now. So close some days we wander into it. Every day it feels like we're either getting the shit kicked out of us or kicking the shit out of them. Last week, three NVA tanks crested a rise just across the border and opened up on us. It would have been easy to take them out with artillery or air support, but the brass wouldn't do it. We're not allowed to attack across the border. Eventually, we scared them off with some LAAW shots. Pretty ineffective at half a klick, but it did the job. What a hell of a way to fight a war!

I was promoted to E-5 last week, second in command of our platoon. I also extended for six months. I know, sounds crazy, but there are guys here who I can help.

How about my sister?! She's dating an old classmate of yours—Ray Reamer. You remember old Ray from the playground, I bet. He's 4-F and won't have to serve.

Well, that's the news. Good luck out on the river, dude. Keep your socks dry.

Stan

Katy's dating Reamer the Ripper, my old grade school nemesis? What the fuck?! I had a real soft spot for little Katy, always had. But Reamer?... That certified dickhead? Things were sure going to hell back home.

The Navy letter intrigued me, so I opened it next.

"Say, how about this?" I said to Bird and JT. "I've been promoted to gunner's mate third class!" I thought on it, then, "I never wanted to be a gunner's mate."

"You can't be too picky when you get a Ho Chi Minh promotion, Cam. After all, you didn't do a damn thing to earn it," JT said.

"Bullshit. You know that's not true. I put my ass on the line, man."

"Sorry," Bird said. "From what I've seen your ass ain't worth anything more than gunner's mate. What else would you be?"

"I don't know," I said, thinking. "Haven't thought about that. My brother was a yeoman.

"Say, my buddy Stan...you know, the kid who grew up across the street from me...he's a jarhead up by the DMZ...says he's extended six months in the Nam."

"That's just fucked up, man," Bird said.

"That's the guy you just missed in San Francisco. The guy who volunteered for Nam. Huh, I don't know," JT said, "I've thought about extending myself."

Bird and I were too stunned to respond.

"I guess I really dig the action," JT said. "Most exciting thing I've ever done. Things...like golf will seem a bit dull after this."

"Gimme fuckin' dull," Bird responded. "Yeah, fuckin' dull. That's what I crave."

"You'd do that?" I said. "Extend? I never really thought about it."

"What the fuck!" Bird exploded. "You two are just talkin' nuts here and I'm gettin' scared."

"C'mon, where's your patriotism?" Jay said.

"Patriotism?!" Bird spat. "The two of you together don't make half a patriot. You both told me you don't believe in this war. So don't start wavin' the stars 'n' stripes in front of my face. JT, you got a wife back home that loves the shit outta you and wants you back all in one piece. Think about that...and let's not bring this subject up again. I *mean* it!"

The air went out of our conversation then, each reflecting on his situation: his past, his future.

"Right, Bird," JT said. "I can't think what got into me just then. Extend?... No fuckin' way. Richelle would kill me. Well, I gotta get goin'. My patrol's about to start," he said, looking at his watch. He grabbed his helmet and flak jacket off the deck. "You guys have the mid? I'll see ya tomorrow maybe."

"Yeah. Good huntin', man," I said. He flashed us the peace sign and left us with a smile.

At 2200 hours the crews from the boats about to go on patrol met on the mess deck with the lieutenant. Something new was coming down.

"Okay, listen up," he said. "The VC are finding ways around us to supply their forces in the delta. Intelligence says the occurrence of small, almost empty sampans carrying ammo and weapons is on the rise. The VCs learned we stop less of those type of craft. So, we gotta spend more time checkin' small boats, people...especially the ones that look almost empty.

"Also...the enemy's goin' more and more to small canals and backwater channels to move stuff. Command is bringing in heavier monitors and swift boats to deal with river traffic. PBR's new prime responsibility is for canals and channels."

There was a collective groan, of which I was part of. It meant our job was about to get much more dangerous.

"Startin' with this watch, that's what we're doin'. I'll go over details for each lead boat and its cover before the patrol. Okay, that's it for now. Crews of the 57 and 58 boats, I wanna see you guys up here, now."

That was us. Crews filed by as we pushed our way upstream toward the lieutenant. Bird was at my elbow.

"I don't like this shit, Cam. They single you out...count on it not bein' good."

"Gentlemen," he started. "The colonel's come up with an idea that falls in line with our new patrol responsibilities. It's a bit of trickery that could pay off. When we patrol these backwaters, the enemy is gonna hear us comin' long before we get there...and it's easy to hide a small boat in the marsh. So, we're gonna try something the colonel calls 'Waterborne Guard Post.'

"We'll try it tonight with your two boats. I like your crews and experience...so, you're just the ones we want runnin' this thing first. Here's how it works...two boats come up a canal together at a slow pace. At a likely spot with some tree or jungle cover, one cuts its engine and floats to the water's edge...while the other boat, at the same time, speeds up and pulls away down the canal. If Charlie is around, it'll sound like the two boats goosed it and fled the scene. The boat left behind silently waits and listens for any hidden traffic to start moving. I know it's a hit-and-miss thing, but if we pull it off successfully a few times it'll give the VC something new to think about. I'm comin' on your patrol tonight for a trial run of Guard Post. Eddy," he said, turning to Boats, "I'll be on your boat and we'll be Guard Post. It could be interesting."

We had been waiting cloaked in darkness for nearly a half hour. The radio was off, and we were as silent as the dead, all straining to hear something in the night. My nervous fingers tap-danced on the side of the gun tub. I assumed if this strategy worked as dreamed up, the gooks would bolt like jackrabbits as soon as the supposed PBRs had skedaddled. A sampan wasn't going to wait for a half hour. The lieutenant, perhaps being overambitious and looking for a home run his first time at bat, wouldn't call it off. Our cover boat, the 6757, was laying off in the river about a half klick upstream, waiting for word from us.

It was breathlessly quiet. Even the insects and birds seemed in on the gig.

"Sir," Boats said in a hush, "perhaps next time."

"Just a minute more, Boats," the lieutenant whispered.

Several minutes later there *was* a noise. The sound of a small engine being cranked to life. Then, the unmistakable putter. I was disoriented as to the location—upstream or down? The lieutenant and Boats huddled with Lenny. They whispered and pointed, listened, whispered some more, and pointed more. Boats moved to the controls, and two angry diesels roared to life. The PBR hit the canal like an alligator after a dunked poodle. Boats was on the radio.

"Side Arm Pete, this is Side Arm Sam; we have a contact. He's headed downstream. Get your boat to the canal mouth and head him off if we don't catch him. Over."

I had the spotlight from my mount trained on the canal, and the sampan soon came into view. It was big fish, little fish time. Quickly, the VC jockey ditched the boat on the side of the canal, jumped, and did a rabbit number. We hit the edge right behind him and I was off the boat in one motion and after him. There was nothing but high grass between us, and I soon caught up. When I tackled him it was like hitting a bag of feathers. The forty pounds I'd added since coming to Nam made me about double his weight. I grabbed him by the shirt and hauled him to his feet, sticking my .38 in between two wide, frightened eyes.

"I don't suppose you'll be giving me any trouble," I said.

The dink silently shook his head while holding his hands high.

The sampan cargo consisted of five B40 rocket launchers and close to fifty rockets. It was a successful launch and validation of "Waterborne Guard Post." Later, our crew all agreed we were probably the recipients of incredible good fortune. The lieutenant would have none of it, though, and neither would command. Guard Post was a new staple in our bag of tricks.

We delivered the sampan and its driver to the ARVN complex at Binh Thuy. It was there we heard the news we'd missed while playing our game in the canal. Two boats had been fiercely attacked in a probable ambush up the canal we called Boogie Man. The lead boat had been hit by a rocket and immediately immobilized. The cover boat made it out with heavy damage and casualties. When the Seawolves and PBR support arrived, they found one dead crewman. Three others were missing. One of the three was JT.

"Fucking Cowles," I hissed. "Up Boogie Man right on schedule, that fuck. Okay if they fry his ass, but JT and the others were along for the ride."

Our patrol ended at noon and I immediately went up to the TOC to get the latest on JT and the others.

"They sent in a company of ARVN Rangers to look for 'em," the lieutenant said. "We brought in the Seawolves to search, too... when we could. We've got nothing. No bodies, no trace. The boat was half submerged in the canal when we pulled it out. They may have all been killed and swept down river. We may never find 'em. Officially, they're MIA until something turns up."

I read the combat action report. The only one who made it out of the attack unscathed was SM1 Dave Wing. I found him surrounded by sailors on the mess deck. When I could get a word in, I asked what had happened.

"It was just an ass-whoopin', kid. They set a trap. I mean to tell you it was heavy shit. I got bullet holes in my pants and flak jacket...shit in my drawers," he said, only half joking.

"The other boat," I cut in with a serious tone. The laughing stopped. "JT...and the others. What happened to 'em?"

"I don't know," Wing said with a shrug. "The boat exploded. I saw guys blown off the thing. They probably died right then. There were so many tracers in the air it looked like a plague of fireflies. A rocket went through our hull, didn't explode...thank you, Jesus! Two guys on my boat went down right away..."

"The rear gunner...on the lead boat...JT," I interrupted. "My best friend. What happened to him?"

"Uh, yeah, he was right in front of me. He was blown sky-high, kid. That much I remember. I can still see it. He probably bought it right then. Sorry," he said.

"Maybe not," I replied. "Stanger things've happened."

Later, I lay in my rack, exhausted but unable to sleep. Every time someone entered the space I thought it might be JT, or news of him. For one of the few times in my life, I said a prayer.

"Dear Lord...my friend is in trouble. He needs your help. I never ask for much, but I need a real favor right now. If you never grant me another thing, grant me this...bring my friend safely back. Please God, bring him back."

Sometime during the day I fell into a troubled sleep with some incredibly bad dreams. I awoke with a start when Bird shook my rack.

"Whoa!" Bird said. "You were thrashing around pretty good. Bad dream?"

It took me a moment to come to my senses.

"JT?" I asked.

"Uh...no, there hasn't been anything, Cam. It's time to get up, man. We're back on patrol in an hour and a half."

Except for US or ARVN naval craft, no boats of any size were allowed on the waterways at night. Of course, the enemy regularly tested us and sometimes got caught. But this night there was no traffic. Even the common sounds of gunfire and the flash of explosions were minimal. We cruised the canals. We tried Guard Post, twice. It produced nothing. It was like the war had ended. An eerie, mystic calm settled onto us. We floated with the current, listening. The river gurgled, a bird here or there sounded, and the muggy air swallowed up everything else. There was no lively banter on this patrol. I sat in the gun tub, alone with my thoughts and worry for my AWOL friend. Radio traffic was light, the occasional squawk making us jump.

Light was showing in the sky by 0500. By 0530 we could see the faint outline of jungle horizon followed soon by details creeping into the dark mass along the waterfront. When curfew ended at 0600, the river would come to life with traffic as families headed for market, work, school, whatever.

We were close to Suicide Bend, laying perhaps three hundred meters off shore. As always, we kept a wary eye on the Bend.

I was the first to notice something odd standing out by the river's edge. In the light, it was hard to say there was anything there, but as minutes went by three ghostly images seemed to appear in a row at the water's edge.

"What do you think?" I asked of Boats, who was looking through the binoculars.

"I can't make it out, Cam. Not enough light yet. I'm gonna call it in."

As he grabbed the mic and reported the sighting to the TOC, I snatched the binoculars for a look. Vague vertical smudges were all that could be seen through the night haze that still lay on the river. The TOC decided it was worth investigating and sent additional boats our way along with the Seawolves so we could get a closer look without getting our butts shot off. Command thought it more than a notion this might be a trap.

The 26 and 27 boats joined us, and when the choppers arrived we headed in—slowly, but with purpose.

"The three things...," I said, looking up from the metal tray in front of me, "that I hate about Navy food...scrambled eggs that always taste like they come from a can. How do they do that? And shit-on-a-shingle...that chipped beef swimming in grease we hafta look at every fuckin' morning."

"And the third thing?" Bird said, looking at me from across the table, his head resting on his arms.

"I was thinking of C-rations, but maybe that's not Navy food... or classified as any kind of food at all."

We were quiet then. The mess deck was nearly empty. A worried exhaustion draped itself over Bird's face. He fought to keep his eyes open. I was tired, too, but so doped up I couldn't find the peace for resting. I would describe it as something of a sad euphoria...a combination of drug-induced giddiness and all-consuming depression. Perhaps guilt, also. I looked at Bird and the concern in his sagging eyes. The vision flashed in my mind, again.

"It *was* real...wasn't it?" I said in a hush.

Bird didn't move, staring with all the emotion of a statue, then...

"Fuck. You *know* it was. Don't start that shit again."

Once again, as if a faucet had turned on, tears streamed down my face. A loud sob escaped unchecked, and concerned looks from a table across the room were directed our way. Bird's eyes watered, too, but he held back.

"Let it go, Cam. Push it out...and bury it deep, hear?" he said in a whisper. "'Ya gotta do this, man. If you don't, they're gonna ship your ass to some psychiatric hospital. Get it together...we wanna keep you here. Your salvation is here; I can feel it."

"Am I crazy?" I asked in a hushed voice. I really wanted to hear Bird say I wasn't crazy.

"It's the antidepressants, Mark. That's all. We need to get you off that shit. You're fine, man. Decide today is the last day you'll let this thing get ya. It ends today! Promise me that. Let's promise each other this is the last day."

"Okay. Okay. This is it. Sorry, man," I said between sobs. I got control of myself and lowered my voice to a whisper. "Thanks for being here, Bird. Thanks, man."

"Yeah, yeah," he said.

Time passed, and I noticed the cold tray in front of me. Had I eaten? Was I hungry? What the fuck did it matter.

"It was real," I muttered to myself.

Bird sighed.

I was pancaked low in the tub as I swept the beach peering through the twin .50s. The taste of combat was in my mouth; my fingers caressed the triggers. Choppers beat at the air overhead, and two dozen pairs of eyes darted here and there, looking for the expected green tracers. A hundred meters out the light was still too dim in the swirling mist to make out the images. The tide was out, so as we got closer the figures loomed like crucifixions. We were coming in quickly now. My eyes continued to scan the bank of the canal, left to right, my helmeted head barely showing above the tub rim. When Boats reversed the Jacuzzi jets and the boat slowed at the bank, I looked up and saw the three figures close for the first time.

Three bodies were skewered like shish kabob on thick poles. The poles ran up the rectum of each body and through the neck, where the head had once been. In a twist, adding to the macabre specter before us, the severed heads were stuck on top of the poles, backward. Each body was soaked in blood and muck. Standing out plainly on the body farthest to the right was a PBR tattoo, upper right shoulder—the tattoo JT insisted on getting before we shipped out.

My lungs collapsed on themselves, and I heard a shriek of unspeakable horror grab my mind and drive it into a lake of fire.

Time and place evaporated. How long did I look at those bodies?... At the one body? Blips, like scenes from a damaged movie, are all that remain...firing the .50s into the bank and tortured grass, the sound of insane screaming from somewhere inside me, and, with .38 in hand, being tackled by Bird somewhere on Suicide Bend. Then, a blessed release...the soothing depths and darkness of a scorched soul, vast empty spaces where the conscious is unconscious and the here and now matters little.

1969

Cholon, South Vietnam

Luang Nu Chi basked in the comfortable sunshine of a pleasant, warm Sunday morning. It was monsoon season and the sunshine was a rare treat. She was at her usual table in the quiet roadside café reading the American *Stars and Stripes*, a pirated copy presented by a friendly American coworker. Drinking her favorite green tea, she would often pause, tilting her head up to soak in the sun's gift.

Her thoughts wandered to the unusual peace and tranquility of the moment, a calm taken for granted in most of the world. She wondered when, or if, such necessary comforts would ever be "normal" in Vietnam. Nu Chi was not old enough to remember a time without war.

The people who passed reflected the morning's serenity as well: children laughed; an old couple walked arm in arm, smiling. Even a taxi driver hummed to himself. Nearby, a chorus of birds happily serenaded.

"It is a wondrous day for improbable things, is it not?" came from the man seated at the next table, spoken in English, his back to her.

Nu Chi was surprised. She hadn't noticed the man sit down.

"Yes, it is...are you speaking to me?" she asked.

"Of course," Dat said, turning to her. "There is no one else I know here."

This time she recognized Dat immediately and was astonished. The audacity of the man! She had never known anyone who could be so reckless and yet so casual in the same moment. He was nattily dressed in black slacks with a green shirt and smiled brilliantly.

"Good morning, Nu Chi. You would agree, I think...it is a most unusual day."

Nu Chi said nothing. Contradicting emotions swirled in her head, and she was unsure what she should do next.

"Would you mind terribly if I joined you? I promise not to be a bore," Dat said, scooting out a chair across the table.

"A *bore*?... Hardly! You are out of your mind!" Nu Chi hissed while looking nervously around. There was only one other man at the café, sitting some distance away and decidedly not interested. "I should turn you in this instant! I do not fraternize with NVA colonels."

"Even worse, you are fraternizing with a general now," Dat said pleasantly, with a mischievous smirk and a wink.

"Oh, aren't you the smart one! Do not joke about this. *You* are an enemy of my country."

"We are of the *same* country. I am in the mood for humor this morning," Dat replied. "I do hope, though, that you will be a good sport and not raise a...what is the slang...ruckus? After all, as bad as this could be for you, I do think it would be much worse for me."

"This is not Tet," Nu Chi stated firmly, unblinking. "You do not control me, or the streets. I could have you arrested!"

Dat smiled. He leaned back in his chair, tilted his head back, and deeply breathed the rain-cleansed air. He, too, listened to the birds as the serenity and sunshine of the place soaked him through as well. He could imagine the two of them sitting quietly here, reading the paper every Sunday morning. With his feeling of contentment there was also a dose of excitement. Nu Chi's mere presence was intoxicating. She was more lovely than he'd remembered, a silken blossom in white.

"The way I feel at this moment, nothing else matters," Dat responded, looking adoringly at her. "I wanted to see you...and whatever comes...it is worth it."

Unsettled by the blatant affection he was showing, she replied, "What are you thinking? Do you believe that we have a relationship?... Something going on?... Because we do not!"

"Of course not. When has there ever been time for *anything* between us? But it is something I plan to change, today. Let's start by...say, *Stars and Stripes!*" Dat said, picking up the paper. "I have seen these before. Interesting reading. I like the comics, though their humor is a bit difficult to understand. I mean, a man gets hit on the head by a pan and that's funny? How did you come by this? Can I read it?"

Nu Chi seemed to sag and shook her head, looking down.

"Nu Chi," Dat said, quietly. "I am just having fun...in a good mood. I am not here to cause trouble or sadness. I am going north...leaving for Hanoi today on orders from my friend Minh. It is quite unusual. So, I wanted to spend just a few hours with you...

the most captivating creature I have ever known. The temptation, the idea of seeing you again...I had to come.

"You had such a blissful look, sitting here," Dat continued. "What were you thinking?"

"Ohh, I don't remember now. I cannot think. I need to go," she said, rising. Dat rose with her.

"You cannot come with me!" she said.

"Then, you must come with me," Dat responded. "I have given the entire day up for you...my first day off-duty in months. Come, there is a park down the street where we can talk."

Before she could answer, Dat put her arm in his and they proceeded down the avenue.

"If I see someone I know, we will be in big trouble," Nu Chi said.

Dat pulled his *can couics* from this pocket.

"You needn't worry, I am Luang Lo, your uncle from Xuan Loc. It is quite official, I guarantee. If it is a relative, I am Tran Thi Tam from Loc An...here to buy farm implements for my collective. I have papers to prove either. How do you like my Southern accent, now? I think it is quite good, don't you?"

Nu Chi sighed. "No wonder your army is so hard to beat."

They found a quiet spot in the old, rather shabby park. Nu Chi sat on a bench, looking around, her hands nervously twisting on her lap. Dat sat on the edge of an ancient fountain that had not worked in decades.

"If my father knew about this, he could lose his job! I could be labeled a traitor! This is a capital offense. I could hang! Nu Chi... what are you thinking?!" she said, but made no move to get up.

"There, there," Dat said quietly. "No one knows me here. My papers are genuine...and I am certainly not about to shoot up the place. We are just two people talking. A man and his companion. You could help by relaxing a little, you know."

"I will try," she said at last, sliding her shaking hands under her legs.

"Thank you," Dat said. "You have no idea what a gift this is."

"Gift?" Nu Chi said.

"Yes, spending time with you is a precious gift. I have thought of you often...while damning our circumstances all the while. I am quite certain now, my feelings for you are genuine...and, I admit, puzzling. From the moment I met you...well, it was as if the heavens opened. The most incredible single occurrence of my life...as if God had opened a door and let me peek inside at my future."

"You...are *crazy!*" Nu Chi said in something of an alarmed whisper.

"Oh, I quite agree! A craziness like nothing I've ever experienced! I have tried very hard to dislodge these feelings, to forget you, Luang Nu Chi." Dat paused, looked at his hands tightly knit in front of him. But, it is *impossible!* My heart would just as soon forget to beat."

"But you *must* forget me!" Nu Chi cried. "What kind of affair could we have? None! There is no room in this world for anything between us."

"Yes, maybe in *this* world. But there *will be* another world... the world after the war. It is a matter of time...not much time, I believe. We are winning and soon..."

"Winning! Be serious, Dat! Every day you lose battles, territory. Men defect from your army by the thousands, and don't forget you are fighting the most powerful nation on earth. This war will go on and on."

Dat let her finish. He was quiet, then... "That all means nothing, Nu Chi. The Americans have never understood *Dau Tranh*, our struggle. They actually think we will give up...or, negotiate a peace that keeps the country divided. Uniting the country is what we live for, and we will fight a hundred years if necessary. They will not, cannot, ever say the same. Unrest and protests in their country grow by the day. How long will they hold out? Eventually, they will leave. When they do, the war will end in our favor. We must plan for this inevitability."

Nu Chi shuddered, hearing her own worst fears boldly proclaimed.

"That is a nice ending for you, Dat," she said. "Your years in the army would assure you a good future. Quite the opposite for my father and me. Most likely he would be imprisoned for a long time, or executed outright. I imagine I would be punished as well.

"Communism!" she spits out. "I could never live in such a society. It is impossible, Dat."

"It is not as bad as you think. I have lived under communism most of my life, and I will help you and your family. I would do anything for you."

"Yes...I believe that," Nu Chi said. "But you cannot change communism. If the North wins, I will escape."

"And go where?"

"America, of course. I love America. I read everything American I get my hands on. There is a position, opening soon at the ministry, working with my father and the American government on finances. Such connections could save me and my family... should your army win this war."

"You cannot leave Vietnam, Nu Chi."

She looked in surprise at Dat, as if he'd said something startling.

"Listen to me," he said, coming to her side on the bench and grabbing her hands. "You and I are meant to live our lives out together. I know this!"

"Well...you are setting yourself up for terrible heartbreak then," she said.

"Nu Chi," Dat said, grabbing her shoulders. *"I cannot live without you!"*

Nu Chi gasped, surprised by Dat's intensity.

"From the moment we met...your wit, fortitude...the way your hair frames that lovely face...the good humor I caught in our first conversation. Only one other person ever affected me the way you have, and though she is long gone I remember the feeling. Now, I know what life has in store for me and it is wonderful! I do not believe our meeting was an accident. Something so perfect, the meeting of such unusual people...arranged by God...cannot be an accident."

"God? You invoke God?"

Dat placed his hands over hers and pulled them to his heart.

"You have been waiting for me. You know what I say is true."

"Impossible!" Nu Chi scoffed. "A Northern general? How have I been waiting for you?"

"Ahh...I hear your heart, I see your eyes, and they are saying something quite different."

Nu Chi looked uncomfortable, tried weakly to pull her hands away.

"There is more to life than romance...and...no life at all for us!" she exclaimed. "No life!"

"Once again, miss...you are exactly wrong. It will not be easy... and I do not see what the future holds for us, but I *know* there *is* a future. A time for you and I will come," he said with a conviction that again surprised Nu Chi.

Nu Chi lowered her face and placed it against Dat's shoulder. He put his arm around her.

"Do not do this to me, Dat," she said with a sadness dipped in a lifetime of disappointment. "Do not raise my hope where none exists. Why must you be who you are? Why is God punishing me in such a way?" she said, tears now streaming down her face.

"*Punishment!* No, no. Quite the opposite. It is *wonderful!* God brought us to one another for good reason. You will see. Trust me. Our life together will come to pass and will be amazing."

"Why not defect?" Nu Chi said, raising her head and meeting his eyes. Immediately, his face went dark, and she knew she had said the wrong thing.

"You know that is impossible," Dat said slowly, mournfully. "I have dedicated my life to uniting my country. The foreign invaders must be beaten...like the Japanese and the French! We are *one* Vietnam. I do not like Communists either, but I would have fought alongside the devil himself if it meant freeing my country."

"Then, I do not see...," Nu Chi started.

"All things in time, Nu Chi. Patience. I know it is there."

The long-anticipated day Dat had fixated on could not have turned out better if he had scripted the whole thing. They spent a magnificent morning and afternoon deep in conversation, meandering the boulevards and streets so occupied with one another they hardly noticed the multitudes. The dark sky and hard rain that should have dominated stayed away as if unable to impose upon their union.

They had much to say, lifetimes to understand. Dat was astounded to discover that Nu Chi could trace her family back centuries, to an ancient Chinese dynasty in which a forebearer had favor within the royal realm...to a time of scandal and banishment from China...and a time of rebirth and favor with the mandarin lords of Vietnam. In return, Nu Chi discovered what drove Dat's considerable ambitions for a unified Vietnam, learning a side of her country's history never before revealed to her.

They uncovered the innermost reason for their mutual attraction. Both were loners, and lonely...finding it difficult to develop a rapport or friendships with others. Likely, it emanated from their mutually strong, opinionated personalities that acquaintances found a bore, but created a spark of emotional and intellectual stimulation when the two were together. For Dat, it didn't hurt that she was very attractive.

Nu Chi eventually forgot her concerns and discomfort in the presence of a man who dazzled her with his courage, confidence, passion, character, and amazing knowledge of America; a man whose love for her surpassed any other concern. She had long felt a disappointment in the way life had played itself out, feeling odd and unappreciated by those outside her family. Here, at last, was a man who didn't need to dominate and control; who wasn't offended by her strength. Instead, he thoroughly loved her as she was.

Evening approached, a time for farewells; Dat revealing he had long overstayed his leave. They were standing under a tall canopy of trees on a central boulevard, hands impossibly entwined like the puzzle of their romance.

"There is an...associate here in Cholon who has agreed to carry messages between us," Dat said. "It will not be easy for us to communicate, and regrettably dangerous...but we must! I cannot live without something from you, if even on the odd occasion. It is as if I only breathe when you agree to it...have a future only if you approve of it. If you could reach inside me, you would understand... how I know there is a place for us in all this. Put your faith in me, Nu Chi. Trust me. When the time comes, I will find you, and we will never be apart again."

As they stood eyes locked and the terrible separation momentary, the rain at last began to fall. Dat looked skyward and smiled.

"The heavens weep at our parting, Nu Chi, but the future is a bright, sunny promise."

It was then he took her in his arms and they kissed. Though both were love novices, their kiss was ardent and perfect. When Dat had at last vanished from her sight, slowly falling tears slid unnoticed with the rain on her cheeks. Dat had said he did not want to cause trouble or sadness. Yet, he had managed to do both.

1969

The Bassac River, South Vietnam

The mind can be a terrible thing when given deadly purpose and the means to act on it. I "recovered" into a state of violent anger, my dislike and distrust for the Vietnamese turning to a vile hatred that consumed and dominated me. I wasn't entirely sane and knew it, as did those around me. Boats complained to Chet and asked for my relief. But since I wasn't acting in a manner that created a hazard to the crew...well, what was one more crazy son of a bitch in Nam...and maybe we could use a few more like him! War is hell. Get used to it.

The carefree personality that had always identified me vanished. I thought only of punishing and killing gooks. In a firefight near Binh Thuy, Lenny had to slap me on the head long after I'd put enough holes in a sampan to sink it three times.

Bird talked to me nonstop, except for the times I caught him staring at me, expressionless. I didn't hear much of what he said. The voices in my head were talking over him.

As a part of Vietnamization, ARVN had been replacing American boat crews on PBRs since I'd arrived. As soon as possible, the politicians wanted to turn the war over to the South Vietnamese. Word came from Chet that a dink would replace Lenny when he rotated out. I was not pleased.

"How do we know this little shit will be anything other than a VC infiltrator?" I said to Boats. "You can't trust one of these people. Swear to God, Boats...I'll plug him with my .38 the first time he fucks up."

One evening we were called to the ARVN complex across the river from Binh Thuy and asked to take a suspected VC prisoner to a temporary prison complex downriver. The prisoner was just a young kid, but angered and filled with hostility. Sitting on the edge of the gun tub I watched as Chet and Boats helped the kid onto the PBR. As soon as their attention wavered, he broke free from their grasp and dove headfirst, with hands tied behind him, into the Bassac. Immediately, Chet pulled his .45, but the kid had disappeared in the brown silt.

As they all looked off the portside edge where he'd vanished, a thought struck me. I pulled my .38 from the holster, crept to the starboard side, and took a quick look over. There he was, head bobbing just above the brown surface.

As I sighted down the barrel of my gun, he saw me. That was good. I needed to see the desperation, the momentary, wild realization of fate in his eyes. He had to know these were his last moments on earth. I pulled the trigger twice. He jerked hard and went under. Everybody ran to starboard. I jumped to finish the job and had to fight my way through them to where a maroon stain was rising on the water. Rapidly pulling the trigger, I fired into the stain until the weapon was empty. When it was over, I blew the smoke from the barrel like a cinema gunfighter, broke the gun open, dumped the spent cartridges into the Bassac, and started reloading. Only Bird spoke.

"Man, you are one sick motherfucker. There's a blackness about you like nothing I've ever seen."

I ignored him. I wanted to finish reloading. I would be ready. Always ready.

One day Bird was in my face, insistent. "I said, we have R&R coming," he repeated, grabbing my chin. "I've talked to Chet and he agrees it's a good idea you and I get away from here a while. How about Bangkok? Next week?"

"I'm not goin' anywhere," I said calmly.

Bird looked surprised, then angry.

"What the fuck's with you, man? I said Bangkok! Whores for a week and all the ghanji you can smoke. We've earned it, Cam. You with me?"

"I'm not in the mood for fun, just yet. I'll think about it," I said, walking away. But I wouldn't.

Those were lonely, bitter days on the river. The image of the crucifixion haunted me. Not a day went by without several mind flashes of those bodies. I lived in an oppressive, mean world. I stopped writing letters and soon after began receiving anxious letters of concern from my parents, Joe Wills, Stan the Man, and Katy. My parents contacted the Red Cross to ask if I'd been hurt. That's when Chet got in my face.

"I'm gonna ship your ass outta Nam, Cameron," he announced. "If you're not writing home you are seriously fucked up."

"Really?" I responded with mock surprise. "Gosh, Lieutenant, I guess I just got wrapped up in my job. I'm okay, really. Look, I'll write today. Promise."

"Right," he said, eyeing me. "You do that. I want to see them before you mail 'em...and that'll be before your next patrol. Got it?"

"No prob, Lieutenant."

There was no way I was leaving Nam anytime soon. I wanted to avenge JT's death at least a hundred times. Outside this world, there could be no killing. In my mind, no opportunity for absolution. I was desperate to remain. Writing a letter, though, would be hard. I'd have to do some serious faking.

The letters I'd received lately blew my mind. Letters from my parents mentioned the record snowfall they'd received; news of my new niece; Grandma's hearing problems. Katy wrote about her situation at home and a desperate need to escape. I couldn't stomach such pathetic drivel! They had problems?! Grandma's hearing loss hadn't been caused by punji sticks. There were no remote-controlled satchel charges hidden in those snowdrifts. Katy's father was a mean son of a bitch, but he wouldn't booby-trap her bedroom.

And what to say about my life? "Gee, Ma, you wouldn't believe what that JT went and got done. Yup, got his head cut cleeeean off and one helluva enema. Me, well, by golly I had a good day today! I killed a whooole buncha people and it felt reeeeal good!"

The canal patrols were getting very dangerous. Everyone was on edge. Guard Post had worked several times with big caches of food and weapons being confiscated. As the VC got more and more desperate to move supplies, the firefights got nastier.

It was an afternoon patrol that found us up a small canal not far from Binh Thuy. We'd been there the week prior and had sacked a big stash of supplies when a sampan led us to a hidden VC storage dump. There was a perfect spot to sit and listen at the confluence of two canals. The nipa palms and overgrowth somewhat hid the boat and gave us access in four directions.

As we pulled into the spot, Boats cut the power as the 57 sprinted away, with the rear gunner flashing me the peace sign. We drifted silently to the bank, buddying up to the nipas. The tide was out and the bank was maybe three feet above the deck of the boat.

Lenny tied a lead rope loosely to one of the palms to keep us from drifting away. I kept my guns turned on the canal while Bird had his .50 pointed rear. I sat on the edge of the tub and put my foot up, listening. We had learned that ten minutes was all you gave Guard Post. That's all it took if it was working; the gooks bought it right away or not at all.

Lenny was softly singing a tune.

"Chain, chain, chain..."

"Shhhh," Boats reprimanded him, and both smiled.

I heard a rustling behind me that made me jump to my feet.

"What the fuck!" I hissed, pulling my .38 quickly from the holster.

"What's up, Cam?" Lenny asked, grabbing an M16.

"Did you hear that? There was movement up there," I said. I looked closely at the underbrush on the bank, but there was absolutely nothing to see. The nipa and undergrowth were so dense I couldn't see anything off the bank. We were all quiet, looking at the bank, but there were no further sounds.

After a long moment, Lenny said in a hushed voice, "Probably an animal."

"Five more minutes," Boats said, "and we're outta here."

Boats and Lenny turned back toward the canal. Bird looked at me and shrugged. I was still wary. Several times I looked over my shoulder, listened intently, but there were no further sounds and I relaxed a little.

I never liked surprises, and this was the worst I would ever get. Close in, several AKs opened up. Across the canal, a half dozen AKs and a machine gun. At the same time, a black-pajamaed kid launched himself through the nipa and landed with both feet on the deck right by me. I had time to turn toward him and see a bayonet being thrust at me. I should have moved out of the way, but I was frozen like a statue as the blade struck my flak jacket near my neck and stuck in the canvas cover. Quickly, he pulled the rifle back and made another lunge. This time I jerked sideways, but the bayonet found my exposed left shoulder. The blade sunk in, nicked the bone, exited out the backside, and then, as he pushed, blew out the side in a bloody gush.

After the surprise came the pain. Excruciating pain unlike any-thing imaginable shooting through my left side and shoulder. Instantly, my mouth was open and I was screaming with an intensity and pitch only someone in real agony can cut loose.

The expression of the little VC bastard burned into my brain; a face painted with hatred and satisfaction. A slight smile creased the corners of his mouth.

Rage consumed me as the little shit pulled back to let me have it again. Instead, he was blown backward onto the canal bank. The .38 was in my hand and I'd pulled the trigger repeatedly with the gun stuck in his belly. He collapsed like a ragdoll in the space between the boat and the bank, disappearing into the water.

I had no time to recover. At the moment the gook flew backward, I saw a rifle poke through the bush, aimed at me. I pulled the trigger several more times and the rifle disappeared. Rounds flew everywhere as I ducked into the tub, spun the guns toward the near bank, and opened up. I swept the shore and tree line back and forth with one long burst.

I hazarded a quick jump up to look into the wheelhouse. I could see Bird firing at the opposite shore, but Lenny and Boats were nowhere to be seen. *Why aren't we getting the hell out of here?* my mind screamed as the boat remained silent.

I spun my mount to the opposite bank. There must have been a dozen different lines of green tracer fire, half coming my way. I opened up, firing while screaming in pain and anger. Shells ricocheted all around me, and I felt a sharp sting in my left forearm. Now, more shots came from behind me, one glancing off my helmet, tearing the pot off my head and ringing my bell.

I spun back and hit the shoreline again, wildly sweeping back and forth, my breath coming in micro-bursts with the effort. I released the trigger and glanced into the ready trays; they were half empty now.

"Bird," I screamed. "Get to the controls. Get us the fuck outta here."

I'd no sooner said this when a tremendous explosion erupted near the wheelhouse. I may have lost consciousness. When I was able to focus my mind again, I saw that most of the wheelhouse and the canopy were gone.

I spun back to the opposite shore and raked them again. *We've got to move or we're dead,* I thought.

"Bird!" I screamed, jumping up one more time to look aft. Bird was just making a move toward the wheelhouse. He jumped on the engine cover and was brought down by a large-caliber round I saw exit his left thigh in a bloody spurt. He hit the deck hard, screaming in pain. Something imitating a couple kidney punches struck me in the back, stinging and knocking the wind out of me. I sat heavily back into the tub, feeling dazed.

Then I heard the engines being cranked and coming to life. Bird was standing upright in the wheelhouse, tracers flying all around him. He gunned the engines, put the boat in reverse, and cranked the wheel. We left in a hurry, but before clearing the bank, Bird was hit and knocked down again.

The boat continued in reverse, cutting a tight circle in the canal like a bad Brahma. I saw a whirling confusion of shoreline, canal, palms, and tracers from every direction. I ducked low in the tub, hiding, suddenly so scared by my predicament, at being alone, I couldn't move. I was shaking in fright and wishing it would all go away. But just then a thought of JT went through my mind like a splash of cold water and I knew I had to do something. I didn't want to die in Nam; leave as Jay had. I didn't want the VC to win this one, not while I could still move. I had to right the boat and get us the hell out of this place.

As I pushed myself out of the tub, a spike of searing pain grabbed me in the left shoulder, taking my breath away. My left arm and side were soaked in blood and nearly useless. I made a dive for, and caught, the jagged edge of the shattered wheelhouse. Desperately hanging on, I was able to pull and push myself over the wall, where I landed on the bodies of my crewmates. Bird was writhing in pain, shaking violently, and bleeding from the mouth. "Fuck me. This hurts. Get us out. I don't wanna die here. Motherfucker!... Don't let me die here. Don't let me die," he rasped.

Bullets continued to fly and ricochet everywhere. From as low a position as I could, I reached up and throttled down, took the boat out of reverse, then cranked the wheel to a neutral position. I saw a channel to my left as the PBR slowed its twirling. This was the moment! I got up, opened the throttle, and turned the boat in the right direction. It gathered itself to leap forward, but not fast enough.

I was struck by so many rounds it was hard to tell where they were coming from or what they'd hit. Several tore at my flak jacket.

I felt a bee sting my cheek that pulled my head sideways; something hit my right hand and it flew off the wheel. I ducked, flopping to the deck.

The boat surged forward, quickly. Looking out the side of the wheelhouse where there had been a wall, I saw we were headed into the bank. I reached up and jerked the wheel, righting the boat and sending us full speed out of trouble. In a matter of seconds we were flying along the canal.

I took a moment to look at my crewmates. Bird seemed to be the only one conscious. He was shaking hard, mumbling curses, a growing red stain below him. Boats and Lenny lay quietly in pools of blood where they'd fallen.

When I looked up again, I was on a collision course with the 57 boat that was flying to our rescue. I reached to throttle back but my bloody hand slipped off the control and we continued at full speed. I quickly jerked the boat right and the two boats slid by each other in the narrow channel at close to thirty knots with the gunwales scraping one another. I spun my head aft and saw the 57 going into a hard reverse and turning spin. I reached for the throttle and my hand slipped off again. It was then I realized my right hand was nothing but a bloody mess with missing fingers.

Slapping at the controls once more, I was able to put the boat in reverse. Quickly decelerating from full speed, I almost went over the top and onto the forward deck as the bow dipped nearly under water. As we picked up reverse momentum, I pawed the lever again and put the boat in neutral. Now, the engines roared as my mind scrambled. Though I knew the controls, they may as well have been knobs on an alien spaceship. A tremendous anxiety filled me and I began shaking violently. I grabbed my left arm with my bloody right hand, trying to calm myself, but the shaking only got worse.

At last a hand was placed on the throttle and the engines died to an idle. The same hands took hold of me. I stumbled over bodies, stepped on the Stars and Stripes, and was set on the engine cover. I felt an uncomfortable sensation in my mouth and gagged. Leaning over, I spit a river of blood that contained a couple teeth.

1998

Outside Bozeman, Montana

I keep living the canal fight over and over like the rerun of a bad Ginsu commercial. Almost thirty years later, it occasionally shows up in my dreams. Once in a while, when I have a lousy day, some particularly nasty person I've dealt with plays the part of the VC with the bayonet.

I was in combat less than six months in Nam, yet I remember almost everything that happened there. The stink of Nam and the smell of the VC is in my nostrils. I can hear the voices and see the faces of everyone I knew. The rattle of the M60 and deafening roar of the .50 cals going off on either side of my head. The *whop, whop* of chopper blades and the growl of those diesel engines. Forget Nam? Not likely.

As messed up as I was, everyone else on the ward seemed worse off. In a way, it was great therapy. The guy occupying the bed on my right had no feet, one leg having been amputated at the knee. The soldier on my left died the day after I arrived. Everything being relative, I was in good shape. If I could have remained on that ward a few years, things might have been easier.

The first couple days had been tough. I was in shock, dazed, and in constant, biting pain. It would have been better if I had been unconscious. There were lucid times when I thought about death. I didn't think I would die and they kept telling me I wouldn't. You wonder, though. Many soldiers have died in wars being told to the very end things would be just peachy.

I was finally settled into a bed. A fitful rest followed and, after time, I was able to take stock of my situation. Among the first things I realized was that the dark specter of JT's death, which had dominated my life for weeks, was gone. Lifted like a veil. Or, perhaps replaced. Even though I was flat on my back, doped up and hurting, I was certain now I was going to live.

However, it bothered me that those who saw me for the first time flinched. There was something about it that made me damned uneasy. Holding my right hand up, I saw it was wrapped in a bandage that looked like a giant Q-tip. The thing scared me. I knew I was missing fingers. How many and which ones, I wasn't sure. On the PBR I had been too afraid to look closely. Wrapped as it was, there was no way of knowing. A hand could be normal under such a bandage. Maybe I had fantasized the missing digits. I'd been under stress, in shock. The fingers all seemed to be hurting, in unison.

I had a sensation like cotton balls stuffed in my mouth. My left arm was bound tightly to my body, so I had no way of knowing what was in my mouth other than to feel around with my tongue. When I did, I found the cheek was rough, prickly, and there was packing of some kind stuffed in there.

When the nurse finally showed up, I wanted to ask her for a mirror, but only a croak escaped. I tried again, but no recognizable words came out. She helped me to a sip of water, and I was finally able to put a voice to my request.

"Okay," she said after a moment, looking unsure, "but you have a lot of bruising...and stitches in your face. It doesn't look too good right now."

After seeing my reflection and letting loose with a steady stream of four-letter words that, even though unintelligible, were understood, she said hurriedly, "Once you heal this will all look much, much better. The doctor says you'll hardly even notice the scar."

I spit the packing in my mouth onto the floor. "Bullshit!" I said, loud and in a rather clear voice. "Look at this shit! I can't go around like this! I'm a fucking monster for godsake. Hold that mirror up again."

I was repulsed anew. Stitches in a semicircle about the size of a fifty-cent piece were planted in my swollen left cheek. The skin was red and puffy with dark black and blue bruising all around. Something else caught my attention.

"What the fuck's wrong with my ear?"

"Well, your earlobe got nicked, that's all."

"That's fucking all!" I said, incredulous and tried unsuccessfully to rise. "I have no fucking earlobe to speak of. Shit."

She took the mirror away then.

Later that morning a doctor showed up at my bed, smiling. I wanted to yell "What the fuck are you grinning about?" but I didn't.

"She made a mistake," he began. "We needed to have a talk

first. But you've got to understand...these nurses see the worst kind of trauma here. Every day they deal with guys who've lost legs, arms, maybe a part of their face, or their balls. To the nurses, you're a welcome sight. You're pretty much whole.

"I understand your being upset—anyone would be—but once you heal...that cheek, for instance. The stitching was done by the best plastic surgeon in Saigon. When it heals, and it'll take a little time for all the redness to leave and swelling to go down, it'll hardly be noticeable. You'll probably only see a faint circle."

"How'd it happen? What did this?" I asked.

"There was no entry wound, so we surmise a projectile—likely a bullet but it could have been shrapnel—came in through your open mouth and exited your cheek. Talk about lucky! It took out three molars and some skin. Not to worry, though, we just stretched your skin and stitched it up.

"About those teeth, we only have one oral surgeon and he's quite busy. You'll probably have to get 'em taken care of stateside.

"That earlobe is nothing. Simple plastic surgery can be performed to lengthen it and match it with the other side. We wouldn't want you to go through life tilting to one side now, would we?"

I was feeling better about my face and ear, but the tough questions were next.

"What about this hand, doc? What's the score? I thought I lost some fingers out there...but, I don't know. I can feel them all right now. They..."

"Uhh...look, you weren't imagining things on the river. A large round did a nice little guillotine amputation of your first and middle finger. It was an easy fix. We just picked out the bone fragments, cleaned it up real good, and did a primary closure over the knuckles. It should heal quickly. The dressing will come off as soon as possible so you can start rehabilitating it."

I was quiet a few moments.

"But...I can feel them."

"Yes. Likely you can and that's common. It's nerves and, you know, memory. Your brain still thinks they're there."

"You said rehabilitate? How? What do you mean?"

"Well, I don't mean like a leg amputee who works with a prosthetic. The hand needs to heal and get strong again. You'll have to get used to picking things up, catching, turning knobs...that kind of thing. Luckily, you still have your opposable thumb, so you can grasp. That's important. Writing won't be a problem. You'll pick it up quick, I'm sure."

"Yeah...how about shaking hands, doc? And when I meet a girl, you know, before she's totally grossed out, how do I explain this?"

There was a long silence. He looked tired.

"Okay. Listen...at this moment maybe you're feeling a little low, a little sorry for yourself. And, okay, you deserve a bit of that. But look around, man. There's much worse come out of here, Cameron. Guys who would quickly change places with you if they could. If some of 'em hear you feeling sorry for yourself, you'll get drilled... and deserve it. Your wounds aren't life threatening—they're hardly even life altering. Feel lucky. From what I heard, you should."

I felt pretty low just the same. Everything is relative. So even though I should have felt "lucky" like the doc said, I was pissed about the fingers.

"Doc, the shoulder is fucking killing me. Can we up the painkillers?"

"Let me take a look at your chart. That shoulder has us worried—I won't lie to you. A bullet wound is pretty clean, a lot cleaner than a bayonet. The VC are known to dip bayonets in some nasty shit...human waste, sewage. We're afraid of infections, and it might be a while before you show symptoms.

"Other than that, the wound was a simple one. The blade went straight through and blew out the side. Luckily, there aren't any important nerves there. You'll probably always have some numbness and, of course, heavy scarring. It's likely you'll always lack full motion and strength.

"Oh, just remembered. You'll be leaving Nam real soon."

"What?"

"We've scheduled you out of Tan Son Nhut tomorrow afternoon. We need the beds and you're healthy enough to be moved to Okinawa for recovery. When you're better, stateside."

There was a lot on my mind. I had to find out what had happened to my crewmates before I left. If they were still in this hospital, I had to see them.

As busy as the nurses were, they agreed to locate the rest of my crew. I again prayed to Jesus to deliver good news to me. Later that morning, I got a report.

"Second Class Murfitt and First Class Duba were seriously wounded and are recovering in Ward 3. I'm afraid you won't be able to see them, but I do know the prognosis for a full recovery is good. Tyrone Sparrow is in this ward," she said, pointing. "The other side about twelve beds down."

"What's his condition?"

"Um, nasty wound in his left thigh...took out a piece of his femur. He nearly bled to death. His leg's in traction. But the other wound is the bad one. A round went in at the shoulder, spiraled through a lung, and lodged in a rib. He's having trouble breathing, but he's likely to make it also. You can see him, but I'm afraid he won't be able to talk right now."

The wheelchair rolled up to Bird's bedside. He looked like hell. His rich chocolate skin was a muted, dusky gray. He lay still as death, eyes closed. I sat and watched a while, the only sound a wet rasp as he inhaled.

What did I owe this guy? Why had I thought it should be him to get the boat moving? Why did I stay in the tub? They were tough questions I would have to deal with. It was also on my mind just how badly I'd treated him recently.

He opened his eyes, his gaze slowly shifting to me. There was no recognition in his face, just a blank stare.

"You look like shit," I said. "I never thought you looked good to begin with, but you really look like shit now."

Slowly, he extended the middle finger on his right hand. I laughed out loud and groaned with pain at the same time.

"I guess that means he's a good friend o' yers?" came from the bed behind me. I turned to see a soldier whose face was swathed in gauze. Only his right eye, mouth, and chin looked out from the bandages.

"He's the best I got," I said.

Turning back to Bird, I added, "I'm sorry, Bird. Sorry for everything I've said...everything I've done. I owe you my life. You're the bravest son of a bitch I've ever known."

Later that same day, sickness swept over me with the quickness of nightfall on the river. It was the beginning of my two-month bout with hepatitis. I vomited constantly, lost all the weight I'd gained, and was jaundiced. The memories I have of Okinawa are small snatches of a hospital ward and going to the airport the day I returned stateside. I was the last of the 6758 crew to reach the states.

Eddy "Boats" Duba recovered and was placed on disability retirement from the Navy. He became a long-haul truck driver who ran I-10 between Riverside and Houston until retiring in 1989.

Lenny Murfitt returned to Philadelphia, finished college, and is currently a partner in the accounting firm of Sackett & Moore. He and his wife put three kids through college.

Bird? Well, the Birdman is another story; a part of my life since the war. One leg is shorter than the other and he walks with a limp. He lost part of a lung that, he claims, keeps him from doing any heavy work or exercise...a convenient excuse for his being overweight. He did attend college, graduating from the University of Michigan with a degree in marketing. Bird was the only one in his family to ever go to college. Tyrone was from the worst part of Detroit but, with the help of the GI Bill, beat the odds.

When a young lieutenant interviewed me about the ambush on the canal, I told him Bird should get the Medal of Honor for what he'd done. Though he didn't, he did receive the Silver Star. It is displayed in a nice three-dimensional shadowbox with his other Vietnam medals, forgotten and ignored in the hallway of his house, which is two blocks from my own in Chico, California.

1969

Homecoming

The Vietnamese stuck me in the shoulder. I felt the blade slide through flesh, rip muscle...and I screamed. The VC wore a look of malice and satisfaction as he said...

"Wake up!"

...though it was Lucy's voice. My eyes snapped open. Chest heaving, I frantically searched the semidarkness. Not here. Still dead. Just another night and the same nightmare. Lucy had me by the shoulders.

"What is it, Mark? Something's scaring the shit outta you. Talk to me."

"Go back to sleep," I said. "It's nothing."

"Bullshit! That's...you should see yourself."

"Just...go to sleep," I said. "Go back to sleep. I'm fine."

Lucy sighed heavily.

"You're not fine. Every time you sleep here you scream and roll around. Don't tell me that's normal."

I said nothing in return.

"You need to talk to somebody about this."

I stayed mum, chest heaving. Now, she was pissed.

"What the fuck, Mark?" She rolled on her side, taking all the sheets with her.

I mouthed a silent curse to my dead nemesis and lay still, the sweat running cold on me now. My nerves finished their little tap dance, and after a moment my heart ceased pounding so I could relax. I stretched and lay quiet, collecting myself while examining the roadmap of cracks in Lucy's apartment ceiling. I had examined them before and recognized the outlines of Poland, Donald Duck's beak, and Texas/Oklahoma. It sucked to wake up with the dream, but at least I wasn't still in Nam.

The dreams were constant now. They refused to leave me. The bayonet was thrust and I would wake with a start, sometimes yelling out and upsetting Mom and Dad—or Lucy. My only consolation was the viciously sweet reality upon waking that I'd killed the little son of a bitch. Before that redemption, though, I had to get stuck and suffer the bayonet. Having been bayoneted many times now, I wondered: Was he worse off, or I? He had only died once.

Strange days were upon me. I had been home nearly four months, but in many ways I was still in the war. Little things in the supposedly normal world terrorized me. National Guard choppers stationed just a mile from the folks' house, where I was living, occasionally flew close by creating curious attacks of fantasy and anxiety. I would flash on a door gunner, rockets, smoke. Unexpected loud noises scared the bejesus out of me. I had never been a skittish person, or been known for seeing things that weren't there. In many ways I was more terrorized now than when I had been in-country.

I rolled my legs off the bed's edge, coming to a sitting position with all the energy of a man wearing concrete shoes. Naturally, I had always thought homecoming would be an enjoyable return to sanity and sanctuary—the safe, comfortable haven it had always been. Right from the start, though, I knew there would be issues.

"We'd like to welcome home our Southeast Asian tourists," the stewardess said to a loud chorus of cheers and laughter. "It's great to have you back. Please remain in your seats with your seat belts fastened until the plane comes to a complete stop...I'd hate to see any of you guys hurt now. When you leave the aircraft you will board a bus to take you to the processing station. During this procedure, you can make further flight plans to get you back to your homes." Another round of cheering followed that announcement. "On behalf of our pilots and crew, it's been a pleasure having you on board and bringing you back to the states. Welcome home!"

When the plane, at last, came to a full and complete stop, servicemen filled the aisle. Except for myself, they were all dressed in the worn, faded uniforms they'd fought in. I was the only guy in a new uniform; issued just that morning. My left arm was still in a sling, my hand still on the mend, so I was struggling with my bag in the overhead when a big hand deftly picked it up for me. A very large black Army sergeant handed the bag to me.

"Here you go, sailor," he said.

We started a slow penguin shuffle toward the door.

"I see by the beret you served on PBRs."

"That's right," I returned.

"Looks like you caught a little something out on the river."

"You think?" I said, sullenly. "Bad luck, man."

"I dunno...you're here with the rest of us, aren't you? Feel good about that. Remember all the guys who didn't make it."

"I don't think I'll be forgettin' 'em anytime soon, Sergeant. How about you?"

"No...I don't suppose so."

Outside, I was following the line toward the bus when something stung me on the side of the head, knocking my beret to the tarmac. I reached up with my hand and pulled away egg shell and yoke. I saw other eggs flying through the air. Twenty yards away a bunch of kids were lobbing eggs over the fence.

"Killers! We don't want you back here."

"Make peace, not war."

I was momentarily confused. Then I got pissed.

"You sons a bitches...," I said, starting toward the fence. Before I took two strides I was grabbed from behind in a bear hug by the sergeant.

"Hey...not today, riverine. That's a war you can't win."

Other guys stormed the fence, scattering the egging crew to the winds.

"Some day that pathetic bunch will regret what they did here, but you can always be proud you served. Forget about this," he said, picking up my beret and brushing bits of shell off my uniform.

I continued to the bus, puzzled. I was happy to be home, to be leaving active duty, but at that moment I felt the camaraderie of being one of the troops and proud to be a serviceman.

I examined the haunted figure in the mirror, a scary sight for the uninitiated. The circle of stitch marks planted on my cheek, though fading as the doctor had predicted, were still reddish and obvious. The big scar in my shoulder was an ugly blot of puffed skin, and there was a permanent crease where the blade had pushed through. The "Sad Sack" earlobe was still missing. I wasn't Frankenstein's monster, but nowhere near an example of American wholesomeness either.

Then there was the hand. I held it up, spreading the fingers wide. Lucy liked to say sixty percent of a hand was better than a whole one any day, preferring its softer stroke in lovemaking. Okay, so there was one advantage. An urge hit me, and as I placed the stumps under my nose, I laughed out loud at the believable sight of fingers stuck up a nose to the far knuckles.

With the same hand, I reached and picked up a half-used joint from the ashtray on the back of the toilet, deftly snatching it with the thumb and ring finger. No problem, man!... Opposable thumb saves the day. I lit the joint and took several hits as I continued looking in the mirror. I had put thirty or forty pounds back on, so the ribs had gone away. My hair was looking better, too, nearly to my shoulders now. The muttonchop 'burns were filling in. *You are a righteous dude!* I said to myself, and snickered again.

My eye caught the new tattoo on my shoulder, and I turned it toward the mirror for examination. It was an illustration of a PBR cutting a wake, guns blazing like some Sergeant Savage comic book. PBR was above the boat, Vietnam below. I was still amazed at the cartoon planted on my arm. Who'd have thought?

Evelyn, the booking agent at the processing station, just looked at me, her face a question mark.

"You don't want to go home?"

"No, not right away, Evelyn. I need to fly into LA...as close to Fullerton as you can get me."

"Sorry, I can't do that. We are authorized to..."

"Of course you can do that!" I jumped in. "This is what you do."

"No, I am authorized to send you, with a free ticket I might add, to Helena, Montana. Not Los Angeles."

Crap! It seemed my plan had hit a snag. No. Wait a minute, damn it!

"LOOK, Evelyn...what's the hang-up here?" I said, trying to mask my annoyance and failing. "The fuckin' Navy put my ass where I sure as hell didn't want it to be. Now all I'm askin' for is one lousy fuckin' favor...shit! Is it money? That's not a problem...I have cash on me. I'll pay whatever it costs extra. Fly me to LA... today...give me a couple days there...then book me to Helena. And I'll need a car. You can't do shit in LA without a car."

She excused herself to talk to her superior. There were more questions and headshaking, typical military exercise. Get out of the mainstream and the wheels come off. In the end, though, they gave in.

"I can get you into a regional airport in Orange County," she said. "That would be better than driving all the way across Los Angeles."

"Now we're talkin', Evelyn!"

The flight arrived early in the evening, and I found the rental just where Evelyn said it would be. But in the dark, wrestling with a map, I had a hell of a time finding my way to Fullerton, where I sort of remembered the way to JT's home. I arrived there just after 9 p.m. The lights were on, so I got out of the car.

But I didn't move toward the door. It suddenly dawned on me just how difficult this might be. My old self-consciousness emerged, and suddenly I was unsure of myself and what I was doing. I could have turned and fled, but I owed this to JT. He had been the best friend I'd ever had. I would likely never be closer to another man, or feel more anguish over a loss in my lifetime. He deserved this. I knew his folks would know nothing of how he had served, or why he had died. So, I willed myself to walk to the door.

But I didn't make it. I turned back and climbed in the car. "I can't do this," I kept saying out loud. It's too hard. They won't care. Are they expecting me?... No! Fuck.

Then the door opened, and Mr. Johnson stuck his head out and looked at me. He walked up to the car.

"Is there something I can do for you?" he said.

"Uhhh..."

"My neighbor called...said something strange was goin' on out here."

"Mr. Johnson...I'm sorry for this...I, uhh...I'm Mark. Mark Cameron. JT's friend. We met once last year and, uh..."

"Mark Cameron!" he said. "I'll be damned."

"I know we only met briefly...but..."

"Where the hell are my manners," George Johnson said. "C'mon son, get outta that car and let's get inside. Hell, you were in every one of Jay's letters. What a surprise! A great surprise."

My concerns proved valid. My time with the Johnsons would be difficult and full of emotions, conflicts, and revelations I had no experience with. It became evident right away that Jay's parents were having difficulty in their relationship. While polite and welcoming, Mrs. Johnson didn't want to hear anything about the war on the river or the part her son played in it. She tried changing the subject but failed. Mr. Johnson wanted to hear it all. She left the room and I didn't see her again the rest of the evening.

"It's not hard to see, Mark. This isn't a happy home anymore," George Johnson said. "Everything's changed. I think I'll sell this house. I built it with the idea it would be the perfect home for my kids and grandkids. But life isn't so abiding. It's all sadness now. A missing son I'll never see again. God...I do miss him!"

Mr. Johnson, Jay's little brother, Charlie, and I talked late into the night. Eventually, I explained the risks Jay's boat captain took and how JT had complained of the repetition of their patrols and its danger. How I had reasoned it led to their destruction. I was surprised to hear there was an open-coffin service. Evidently, a talented funeral director had done his job well. In time, George's personal feelings poured out of him.

"I've never known such raw...anger and hatred," he said. "It was exhausting. It's still with me, you know. The day after we got the news I got in my car...not really even thinking about it...and drove over to Peter Kennison's house. He's an old acquaintance, a judge..."

"Sure," I said. "JT told me about him. He's the guy that got JT drafted."

"Yeah...he told you. Well, I had harbored strong feelings toward Pete since then...and there I was in front of his house. I walked up to the door, asked the maid if I could see Pete. He arrived with that fucking smug look on his face, and I planted my fist right in the middle of that big nose. Broke my hand.

"Well, hell.... I thought, 'That's it, I'm goin' to jail...and I don't give a shit.' But, to this day, I haven't heard a thing from Judge Kennison. Nope, nothin'."

When I asked about Jay's wife, Richelle, there was a lot more hand-wringing.

"She loved my son, and I think he loved her...their entire lives. Damn, she took it hard...then one day just up and left. She calls once in a while...the last time from Houston. She sounded like she was high. I hope we see her again one day. There's another casualty of this war, Mark...one that doesn't make the papers or end up in the statistics."

I was offered JT's room to sleep in, but it was out of the question. I spent what remained of the night sleeping on the sofa and had my first dream of JT in a while, head spinning on the spike and all. Mrs. Johnson graciously greeted me in the morning and fixed me breakfast. We talked about everything but her son.

That morning, Charlie and I drove to JT's gravesite. You could still see the lines where the sod had been laid in strips. A temporary marker was at the head. I flashed on the handsome face—the great JT smile that always lit up a room—and his laugh. I envisioned the last day we had spoken and the peace sign he flashed while walking away. He was such a great guy. One I would never see or speak to again. How do you measure such loss? A sob left me and that was it. Tears came hard and furious. Charlie grabbed me in a bear hug and we sobbed into one another's shoulder.

We left the cemetery and drove into the city, where I found a tattoo parlor. After a few exploratory sketches, the artist and I came up with a pretty good facsimile of JT's tattoo. I had him plant it on my shoulder. Charlie had wanted the same, but I refused to let him; you had to earn such a thing. I'm not sure he totally understood.

I felt the mellow rush and tingle of the weed. Ah, now that's a great way to wake up! I walked to the doorway and looked over the lounging Lucy. Dark haired and kinda cute, Luce provided an invaluable element to my recovery: sex.

She had been one of my girlfriends in high school. We almost had sex once at the drive-in movie. Well, there was no *almost* about it anymore. I walked to the bed and sat down next to her. She stirred and rolled over.

"Want a hit?" I asked. She looked at me with tired eyes.

"Fuck it, might as well," she said, putting out her hand and exposing a breast. "I want to thank you again for the scene in the bar last night. That's the first time I've ever been thrown out of any place."

"Kirby!" I seethed anew, the fresh memory hitting me. "What a fuckin' asshole he turned out to be."

"You should ignore guys like that," she squeaked, holding in the smoke and passing the joint back. "The bar last night and, damn it, Mark...these nightmares. It's embarrassing."

"Hey! You think I'm havin' a good time here?! This world's fucked up. That son of a bitch called me a baby killer! A kid I've known most of my life, for godsake. Everybody sits around here

thinkin' life is just peachy. Well, it ain't! Let me tell you, darlin'...
half a world away some heavy shit's goin' down. Nobody in this
fuckin' town understands that! Nice American kids are gettin'
fuckin' blown away and you all go on like it's no big deal. I come
home and everybody's just so sweet and nice...but let's not talk
about any of that bad shit...that baby killer stuff. Please, no details...
and no parades, motherfucker! Nobody gives a shit I'm back...or I
survived. This war...it's like a movie, somethin' out of a magazine
to you...to everyone here? It's nothin' but a fuckin' TV war. Just
another show. But not to me! I had a friend...a friend...see..."

I was back in it. The choppers were overhead streaking mis-
sile trails, and the .50s were in my hands, blazing. Tracers swirled
around me and I screamed at the top of my lungs, though it was
lost in the violence. There was an explosion and its fireball enveloped me, then disappeared. Lucy was in my face, shaking me.

"Mark! Mark! Stop...please stop. Shit, oh dear..."

I gasped. What the hell happened?! This was new.

"Look, baby," she said. "Don't get so upset. Don't go nuts on
me. You're safe, really. You're safe."

"Am I? I'll tell ya, Luce...I'm not sure where the hell I am these
days. I don't think I'll ever feel safe again."

"C'mon," she said, smiling sweetly, but with a tremor in her
voice. "Let's roll another joint. Yeah. Let's get stoned and forget
about it.'

Suddenly, it was like I'd been thrown into an icebox. I could
have cared less. It was operation normal in this fucked-up world.
Either I was a raging lunatic or I was totally complacent and could
give a shit what happened the next moment.

We smoked more grass and we made love, and it made up for
everything else that happened that morning. Maybe it had come
late for me, but sex was number one on my list of favorite things,
and Lucy was more than accommodating. Much later she walked
to the chair, where her robe hung. I loved her naked body: the full-
ness of her breasts, the curve of her buttocks, the tight curly mass
of pubic hair. That body was the most beautiful thing in my world.

"Today's the day," she said, covering the beautiful body with
terry cloth. "You goin' to the VA hospital...or, blowin' it off like the
last five times? You need this, baby, and I ain't shittin'.'"

"Yeah...maybe I'll go this time."

"Right. Tell 'em about those nightmares and this shit goin' on. Ya gotta talk to someone! And, please, one favor...have 'em fix that ear. That thing just fuckin' freaks me out."

Lucy Cox's GTO sped away from the folks' house with a nice rumble and a chirp of the tires. She was an hour late for work, not that it mattered. She had a good job working for her father, who indulged and overpaid her. My job was at the ice cream plant, the same one Bud Brody had worked at in high school. I was stick man on the Popsicle line, and my shift started at 1 p.m. I made enough money to party. I saved nothing and my future was a question mark. It didn't sit well with my parents.

"You can't hang around here all your life!" Dad said, standing in a familiar pose: hands firmly planted on his sides like a super hero. Dad was the type of guy who loved to have a good time, but this look was devoid of all humor.

"Skip...we've talked about this and I don't want you saying that again," Mom said.

Mother, taller than Dad, was my personal protector in life. With Mom, I could never do wrong.

"I know, I know. Look, I'm trying to be understanding here. You're dealing with a lot of issues, son...but life goes on. You need to put these things behind you..."

"Damn it, Skip," Mom cut in. "He's trying! You and I can't possibly understand what's happened to our boy. We need to be patient."

"Patient?" Dad said. "I *am* being patient."

I had to chuckle at that one. My dad wasn't exactly a patient man, never had been. They went on debating as I lounged in the chair, distracted by a rerun of *Batman* on television.

"The least we can do is give his therapy time to work and support him until he's ready to go back to school. That's not much," Mom said.

"Well, I just think his life's getting away from him and he needs a little kick in the butt. I'm sorry, but that's what dads do."

"That might be okay if he was lazy...but it's more than that," Mom said.

"Well, something sure as hell is wrong with'm," Dad said, looking at me now.

"The psychologist at the VA says it's the war...and depression. He calls it a traumatic syndrome," I said.

"Traumatic...shit, I didn't see any of that after the war," Dad said. "Guys didn't sit around like this after World War II. They went right to work. They were tough."

"And they drank gallons of whiskey," Mom added.

"They were due a good time," Dad put in.

"How do you know they were havin' a good time?" Mom said. "You never went to war...thank God for that...so you couldn't know. Our son's seen and done horrible things and lost a of couple good friends in the meantime. One he's known all his life. We need to understand and let this run its course."

Dad thought on this a minute. He went over and turned the TV off, walked up to the chair, and knelt down in front of me.

"I'm truly sorry about the close friends you've lost, Son. Don't think I don't care about them...but I care about you more. You're mine and you're right here, alive. You need to reclaim your life, get better. Whatever that takes. And I'm with you. I'll support you... and I'll push you. Hell, I'll carry you if I have to...to make this right."

He stood and my gaze followed him up.

"I do care," he said. "A lot."

"I know you do, Dad," I said, tears again coming to my eyes. "Thanks. I am trying...I really am. I wanna get it right."

"Okay then," he said. "That's all I needed to hear."

The neighborhood was a tomb, or at least as quiet as one. The season of our childhood had passed, and like seeds from a dandelion yesterday's children had scattered with the wind. Even the youngest, little Katy Wicks, had gone away. Katy married the day after I arrived home. Ray Reamer was the lucky man. I attended the wedding with my family and my old college roommate, Tim.

The child bride was radiant, beautiful. She made quite a scene when she saw me for the first time in the receiving line, her expression revealing shock and sympathy for my appearance. Later we had a moment to talk out on the dance floor.

"It's so good to see you," she said. "When we first heard you were wounded I cried and couldn't sleep for days I was so upset, honest. Ray said I was being silly, that you'd be fine. But I was scared, ya know?"

"Thanks, Katy. It's always nice to know someone cares."

"Looks like you need some of your mother's good cooking. You're as skinny as I've ever seen you. I can feel every bone."

We twirled a bit. Though I felt a little self-conscious with every eye on us, it was nice being close to her. She smelled wonderful, like mountain meadows, cinnamon rolls, new cars...all my favorite fragrances. Her skin was smooth, tanned, and glowing. Her smile blinding. Somehow I felt at ease with her, and before long she was laughing in my arms.

"What are your plans now?" she asked.

"I just wanna get my act together. Health and happiness... that's all I'm shootin' for. I'm up for some serious partying with old friends. This fall I'll go back to school."

"Back into art?" she asked.

"No. I've settled on film and television."

"Ah, interesting. You've always been something of a drama queen," she laughed.

"Sorry, *war hero*," came Ray's voice from behind me. "It's time I danced with my wife."

Reamer pushed between us and I backed off.

"Sure, Ray. You've got a fine woman here."

He gave me a smug, dismissing look and was about to say something.

"Treat her right," I continued, "or I'll look you up and kick your ass."

Katy was shocked. Ray growled and quickly spun his wife and himself away. But as they moved on the dance floor Katy looked back with an expression that seemed full of regret. I was imagining things, perhaps seeing myself in her expression, but I would re-member that look long afterward.

A short time later, the newlyweds left in a hail of good wishes and rice. Tim and I snuck out the back.

"Let's go out tonight and have some fun," Tim suggested. "I know a place where we can get served."

It was then I realized the oddity: With everything that had

happened in the last year, I still wasn't old enough to legally buy a drink in a bar.

As always, my parents had left the door unlocked. I opened it slowly and slid silently inside. The house was empty and quiet. I turned the old rocking chair toward the yard, as usual, and settled in with my favorite view of the lilacs and their peaceful enclosure. At moments like this, the world around seemed small and insignificant, in a time capsule of my making. There were blessed times in the chair when I thought of nothing, the world being a blank page. There were tortured times with guilt and depression falling over me like a blanket, smothering all light and possessing me with anger and remorse that filled my head like a tumor blotting out all other thought. Today would be a good day. Dope helped.

In my second month home I answered a knock at the door and found my brother and the commander of the local Naval Reserve unit. They were grinning ear to ear like two schoolgirls with a scathingly sweet secret.

"Gunners Mate Cameron," the commander said, "I'm here to order you back to active duty."

I must have had the right look on my face because they both burst out laughing.

"Well, invite us in," my brother said, grabbing me and pulling me into the living room. "Commander Johnson has some great news. Damn, I'm just so proud!"

"Gunners mate," the commander said without hesitation, "it is my privilege to inform you...you have been awarded the Navy Cross for your heroic actions on the Tu Duc canal this past 14 April, 1969. Congratulations, Petty Officer, you have your country's, as well as my very own, thanks and appreciation for your bravery and courage under fire."

I was too shocked to respond. Honestly, being ordered back to duty would have been less shocking. My brother grabbed my limp body in a big hug.

"Isn't that somethin'!" he said. "The Navy Cross, Mark!"

"Scuttlebutt was you were considered for the Medal of Honor," the commander said. "They're reluctant to award that one, though, if you come out alive. That's how it goes down sometimes. My guess is you'd rather have the Navy Cross, right?" he finished, with a smile and a laugh.

There followed an uncomfortable silence in which I was expected to say something. My mind was quite blank, though, and I just looked one to the other.

"Uh, anyway, what we're going to do," the commander added, breaking the silence, "is read the citation and present the medal to you during our next drill, this coming Tuesday. We'll have your family there, the newspaper...it's a wonderful thing for our unit, the city.... I imagine the story will run statewide. Again, congratulations."

I didn't want to seem like a complete idiot, so I finally spoke. "Thank you...sir."

Actually, the story and picture got on the AP wire and were carried by newspapers all over. Al Johnson interviewed me for his *Coffee Break* program on KBLL radio. The interview was rebroadcast in a four-state area over the Intermountain Radio Network News. In response to all the media, I got maybe a hundred letters from veterans, veterans' organizations, patriotic moms and dads, old college friends, antiwar organizations, protestors, and more than a few real nut jobs. I was thanked, blessed, condemned, and castigated.

Personally, I was humiliated. The things they said in the citation were all lies. I went along with the show. It was what everyone expected. It wouldn't have been civil to have made a scene or to have refused the commendation. That would have created a scandal in our neighborhood and embarrassment for Mother.

I thought the medal was the worst misplacement of credit or heroism imaginable. Bird was the hero. I had told them that. The Navy had fucked it up again. He wouldn't have been nearly killed if I had gotten to the wheel and taken us out. I had been closer to the wheelhouse. It should have been me, but at the moment when I'd needed courage, I was too scared. Instead, I yelled for Bird to do something. I expected someone else to save my butt. We could have all died because I did nothing.

Worse was the remembrance of cowering in the gun tub as the boat spun circles on the canal. It wasn't bravery that moved me to act, but fear—fear of dying, of ending up like Jay. Calling me brave was an insult to the really courageous men. Getting the

Navy Cross was the most disgraceful thing that had ever happened to me. I threw the medal under a pile of underwear in my dresser. Mom dug it out and had it framed in a box with my other medals. They mocked me from a wall in the dining room. I couldn't stand to look at them and was disgusted at their very existence.

I had to talk with someone about my feelings. My family couldn't possibly understand. So, I decided to call Bird. I needed to apologize to him anyway. If he had heard about the medal, I didn't want him to think this was my doing.

It wasn't easy, though. The Sparrows were plentiful in Detroit. After many errant calls, I found an uncle of his who gave me Bird's number. I caught Tyrone at home on a Sunday afternoon.

When I got the nerve to bring up the canal firefight, his response gave me some small measure of peace while supporting my own theory of who the hero had been.

"I never heard you yellin' at me, man," Bird said. "I never heard that. There was too much racket. It was my own idea to get to the wheelhouse. Hell, my ass was hung out on the fantail anyway. In my mind you deserve the medal, Cam. I told 'em to give you the best medal they got. We're lucky sons-a-bitches...all of us...and I really don't understand why I'm alive. I know I shoulda died right there...and I can't get that out of my mind. It was my destiny to die there. I felt it the whole time I was in Nam...but never tol' anyone. You changed that...not that I'm complainin', understand."

Our conversation was the beginning of a long recovery for me. A recovery made harder by the nightmares, politics, social unrest... the times. I wanted to put it all behind me, to get on with things. It would be slow in coming, though, and the death of another friend didn't help.

A sanctuary ringed by lilacs. Stanley and I had played here. I could almost see his youthful ghost now, racing among the bushes. We had slept under the stars, getting up in the middle of the night to raid his father's garden. This yard, this house, the home across the street, the ball field...Stan was everywhere, and nowhere.

I loved my mother's cooking. After a month of roast beef, fried chicken, and potatoes the pounds were going on quickly. Tonight, we were having her famous navy bean soup with cornbread smothered in syrup. For a change, Mom and Dad seemed relaxed. There were no discussions about school, getting my life in order, or the way I was dressing. There was laughter and a lightness that had been missing almost from the day I had returned home.

When the phone rang my father was annoyed.

"Why the hell do people call during dinnertime?"

As always, Mom got up and answered. Dad and I continued our conversation.

"So, anyway, Dad...I was wondering when you were going to get with the times and grow your hair longer?"

Dad looked stunned. He had been on my case lately about my lengthening hair, not wanting a hippie for a son.

"Me?!"

"Yeah, you," I said, seizing the offensive. "You're outta step, Dad, and it's time you got with the program. I've noticed a few of your old friends with longer hair."

"What? Who?"

"Joe and Leroy Longmire, for two. Joe's got some nice 'burns goin'."

"Yeah...but me? The guys at work..."

He froze midsentence. There are expressions that say things in an instant. Dad had glanced at my mother. I turned slowly in my seat to see my mother's face as she hung up the phone. All the color was gone.

"What is it?" my father said. "Your mother?"

"No...that was Mrs. Brody," Mother continued, sitting down slowly. "She just heard...we've lost a boy from the neighborhood." She looked at me. "Stanley's dead, Mark. Killed in action."

I wanted to count crocodile ten and make Stanley alive again, like we had during our childhood war games. But this was real war he'd been playing this time. There was a military burial at Fort Harrison National Cemetery. I caught Katy's face only once during the ceremony and her grief broke my heart. The old man, Willy, looked defiant, angry. The rest of the family appeared frail, vulnerable, and virtually crushed.

As the graveside ceremony ended and folks disbursed, I made my way over to Katy. On seeing me, she smiled through a tear-streaked face. Husband Ray frowned and set his expression in a grimace.

"Hello, Katy," I said.

"Thank you for coming, Mark."

"Hi, Ray," I added.

"Yeah," Ray said. "I'll be in the limo, Kate. Don't be long."

He walked away quickly, turning back once with a nasty look.

I'd had doubts about approaching Katy. While I had firsthand knowledge of dying, death, and the sorrow that follows, I was not in a good place for talking about it with anyone. There was an uncomfortable silence between us as we searched each other's face.

"I'm sorry," I said at last.

"Yes," Katy added. "Sorry."

"You know, he's in a better place. He'll never have to suffer again...never face disappointment, anguish. That's what we said in Nam...now he's in a better place," I said. It was all I could do.

"He was just coming into his own," Katy whispered. "His last letters were all about getting out of the Marines, going to college, living it up. He never had a chance to be happy, but he was ready for it."

She broke down then and collapsed in my arms, weeping. As I cradled her head on my shoulder, I saw husband Ray bang the top of the limo, jump inside, and slam the door.

"Will you come to the reception?" she asked.

"No. I, uh...I can't do that. I don't do well in crowds."

"You've changed," she said, pulling back from me. "Since I last saw you you're a different man, Mark. When did this happen?"

"There's nothing really wrong, Kate. I just...I need to work through a few...issues. Sorry, again. Take care of yourself, huh? I'll give you a call sometime."

"Don't live your life like this, Mark Cameron. Those who love you care."

"Oh, yeah," I said. "Thanks for that. Uh, well...bye, Katy. Bye."

I turned and left quickly. I had the sensation of sinking or being pulled into a whirlpool. I broke into a trot and jumped into my Beetle, sweat now pouring out of me. I gasped for air. A sob left me and I cried a long, long time among the dead, for the dead.

It seemed I had become a large, sucking vortex, with everything bad being pulled toward me by some unseen, other-dimensional force. I couldn't get my feet under me, as Dad would say. Stanley's death, heaped on top of what I was dealing with, sent me headlong into a dark, muddled despair. Demons nipped at me day and night, but thankfully there was marijuana, speed, reds, LSD, and hashish to put me into an altered reality. The VA psychologist said those things weren't doing me any good. I felt otherwise.

Four months after Stanley's death I received a curious postcard from Joe Wills. The front of the card pictured three hula girls. It was postmarked Honolulu, Hawaii, and it read...

> *Mark—I'm done with Nam and will be out of the Army next week. Not coming home. Have a good life.*
> *Joe*

"Have a good life"... What the hell did that mean? I tried reaching Joe's mother, hoping for some clarity, but it was a dead end. She had married again, and my mother thought she had moved to Colorado. There was no listing for Joe's brother, Paul, in the phone book, either. Dancing hula girls was the last I heard of Joe Wills.

1969

Cholon, South Vietnam

Nu Chi was buoyant, riding the crest of love for the first time in her life. She was confused and conflicted to be sure, but every time she thought of Dat and their day together, she would smile and feel giddy.

Her father noticed the invigorating change in his daughter, correctly suspected a man as the reason, and was very pleased by the notion. He had been losing hope for his daughter's future and had prayed to his ancestors for help. She needed someone, and he, grandchildren. Now he looked forward to the day, soon he hoped, when the young man and his daughter would present themselves for his approval.

It had been exactly one week since Dat's departure when a man approached Nu Chi's table at the café and presented a letter from Dat. The man told her if she had a response, to bring the letter with her the following Sunday and leave it at the edge of her table. He then abruptly turned and disappeared up the avenue.

Nu Chi opened the letter and read...

> *June 29, 1969*
> *My Love,*
> *How is it that I have just left your side and feel so impossibly alone already? I am like the addict and you are the only source of sustenance. How will I survive the coming separation? I fear this hardship more than any I have yet endured.*
> *As I write I am still nearby, but soon a flight will take me far away. I wanted to send this now so that you would receive a letter quickly. All future correspondence will come infrequently and at times with long delay. Between, I will imagine you in my mind, as fresh and lovely as last I saw you.*
> *Our day together was all I hoped it would be and confirmed everything I have wished and longed for since our first meeting. You must keep faith, Nu Chi. Like the rising and*

setting of the sun, the coming and going of the monsoon, I
<u>*will*</u> *return to you. I promise this on my life.*
     Love,
     Dat

Tears from the many emotions swirling within her fell as she read the letter. Nu Chi knew Le Van Dat well enough to know he would pursue his dream at all costs, make an incredible effort to see it fulfilled. But life is not just, fair, or equal. She knew the likelihood of her ever seeing Dat again was slim and, if he was right in his assessment of a Northern victory, a time might come when she would have to choose between her freedom and his promise.

Hanoi, North Vietnam

Dat rode in reasonable comfort on the back seat of the old Russian-built Moskvitch limousine as it slowly wound its way around potholes and over filled-in bomb craters. Repairs left the highway looking like a harvested potato field. Occasionally they came across youth shock brigades repairing the roads as best they could.

As the car passed fields, industrial areas, and neighborhoods, the impact of America's bombing and the austere effect the war was having on his country were everywhere. Women worked in the fields with rifles stacked nearby. Gangs of laborers moved to resurrect twisted, shattered buildings. In the once bustling capital city, few people were in attendance. Dat wondered where the populace had gone.

That Dat had been picked up at the airfield by a government limousine revealed just how far up the chain of command he had risen. He saw many bicycles, now and then a truck, but not another single car.

They pulled up to a familiar ministry building. A young officer was waiting at the curb and hurriedly opened the door, snapping to attention and throwing a salute. Dat gathered himself and stepped from the automobile.

"Welcome to Hanoi, General. I am Major Phong. If you will follow me please, General Minh is most anxious to meet with you."

As Dat entered the room, Minh beamed at his friend and struggled to get up from his desk.

"You did not have to get up, General," Dat said, leaning across the desk to shake Minh's hand.

"Ah, it is not so bad today, Dat. I am learning to live with my infirmity. I feel lucky to be alive. It is wonderful to see you. Please, have a seat."

The two settled into their chairs. Minh pointed to the cigarette box on his desk.

"Help yourself. They're Players...your favorite, as I recall," Minh said.

"Thank you," Dat responded, taking a cigarette.

"So," Minh started, "how is it to be back in Hanoi?"

Dat exhaled and felt the welcome nicotine rush from the smooth tobacco. It had been some time since he'd enjoyed a good smoke.

"I haven't had the opportunity to look around, of course, but it seems the city is much quieter...and a little bleak, perhaps."

"True enough. It is appalling what the bombing has done to our country. The people see all their hard work being destroyed and are confused and angered by it...a good motivational tool," Minh said. "I understand your reaction...but, I was referring more to the sensation of being home, back in friendly, familiar surroundings. It has been years."

"It is always nice to be home, General. If I might change the subject, though, how is your health? Have you fully recovered?"

As Dat asked the question, he had already formed his own opinion from the physical appearance of Minh. Now just forty, Minh looked well beyond his years. His hair was almost fully gray. He looked frail, his eyes sunken. Dat supposed the trauma of his wounds had erased many years from the man's life.

"I am much better, my friend. Thank you for your concern... and your letters. They were welcome and most appreciated."

"Are you fully installed in the Politburo, then?"

"Yes, just," Minh said. "It is still difficult for me to get around much. But the doctors tell me my health will improve. I must say, you look the very picture of health."

"It is true," Dat responded. "I am feeling better than I have in years."

"Really? The dour old Dat? What is the reason for all this well-being?"

"Being home...of course." Dat quickly moved the conversation along. "There is much in the wind of peace talks with the Americans. I am sure there is nothing to this..."

"Of course not," Minh interrupted. "The Americans do not understand our cause...never have! The peace talks are merely another weapon in the struggle for unification. They must think we are quite naive. We know about the demonstrations in America. We know about the new president's promise to get America out of this war...and his plan for immediate troop reductions. With all this well known, it is an insult that they would think we will compromise anything. It is the disdainful pomposity of a powerful aggressor nation.

"I have seen a copy of the letter President Nixon sent to Ho. He wishes to move negotiations along or there will be 'grave circumstances.' We are planning a very pointed response to Mr. Nixon's request...attacks at over a hundred Southern locations to be launched on August 12. Of course, it is just harassment. The truth is Giap will not launch another major offensive in the South until the Americans are gone...but, that offensive is already in the planning stages."

"That is something that cannot come fast enough," Dat said. "I look forward to concluding my life's work."

"Yes. Well, let's talk about that," Minh said. "Since it is rare for a senior officer or anyone at all to be recalled from the South, I am sure you are wondering why.... What is this all about?"

"I was...surprised by the orders. I assume I am to be given a new command. People's troops, I hope...but why call me home?"

"I am sure you found commanding NLF forces a bit daunting. Such a waste of talent. A man such as yourself in command of the ineffective Viet Cong."

"I never saw it that way, General. I have taken on the burden of *Dau Tranh*, the struggle, as well as anyone."

"Dat, please," Minh pleaded. "No one, especially me, is suggesting you have not been doing your duty. You are the very representation of *Dau Tranh*...despite your Communist failings. However, I believe someone such as yourself should be put to better use. Talent is not wasted in a utopian society, eh? Your new posting will be here in the Hanoi area, but the position is just window dressing."

Minh leaned forward, intent. "It is a well-known fact the Politburo is growing old. The inbred government needs new blood. It is every citizen's duty to advance capable leaders for political position."

Dat did not want to think about where this conversation was headed. He had never held political aspirations, nor had he ever led Minh to believe he did. His chair was growing decidedly uncomfortable.

"I want you here...to attend parties, functions, meetings...to be seen and to become known by those in power. I will talk you up... be your champion. The rest will be easy once the right people see the stuff you are made of. The country needs no-nonsense leaders from the military at the highest levels."

Minh took a cigarette from the box and leaned back in his chair, taking time to light it while he observed Dat.

Beads of sweat broke out on Dat's forehead as the implications of Minh's plan imploded in his mind. This was a disaster! He wanted nothing to do with a posting in the North, thought it impossible. He had been wondering how far from Nu Chi his orders would take him, hoping all the while for something in the Saigon area. Further, he wanted nothing to do with a seat in the Politburo. It was absurd! Surely, he thought, Minh has lost his mind. I must tread lightly, though. Minh is not someone to trifle with.

"General...we have been very candid with one another in the past. You know well my feelings on communism...my commitment only as a soldier. The idea of me in the Politburo?... Well, I am grateful and appreciative that you would consider me worthy, but..."

"But...have I lost my mind?" Minh interjected.

At this, Dat blushed deeply, causing the general to laugh out loud. "Ah, Dat, Dat. Yes, I know you well. But listen for the moment. Diversity, free thought, contrary opinions...every government needs someone who will advance new and different ideas. That could be you! At Dien Bien Phu it was Le Van Dat who suggested the unthinkable...an escape along the river. It saved the garrison. Time and again you have demonstrated raw courage and clear thinking when it was needed. I know of your failings to communism. I also know your dedication to your country, to unification, *Dau Tranh*...and that is more important. That is why I want to present you for membership in the Politburo. We will keep your feelings on communism to ourselves, eh? No one need know."

Again, Dat began to protest. Minh cut him off.

"No. It is useless, Dat. I know this is not what you desire. Not the role you envision for yourself. It is, however, a role others see you performing perfectly. Now, I will not be deterred...and you will cooperate with my plan. It is your duty as Vietnamese...your *Dau Tranh*."

Dat's frustrations boiled over.

"I am just a soldier, Minh!" Dat stated, his voice rising. "The first time I stood in front of you...that was all I asked to be. It took more courage than I thought I had to refuse your order to join the porters. I wanted a rifle. I wanted to be a soldier. It takes as much courage now to refuse you again. Bust me to private if you must, but send me south. I am just a soldier and my place is in this war."

The two sat silently, staring one another down. Dat's face reflected defiance, resolution, and purpose. Disbelief, anger, and disappointment were on Minh's as he pursed his lips and scowled.

"Damn you, Le Van Dat!" he said at last, but his expression softened at the same moment. "You have done it again, haven't you? Will we ever get too old for this game? Before I die, let me give you just *one* damn order you will not refuse."

When the laughter subsided, Minh looked warmly at Dat.

"Those days...as sergeant, then lieutenant...with you in my command...they were the best years of my life. I have never felt more comradeship...been as close to other men or been as inspired. It was a special time and you were there to help make it so.

"I will not bust you to private...*and* I will not send you south again...just yet. Let us compromise. The war has a few more years to play out. The Americans will not go away easily. Give me a few years in Hanoi and I promise, I will send you south to command People's Army troops once more. You will be there when our flag is raised in Ho Chi Minh City...providing you agree to embrace membership in the Politburo when it is offered. Is this acceptable?"

No, it was not acceptable in the common sense of acceptability. But Dat felt the same comradeship, the same emotions as Minh. He owed the great man much. Though he didn't know yet how he would endure the long separation from the woman he loved, he knew he had to accept Minh's offer. There was nothing else to be done.

"I agree to your proposal, Minh. Thank you for understanding...and for everything you have done for me. You are my best friend and ally. I will cooperate to the best of my ability...but, you must keep your promise as well and send me back south...soon as possible."

"Ah," Minh said. "You are more trouble than you are worth. Here."

Minh slid an official document across the desk.

"Your orders. You are to be the new commandant of the Xuan Mai Indoctrination Center, our largest recruitment and training facility. I know this is a command you do not want, but it is a very visible and important political position. I had to call in a few favors to secure it. Your reputation and experience will serve you well at Xuan Mai. You will be a tremendous inspiration. We need men such as you shaping the minds of our youth. Vietnam does not have enough heroes to look up to."

"I doubt anyone in the North has ever even heard of General Le Van Dat."

"Oh, don't be so sure, my friend. They know...or soon will."

The next morning Dat picked up the newspaper at his door and was greeted by his image on the front page. The photo had evidently been taken as he had stepped out of the Moskvitch limousine in front of the ministry. The headline read "Heroic General to Command Xuan Mai."

"Minh," Dat mumbled under his breath.

He had been given a furlough, two weeks in which to rest and recuperate. Briefly, he entertained delicious thoughts of flying to Bangkok, securing passage south, and spending time with Nu Chi. Sheer fantasy. He reminded himself he must be extremely vigilant with this affair. Discovery of the liaison would mean the end of his career and likely prison.

He sat down and penned a letter. It proved the most difficult he would ever write. Again and again he started, not finishing a final draft until noon.

July 3, 1969
My Darling Nu Chi,
I start every day by reconstructing you from memory. As I lie in my bed your face comes together in front of me like pieces of a puzzle. It never fails to bring the first joy into my day.
I am afraid of how to word this so as to not bring you more despair than I already have—better just to write it. I will not be coming south to see you again for some time. My superior, an old and important friend, has plans for my promotion and intends to keep me close by for the time being. His intent is flattering and honorable. He wishes to see me installed a member of the highest authority. Though I long only to join you—obsess on it daily. But, I have no choice but to remain and meet his demands. There is a history between this man and I that goes beyond duty. I will explain one day.
I have been given a position here that is honorable, much sought after, and away from the war.
Now that the foreseeable future is clear, please do not shun me. Do not cast me aside. I could not endure it. I live only for you. To see you and hold you once again. I repeat what I promised at our parting, the future is ours. Our love will abide.
A favor, please. If it is not too much, I would like a photograph of you. While I can reconstruct your face perfectly in my mind, my eyes hunger for the sight, too.
Keep well, my love. Think of me often, as I do of you and pray the time passes quickly.
All My Love,
Dat

Colonel Boa Hanh was the epitome of self-control. His face was as rigid and unyielding as a porcelain Buddha. Neither smiling nor frowning, his expression was set in a look of intense interest or acute respect. Those laying eyes on him, and there were many doing so, were very curious to know what was going on inside the man's head. They would go on wondering, for Hanh would give up nothing. It was a game at which he was very good: the outward calm and uncompromising control masking the emotional volcano that erupted within. He was the unreadable man, the cool manipulator, the master politician. He was also second fiddle.

Before him stood General Le Van Dat taking over command of Xuan Mai—the Xuan Mai command that was supposed to have been his! The command he and his mother had worked so diligently to secure. The next step in what all saw as his eventual ascendance into the Politburo. It was a disappointment predicated by one of those unforeseeable events that sometimes befall a politician. The hero of Tet had returned and asked for one favor. How could they deny the one-legged superstar? And now their champion's comrade and fellow rice farmer stood resolute and with great humility, it seemed, accepting the prize Hanh and Gao Jinh had schemed and worked so hard toward. Damn the luck!

General Tran Van Minh's warm smile was also something of a mask. The smile was for Dat and the politicians in attendance who had thrown their support behind him. Poor Dat, Minh thought, he knows nothing of the political minefield he is entering. After his installation, I will have a little talk with the new commandant. He must know the intrigue and danger his position holds, who his new enemies are, and what they seek. The powerful Gao Jinh and her son were no doubt already conspiring in Dat's demise. This was a new kind of warfare Dat would have to learn. But look at the man! Dat was the very picture of confidence and accomplishment. The resourceful little sergeant would find a way to win this battle, too.

Unknown to those gazing upon him, General Le Van Dat's own subdued appearance was more the reflection of true sorrow. What passed for admirable humility was, instead, all-consuming depression. Dat had conceded to Minh's ambitions for him, but now at the change of command, he felt disheartened and desperate. It was not just the acceptance of a post he did not covet; it was the official validation of a long separation from the woman he loved. Only those who have suffered such heart-wrenching circumstance could ever understand.

The reception that followed was a whirl of Hanoi politicians and military leaders that General Minh lined up in an endless stream to meet the new commandant and rising star of the Hanoi political theater. Dat was intensely relieved that Ho was too ill to attend. It took all of Dat's willpower and stamina to hold his smile and weather the onslaught.

He noticed Xuan Mai's second in command, the head of the political cadre, Boa Hanh, standing in the background with his formidable mother. Dat had always been at odds with the political commissars, so it was not unusual that he found Hanh an annoying, presumptuous little fanatic. However, he knew this one would be worse than the usual extremists who held such positions. The son of one of the revolution's well-known heroes, Hahn was a politically savvy insider with tremendous clout.

Hanh's mother, of course, was the renowned Gao Jinh, whose husband, also named Boa Hanh, had been with Ho from the very beginning. They had been students in Paris and, together, both had fought the Japanese, then the French. The elder Boa Hanh had died in a B-29 raid in 1953. At the request of Ho, Gao Jinh had resolutely taken her husband's place in the Politburo. Flashing subtle intelligence and an uncanny talent for politics, she now wielded incredible influence and was seriously considered as a candidate to replace the aging, and ailing, leader.

As the two of them approached Dat, he put on his best face.

"General," Hanh said, "I would like you to meet my mother. Perhaps you've..."

"It is *indeed* a *great* pleasure," Dat said, cutting off the younger man. "Every soul in Vietnam knows of the great Gao Jinh."

"Too kind," Gao Jinh replied.

There was foreboding behind Dat's blinding smile. The "Matriarch of the Politburo," as she was known, had the most unusual face Dat had ever seen. Her smile held perfect, straight, white teeth in a handsome jaw under a small button of a nose. But above the nose were two of the coldest steel-gray eyes he had ever encountered. He had seen many photographs of Gao Jinh, but the lens must have been tricked by the color and mystery of those eyes. They seemed like twin tornados wishing to suck Dat in.

"I have recently become aware of your exemplary record in the field, Le Van Dat. The Vietnamese people are fortunate to have such a warrior on our side. Why, you seemed to be winning the war all by yourself! It is such a loss for the army. You must be disappointed...as we all are."

"I could never refuse an order from the great Minh," Dat replied. "It is an honor to serve my country in any capacity."

"Oh...next you will want my job," Gao Jinh said, to the laughter of those around. "You know...the only discomfiting 'notations' in your official record are the many complaints from the political cadre serving so valiantly alongside you.... Why is that?"

"Sometimes, madame," Dat replied, smiling broadly, "military decisions in the field, of necessity, are not consistent with the, uh... political condition, eh?"

"That's odd," Gao Jinh replied, also smiling broadly. "I thought we were Communists first. Doesn't the political commissar always hold rank in the field?"

"Not always, madame, and often, when the bullets fly, they are not about when decisions must be made."

At this, Boa Hanh momentarily lost his composure, looking as if he'd been slapped. Dat's insolent, arrogant response to one of the most powerful members of government was shocking! He was personally affronted as well, the implication being the political cadre acted cowardly in the field. It was true Hanh himself had no experience in battle, but he felt if the time ever came he would act honorably, as did all commissars.

Gao Jinh's eyes seemed to darken while the rest of her face remained frozen in an exacting smile. Dat knew he had affronted her and her son, but he was new at this political game and had little patience for it. In the pinch, he reverted to what came naturally for him: He would be the aggressor.

"Well," she replied at last, "I am sure that when carefully reviewed your record will stand on its own. What a pleasure it will be having you here in Hanoi, General. Congratulations...I hope your stay will end in a satisfying manner."

Gao Jinh excused herself and left with a severe smile. The passing look from Hanh was stony and dead cold. They retired to a corner of the great room, removed from the others.

"I am going to enjoy bringing this man down," Hanh whispered. "He acts as if he is still on the battlefield. What do you think, are the complaints in his record enough to remove him on moral grounds?"

"No. All complaints were dismissed out of hand by his commanding officers. Whining commissars do not bring down heroic leaders. Hopefully, you will learn this someday."

"Is there anything else, Mother? Are you holding back?"

"Stop it!" she hissed. "You are starting to sound pathetic...weak and grasping. Our only problem is we do not know enough about this man. He materializes out of the fog of war like someone lost in a commode the past twenty years. But I tell you, he is not all he seems to be; they never are. Le Van Dat has his little secrets, and all we need do...is *find* them."

"But...how? I have gone through his record. He has been a soldier in the field his entire career. Not married...been in the South a long time."

"Be quiet and listen!" Gao Jinh cut in. "It might have something to do with the political cadre. It is interesting—is it not?—that the only blemish on his record is the continual disagreements with commissars. More likely, though, it is something personal... family issues, money, a woman.

"We just need more information. Listen...you are still second in command, so you will become the general's close companion... perhaps even a confidant, eh? Yes...you must play the role of trusted friend. Starting tomorrow, Le Van Dat will see a different Boa Hanh. A cordial, helpful, complimentary Boa Hanh who is *much* more like him than he first thought. You must be agreeable, understanding...not all at once, understand. Play the politician. Patience. Get to know your enemy...so you can destroy him."

She turned to look at Dat and felt the intensity of competition that had always made her a ferocious adversary.

"The man will have trouble adjusting to an office on an army base. You will help," she said, absently. "He is uncomfortable in the public eye; you will guide him. He will be depressed at times; you will cheer him up! What a *friend* you will be."

"I understand perfectly," Hanh said with a sadistic smirk. "I just *love* the guy, don't you?"

"Oh, yes. And like the butterfly emerging from its cocoon, General Le Van Dat's story will unfold to us."

Dat was just greeting the minister of finance when he saw a woman standing alone out of the corner of his eye. Lee Nah was of course much changed since their days in the delta, but not in a disagreeable way. In fact, she was stunning. A beauty in her youth, she had matured into a magnificent woman with the looks of a movie star. A second glance confirmed she was studying him closely with an unblinking gaze.

While conversing with some minister, Dat had no idea what was coming out of his own mouth or what the minister was saying in return. While he should have expected Lee Nah to be in attendance, the thought had not crossed his mind. The discomfort he felt with the whole Xuan Mai affair took a new and very personal direction. It seemed now he was wishing the minister well, or some such thing. As the old man left, Dat hesitated to look again in Lee Nah's direction.

"Congratulations, General," came from Lee Nah, soft and without emotion.

He turned and met her gaze as she moved forward, hand extended. *Breathtaking* was the word that came to mind. Close up, she was perhaps the most beautiful woman he had ever seen. While she wore the straight, medium gray suit of the political elite, its simplicity only seemed to enhance her beauty, like a masterpiece on a blank wall.

Dat was momentarily speechless. The corners of Lee Nah's mouth turned up slightly. "You have certainly earned your place in Hanoi. Everyone is talking about your heroic exploits. It seems you are much admired," Lee Nah said.

"Yes. Uh...thank you, Lee Nah. Certainly, not as much as yourself, though," Dat replied.

"Um...ancient history. You look good, Dat. War must suit you. I bet you can't wait to get back to it."

"Lee Nah..."

"Again...congratulations. I hope things go well for you in your new post. I'm sure you have much more to give your country...and the cause."

With that, she turned and walked away. Slower than necessary, he thought.

As Dat discovered, the commandant of Xuan Mai circulated in the highest echelons of the military. Besides his command headquarters, he was given a second, much larger office next to Minh's. He quickly found out the job of commandant held little work and few responsibilities. It was mere window dressing, and this confused Dat to no end. He was unsure what was expected of him, where to direct his energies.

"It is easy," Minh said. "If you are expected at a meeting, you will be there. If Giap asks you to work on a plan or project, you will throw all your time into it. Your talents are for military operations and planning. You are much too important to run a recruiting center. Let Hanh run the damn camp, as he has done for some time now. Let's just keep him there, shall we?"

These were the first offices Dat had ever occupied. His first desk job. There were adjustments to be made. To Dat's surprise, Boa Hanh had humbled himself and stepped forward, proving invaluable in easing Dat's transition. No doubt it was part of the political game Minh had spoken of, but increasingly he found Hanh an indispensable aide. He knew he must practice vigilance with Hanh, but the man had given him nothing but support and allegiance.

One of the first acquisitions Dat made was a cigarette case. Not finding what he needed in the markets, Dat had commissioned the construction of a teak desktop case of his own design, handsomely carved with inlaid mother-of-pearl.

Minh had taken exception.

"What is this monstrosity? Do you assuage your ego by purchasing a larger cigarette case than mine? It will not make up for your small member, you know."

"I figure I can use it as a foot stool if needed," Dat laughed, flipping the box open.

"Oh, my," Minh said, peering inside. "Cigarettes by the bushel...and cigars too? Where did you get those? And...is this pipe tobacco or ganjhi?"

"I assure you it is tobacco," Dat said. "You must forgive me, Minh. I have admired your own case these many years and finally I have a desk fit for one of my own. This one's a bit large, I know. But after all those years smoking that damn Burmese stink weed, I wanted to make sure I never ran out of the good stuff."

During his second month in Hanoi, Dat received his first letter from Nu Chi. The letter was inside an official government pouch from his Saigon operative and marked for his eyes only. In the late hours of the day, with the lights extinguished and the ministry nearly empty, Dat held the letter under a solitary desk lamp. Her delicate cursive styling was artwork, the lightly scented pink envelope enchanted and teased. He opened it with feelings of elation and anxiety.

September 9, 1969
Dearest Dat,

I, too, mourn our separation and think often on our mystical day together. A day seemingly divined. I also think of the other times, such as our first meeting when I was charmed by the rice farmer. I should have known you were no farmer—what a silly girl I must have seemed. Then the surprise in Cholon. I am still angry at your deception and amazed at where it has led.

It all seems impossible. I am in love, the most joyous time in my life. Yet, I cannot tell a living soul. My father suspects and keeps dropping hints as if I will bring a suitor home one day. Imagine his surprise!

How can it end well, Dat? Your faith in our union, your love and devotion is overwhelming. As the days go by, though, I cannot but wonder if I will ever see you again.

Please, come and take me away. We can leave Vietnam altogether and make a new life in a world without war, without sides, but with a future! I am ready to leave tomorrow. Come for me!

My heart belongs only to you, but I fear it's withering with the longing. Keep well, my love.

Nu Chi

Escape to a world without sides? What a lovely dream. Vietnam was a round hole and they were its square pegs. But after the war... well, he could take a Southern bride, even one who had worked for the defeated South. But Nu Chi, as she had said quite emphatically, would not live in a Communist society. Dat wondered, without the war, could he? Minh's Politburo dream was not realistic, could never work. He did not fit in the system. *Could I leave?* he thought. And the thought amazed him. He had never had such a thought before. His ancestors, the same ones who had guided him and protected him throughout the war, must be recoiling in horror at such a preposterous idea. He felt shamed and uneasy. It was not prudent to tamper with such things.

Quickly, he folded Nu Chi's letter and, sliding a perfectly fitted piece of wood at the back of his new cigarette box, saw the secret compartment pop open. While putting the letter safely away, he also locked away all thoughts of ever leaving Vietnam.

1998

Rounding that last curve on I-90, before you exit North Seventh into Bozeman, you look right at Montana State University. Rising like silos in a field are three high-rise dorms: hedges, north and south, and Roskie. To their left, looking like an overweight flying saucer, is the fieldhouse. It is the same view that greeted me when I returned to school in 1970. Everything else has changed.

In those days, North Seventh was dotted with empty lots and open fields. Street traffic was typical of a small town, irregular and slight. Farms with their rich soil encroached Bozeman on every side, as if the land wouldn't abide houses where there should be cows or alfalfa. It was a quaint agricultural college town that I grew to love.

What a difference thirty years can make. Today, Bozeman is a boomtown filling up with elite, mobile-rich immigrants. Traffic is horrendous, housing prices outrageous, and the snobbery unbearable in this one-time, one-horse burg. The rich farmland is being covered with housing tracks far out into the valley. It has become the poster child for the ruined innocence of the American West.

I planned on pulling into the old SuperAmerica gas station I had used throughout college, but it had lapsed into a boarded-up relic. I found a Thriftway station half a block further and pulled in for gas. I wondered if it was associated with Van's Thriftway, my convenience store of choice in Northern California. But the logo was different and this was a Conoco station, not Shell. Gas, at $1.36 a gallon, was exactly a buck more than it had been while I was in school.

I was directly across the street from where Manny's had once been located, a popular greasy spoon Clark and I had frequented. Its demolition likely prompted all the dietitians in town to stand and cheer, though it would be a mistake to think students had come for the food. Manny's had the unique character of a hangout, largely shaped by an aged, foul-mouthed waitress named Sal.

Sal liked Clark, and vice versa. They were two hard-bitten characters sharing much the same view of the world. While giving each other a wink, they gave the rest of the world the finger.

I met Clark Douglass in a student watering hole known as the Hof, or the Hofbrau. At the time, I had only been back in school one week, and though I thought many of my old freshman pals were likely still around, I had no desire to look them up.

During my first Friday night back in school, I had gone to the Hof to drink beer by myself. I was an hour into my hops and barley rumination when I heard singing. A few others and I turned to see a grizzled man serenading us from his wheelchair. While the others laughed it off and went back to their drinks, I studied the guy.

He was by himself, facing me from behind one of the large, circular wooden tables in the middle of the room. There was a pitcher of beer and a glass in front of him, but he was drinking straight out of the pitcher. The guy had long, stringy hair and an unkempt beard, sandy red in color. He wore a Marine fatigue jacket with official insignia and a few unofficial additions. A big peace sign badge was over the name DOUGLASS and a Zig-Zag man was on the shoulder. As I watched, he finished a big drink and launched into another song.

Aiee, yiee, yiee, yiee
In China they do it for chili
So sing me another verse
Just like the other verse
And waltz me 'round again, Willy

"That's it, pal," said the bartender. "One more chorus and you're outta here."

The guy laughed and looked around the bar, shaking his head. He tilted the pitcher again and took a long draft. This time, when he brought the pitcher down, he was looking me dead in the eye. Momentarily, neither of us blinked. He laughed slightly, went quiet, and returned to studying his pitcher of beer.

I finally realized what it was about the scene that seemed out of place. Beneath the table there were no feet resting on the chair's footrests and no legs to be seen, either.

"What the fuck you lookin' at?" he said suddenly.

I was embarrassed, then tickled. Evidently, my beer buzz was kicking in. I got off the stool and walked over to his table.

"Is there a place at this table for a riverine?" I asked.

"You Nav?" he replied.

"Yeah. If you're expectin' someone...fine. I'll..."

"No...no, no...fuck, no one. Have a seat, you river rat. An' here, have some more beer," he said, sloppily pouring beer from his pitcher into my glass as I sat down. I didn't object.

"Been back long?" I asked.

"Yeah, a year...uh, maybe two...fuck, I dunno...a while. My name's Clark...Clark Douglass," he said, extending his hand.

I hadn't shaken anyone's right hand with my own since Nam. My left rose to grab his hand, but I thought better of it. I pulled my right hand out of my pocket, where it had been all night, and extended it. Clark looked at the hand and a different expression came over his face. He nodded and grabbed my hand firmly.

"Mark Cameron," I said.

"Glad to make your acquaintance. So, how's life treatin' you, Mark?"

"I'm gettin' along," I said, after a pause.

"Yeah," Clark said, tipping the pitcher. "It's been a real bummer for me, too."

I had to wonder what I was doing at this table. Was I looking for a drinking partner? Was I there to offer pity? Try to save the man? It didn't take much detective work to see the guy had some real issues he was dealing with. As fragile as my own psyche was at the moment, could I do anything for him? *Maybe he can do something for you* came the answer. I'd stick around and see what happened.

"Third battalion, Fifth Marines out of Da Nang," Clark announced. "Spent most of my short time in-country patrolling the Que Son Valley. The NVA was pretty well dug in. They needed the rice."

I told him about the PBRs. We traded stories. He howled when I told him about shooting down our own chopper.

"My first action was interesting, too," Clark said, stroking his beard while looking into his memory. "It was March of '67. They flew us into the area south of Dak Sut. Came under machine gun fire not two steps outta the LZ. It was intense and coming from a densely wooded hillside. I'm not sure I got my face out of the turf the first ten minutes. Shit, we tried to silence that machine gun every which way. We launched grenades, called in artillery, called in the Cobras...nothing worked. Now, we're startin' to wonder who or what the hell is shooting at us. Finally, the sergeant put a perfect M79 round right on top the guy. We found the gook had been firing out of the turret of an old tank of ours. The dinks'd buried it into the hillside. They are resourceful little buggers."

So the stories went, back and forth. Once, a young coed walked by just as Clark was describing a sucking chest wound. Her expression said a lot about the times we were living in: young men with war experience and their peers who were revolted by them.

I knew we would eventually get to the main course: how Clark lost his legs and I got messed up. Clark's story was sad but, as Nam stories went, not so unusual.

"Ya know," he sighed, "it was just one of those things. We were on patrol north of Binh Son, walking through small villages and rice paddies. I stepped on a land mine planted on the bank of a stream. Three guys in front of me missed it. How about that for luck? I'd been in-country a little more than three months. That was, what?... Two and a half years ago. Lost both legs, a testicle, and damn near my pecker. I went to Nam six foot, 145. I left it four-two and ninety pounds," he finished, with a bitter laugh.

Clark was from New York City, the fourth-generation son in a family financial empire known as Milton Trust.

"My father is Milton Douglass III. In my family, it seems everyone but me is either a something-Milton or a Milton-something. I was named Clark after my maternal grandfather.

"I had an uncle on my mother's side who was a Marine in World War II. He was only in one battle, Iwo Jima. I don't know what you know about Iwo, but it was a fuckin' slaughter. My uncle was wounded the second day of the battle and was lying on a stretcher on the beach with other GIs. He said the Jap rounds kept coming in and guys on stretchers were being blown sky-high. So, my uncle got off his and made his way onto an LST. Some Navy dude told him he'd have to wait his turn. My uncle said, 'You don't understand...it is my turn.' I loved hearin' those stories when I was growin' up.

"My father forbid me to join the Marines, so naturally that sealed it. He won't listen to me anymore. We don't talk. I think he's embarrassed by my situation. Fuck'm. I'm here livin' on disability and goin' to school on the GI Bill. I chose Montana State because it was about as far away from New York as I could get."

The same night we met Sal at Manny's. After closing the Hof, Clark suggested the diner he'd seen nearby. I walked; he rolled.

"You ever gonna try artificial legs, Clark?"

"Don' know. I think they'd be a real hassle. The coaster's trouble enough, for now anyway."

We got to Manny's and discovered there weren't any tables, just a counter. But there was a spot near the middle where a stool was missing. Clark rolled into it like it was made for him.

"Look at this," Clark said. "Like it was waiting for me. I got a feelin' I'm gonna like this place."

"Boys," Sal said, introducing herself, "you look hungry and horny. All I can do is feed ya. What'll it be?"

1970

Bozeman, Montana

"People treat me like a freak. I know how lepers feel," Clark said. "So, I treat the perpetrators like shit. I've found it takes a lot of air out of their elitism, or pity, and somewhat levels the playing field."

This was my new friend. The one shouldering the bowling ball-sized chip.

"Usually we pitiful few see two reactions. One, they look away.... Cripple? What cripple? I don't see a cripple...or, maybe look through us like we don't exist...or, wish we didn't exist. And the opposite...abject empathy, retched sympathy, patronizing subservience.... Oh, here, let me wipe your ass, please. I hate both reactions. I hate the fucking world."

In his current state, not a people person.

"So, those who treat me like a little puppy...while thanking them profusely for their caring attention, I manage to roll onto their toes." He paused, chuckling. "They grimace and smile. They don't want to appear rude. They *never* complain. It pisses me off!"

I didn't think he was really that bad a guy. It was just his dark period.

Coming out of an orbit our college peers didn't appreciate or understand, we sat like a couple of burned-out rockets, scorched by our fiery reentry into society. We quickly became friends. Clark and I were two men clinging to the same piece of wood in the collective ocean of our new world. We sat out of the mainstream at our regular table next to the vending machines, having coffee in the Student Union.

Our coffee conversation was free-ranging and covered an endless array of subjects, but often turned to something that directly or indirectly involved the war. I was growing weary of the seeming inescapability of it all.

"So, you hittin' on any chicks? Got anything goin'?" Clark asked, out of nowhere.

Damn! That was just a little personal and a little sensitive at the moment.

"No," I said. "Uh...I'm having a little difficulty talking to girls right now. Not all girls. It seems just the ones that matter."

"Really?! The ones that *matter*? Interesting. I fantasize about women all the time, not that it'll ever happen for me."

"You don't know that," I said.

"Wake the fuck up, Cameron! While we're both missing a couple digits, mine make me just a tad bit less desirable. Who'd want me? Which of these lovelies in here would want to take care of the crip the rest of their lives?"

"I think you'd be surprised. Your attitude scares them off more than anything else, Clark. Be cool, man. Give it time."

"Give it fucking time!" Clark said. "Since this happened that's all I've heard...give it time. Well, I think now would be a pretty damn good time!" he said, banging the table. "I don't wanna wake up forty years old and wonder if it's *time* yet. I can't wait that long!"

"Knock it off!" I said. "You just make it worse with all this bullshit. Give it a rest; get past it...or life really will get away from you."

"Sorry...Dad."

I wasn't sure how much more of Clark I could take. Every conversation included two or three such outbursts, and I was often ruefully blunt in response. To his credit, Clark seemed to take my rebukes in stride.

"So," Clark said, calming down, "you can't talk to girls. No, excuse me...the ones *that matter*. Why not?"

Inside, I cringed. It was like having to explain body odor or the clap. I would rather have avoided the subject altogether. Clark tapped his fingers, waiting for a response.

"I don't know what to say. I never had this problem before. I feel their look on my face, my hand...I should break the ice, say something funny. But it's like everything I can think of is so...stupid and pointless."

"But, what about that girl in Helena...uh, Lucy?"

"Lucy's good in the sack. No, she's *great* in the sack, actually. But that's not what I'm talkin' about. We never have anything beyond sex."

Clark looked at me, eyebrows raised. "What the *hell* is wrong with that? Jesus H., Cameron. I'd...oh, man, you got it rough."

"I need the kinda girl you really like to spend time with...talkin' about life, family, art, books, sports, politics. Someone to care for...

and, if I'm lucky, maybe love. That's what I'd like, right now. But...
when I meet that kind of girl I turn into an idiot."

"Well," Clark said, sighing, "give it time."

I was concerned the war would go on in my head forever; afraid
the trauma would not end. The insecurity, the nightmares, anger
and paranoia had to end sometime, didn't they? Would I ever feel
comfortable in society, or in the presence of a beautiful, cultured
woman?

With these thoughts filling my head, I walked out the front
door of the Student Union and smack into the middle of a peace
rally. It was like stumbling into *This Is Your Life*. I found myself
standing before an audience of about two hundred sign-carrying
war protesters and next to a long-haired kid with a bullhorn. Everyone was looking at me. Finally, he said, "Hey, man, wanna join
us...or somethin'? We're havin' a rally here."

"Sorry," I said. I walked down the steps and through a crowd
that parted before me.

"He's one of 'em," someone in the crowd said. I increased my
pace.

"He's one of those murdering assholes from Nam...aren't ya?!"
came the voice, more insistent now.

I kept walking, though every face turned my way, willing me to
stop. It felt as if I were dragging anchor.

"Hey, man."

A hand grabbed me by the upper arm and I stopped. I looked
at the hand holding me back; followed it up to a pimpled face
sprouting sparse blond whiskers.

"You're one of those killers, aren't you? I've seen you around...
heard guys talkin' about you. You don't belong on a college campus."

I pulled away from him, trying to leave. He caught my arm
again. I could feel my face reddening as the anger rose.

"I think we deserve some answers. You don't come to a peace
rally unless you want peace. How about you, man? You want
peace?"

"Yeah," I said, looking pointedly at the hand holding my arm
and then back to the bandanna-headed menace. "I want peace.
More than any of you. I had to deal with a lotta hell. Peace is all

I'm really searching for, man. So, whaddya say...how about takin' your hand off and leavin' me alone?"

"Here we have a killer," the kid said. "Certifiable. Did you like it, man? Get your rocks off blowin' away kids and old ladies like Lieutenant Calley and his goon platoon?"

"He wasn't at My Lai, puke."

It was Clark. He had rolled up to us.

"You don't know who you're talkin' to," Clark continued. "This guy's a decorated hero. Saved his whole crew..."

The kid interrupted Clark with a scoff.

"Here's what this war is *all* about," he said, expanding his arms to include Clark and me. "Without guys like the two of you...who gladly go to war...we wouldn't have wars, now would we? Someone make you pick up those guns? Someone make you sight and pull the trigger? Tell us, man...what made you *kill*?"

"It wasn't for the sake of little jerks like you," Clark said.

Now the crowd around us was getting into it. We were just what this rally needed.

"Ya shoulda said no!"

"War's not the answer."

"You won't get any pity from us...," the bandannaed brainiac said.

"I sure as hell don't want it!" Clark spat out.

"...because you guys got what you deserved."

"Jesus! What I wouldn't give for two good legs," Clark said, rolling up to the kid and grabbing at him.

In response, the kid gave Clark's coaster a hard shove with his foot. The thing slid sideways and tipped Clark onto the concrete as the crowd gasped, perhaps sensing the kid's reaction was over the line. I don't think mine was.

I grabbed the hair at the back of the little twerp's head and punched him hard in the face with my left fist. He crumpled at my feet, hands flying to his gushing nose. There were gasps followed by murmurs of protest all around, but no one approached. I stood with fists clenched. I would take them all on.

"Hey, no violence, man," bullhorn boy said, broadcasting to the campus. "Haven't you guys had enough of that?"

"Shut the fuck up!" I yelled back at him. "You call this a peace rally?!" I said, looking around. "What kind of people are you?"

The crowd was silent as I went over and helped Clark back into his coaster. A coed lent a hand.

"Damn it!" Clark said. "Let me roll over that little cocksucker a couple times."

"We've dealt with enough shit already," I said to the crowd. "We aren't asking for your sympathy...or support. But, ya know, if you guys wanna have a *peace* rally, try goin' to war first...or ask us about it. Guys like us...we remember what peace is. It's all we're lookin' for."

"Right on," Clark said.

I rolled Clark away from the scene, both of us looking past the parting faces. When we had left the crowd and were in a quiet part of the campus, I heard a sob from the seat below. Clark was crying. I stopped and stepped around the coaster, crouching to face him.

"What's this?" I asked.

He lifted his tear-streaked face to me. "This is one of the things I fear most. I'll be confronted with assholes from time to time and I won't be able to do a fuckin' thing about it. And, oh yeah, they seek out people like me because they know I can't do a goddamn thing to 'em. It's so fucked! I wanted so badly to jump up and punch that little shit. Thanks for that, man...but will you be there when it happens next time? Or the time after? No...this is my fucked reality."

"Hmm...," I said. "Nope, you get nothing from me, Clark. 'Cause, ya know...I *know* you. You're one mean, nasty son of a bitch. Nobody's ever gonna take advantage of you.... In fact, I feel sorry for the world out there that'll have to deal with *you*.... By the way, thanks for rollin' to my defense. That took courage."

"It's nothin', man. Us vets have to stick together. You're right... about me. I'm gonna have to get sharper dealin' with people. But brother, what I wouldn't give for two good legs."

1998

My drive out of Bozeman was a parade of old haunts: the Allen Theater, 4B's restaurant, Baucus Pub, and the old St. George and the Dragon, my favorite beer and pool hall, though it was now a clothing store. A town becomes part of the college experience, especially the bars and eateries. There was Manny's, the Hof, and Molly Brown. Many nights spent with marijuana, tequila, and beer. I was always accompanied by Clark and often by my freshman year roommate, Tim, who drove over from Helena on weekends to party in the college town. Every weekend we hit it hard and did our best to bed every woman we could.

Though I'm embarrassed about those hedonistic days, I actually miss them. The largest portion of our lives includes huge, consuming rations of responsibility and career and societal pressure. Yes, it was *damn* good to be young and stupid once. To spend most of my waking moments in the pursuit of nothing more than a good time. Every person should experience such a time in their life.

From Junior High through my first year of college, my old friend and roommate, Tim Woodley, had been a constant companion. But he just wasn't that interested in school and had dropped out after our freshman year. That hardly meant Tim wasn't sharp enough. He was plenty smart. Tim was a geek—a geek that still lived with his parents in Helena. He'd sported the same glasses and haircut since I'd first met him, though his hair was a little longer now. Most weekends I was at school, Tim would show up for some good times and sleep on the floor of our apartment.

"Let's go. Where's Clark?" Tim said.

"Over in the corner...sleeping," I said.

"Passed out again, huh. Where's the girl he was with?"

"There," I said, pointing out the young lady dancing wildly with some cowboy.

"Too bad. I thought he might get lucky."

"Clark's gotta learn to pace himself. He can't start the night matching us in shots of tequila. He forgets he doesn't have legs to put booze in," I said.

"That's mean," the woman on my right said. Her name was Mary or Marty; I couldn't recall at the moment.

"Not the way I mean it," I said. "I'm Clark's friend and roommate and I'm only stating the obvious. Tol' him the same myself."

"Let's split," Tim said.

"I'll grab Clark," I said.

We rolled him out to his van, a brand new Ford Econoline with a power platform for the coaster and hand controls for the driver. Clark could actually drive himself anywhere he wanted. I couldn't guess what the rig must have cost, maybe seven or eight thousand. A lot. Clark's dad bought the van and had it delivered. In the time Clark and I had known each other I'd had the opportunity to talk with Clark's father on several occasions. It seemed to me, contrary to Clark's opinion, that he cared deeply for his son.

Tim winched the snoozing Clark up into the van. The young lady of the moment, whom I now remembered was named Marty, planted a big kiss on me as we stood by the van. She worked her tongue inside my mouth while moving her leg suggestively between mine. I wondered what had happened to the gum she had been chewing. Oh, yeah...there it was.

"Wanna come to our place?" she said, again chewing the gum like a cow on speed.

"Sure, right on. But, don't you guys work tomorrow?"

"It's all right. We do this all the time. Life's short. The fun's waiting."

I drove the van. Tim rode shotgun and we had Clark secured in the back. I followed the girl's Datsun down Main toward the east end of Bozeman. Clark stirred and swore.

"What?... Where the hell? Wha' happened to...uh..."

"You passed out again, Clark. She split with some cowboy. You didn't take any downers tonight, did you?"

"No. Damn, I liked her." His head drooped and he was gone again.

"That Marty's real cute," Tim said. "I'd rate her a seven."

"I give her a five-five," I said. "I don't like the gum thing. I know these girls we pick up aren't, uh, refined, but it'd be nice if they knew a few three-syllable words. I'd give yours a six, at least."

"Naw. No more than a five. I mean, that laugh! I couldn't take it for more than one night."

"You're wrong. Those tits are a five all by themselves," I said.

"Point, er, points taken. But we're agreed, it's tough findin' a ten, man. I mean, how many have we even known?"

"Hmm...my high school girlfriend was a solid nine, nine and a half."

"Jan Fred? A ten," Tim said.

"Then there was my school-boy crush, Julie Wicks...Katy's sister," I said, wistfully.

"The cheerleader? Eleven with a star," Tim said. Then, "Shit! I forgot to tell you. Just before I left Helena today I heard that Ray Reamer was in a car accident. He's in the hospital and word is he won't make it. I heard he's brain dead."

I slowed the van, listening to Tim's words.

"I guess he was driving drunk on the highway that goes around Flathead Lake and nailed a tree doin' about eighty."

"What about Katy?" I said. "Tell me she wasn't with him."

Tim deliberated. "I don't think she was. I heard the news from Don Davis and his girl. Shit...they didn't mention Katy and I didn't think to ask."

I'd pulled over to the side of the road and was just staring at Tim. Looking away, I could see the reflection in the windshield of my hands gripping the wheel, and the face of a lovely young bride as she danced off with her new husband.

"Sorry, Mark. I should've asked. I was in a hurry and it just skipped my mind. I'm sure she's all right. They didn't mention her."

The Datsun pulled up next to the van. Marty was saying something. I rolled down the window.

"Huh?"

"I said what're ya doin'? You coulda lost us."

"Yeah, uh, sorry. Go ahead. I'm with you."

Marty gave me a funny look and a shrug, rolling up the window as she did a U-turn in the middle of Main Street and sped away. I pulled out and followed.

Tim and I were quiet then, thinking. The now familiar dread hit me and I shuddered. I didn't need to lose another friend. Certainly not Katy Wicks.

"There's a ten I know," I said, breaking the silence. "Katy Wicks. Ten all the way."

1973

Bozeman, Montana

I downshifted and pushed the pedal to the floor. My bug slowly picked up speed as I swung around the Cadillac with its *Nixon's The One* bumper sticker. As I cleared the Caddie's front bumper, I abruptly pulled in front of the car, spraying snow and gravel on the offensive vehicle. I wanted the driver to get a good look at my *Don't Blame Me—I Voted for McGovern* bumper sticker.

I turned off Wilson Avenue going a bit too fast, the bug scraping bottom while bouncing wildly over the ruts of ice and snow. As I roared down the street the car careened left and right like a bucking bronc, trying to lurch out of the deep icy paths made by much bigger cars. Approaching a side street, I attacked the side window with the scraper I kept in one hand, looking quickly for oncoming vehicles. As I reached the house I threw the car into a sideways skid, launching it quickly up the sloped drive before skidding to a stop. I turned the engine off just as the first hint of heat escaped from the defrost.

Carrying a stack of books resembling A–L of *Encyclopedia Britannica*, I made my way to the front door, glancing up the main mall of campus as I did so. A pearly sunset washed the boulevard between grand, silhouetted buildings. I paused a moment, attempting to frame and save the vision for some future film project.

The place Clark and I rented wasn't much, just a small postwar home with two tiny bedrooms. But if it's all about location, we were living the high life. Our house was just a stone's throw from campus in housing-starved Bozeman. It helped that Clark was a double amputee war veteran with a Republican mother who personally knew the secretary of Housing and Urban Development.

As I opened the door the sounds of Zeppelin and the smell of dinner enveloped me. The song was "Ramble On." I couldn't decipher the aroma.

"If that's Hamburger Helper again, you are in deep shit," I yelled, walking to the kitchen.

"Don't worry, I'd never do that more than three nights in a row," Clark said.

NAM, *The Story of a Generation*   271

"Good."

"We're having Tuna Helper. See, it's new."

"Shit."

I dropped the books and flopped into a chair at the table. "I just kicked rocks and snow on a Caddie with a Nixon sticker. It felt good."

"He's okay. His man won."

Clark, politically savvy and of Republican roots, made a game of getting my goat.

"If Johnson hadn't signed the Civil Rights Act the Republicans would still be nowhere on the map," he said. "The guy single-handedly lost the South for the Democrats...maybe forever. And McGovern, please! 'I support Eagleton one-thousand percent.' Ha!"

"Hell, why don't you just join the Young Republicans and get it over with, Clark."

"Ouch. That wasn't very nice."

"Better a nine hundred percent McGovern than that...criminal in the White House," I said.

"Hey, that criminal in the White House got the peace accord signed and finished the fucking war for us."

"Bullshit! The Democratic Congress made it impossible for him to continue the war. Nixon had no choice."

"Nixon's administration ended it. That's just sour grapes."

"Ended? What kind of end? What kind of peace?" I said. "You think the North Vietnamese have any plans whatsoever of honoring this agreement?"

Clark didn't respond right away. I'd hit the nail on the head. The peace accord was as phony and politically shallow as the whole war had been.

"It doesn't matter, does it? We've all known for years this war was lost," Clark said. "By '68 we really knew, didn't we? I'll tell you how I feel. I feel like the beaten and bloodied boxer who was still... standing...at the end, damn glad the fight was over and not giving a shit if he won or not."

It was how I felt, too. Bud Brody, of course, had been right so many years before. Winning in Vietnam was impossible. Our smartest politicians, or best military minds, our bravest soldiers could not win such a war. Like the tough lessons you learn in life, I just hoped this mistake would never be repeated.

We ate all the Tuna Helper; it was a nice change of pace. Clark cooked, so I washed the dishes. Finishing the job, I yelled to him in the next room.

"I have to go to the library tonight. You wanna come?"

"No...I was at the, uh, library this afternoon," he shouted back, "and the most amazing thing happened!"

I came to the doorway. Clark turned his chair to face me, mischief about his face. I knew the look and was instantly on guard. There was a prank about.

"I happened to make the acquaintance of a stunning coed," he continued.

"Really? Someone special?"

"Oh, yeah...you could say *that*."

"Sooo..."

"I asked her over," he said.

He looked at me in an even more mischievous, twinkly sort of way. Uh-oh.

"All right, Clark. I've seen this before. What's up?"

"Well...you know how it is. It's complicated. She's coming over to the house Saturday night and I want this to be special. Candlelight, soft music...it's gotta be nice. And, you're gonna help me pick up this place. We don't want her thinking we live in a pigsty."

"Uh-huh. Okay. She must be something 'special.'"

"I want lots of atmosphere. Let's have wine, little crackers and cheese...the works."

As I stood looking at him I knew I had to ask the question. "Uh...all right, just asking—not being judgmental—but, what about Heather?"

Immediately his manner changed. I got Clark's quiet, contemplative look. The pregnant pause.

"I resent that question," he said. "Coming from you...a guy who's never been faithful to any girl I've ever known about. Heather and I are none of your business."

"Yup, got it. Just asking, man. What time is...what's her name?...coming over?"

"Eight o'clock sharp, and I want to make sure we're ready in plenty of time. So, don't screw this up and spend all afternoon with the guys shooting pool and drinking beer."

"No, no...c'mon, Clark. I'll be here. We'll get some nice incense to go with the candles. We'll put Gordon Lightfoot on the stereo and have wine on ice."

"Yeah, that's the idea. Man, I can't wait to see her again. It was just...unbelievable, this chick. Instant karma. We clicked and she is one nice babe. You're gonna like her," he said.

While I was happy for Clark, I was disappointed for Heather. She had single-handedly brought about a return to sanity in Clark. I thought I saw lifetime commitment from both of them. However, I would not be playing "Virtuous Man" anytime soon. Not with my track record. Like Clark said, it was none of my business.

Hanoi, North Vietnam

The crowd moved smoothly through the doors and out onto the plaza. The new play's premiere had just ended and the elite of Hanoi's social strata dispersed in chatty groups. Among the early departures, Dat and Lee Nah walked side by side. Nah grabbed Dat's hand and put her arm through his.

"Lee Nah!" Dat exclaimed, looking around. "You should not do this. There are too many people around for such a show of affection."

"What, you dislike my touch? There is nothing wrong with showing affection in public. I am not afraid of what others might think, and I do not believe the state minds. If people talk, it does not bother me. Did you like the play, Dat?"

Dat had hated the play. It was the same overblown state-sponsored propaganda; the same tired old story, just different characters and costumes. The Americans were portrayed as nothing more than vicious dogs. Dat wondered if anyone at the play had spent even a minute with an American. But, he knew well the reasons why every play and movie produced glorified war. It had long since gotten old with him, though. He longed for a cultural experience that dipped into the classics of the world, or maybe even comedy.

"The play was fine," he said.

"I loved the costumes and sets...the choreography," Lee Nah said. "It was one of the best plays I have ever seen."

In the group just behind the couple came the generals Minh, Giap, and Tran Van Minh.

"Say," Minh exclaimed. "It appears something is blooming between our two rising stars." All three smiled at the thought.

"Such a nice couple. Really, the perfect pairing...don't you agree?" Giap commented.

Each nodded in agreement.

As they settled into the back of their limousine, Lee Nah snuggled in next to Dat, content. This made Dat uncomfortable, and he decided he must reveal to Lee Nah his situation before their relationship was compromised even further.

"Lee Nah," Dat said, looking into her lovely face. "My feelings for you...well, I do not think I have to explain. We have, as they say, history. But we are not fifteen years old anymore. Much time and many experiences have come through the years...years in which, honestly, I did not think of you. You were out of my life. Who could ever have anticipated what has happened? This is all new, you and I...and unsettling."

"Unsettling?" Lee Nah said. "I do not understand what you mean."

"It is...not easy for me to explain," Dat said. "My feelings for you are...torn."

"Torn? Now I am more confused. What are you trying to say, Dat?"

"There is a girl...," Dat said, and abruptly stopped, not knowing how to continue.

Lee Nah, seeing guilt on his face as he looked away, sat upright and turned to Dat. "Another girl?"

"Yes. There is another woman in my life, Lee Nah. It is very difficult to explain."

Lee Nah was shocked. Though she had wondered what Dat's hesitation and awkward moments meant, another woman never entered her mind. Dat was a soldier; a dedicated soldier who had had very little time for romance. She was speechless. Dat spoke first.

"As you probably have deduced, she is in the South. A chance meeting, but someone I have very strong feelings for. We have made a commitment to one another."

"A commitment? Who are we talking about, Dat? Is this one of the cadre in the tunnels?"

"Uh, no. Nothing like that."

"Nothing like that?! What else is there?"

"She's a Southerner. Born and raised in Cholon."

Lee Nah was speechless again. The unlikelihood of such an arrangement and its political and military ramifications were astounding.

"I can hardly believe what I am hearing, Dat. You have a Southern woman you've made a commitment to? Who is this person? Will you marry her...is that the plan...the commitment?"

Dat said nothing.

"Tell me about her. I must know."

"A chance meeting on a street corner," Dat started. "She was pleasant. I was playing the role of a peasant farmer, doing a little reconnaissance...and though she was a young, cultured woman, she was...very nice to me. I thought that was extraordinary.

"Since that meeting I have seen her two other times..."

"You've seen this woman a total of three times?"

"Yes."

Lee Nah sat back in her seat, shaking her head. "Three times. When was the last time you saw her?"

"Just before I was assigned to duty here."

"And you feel that these three meetings are enough to push aside our lifetime of deep feelings for one another...our own commitments?"

Dat thought on this. "Nu Chi, the young lady, and I have no... solid plans for the future...as of yet. Like I said, Lee Nah, I am torn."

"Seriously, Dat? You would consider this woman over me? I cannot believe what I am hearing because it makes no sense. If it got out that you were involved with a Southerner there would be some very tough questions for you to answer."

"Yes, I am very aware of that, Lee Nah."

"You do not think I might be the one to reveal this to Minh or Giap?"

"Yes, I understand, but what else am I to do? You have obvious romantic feelings for me...and I will not deny the feelings I have are...somewhat mutual...but I cannot be unfaithful to two women. I am not some gigolo who plays around with women's feelings."

Lee Nah sighed, and looked beautiful.

"Please, do not mention this to anyone else, Dat. I will not betray you...or give you up to another woman. I would like to think your feelings for me are the same I have for you...without this... *inconvenience* attaching itself. The likelihood of you ever seeing this woman again is remote at best, and I believe with time you will see what you have in Hanoi, in me, is far more desirable. Time has a way of changing things. I would like to think our best times are yet to come."

Boa Hanh stood in the doorway, the orders crumpled in his hand. His mother, distracted and fussing with her secretary over the wording of some document, didn't see him. As the two prattled on, Hanh became incensed at being unnoticed, his anger boiling over.

"Linh Mao!" he shouted.

The two women looked up as one—surprise on the secretary's face, immediate anger on his mother's.

"You will leave us...please."

The secretary looked in question at Gao Jinh, who nodded and settled back in her chair as the secretary, glancing up once with frightened eyes, scurried from the room, closing the door behind her.

A little of the rage and bravado went out of him as Hanh observed the smoldering fury in his mother's eyes. He swallowed and steeled himself as he strode forward with the damning orders raised in his fist.

"New orders!" he said. "I am being sent south! Do not tell me you know nothing of this."

"And *do not*," Gao Jinh said, "raise your voice to me, Colonel. I am not one of the young cadre zealots you are humping in the barracks."

The temple of fury and resolve Hanh had built while storming his mother's office collapsed, and was carried away like a castle of sand in the onrushing tide.

"Yes...I know what goes on in the back rooms at Xuan Mai. Instead of doing the work of discovery on Le Van Dat, you diddle away the time in other pursuits. Disgusting!"

Hanh looked away, mumbling a curse, while Gao Jinh nimbly picked up a cigarette and placed it carefully in a slender jade holder.

"Surely that is not the reason I am being sent south?" Hanh

said. "Why are you doing this? Especially now that Xuan Mai is finally to be under my command!"

Gao Jinh sighed while inspecting her fingernails. "We are refitting and reinforcing our troops in the South, Hanh. High-ranking political officers, such as yourself, are much in demand...after our latest catastrophe. It is a great opportunity for you," Gao Jinh said, lighting her cigarette with a flourish.

"But...we have rebuilt in the South many times...throughout the war."

"Yes, but this will be different."

Hanh felt his frustration rising again. "You will send me off to battle then...your only son," he said.

Gao Jinh glowered and sat forward, slamming the desk with her hand. "YES!... You cowardly idiot!"

She turned and launched herself out of the chair, pacing quickly to the windows. She stood with the cigarette holder balanced in her left hand, her right planted on her hip. A slight bend of the leg sent a knee peeking through the slit in her tight-fitting dress. The drabness of gray silk was her only concession to the uninspiring official Maoist party uniform, which she adamantly refused to wear.

Hanh trembled with indignation.

"I do not understand, Mother. Everything we have worked for...and with the rice farmer now permanently attached to the general staff..."

Gao Jinh sighed heavily, cutting him off with a pitiful look.

"You lost that battle, Hanh! Everything has changed," she said. "If I did not know better I would not believe you are my son...or your father's. How could it be that you do not understand what has transpired?"

Hanh said nothing. As practiced as he was, he found it difficult to keep his frustrations from reaching his face.

"Forget Xuan Mai!" Gao Jinh said. "The South is finished! Consensus in the Politburo is the war cannot possibly last more than two or three more years. The commandant's post at Xuan Mai means nothing now. Politically, the position has diminished to that of a lighthouse keeper! The next challenge, the next heroes, will be those waving our flag over the presidential palace in Saigon. From them we will find our future leaders. You are my son and I must save you. It is time you joined the war."

"But, Mother...the B-2 front? Saigon? General Tra? I am to serve with this...Southerner?!... This outcast! Certainly, a better posting, any posting, could have been found."

Gao Jinh sat on the divan by the windows, crossing her legs Western style.

"One of us is a politician and has wonderful foresight," she said. "When you are accepted into the Politburo, you can thank me for this and I will expect...much."

"Thank?" Hanh started, thought better, and caught himself. "Mother...Tran Van Tra is the single most reviled commander we have. He is advancing the same tired Saigon strategy he sold the Politburo for the '68 Great Offensive. It did not work then; why now? Saigon is a fortress! Who will believe in this man and his delusions?"

"I am not sure which, or why...but there is either too much of the scientist or the Communist about you, Hanh. Or perhaps you are just lazy. Where in hell is the politician?

"Tra is correct and has more supporters than you obviously believe. Do not put so much faith in the Thieu government. US aid cannot save him now. His corruption is contagious and has spread to every facet of the military...though there are many of my comrades who do not see it. Fools. The war cannot be won until Saigon falls. When it does you must be there! As a high-ranking political officer you will receive much credit...and with it, rewards."

Hanh further crumpled the orders in his hand, his anger again rising.

"Saigon. Many men will die taking Saigon."

Gao Jinh let him simmer as she painstakingly inspected her nails again.

"But not you," she said at last, now looking at her son with wide eyes, seeing something not quite there. "You...will not die before the war ends. You are a survivor. You will find a way to save yourself...and," she said, smiling, "steal the glory. In *that* way you *are* so much like your father. Survivor?... Without question. And... perhaps, hero?"

January 23, 1973
Dearest,
My sorrow is as profound as my country's despair. Our

hopes have vanished with the signing of the shameful peace agreement. It is the end for us in the South. Father has seen a copy of the proposal and agrees with our president that it is nothing more than a surrender document. The American president has made private assurances to Thieu. Promises of continued financial and military support. It is an empty guarantee from a fading president. Your victory is assured.

Father has secured American visas. He wishes to leave Vietnam immediately and, of course, the family will go as well. You remember my promise to never live under communism? It was not a hollow declaration made lightly.

I have prayed and meditated over this a long while. If there were any other way, any other course, I would take it. But there will be nothing but trouble and ruin in my country, and I will not stay behind to see the Communists parade through the streets of Saigon.

Father has fixed his sights on San Francisco. There is a historic and cultured Asian population in the Bay Area. My only hope now is that God will protect and save you, enlighten you, and bring you to my arms in America.

Forever Yours,
Nu Chi

Bozeman, Montana

"You didn't get that mess off the end table yet," Clark said, pointing at the offending stack of old papers and notebooks.

"For chrissakes, Clark. She knows we're students. It's not supposed to be spotless."

"I told you I want it nice. Let's start with a good impression, huh?"

I took care of the mess, dumping it in a closet, and turned to look the room over. Neat and tidy. Incense burned, a bottle of Matteus chilled in an old ice cream bucket, about a dozen candles burned as Helen Reddy sang from the stereo. Perfect.

"Yes," Clark said. "We are ready and...just in time," he finished, looking at his watch.

I looked at my own.

"Actually, plenty of time. There's more than a half hour before she arrives. I told Ken and Jim I'd meet 'em at the Molly Brown. So, I guess I'll..."

I was interrupted by the doorbell. Clark and I looked at one another.

"Is she early?" I asked.

"No," he said. "I don't think she'd be this early. Must be somebody else."

I opened the door to a smiling Heather, who pushed by me saying, "Hi, Mark."

Holy shit! Bad timing.

"Oh, say...it's very mellow in here. Nice," she said.

With her back to me, I did a little charade to Clark that essentially signaled *What the fuck do we do now?*

Ignoring me, Clark smiled and greeted Heather warmly. "Hey, babe. It's all for you 'cause you are a righteous woman who needs lots of romancing."

"We're expecting friends, Heather. Friends of mine," I said. "But, uh, of course it's always nice to see you."

She gave me a puzzled look, then, "Yes, okay. Well, I'm gonna just run to the bathroom quickly. Be right back," Heather said, pecking a smiling Clark on the cheek as she went. He watched her walk away and sighed contentedly.

As soon as she was gone, I jumped Clark.

"What the fuck are we gonna do now? Didn't you tell her you were busy tonight or somethin'? And, I don't care what kind of '70s relationship you've got going on here, Clark, you're in some deep shit my friend. What'll we do? What'll you tell her when this other chick shows up?"

"Whoa, whoa, whoa. Slow down, Mark. Everything's under control. I guarantee you I can handle Heather and this situation. Just be patient and watch," he said.

"Oh, yeah. I'm gonna watch all right...watch you get toasted, you dumb shit!"

"You're overreacting, Cameron. Trust me. I know what I'm doing here."

Well, what else could I do? "Sure, pal. I'm cool. It's *your* problem," I said, flopping into my inflatable chair.

Heather came back from the bathroom and spied the Matteus. "Oh, are we having wine?"

"Yes, my darling," Clark said, rolling over to the wine. "Get some glasses, sweetheart."

I rolled my eyes. What the hell was he doing? I checked my watch at the same time Clark was checking his. Twenty-five 'til. There was still time. Meanwhile, I was desperately searching my mind for old excuses and cover-ups I'd used. Heather returned with four glasses and put them on the table as Clark finished opening the wine.

When the doorbell went off a second time, I jumped. Time to seriously panic! Clark looked coolly at me. Heather smiled, radiantly.

"Well, Mark...aren't you going to answer the door?"

"Sure, Clark. I'll get the door," I said. I hadn't come up with anything. I went to the door resigned to being the witness of a calamity. Saying a silent prayer for deliverance, I opened the door... and my prayer was answered.

There are moments in life that change everything, irrevocably altering the course you were traveling and replacing it instantaneously with a new set of tomorrows. Standing before me was a woman so beautiful—heart, soul, and skin—I realized I had spent years measuring the beauty and worth of every other woman against her.

"Hello, Mark," Katy said. "Weren't you expecting me?"

Hanoi, North Vietnam

Dat faced away from his desk, soaking up the sunshine and enjoying the fresh air. Workers quietly scurried around him, repairing and replacing the glass of his office windows. He was reading the post-invasion inspection report of the failed 1972 Easter Offensive. Dat found General Dung's bold and candid analysis of the defeat a delight; straightforward and deadly accurate in its conclusions.

The offensive had kicked on March 30, 1972. With America now disengaging and facing only ARVN forces on the ground, the Politburo had seized an opportunity to finish the South while the Americans were still officially deployed. With the massive infusion of tanks, artillery, and supplies from Russia, victory was thought possible—a victory that would have been a huge embarrassment for the Americans.

But once again, age-old problems had arisen: supply, communications, logistics. Giap's faltering battle plan had been laid bare, resulting in the heroic general being sacked as commander of the army. Mostly, though, as the report pointed out in one short paragraph, the Americans had a big hand in the defeat.

No small amount of responsibility for our defeat can be put on American air support. The B-52 attacks on the People's Forces, close support of ARVN ground troops, supply air lifts and medical evacuation by the American air forces greatly affected the enemy's strategic situation and morale. ARVN forces seemed motivated and fought well in this conflict.

The damn Americans! They had ruined the day once again... and had taken Nu Chi from him as well. In the aftermath, sorrow and anger consumed him. America seemed bent on taking away any happiness he might find in life. Nu Chi wanted him to migrate to America! No! It was the hopeless fantasy of a young woman.

He knew he could not continue to dwell on this turn of events. It had affected his performance. His health had suffered as well. Either he would come to grips with his new destiny or...

"Deep in thought, I see," Minh said from the doorway. Dat spun in his chair to see the general taking a seat across from his desk. "Feeling any better, my friend?"

Dat ignored the oft-repeated question.

"Just reading Dung's inspection report; an enlightened review."

"Uh-huh...you did not answer my question. Something continues to bother you, Dat. It takes an old friend to see it clearly. I wish you would confide in me."

"I am fine, Minh. This bombing...and work, you know. Perhaps a small retreat would be good for me."

"Of course," Minh said immediately. "A few days away would do you wonders. Get out of this mess, forget things, and just enjoy yourself for a change."

"I am thankful the bombing is over...or seems over. Maybe our lives can move forward now," Dat said, turning to the windows.

"No one was spared," Minh said. "We are lucky only the windows went. This building seems to be one of the only governmental edifices still standing. The Americans did quite a job this time."

Nixon, furious at North Vietnam and Le Duan for snubbing Kissinger at the peace talks, had started the Christmas bombing campaign on December 18, while American college students were on their holiday break. The bombing had continued nonstop for eleven days. Unlike in the past, though, the Americans seemed to finally understand what they needed to do. Every facility, structure, road, airport, or standing "thing" of perceived military or industrial value in the North had been bombed to rubble. The fighters, bombers, and B-52s had come in wave after wave, days and nights on end. In the final three days of the campaign, the North had run out of SAMs and had literally nothing with which to bring down the American planes or stop their new "smart" bombs from hitting choice targets. Haiphong Harbor had been mined. All roads, railroads, and airfields had been ruined. The entire military industrial complex of the North had been eliminated.

"I am glad," Dat said, "they did not do this earlier in the war. No heroic or gallant effort by the people could have overcome this devastation."

"Yes, it was all too late. Good fortune was on our side. The righteous always prevail."

"So," Dat said, looking up with a smile. "Office rumor is Nixon drove us back to the bargaining table...that the Christmas bombing did the job. You agree?"

"You think I would so easily reveal Politburo secrets?" Minh replied. "Nixon is a madman. With all the pressure he faces to scale down the war...to launch an eleven-day, nonstop bombing campaign...is the absolute last thing one would expect. Yes, yes... much like his Cambodian invasion. He is a dangerous, unpredictable man.

"But...there were many other factors. It seems Nixon has won over the Chinese and Russians. Both were ominously silent to the Christmas bombing...something that would not have happened in the past. There has been...a political shift.

"And, no, we would not have defeated the South while the Americans remained. The Easter Offensive proved it once and for all. So now the old guard in the Politburo knows it, too. The bombing *inspired* us to peace."

"But the peace agreement is very accommodating for us...you agree?" Dat said.

"Accommodating?! My friend, it's like having Kissinger shine your shoes. As decisive a defeat as the Easter Offensive was for us...as bold and ruinous as Nixon's bombing campaign...it was all too late. The American people had obviously run out of patience. Exactly as Chairman Ho had predicted."

"Now...will they return?" Dat said. "I have studied the Americans a long time, Minh. As they have shown repeatedly, they are proud and determined. Keeping a few carriers off the coast would be easy enough. As you said, Nixon is unpredictable."

"I agree. It is why the Politburo is seeking a political victory in the South instead of a military one. You have heard?"

"Yes," Dat said, "though that will never happen. Our Southern brethren despise Thieu and his government...but communism scares them even more. We will have to beat them with our military might. It is a matter of time...*and* what remains of the American will."

February 22, 1973
Dearest,

You spoke of destiny on that wonderful Sunday in Saigon that seems so long, long ago. My belief in such a destiny has since grown for, at the last minute, an American friend of my father, who persuaded him to allow me to remain and continue my work for the treasury. He said our work was vital to the successful cooperation between countries and that he could not afford the loss of both of us. With much proselytizing and an iron-clad promise to put me on the first flight out if the country falters, he coaxed father into an unlikely agreement.

My family has left for America. Father will be settling the family in Sacramento, California. When the time comes, I will join them there.

My emotions are so pulled in opposite directions these days! Our world is in constant turmoil and I am often depressed. My country cannot stand without the Americans. We know this inevitability and it is having a very bad effect on morale. Many people are out of work and inflation is ruining the economy. We have also lost faith in Thieu. No one, even the highest-ranking politicians, thought the Americans would abandon him.

Everyone I love is far away now and I have never been so lonely. I long for my family, just as I long to look upon your face one more time. Of course, you had more than a little to do with my agreeing to stay behind. You are the one love in my life and I could not bear the thought of leaving you so far behind. But once again I must state the inevitable, the obvious. Before the South falls I will leave Saigon.

So, why do I remain? What do I hope to accomplish? Do I await the final twist of the destiny you so strongly subscribe to? When your soldiers raise the Communist flag in Saigon, I will remain only in spirit. Where will you be then, my love?

Yours as Ever,
Nu Chi

1998

"How're the kids? Stan's team win? Did he score?"

"Sorry. They were shut out again."

"Crap. I'd like to see 'em win one."

"It doesn't matter. He has lots of fun. You should see him smile when the game's on. You're on the road awfully late today. You'll be tired in the morning."

"I took a side trip to the old neighborhood today."

"Really?"

"Yeah, I don't know what possessed me. The old place is different...and yet, much the same."

"Did you stop to see my father?"

"No. It was, you know, just me and my memories...and I didn't want your father messing it up. Talked with old man Anderson—geez, he looks old. He said Mabel Brody had died and that Buddy was back in Helena...has been for a while, I guess."

And so it went. Another call home from the road. This was one of the things I hated about my life. One of the things I'd decided this day to change. My kids were nearly grown, and I hadn't spent enough time being a dad, or husband. They deserved more.

The memory of the day Katy had arrived on my doorstep always brings a smile. It's perhaps my best memory ever. How utterly taken in I had been! You'd think I'd have caught on. The stunned, mute look on my face added to Clark and Heather's amusement, and they laughed themselves sick. I'd had to live with Clark's annual recreation of the moment ever since.

I knew the instant I opened the door, and she stood before me, that I would marry her. Somehow, I just knew. It didn't take long for us to bridge the gap that separates friends from lovers.

I had to be careful and force myself to go slow. I was nagged by an overpowering desire to wrap Katy in my arms, but I didn't want to freak her out. Play it cool, boy. But I knew, hoped really, that things would be much different between us now.

The flickering yellow glow of the candles sent shimmering

highlights cascading through her short blond hair. My arm was casually placed on the back of the sofa, and on occasion, I lightly stroked the hair at the back of her neck or touched her shoulder. I had to have that touch. At times, she put her hand briefly on mine or brushed my leg. Every touch, no matter how slight or brief, created a shiver. My heart swelled in my chest, seemingly cutting my breath short.

Clark and Heather had left, I thought. I was sure I had heard them say something on the way out.

"I wasn't sure I'd ever see you again," I said. "The last time..."

"I know, Mark. I know... and I'm so sorry about that."

"No, it was me. It was my ignorance coming out again. Emotion and immaturity are a really bad mix. God, I acted like such an idiot!"

"It was an emotional time for both of us. I think we can be forgiven."

I cringed as my thoughts went back to that day, when Ray Reamer died— no, before he died— all I could think about was Katy. She filled my thoughts; became my infatuation. In the process, the manner in which I'd always seen and treated Katy morphed into something very different. Something that had always been there, below the surface, working for a long, long time. She was the woman I'd been looking for all along— the woman I wanted to spend the rest of my life with. That thought slammed me like the recoil of a .50 cal. Katy? Little Katy from across the street? Yes. Absolutely! What an idiot I'd been. Why hadn't I seen this before!

With the revelation came sweeping anxiety. I *needed* to see her. Now. Today. I didn't want to spend another moment without her. I wanted to drive to Kalispell and throw myself on her.

Luckily, it's a long drive from Bozeman to Kalispell. Maybe a call first would be a good idea.

But, I didn't get through to her. Older sister Julie answered and coolly asked me to call back another time; Katy wasn't taking calls. I wouldn't be deterred. I asked again to speak to her, and now Julie got upset.

"Shit, Cameron! Give her a fuckin' break. She just lost her husband."

Then she hung up.

I couldn't let it go. I *had* to talk with Katy; console her and offer my love as a replacement for her loss. So, I called again, and again. I don't know how many times I called. Julie became totally exasperated; using some salty language I'd never even heard in the military. She threatened to call the sheriff and file a complaint.

Finally, Katy took the phone.

"Mark, you've got to stop calling here. My sister is driving me crazy and, no, I don't want to talk with anyone right now. Please stop."

"I'm sorry, Kate. I can't help myself. I really need to see you right now. I think I'm in love with you."

"What? That... Mark, I...I can't deal with this. Stop. Please, go away."

And she hung up.

I called again because I just didn't get it.

"This is ridiculous, Mark Cameron!" Katy shouted.

"Katy, I just..."

"Shut up, Mark!"

I was surprised. There followed the pregnant pause.

"The last time I saw you," she started, soft and slow, "was at Stanley's burial. You were in tough shape, Mark. I could see the struggle in your eyes. You looked like you wanted to run away from the world.

"Well, now, that's where I'm at. I've lost Stanley and Ray, and I'm the one who wants to run away. I look in the mirror and it reminds me of you in that graveyard. I'm no good to anyone right now. I need time and help with this."

"Katy, I can help you! We could be so good for each other. I'll come up..."

"Jesus Christ, Mark! Don't you get it? I don't want to see you. I don't want you dropping in and I don't want you calling anymore."

"Kate..."

"I'm moving out of state with Julie. I need to get away. Take my advice Mark—forget about me. You'll find someone else. Please, for the love of God, do not call me again."

And she hung up.

"So, you're better?" I said.

"I'm better," Katy replied.

"Well, I've come down to earth, a little," I said. "I don't know what got into me. Sometimes these days I just do crazy things. I made a fool of myself."

"Not totally. Once things settled a little, our last conversation played in my head. You'd said you loved me. That isn't something to take lightly. And, instead of focusing on the past, I began seeing something better in the future. It helped me come out of that funk. Then, like you in that crazy phone call, I knew I just had to see you.

"So, this little ruse with Clark… how'd you pull that off?"

"Tim gave me your phone number. Clark answered and said you weren't home. Jeez, he's just a great guy, isn't he?"

"Yeah, well…"

"This was all his idea. He's something of a prankster. But, honestly, I liked the idea. I wanted to see you, not just talk to you on the phone. I wanted to be with you. So, I let him set it up… and, here I am."

We shared a moment with only our eyes and senses communicating. She lowered her eyelids slightly as she stared intently into my eyes. Her mouth opened just a slice, and she ran her tongue lightly along her glossy lips. I thought I saw desire; knew I was sending that message. Yet, I was nervous. I'd known this woman all my life. In a way, she was like a sister. She seemed to read my mind.

"You need to forget about that little girl across the street, Mark. The one in diapers, the one following you and Stanley around, the one with the schoolgirl crush. She's gone forever. Me, on the other hand…you'd better kiss me, Mark. I don't think I can take much more of this."

I didn't hesitate, the little girl was immediately forgotten. The next morning, I awoke to discover that the life I had been looking for since Nam had begun.

1975

Hanoi, North Vietnam

They had never entered into the war for anything excepting total victory. To this end, the North had worked diligently for almost thirty years. The decades of sacrifices, the organization and exploitation of the masses for one purpose, the vast resources needed, acquired, and expended were awe-inspiring if not nearly impossible to comprehend. At times, magnificent failures were endured as if mere bumps in the road, never altering their national perspective or weakening their resolve. Brick by labored brick the wall that separated North from South had been torn down, and now all that awaited their hard-won victory was kicking over the remnants of that wall and marching on through.

In the Politburo and military committee conferences of December 1974, General Tran Van Tra had shocked both the committee and the military operations officer by suggesting the proposed attack on Duc Lop was of no significance and that, if they wanted to make the effort worthwhile, Ban Me Thuot was the choice target. The military committee did not agree with Tra's unsolicited, and largely unwelcomed, idea. But Le Duc Tho, other Southern influences, and select members of the committee, including Tran Van Minh and Le Van Dat, saw the wisdom of Tra's strategy and supported the idea. Of course, egos had been bruised and a bitter debate raged. In the end, though, Le Duc Tho had his way and Ban Me Thuot was targeted.

No one involved in the conferences could possibly have predicted the incredible chain of events this decision would induce. As Tra had foreseen, the fall of Ban Me Thuot, located at the rear of the central highlands strongholds of Kontum and Pleiku, shocked, thoroughly demoralized, and upset the Southern leadership. What came as a surprise to everyone, though, was how vulnerable the South had become since US troop pullouts and budget pullbacks. In an astounding succession of swift victories brought on by Southern incompetence from the top down, military defeat turned into military slaughter, abandonment, desertion, and full-scale panic. In a cascading flurry, the South was coming apart like a mud house in a monsoon. In the North, it was as if they had patiently waited nearly thirty years to view a thirty-second commercial.

The atmosphere in the room better resembled a gathering of students at graduation than the general staff of the nation's highest military authority. Giddy elder members of the staff bounced about like children. Backs were slapped, hands shaken, compliments shouted. Champagne flowed. All were of high spirits.

At the far end of the room on a small sofa, Le Van Dat and Lee Nah sat talking quietly.

"What do you mean you are going south?" Lee Nah said.

"It is something I must do, Lee Nah. I must be there at the end to see our dream of a free, united nation realized. Years ago, Minh agreed it would be so. Now I will see it done."

"But...I do not want you to go...and you know why," Lee Nah said.

"Lee Nah! Really!" Dat said, then sat straight and nodded to himself. "No, I do understand your concerns. They are reasonable. But can you doubt me now? After how far we have come the last two years?"

He grabbed her hand and patted it. He would not show any more affection in this gathering. Indeed, he felt somewhat exposed with the gesture.

"I can come with you in an official capacity," she said.

"Absolutely not! It is still a war, Lee Nah. You know well what that is like, and the South is desperate now. They will throw everything at us. A national hero such as yourself put in such a position of risk? The leadership would never allow it and neither would I. It is far too dangerous."

"It is dangerous for you also. Please, Dat, there is no good reason for you to do this. Do not go!"

Dat sighed. He gathered himself and his thoughts.

"Lee Nah...so many years ago I left the girl I loved to enter a war at just sixteen years of age. I did so because of a hope...a dream of a united Vietnam living unchallenged and free of its occupiers and foreign interests. It struck me to my core, this vision. Now, with the end of this struggle on the doorstep I am going to see it done!

"I was devastated when Minh pulled me out of the South and planted me in an office. I made him promise I would be there for an end of the war I was sure would come one day. Well, that day is here...and I cannot wait to get back to it. Surely, you can understand this from an old soldier?"

"I cannot pretend to forget the woman you had, or *have*, in the South. I want you back and I will not let you go unless we have a date for our wedding set." She paused for a moment and then asked, "When will you go?"

"The war is quickly coming to a close. There is little time to waste. It will be very soon."

"Lee Nah," came a call. It was General Lo calling from across the room. "Come and say a few words for us on this great occasion."

She smiled and rose. Dat watched as Lee Nah crossed the room to join her comrades. Her vacated place on the sofa was immediately taken by Minh.

"Can you believe it?" Minh said, slapping Dat's knee. "I will tell you, comrade, there were many times during these past decades when I did not think I would see such a moment. The world did not understand *Dau Tranh*...they did not know we had this in us.

"One nation, one people. It is happening right before us. Succeeding generations will look to us. They will know and recite our names in history classes. We are the founding fathers, the ones who brought independence to Vietnam after a thousand years. It is all too much," he said, exasperated.

"Minh," Dat cut in with a serious tone. "I am going south...to Loc Ninh...to join Dung, Tra, and Le Duc Tho. As I told you so many years ago, I must be there before the fall. It feels as if I have waited too long already. As it happens, Boa Hanh is returning to First Corps...flying out at 6 a.m. tomorrow morning. I will be on the plane with him."

Minh nodded in Lee Nah's direction. "Does she know this?"

"We have talked, yes. But...she does not know I am leaving in the morning. She is...hesitant. So, better I just go. I will make it up to her later."

"Hmmm. Well, that is between the two of you. I am quite fond of Lee Nah. Well, who is not, eh? You have quite a prize there my friend, and what a beauty! But, yes! Off you go on one last adventure."

Minh looked around to make sure they were alone.

"It is known," Minh began in something of a whisper, "among inner circles, that several elder members of the Politburo will be stepping down at the war's conclusion. I plan on advancing you for membership and, you will be happy to know, many members I have spoken with are favorable to your nomination, including Giap, Dung, and Le Duc Tho. You have some powerful allies, my friend. I know you did not subscribe to this, but can you deny it is everything you could ever want? A leader wishes only to lead, does he not? Well, now you can help us bear and raise a new nation. Exciting days are ahead; challenging days, for all of us.

"But go...and be careful. It would not be nice of you to die in the final battle. No advancing to the front with the troops, eh?! Promise you will stay with Dung's staff in the highlands."

"Thank you for your support and understanding, my friend," Dat said. "I cannot thank you enough. I have never had a better comrade...nor owed any one person so much."

"Yes," Minh said. "Well, no need for that now. We will have many years to grow old together and reminisce. Anything owed is owed each other in turn."

It was late the same night. Dat sat at the desk in his ministry office, alone with his thoughts and nagging doubts. His mind was impossibly muddled; his purpose conflicted. The flight would be leaving in just a few hours and yet he had no plan, no idea of what he would do once he reached the South. Would he search out Nu Chi? And, what exactly would he do if he found her?

Find her? It is a ridiculous thought, Dat said to himself. After all these years?! What of Lee Nah and his future, probably in the Politburo? He had grown quite fond of Nah once again. Was it love? And Nu Chi, how deep was his love for her, a woman he had not seen in years? All things considered, he was afraid to think of what the answer might be.

Shifting the block at the back of the cigarette case, the hidden drawer silently sprung open, revealing the carefully stored letters of his affair. Placed on top was the photo Nu Chi had sent years ago, the image of a smiling young woman of breathtaking beauty and a countenance that spoke of even better things lying within. It was the one memento that never failed to stir him; remind him of what he had left behind.

Be realistic! he reasoned, scolding himself. Stay in Hanoi! To search her out now would be to strike out alone, without anyone's knowledge and, certainly, without approval. His long military career, an opportunity to serve in the Politburo, with Lee Nah, could be lost forever. All this for what likely would be a futile effort to find a woman who had vowed she would be long gone by the time Saigon fell.

Still, he had made a promise. A promise made with sincere and heartfelt intentions. A promise that kept Nu Chi from immigrating to the United States because she had faith in him. Nu Chi knew Dat would carry through on his promise. Looking at her photo, he was reminded of the sense of "one-ness" he felt with this woman. He could never shake the notion that their future would be shared. Even now, he felt destiny tugging at him.

Would he dishonor himself at the eleventh hour with selfish aspirations of a future he never wanted in the first place? Could he at least not try?

"I am not prone to sentiment, as you know, but the excitement of the moment is irresistible," Boa Hanh said, smiling. "For a man such as yourself, it must be a glorious time. A lifetime of duty rewarded."

"Yes, it is," Dat confessed. "Things are coming to an end...very suddenly. By this time next week, I may be wondering what to do with myself."

Hanh smiled in amusement. "Are you traveling with me to Ben Cat, General, or getting off at Loc Ninh?"

By daybreak, Dat had made his decision. He would attempt to find Nu Chi in Saigon. The decision ran so far outside rational, or reasonable, thought it astounded him. He was going to make the effort to find her and, for the life of him, he could not understand how a man such as himself came to such a conclusion. Something baffling and of another sensibility seemed to be driving him to it. He felt literally unable to stop himself.

His one hope, his hole card, was that he would be swallowed up in the fog of war once he reached the front lines and could justify his actions to that of the overzealous patriot who could not bear missing the final battle. He knew there would be more than a few forgiving, understanding souls within the victorious general staff he served.

"I have decided to go all the way, Hanh. Ben Cat."

"I am not surprised. You are meeting up with General Tra, then?"

"Yes," Dat said. "I would like to get into the action. It should be a very exciting few days."

"Thi, would you bring me the troop-strength estimates for ARVN 7th Corps at My Tho?" Minh called out to his secretary.

"General Le Van asked for all the latest ARVN estimates late yesterday," Thi said, coming to the door. "He did not return them. Should I look for the reports in his office, Senior General?" the secretary said.

Minh thought of his secretary rifling Dat's desk.

"No, thank you just the same. I will get them myself," he said.

Minh entered Dat's office and walked to the back of the desk, leaning over to survey the contents lying on top. After shifting several files and papers, he had not found the documents. He sat in Dat's chair and began looking in drawers. No sign of the documents. Did he take them with him? He would look more carefully on the desktop. They must be among the many papers lying about. *This is quite a mess*, Minh thought. *I suppose he was in a hurry.* The large cigarette case lay atop several files. Minh picked the case up to move it, almost losing hold of it before setting it aside. It was after he had set it down that Minh noticed a drawer had slid out from underneath.

What is this? he thought. He could see the edge of a picture peeking out. He put his finger on the drawer and edged it open further, snatching up the photo as he did so. A beautiful girl...and letters. *That rascal*, Minh thought. *Who would have guessed? I often wondered. He never said a word...even to me! Unbelievable! And what of Lee Nah? You scoundrel! I have always read Dat like a book, but this?...'*

He turned the photo over, read the inscription.

Dearest Dat, Let the years swiftly fly. I think of you always. Love, Nu Chi

Nu Chi? Chuckling and shaking his head in wonder at his discovery, Minh was about to replace the photo and close the hidden compartment when something caught his eye. A small smudge of a stamp on the bottom right-hand corner of the photo back: *Ling Photography, Saigon.*

Linh Mao opened the door and silently stepped inside. Lee Nah pushed by the startled secretary and made straight for the matriarch.

"Gao Jinh!" Lee Nah cried. "He has left me. I just discovered Dat left on the early flight to Loc Ninh."

Startled out of a wonderful daydream in which she was being acclaimed as Ho's successor, Gao Jinh was confused.

"Loc Ninh?" she said. "Well...everyone wants to be in the South right now."

"It is not just the war!" Lee Nah fairly shouted.

With a dismissive nod to Linh Mao, the secretary exited the room, closing the door behind her.

"Let us calm down a bit, Lee Nah. It is too early for such excitement. Would you like some tea and..."

"I cannot calm down, Gao Jinh. The man I love has left!"

"Gracious, Lee Nah, I will not abide this shouting. Now, please, calm yourself...take a deep breath...and tell me what in the world has got you in such a fit."

"Dat...told me last evening that he was leaving to join our forces in the South. He wanted to be there when the war ended...to see his dream fulfilled."

"And you do not want him out of your sight for even a few days?! You are a fluttering little bird, Lee Nah," Gao Jinh said, laughing. "Love has you..."

"I am no fluttering bird!" Lee Nah spat. "Dat lied to me! Just last night he said his plans weren't set...then, he left *this morning!* The war is just an excuse. Dat has a woman in the South. He wants to be with her, I know it!"

Gao Jinh was stunned. "A woman in the South? Our Dat?"

"Yes. Someone he met when he was near Saigon."

"A cadre member?... Some young, flirtatious concubine?"

"No, Gao Jinh. A Southerner."

"Oh, my," Gao Jinh said, standing and pacing the floor. "Oh, my...this is quite a development. A Southerner. Not a cadre member or another soldier... Is she a Communist? What else can you tell me?"

"I think he loves her."

"No, not that!" Gao Jinh said. "What does she do? How did he meet her? Do they communicate?... Oh, my! She could be a spy... likely *is* a spy. Got him! Where exactly is Dat now?"

Saigon?! Dat has a woman in Saigon? Suddenly, a new and very different interest took hold of Minh. He reached into the drawer and pulled out the letters. Slowly, one by one, he read through the pile. His initial amusement had turned to apprehension, which in turn became concern and then acute distress. Finishing, Minh slumped back into the chair. Unbelievable! His close friend, a man he had put all his faith and trust in, was carrying on an affair with a woman who worked for the Thieu regime! It is right there in her letters! The conflict, deceit, and corruption could not be more obvious. Undoubtedly she was a spy who had landed a prize victim, a man excellently placed. What had Dat's letters to her included? What had been compromised? She spoke of his defection. Had he gone South to defect at the last minute?

Minh felt light-headed. Everything he knew, valued, and revered in his friend was suddenly a viper at his throat! A trusting, affectionate, nearly lifelong friendship lie ruined in the pile of letters. Over and over he told himself he could not believe it. The smart little sergeant a spy for the South? He knew it was all too wretchedly possible. And who had placed him so high and so well? Who had been his champion? Touted him over others for the nation's highest assembly?

Fear grabbed hold of Minh. The discovery was a disaster of immense scale. *If this gets out, instead of a villa on the seashore I will spend the rest of my days in the Hanoi Hilton.* Hand shaking, he picked up the phone. His secretary immediately came on the line.

"Call Dung's headquarters in Loc Ninh, immediately!" Minh said. "I need to talk with General Le Van *now*. It is most urgent."

"Certainly, General. Right away," Thi said.

While the secretary placed the call, Minh sat staring at the desk, growing angrier by the second. The cunning deception of the man! So thoughtful, humble. How could this happen? I will kill him with my bare hands!

The phone rang.

"Yes?" Minh shouted into the phone.

"Uh, General," Thi said, "I have Senior General Dung's chief of staff on the line. He says General Le Van is not there. He was not even aware..."

"Let me speak with him," Minh broke in.

There was the crackle of a connection.

"This is Senior General Minh in Hanoi calling. To whom am I speaking?"

"Colonel Nguyen Van Diep, General. Can I be of service?"

"Yes, thank you, Colonel. General Le Van Dat was supposed to have taken a flight to Loc Ninh this morning. I was wondering if he had arrived."

"Sorry, Senior General. We have not seen the general in our headquarters today. We were not aware of his travel plans. Should we have been?"

"No...er, it was not exactly official. A personal decision. You know...everyone wants to be in the South these days. Perhaps he changed his plans."

"The morning flight from Hanoi did fly on to a small airfield near Ben Cat. Is it possible the general was going to link up with First Corps?"

"Yes, quite so. I suppose that is what transpired. Thank you, Colonel," Minh said, hanging up. Immediately he picked the handset up again. Thi was on the line instantly.

"Get me in touch with Colonel Boa Hanh. He should be with First Corps near Ben Cat."

"Yes, General," Thi said.

Waiting, Minh picked up the damning letters. How could he! Minh reared back his arm to throw them across the room, but hesitated. No, I must not let these out of my hands. They must be safely hidden, perhaps to be burned later. He picked up the picture. Lovely girl. Yes, who could resist such temptation? An innocent, carefully developed affair. Perhaps a chance meeting or two. Seductive eyes and a tantalizing smile given a lonely man. It would be easy.

On second thought, maybe I have it all wrong. Perhaps Dat thought he could turn her into his spy. She does speak candidly of the affairs of her government. Damn! I must get my hands on the man. Boa Hanh. He is the only one I can trust to catch him now.

"A spy?!" Lee Nah said, shocked. "Gao Jinh...that is impossible. Absolutely impossible! Saying so is...well, it is unthinkable. I have known Dat all my life, and I can tell you that is an absurdity. I do not know what would make you think such a thing, but it is not so."

"Please, Lee Nah. You are young and in love. What I am saying is not out of the question in the least. You are blinded by your lifelong love for the man, but he is not what you think."

"Dat is *not* a spy!"

"Lee Nah...you must be very careful now," Gao Jinh said in a conspiratorial whisper. "You have just admitted to me you are aware Dat has a woman in the South, and that certainly is not permitted of a senior line officer. Yet, you did not inform me or anyone else of this? You are as culpable as the general. Prison for the two of you is a very real possibility. Not the ending you wished, eh?"

The daydream Gao Jinh had been having when Lee Nah arrived suddenly seemed almost real. Uncovering a spy in the general staff while implicating the Hero of Dien Bien Phu would be a sensation of historic proportions. The spy love-nest conspiracy discovered and exposed by the great Gao Jinh. The possibilities made her feel faint.

A sudden and very real concern struck Lee Nah with the matriarch's true words. If Dat was indeed an agent of the South, Lee Nah was in trouble. Everything was on the line.

"Gao Jinh...you know very well I am a true Communist and a patriot in every sense of the word. But, Dat is *not* a spy. I believe this to my core and I will stand firm on that. I have nothing to be concerned with in the matter and...neither do you."

"What?" Gao Jinh said, surprised. "Me? Do not include me in your...."

The matriarch stopped short, mouth open. Lee Nah let the air go out of Gao Jinh.

"Yes...you of all people know how these things can play out," Lee Nah said. "Who has been my biggest supporter all these years? Who sponsored me for the Politburo? Who asks for me and consults with me in her private chambers?"

Gao Jinh was stunned. She seethed, her eyes a raging storm as she took in Lee Nah. The slender jade cigarette holder she was holding snapped in two. She opened her mouth to speak, but no words would come. She removed the cigarette from the holder and took a deep drag, throwing the broken jade pieces on her desk.

"But, like me, you have nothing to fear, Gao Jinh. Dat is *not* a spy. However...it would be...*convenient* if he were back in Hanoi and not shopping around in the South looking for his lost love, eh? Perhaps we should recall Dat?"

"Linh Mao!" screamed Gao Jinh to her secretary.

"The 338th will sweep around Ben Cat, here," General Tra indicated on the map. "They will be the point of our spear."

"Yes," Dat said. "Excellent plan, Tra. I read the strength evaluations last night. ARVN is weakest right there. So, you are bypassing Ben Cat and hitting ARVN at Lai Thieu?"

"Exactly. We will rupture the lines here...southeast of Ben Cat...and move on the 9th Rangers. It will close Highway 13 and isolate Ben Cat."

"Excellent. Do you think I could get closer to the front?" Dat said.

"I rather think this is close enough, for now. By tomorrow, I expect all of us will be on the outskirts of Saigon. You still yearn for action, General?"

"I always wanted to be up front. It is the only vantage point where you can see everything as it unfolds," Dat said.

"I cannot allow that, General. If you were wounded...or killed... it would be a national tragedy."

"Yes...well, I understand, Tra. Mind if I have a look around the staging area?"

"Not at all. Lieutenant Hoai will escort you," Tra said, indicating a young officer.

"I would like to accompany you, General," Hahn said. "But, uh, I think I should remain in the command center. We expect big developments this afternoon."

"Of course, Hanh. I do not wish to take any more of your time. We will talk later. Thank you, General Tra...for your indulgence and consideration," Dat said.

Dat and Lieutenant Hoai exited the command tent and jumped into an army field car. As they drove, the lieutenant indicated staging sites, pointing out the convoys of tanks and trucks leading to the front and where they were headed. Hoai turned off Highway 13 onto a makeshift road lined with trucks.

"This is the supply train for the 338th, General. Troops and tanks are a few kilometers ahead, already taking the fight to ARVN."

"You could not understand, Lieutenant, but seeing this kind of supply support is a remarkable thing. I led a company through this area fifteen years ago with no logistic support whatsoever. We carried what we could on our backs."

"I trained at Xuan Mai, General. We all know your story. I must say it is an honor to be in your presence."

"Thank you, Lieutenant. It is always a pleasure to be appreciated. Perhaps you understand, then...why I want to be at the front."

"Certainly, General. I would like to be there also."

"But, of course, you follow orders."

"Yes," Hoai said. "While the troops parade in Saigon, I will no doubt be stuck out here in the bush somewhere."

They rode in silence down the long line of trucks until they cleared the lead vehicle. The lieutenant pulled the car to the side of the road.

"This is it, General. As you can see this is probably as far as we should go. Maybe a kilometer beyond this point is where the battle is being fought today."

"Lieutenant, this is where I leave you," Dat said.

"Excuse me, General," the lieutenant said.

"This is where I get out," Dat said, getting out of the vehicle.

"I do not understand," the lieutenant said.

"I think you do. I am going to hitch a ride with these trucks and get closer to the front."

"I cannot let you do that, General," the lieutenant said, jumping from the vehicle and running to Dat's side. "I will be severely reprimanded if you do this."

"No, I do not think so, Hoai. I am a general of the People's Army and I am ordering you to leave me here. There is not a single junior officer in this army who would question such an order. This is not your doing, as I will be happy to confirm when asked."

"General...please! What will I say to General Tra?"

"Tell him only the truth and nothing more, Hoai. You know who I am. How long I have served the country...fought in this war? I must be in Saigon for the end. You understand this?"

"I suppose, but..."

"No. No more objections, Lieutenant. But one thing, it would be nice if you took your time getting back to the operations encampment."

The lieutenant reluctantly smiled. "Have a safe journey, General. Speaking for all of us, please stay out of harm's way. If something happens to you, I will likely be held responsible."

"That is ridiculous, Hoai. I do this willfully and gladly. If the army, the politicians, or the people knew the real Le Van Dat, they would understand."

"I will return by a more scenic route, General. Take care."

"Hanh, is that you?"

"Yes, Senior General Minh."

"We have a...political situation to deal with Hanh. Something... knowing your background...I expect you will fully understand."

"Yes, Senior General."

"A serious question of moral character...and national security, I suppose...involving General Le Van Dat has been raised."

"General Dat?!" Hanh said.

"Yes. Now don't get ahead of yourself, Hanh. With regard to his position within the military and the government, it is vitally important that this...*misconduct* by the general...be a closely held secret for security purposes...at this time," Minh said.

Hanh recognized and noted the slightest tremor and falsetto in the general's voice. *Despite his cool presentation, this man is very upset,* Hanh thought.

"Is the general there...in the room with you at this moment?" Minh asked.

"No, Senior General. General Le Van has gone on an inspection of the forward staging areas."

There was a slight pause. "When is he due back? No...forget that. I have very specific orders for you, Hanh," Minh said. "You are to find and *detain* General Le Van Dat immediately. I hereby relieve you of your duty as political commissar for First Corps so that you might apprehend and return the general to Hanoi.

"However...do not divulge your mission to anyone...even General Tra. I will explain to Tra that you are charged with a special mission...a mission of great national importance...under my direct command. I do not think he will miss you.

"You are to commandeer a vehicle, a few soldiers as needed, and detain the general on sight...but, with all due respect," Minh quickly added. "He deserves that. You understand your orders, Colonel?"

"Yes, General. I do."

"Well, then. Carry on. When you have him, you must contact me immediately. And Hanh..."

"Yes, General."

"He may be aware of his dilemma. He may attempt to...get away. You must pursue him with all speed and intent. If he should get into Saigon, look for him in Cholon, at the Finance Ministry, or wherever the Americans are evacuating people."

"Evacuating?! Surely, General...," Hanh said.

"There is no time to explain, Hanh. It is speculation only. Now, allow me a few words with Tra. However, I want you out the door of that compound and after the general this instant!"

"Yes, General. This instant."

Evacuating with the Americans?! Is it possible General Dat is a spy for the South? Mother said the puzzle would come together. She was right all along, Hanh thought.

"Damn, damn, damn," Gao Jinh shouted. "They cannot tell me where my son is! Unbelievable! Tra said Hanh had direct counter-manding orders from General Minh. That is all they know. Well, I will talk with Minh. Linh Mao!"

"There! That is him! Pull in front of him," Hanh said, grabbing the wheel and sending the vehicle directly in front of the oncoming field car. Hanh's driver slammed on the brakes while a surprised Lieutenant Hoai in the field car veered off the road and into some brush, the front of his vehicle coming to rest in a bush, a foot off the ground.

Cursing, the lieutenant was about to jump out of his car and give someone a talking-to when Hanh ran up to his door.

"Lieutenant Hoai! Where is General Dat?"

The lieutenant, surprised and upset, could only stumble out a few sounds.

"What have you done with him?" Hanh roared.

"Nothing. I have done nothing with the general," Hoai finally got out. "He ordered me to let him out. I tried to stop..."

"Where?!"

"The supply train of the 338th. He wanted to catch a ride closer to the action. Really, I tried..."

But Hanh was already in his car shouting orders. As the vehicle sped away, Hoai could only shake his head. *How did they discover the general's plan so quickly?* he thought.

"General, where is my son?" Gao Jinh said over the phone.

"Madam Gao," Minh gushed. "What a pleasure."

"You have done something with my son. I want to know where he is and what he is doing. How dare you commandeer Hanh without even the smallest consideration for me?"

"Oh, Gao Jinh...it is not what you are thinking...and I certainly meant no disrespect. Hanh is merely doing an errand for me. A favor for an old general."

"What favor?"

"Oh, now...uh, I am afraid I cannot divulge that just now. It is a personal matter."

"You cannot push my son around like some lackey! I need his help with a...personal matter. Where is he?"

"Um, well...I am not really sure, Gao Jinh. I am not certain where or in what direction he was headed. He will be checking in with me eventually. I will have him contact you."

Gao Jinh seethed. It had been such a nice morning not so long ago. "Eventually! You do not know *where* he is? You will not say *what* he is doing? Or where he is doing it? This is an outrage, General. I will be informing the Politburo of this."

"I am sorry you are so upset, Gao Jinh. I could not have anticipated your needs. Hanh is, after all, a military officer."

"You will not get away with this, General."

"Please, Gao Jinh...," but the Matriarch had already rung off.

What other disasters will befall me today?! Minh thought, hanging up the phone.

"How close will we get to the front?" Dat asked the driver.

"Uh. Um...within a half kilometer...or so," the driver replied with a noticeable tremor.

"Good. The closer the better," Dat said.

Dat began unbuttoning his tunic, the nervous sergeant glancing repeatedly at the general as he did so. Underneath his uniform, Dat wore the clothing of a common citizen. A light shirt, casual slacks. He finished undressing, rolled up his uniform neatly, and stuffed it under the truck seat as the driver looked on, astonished.

"It is a secret mission I am on. No one must recognize me. If anyone asks, you have not seen me. Do you understand, Sergeant?"

"Yes, sir."

"Good. I will return for my uniform. Take care of it."

The truck came to a stop behind a command car on top of a ridge. An officer was standing alongside it with binoculars to his face. He glanced at them only briefly before returning his concentration to the battle in front of him. After a moment, Dat slipped silently out of the truck cab and into the brush beside the road.

Honking, wildly swerving, the car ducked and dodged between trucks as it sped along. At last they came to the head of the column. Pulling in front of the lead truck, Hanh jumped from the car before it stopped, waving his arms. When the column had come to a stop, Hanh approached the driver, who stuck his head out the window.

"We are looking for General Le Van Dat. We have information he may be on this truck," Hanh said.

The sergeant, looking conflicted, shrugged his shoulders. "A general? Here?"

Hanh knew this look. He approached to within inches of the driver. "This...general," Hanh said in a threatening whisper, reaching for his pistol, "is wanted for questioning. Hiding him or in any way aiding him...could be considered treason. You can be summarily executed on the spot if you lie to me. Now, where is the general?"

The sergeant swallowed and found his voice.

"He got out. He got out! Maybe a kilometer back. He undressed in my truck. There," the man said, pointing. "His uniform is under the seat. I did not know what to do. A general! In my truck? He said he was on a secret mission and I was to tell no one."

"So, what is he wearing now?" Hanh asked.

"A civilian green shirt and black pants."

"Get out of your truck. You are coming with us, and show us exactly where he left your truck."

They walked out into the field past the carnage of war. The driver stopped and pointed.

"The last time I saw the general, he was headed that way... through those trees and down the slope."

"Bring the car," Hanh said. "It appears as though we will be heading cross country."

Saigon, South Vietnam
April 28, 1975

The Second Day

Dat choked back the dust and switched hands once more. He felt like one of ten acrobats balancing on a bicycle. His place on the running board of the ARVN troop transport relied completely on five fingers and five toes. Fleeing Lai Thieu, the crowd had rushed the truck and jumped on. Dat was lucky to have found a hold and a place to put his foot. He checked his watch. They had been traveling more than an hour and appeared on the outskirts of Saigon. As the truck slowed for an intersection, Dat and several others jumped off. He needed to arrange transportation to get him around the city.

Fright, confusion, crying, and screaming charged the atmosphere. Around him, panicked Southerners gathered whatever they could before fleeing into the city. Looking upon the desperate faces, Dat felt like shouting, "There is nowhere else to run. Stay put and protect your property." But this crowd was hardly in a listening mood.

Ahead, he saw a young man, hands folded across his chest, sitting astride a Honda motorbike. Unlike the panicked hoard around him, the boy looked bored. As Dat approached the boy, he tried to remember the many tricks of Southern dialect he had learned so many years before.

"Hello," Dat said.

The boy looked at him, neither smiling nor frowning and did not return his greeting.

"Why are you not fleeing with the others?" Dat said.

"Why aren't you?" the boy returned.

"I am. That is why I am talking to you. I need transportation."

"The bike is not for sale," the boy said.

"That is fine. I need a driver, too."

"Why?"

"I am looking for someone in the city. I have not spent much time in Saigon. Do you know the city well?"

"Yes."

"Good. Would you consider being my driver? I will pay you."

"It is a mess in the city. I am staying here," the boy said.

"I am somewhat...in need at the moment," Dat said. "I would pay you well."

"In what...useless piasters? I might consider US dollars...lots of them," the boy said.

"I have no American dollars," Dat said.

"Then go find another driver," the boy said, looking away.

Dat heard the familiar whistle of incoming rounds followed by two large explosions maybe half a kilometer away. The escaping crowd screamed as one. The boy flinched, then turned the key and flipped the starter pedal on his bike.

"But I do have dong to pay you with," Dat said. "Let's say two hundred in advance. Another two hundred at the end of the day. That will buy a lot of petrol in the days to come."

"Dong?" the boy said. "North Vietnamese dong? How did you come by that?"

"At this point," Dat said, handing the boy several bills. "I hardly think it matters."

The boy shrugged his shoulders. "I suppose you are right. Where are we going?"

"She lives in Cholon, or did," Dat said, straddling the seat. "She might still be there."

"There was a big fire in Cholon. Northern rockets hit it early yesterday."

"Yes, well...regardless, that is where we will start."

Boa Hanh had pinned himself against the wall. His eyes were squeezed shut; his teeth clinched. Beside him, an old sergeant fired off his Chinese submachine gun. Hanh put his hands over his ears as the sergeant continued firing bursts. When the sergeant pulled back and appeared to pause, Hanh yanked on his sleeve.

"Can we push around the roadblock? The man I am after is getting further away."

"What you are asking is impossible, Colonel. This is war. You do not just 'go around.' That machine gun emplacement has to be taken out," the sergeant said.

In a daring move, a soldier ran from a doorway, diving behind a parked vehicle as rounds ricocheted around him and pierced the vehicle.

"Did you see that, Colonel? What bravery," the sergeant marveled. "I will see he is rewarded."

The man rose from behind the vehicle and launched a grenade. While exposed, the heavy ARVN gun cut him down. The grenade found its mark, though, and the gun was silenced.

"A pity," the sergeant remarked, standing. "Too often that is the reward for real courage, eh, Colonel?"

But as the sergeant could see, the colonel had not been listening. The sergeant tugged on the colonel's sleeve. Hanh opened his eyes, looking wildly about.

"Your first action, sir?" the sergeant said.

"Is the way clear, Sergeant?" Hanh said.

"Yes, Colonel...but I see the tanks of the Huong Giang Brigade coming from down the road. Maybe it would be...faster if you rode with them."

The smoldering ruins seemed a perfect representation of Hell. Blocks of charred, gutted, and burning buildings spread before Dat. Here and there people moved among the debris, hopeful of finding mementos. Nu Chi's family home lay somewhere in the rubble. It was an unsettling sight and a dispiriting moment.

"So, now what?" the young motorcyclist said.

"Give me a moment," Dat said.

He walked through hot embers to a small clutch of Hell's farmers combing through the wreckage with rakes. They did not look up as he approached.

"I am looking for Luang Nu Chi," Dat said. "I am her uncle. The family home was here. Has anyone seen her? Does anyone know what happened to the Luangs?"

One tired, soot-streaked face nearby looked up.

"I knew the Luang family, but you will not find them here. You should know they left for America months ago."

"Yes," Dat said, moving toward the old lady. "But Nu Chi remained in Saigon. Are you saying she did not live here anymore?"

"That is right. But, I thought they had all left."

"Fantastic news!" Dat said. "Thank you so much."

Dat turned and hurried toward the motorbike, but stopped and retraced his steps.

"Sorry...one more question. If you were trying to leave Vietnam today, where would you go?"

The old lady didn't hesitate. "If I had contacts...American friends like the Luangs...I would be at the Defense Attached Office right now. You know...the DAO at Tan Son Nhut. They have been evacuating people for most of the week."

"Again, thank you," Dat said, turning quickly.

"Yes. Good luck finding Nu Chi. She undoubtedly has excellent contacts. If you find her in time you might get out with her," the old lady said to Dat's backside.

"Tan Son Nhut!" Dat shouted to the motorcyclist. "The DAO compound."

Flying along Saigon's streets, Dat feared for his life—not from the looters and deserters he saw here and there, but from being impaled on the speeding motorcycle. The young man drove too fast, zigzagging in and out of the melee, sometimes heading directly into oncoming traffic. At one point the street was totally blocked by ARVN soldiers, so Dat's driver veered onto a side street and continued to speed along. They came upon dozens of soldiers—Dat estimated perhaps a full company—shedding their uniforms and changing into civilian clothes. They drove by without slowing.

At Tan Son Nhut, the young driver raced alongside the lineup of trucks and buses to reach the main gate.

"Excuse me," Dat said to the sentry checking a bus driver's ID. "May we pass?"

"What's your business?" the American Marine said.

"I am Luang Lo from Xuan Loc. I am searching for my niece, Nu Chi. She works for the Finance Ministry with the Americans. I believe she is here. It is imperative that I find her."

"Yeah, everyone's desperate today, pal. Let's see some ID," the sentry said.

Dat handed over the ID cards he'd had since visiting Nu Chi in Saigon. After looking briefly at the cards, the guard gave them back.

"You gotta be kidding."

"Please, understand. I rarely get to the city. I am only here because of the war, and I must find my niece. She is quite alone, without family."

"Like to help you, buddy..."

"I cannot take no for your answer," Dat said.

Cars and buses started honking, drivers yelling at the sentry.

"You'll have to get new identification papers," the Marine said, walking to a truck.

"You know that is impossible now," Dat said, following. "There is no time and no civil servants on duty. Please...you must help me."

"Okay, okay. What the hell. Go on. Get outta here," the sentry said, waving him away.

"Drive," Dat said, hopping on the bike.

The evacuation processing center was teeming with refugees, looking like a hill of ants recently stirred with a stick. Hundreds of people milled about outside on the tarmac and inside the DAO compound.

"How will you find your Nu Chi in all this?" the boy said.

"I will start looking...first on the tarmac...those nearest planes. Then, I'll work my way back inside."

"Good luck. Can I have the rest of my money now...please?"

"No. You must stay. She may be elsewhere. I need you."

"I am not waiting around for..."

"Okay, here!" Dat said, stuffing bills into the boy's hand. "That is two or three hundred dong. But if you stay with me...until tomorrow...you could see much more...maybe enough to start a small business. It is an opportunity you will not see any time in the near future, I assure you."

After looking closer at the bills, the boy coolly stuffed them in his pants pocket.

"I'll wait for you over there...by the gym. Don't get lost or, you know...take a plane or something."

Dat felt like a man swimming uphill in an avalanche of worried looks and furrowed brows. Every Vietnamese on the base was focused on their one objective: leaving the country at the earliest possible opportunity. It was an anxious, nearly hysterical crowd teetering on the edge of chaos.

Dat realized he could easily miss Nu Chi in such a surging, milling crowd. So, he took his time, systematically searching in squares measured out in his mind while occasionally calling out her name.

Boa Hanh again had his hands clamped tight to his ears as the cannon in the turret fired another round. *Damn, I never realized war was so loud,* he thought.

"Lieutenant...eleven o'clock...just left of the pink house," the driver said.

"Got it," the lieutenant responded, as his sergeant shoved another round into the cannon. The turret moved in jerks back and forth, then exploded another projectile through the barrel.

"Oh...that is not so good," the driver chuckled.

"Sorry about your house, missus," the lieutenant said.

The men hooted as the sergeant rammed another shell in the cannon. The turret jerked back and forth again, Hanh hitting his head on a toggle bolt as it did so. He was rubbing the knot rising on his skull when the cannon roared again.

"This is intolerable!" Hanh screamed, though no one seemed to hear him.

The tank battalion was on the outskirts of Saigon in a pitched battle with ARVN tanks and artillery. Hanh had all but given up on finding Le Van Dat; too much time had passed; too much chaos. Hanh's only interest at the moment was getting out of the tank and to the rear of their lines, which he would be doing at the earliest convenience.

An explosion rocked the tank, throwing Boa Hanh sideways into the steel wall of the turret. When he came to, he was lying on the engine cover at the back of the tank.

"The colonel is coming around," the sergeant said.

The face of the lieutenant filled the sky Hanh had been blinking into.

"Remember, I asked you to wear a helmet," the lieutenant said. "This is why."

"What...happened?" Hanh got out.

"A round narrowly missed us. Blew the track off the tank. It will take some time to fix."

"I would like transport...back to Ben Cat," Hanh said. "An ambulance. I think I might have a concussion."

"I am afraid that is not possible, Colonel. Everything is moving forward right now. We are a half kilometer behind the front already, and it is hard to say where we might find an ambulance."

"Damn...so, the war is not over?"

"Almost. Take another nap. By the time you wake either the war will be over or we will be in it again," the lieutenant said.

Hanh sighed and closed his eyes. "Damn."

Saigon, South Vietnam
April 29, 1975

The Third Day

Impossibly tired, Dat slumped to the floor in the DAO gymnasium. The owner of the motorcycle lay beside him, sound asleep. Dat had searched for hours through the seething mass of refugees and had not glimpsed Nu Chi. But, with the crowd constantly moving, more arriving in regular waves, he could not be sure she hadn't slipped his sight or just arrived in some remote corner of the complex.

What was he to do? The end was near for the South. The army must be just outside the city. At most, there might be a day remaining before the collapse. Those around him knew it as well. Tension had increased by the hour.

Just after 5 p.m. the previous evening, a flight of five American-built A-37s had surprised everyone by making a bombing run on the airport. Obviously, they had been captured aircraft sent on an improbable bombing mission by his country. The attack caused widespread panic, wild shooting and rioting from troops, and a three-hour cessation of the evacuation flights. Rumor spread that the whole operation would be abandoned. Those who could sleep now slept out of utter exhaustion.

As Dat sat against the wall, nodding, a thought came to him as if a switch had been flipped: She is not here! He had been too occupied in his search to consider his senses, the ethereal mix that had always guided this union of unlikely soul mates. No, he realized coming fully awake, there was no sensation of her in this place. It all felt wrong.

With this new notion, everything and everyone around him took on a remote and disconnected air. *I am wasting valuable time,* he thought, somewhat amazed at the revelation. But where else could she be?

Dat located an American officer surrounded by refugees, all demanding to be heard.

"I know patience is difficult right now," the American said to the gathering through an interpreter, "but I have been assured the flights will continue through the night and will be stepped up tomorrow. Everyone will get out. We're doing all we can. There is nothing more I know or can tell you."

After a few more anxious questions, which he merely shrugged his shoulders at, the crowd began to disband, muttering as they went along. Dat used the moment to approach the man.

"Excuse me, sir," Dat said. "I am looking for my niece. I am sure she is being evacuated...she worked with the Americans at the Finance Ministry. I have looked for hours and cannot find her. Where else might she be?"

To his credit, the overworked, under-informed officer had listened patiently.

"This is most likely where your niece would come," the officer said. "This is the only evacuation center operating right now. The Navy had planned to evacuate thousands up the river, but the NVA closed too rapidly and the ships had to sail with no refugees aboard. There is no escape by river now.

"The only other place evacuating friendlies is the US Embassy...and that's mostly embassy staff. Best stay here and keep lookin'. Good luck. I hope you find her," he said over his shoulder as he left.

Dat didn't hear the man's last words as the excitement rose within him. The US Embassy! Of course! That is where she would go. Her contact was highly placed. No doubt he would take her there instead of bringing her to this impossible mess. He thought of waking the driver immediately, but Dat was near exhaustion and needed rest himself. A few hours' rest, he thought, and then we will be off. He fell asleep at once, but with new hope and inspiration.

Sleeping restlessly atop the engine cover of the Soviet tank, Hanh was instantly awoken by the sound of rockets screaming overhead.

"What?" he said. "What is happening?"

"Rocket attack on Tan Son Nhut, Colonel...just heard over the radio. I was told it is a reprisal for the South's sending most of its air force to Thailand yesterday.

"We are about to move out again, sir. Better get ready," the lieutenant finished.

"Could we remain here a while longer?" Hanh said. "It is the middle of the night, after all."

"Come on, Colonel! We will miss the remainder of the war if we stay here. We are all anxious to get back into battle."

"Hurrah," Hanh said under his breath.

Dat was awake before the first rocket slammed the runway; a sixth sense fashioned from decades of fighting. Several explosions rocked the compound in rapid succession. The motorcyclist bolted upright, wild-eyed.

"We are under attack!"

"Sit tight," Dat responded.

A rocket must have hit very close to the gym. Part of the roof blew off and shrapnel ripped throughout the building. Screams, shouts, and a rush for the doors ensued. The boy tried to rise.

"No," Dat said, grabbing his shirt and pulling him down. "Stay here for now. It is safer inside."

The attack was over nearly as quickly as it had begun.

"Now," Dat said. "Let's get your motorbike and go. I think Nu Chi is at the US Embassy."

They were barely outside when Dat heard the whistle of incoming 130mm shells. In regular succession the shells started slamming the runway, flight line, and compound. Fires burned everywhere as pandemonium swept through the refugees and ARVN soldiers waiting for evacuation. Dat and his young driver mounted the bike and headed for the main gate.

The gate guardhouse had been obliterated in the attack, but the cyclist had no trouble negotiating the wreckage to reach Cong Ly road for the trip back into the city. Dat saw what was left of the Marine guard he had spoken with the day before, lying dead and burned in the wreckage.

As they sped down the boulevard, the young biker wove his way in and out of looters who carried everything and anything of value. The homes and offices of the Americans were already being ransacked, crowds carrying away furniture, fixtures, even carpets. The look on the faces of trapped Saigonese varied from lost bewilderment to wild anger. The city emitted a constant, shrill wailing like a beast in its final throe of death.

Clinging to the biker, Dat wondered how much more of this he could take. He hadn't eaten now in two days. He had slept a few scant hours. The chaos around him failed to raise his adrenaline level any longer. He felt a numbing fatigue throughout his body. Unable to keep his head up, he rested it on the boy's back as they hurried through the pandemonium. Dat was hoping the situation at the embassy would not be so confused, but as they reached the area Dat had visited during Tet so many years before, he saw a huge crowd blocking the street. The bike slowed to a crawl, zigzagging around other motorbikes and Saigonese with their luggage before stopping by the curb across from the embassy.

Dat stepped off the bike and surveyed the end of times. Surrounding the embassy was a throng of thousands of wailing, desperate people trying to get past the embassy walls and its US Marine guard.

"I hope you know someone," the cyclist said to Dat.

Dat said nothing in return.

"I think this is it," the biker added. "There is nowhere else to go. No time for anything else, at any rate. So, now I would like my money. The money you promised."

"Oh...yes," Dat said, somewhat distracted. He reached into his baggy pants pocket and pulled out a large wad of bills. "Here...you might as well take it all. And, thank you. I owe you more than I can pay. Your help was indispensable," he said, handing the bills to the boy.

"Oh...well! Thank *you*, sir. Most generous," he said, his face lighting up. "Good luck! I mean that. I hope you find her."

With that, the boy put the bike in gear and soon vanished in the crowd. Dat turned to the swarming mass in front of him and wondered not how he would get inside the compound, but how he would even get to the front gate. He stood next to a woman who was hugging a small child among her packed bags. Dat sat down heavily on the curb, exhausted. The woman looked him over.

"Do you know someone at the embassy?" she asked. "Can you help us inside?"

"No," Dat said. After a pause, he added, "I do not know anyone here."

"My husband is somewhere in the crowd. He sometimes worked as a gardener at the embassy. He is trying to find his employer. You need to know someone...that is all. You just need an American's help. We are getting out. My husband is a very resourceful man."

"Yes," Dat said, and after a moment added, "Just curious,

madame...why are you so desperate to get out? You would leave everything you own, your country..."

"Of course! Have you not heard what happened in Phnom Penh? Everyone the Khmer Rouge did not kill they banished to the countryside. Two million people were driven from the city. It will happen here, too. It will be a bloodbath when they take Saigon."

"I do not believe that will happen. The South has been assured..."

"Assured by whom? What assurance do any of us have? Why are *you* here?" the woman spat out. "The North would not think twice to kill us all. They hate us. They mean to kill everyone. But we will get out...my husband is a resourceful man."

Dat looked away from the woman as she pulled her child closer. She could not know there would be no slaughter. Here, at the end of the war, the Politburo and the military seemed to sense the bigger picture, the coming together of Vietnam. The nation was poor, shattered, and would need years, decades, of hard work to rebuild. Everyone in the South would be needed. Certainly, there would be some "re-education" of Southern political and military leaders, but no retribution, no killings, no mass graves. He could not explain this to this desperate mother, but he did not blame her for feeling anxious. Like himself, he doubted very much that she would find a way into the embassy, or her way out of Vietnam. Mercifully, it would soon be over and the woman would discover that her fright was unfounded.

What of himself? What would become of Le Van Dat? He was so tired he felt he could not move an inch. He rested his head on his arms and quickly fell asleep.

He jumped with a start as a helicopter swept over him. For a moment he was completely disoriented, not knowing which day it was or where he was. He checked his watch. It was a few minutes after 9 a.m. He had been asleep for hours! Looking up, he saw the helicopter landing on the roof of the embassy. As soon as it settled he could see Vietnamese ducking low as they got out and proceeded inside. Now that was odd! Helicopters were flying Southerners into the embassy, just as helicopters were flying Southerners out. But why? Most likely a logistics problem of some kind, he thought, because it made no sense at all. What an impossible mess.

Among the helicopter's passengers was a young woman. From what Dat could tell at a distance, she was about the size and age of Nu Chi. Who knew, it might even be her? Inside him, a long-developed sense of honor and duty nagged. I have come too far, sacrificed and wagered too much, to give up on the doorstep, he thought. He would try to get inside and, if failing, know he at least tried his best.

With that, he pushed himself up and walked toward the embassy gate.

Senior General Tran Van Minh stood resolute at the windows of his office, looking into the sunlit street below. The people were getting about their work with seeming vigor and good humor this fine morning, no doubt buoyed by the news from the South.

Minh had just returned from a Politburo committee meeting in which no work at all had been completed. The gathering more resembled a New Year's Eve party in Manhattan. No one was wearing a lamp shade, but much to the delight of those present, Le Duan had given Lee Nah a spin around the room.

He had been enjoying the spectacle when he sensed a presence next to him and turned to look directly into the burning eyes of Gao Jinh. The surprise nearly made him shout out.

"Where is my son?" Gao Jinh demanded.

Flustered, Minh stammered.

"Speak up, General," the matriarch demanded. "You have sent him off. You must know where he is. Tell me!"

"Nothing has changed, Gao Jinh. The chaos..."

"Do not attempt to blame this on the situation in the South. The only situation I see is an incompetent general who sent my son on some 'personal' errand and has lost him to the wind. I do not accept your excuses, General. Now...I want only answers! If I do not hear from you by 8 a.m. tomorrow, my patience will be completely expended. You do not want me for an enemy, Minh. I want answers," she said, turning to leave.

While watching the good humor in the street, Minh felt cheated. It was a sensation that added to his misery and further heightened his anxiety. He should be celebrating, too! He as much as anyone deserved to be in a celebratory mood. But celebration was out of the question with the issue regarding Le Van Dat still in doubt and the most powerful woman in Vietnam on his case.

Minh had read Nu Chi's letters several times, trying to glean more information. Instead of clarifying the situation, the matter seemed more muddled than ever. There was a genuine tone and intent to the letters that indicated nothing more than an affectionate union. Her thoughts and reflections on her job and the South's politics seemed to be the innocent, concerned musings of a young woman. Yet, such reflections were sometimes important clues, the kind used in intelligence gathering. Was Dat using her as a spy? What passed between them that was *not* in the letters? Where was he now? Damn!

"Senior General," Minh's secretary said, entering the room at a brisk pace. "It is Colonel Hanh. He is on the phone."

Minh quickly snatched up the handset. "Hanh...where are you? Why have you not reported back before now? What can you tell me?"

The line was not clear, and there were explosions in the background. Minh had to listen closely.

"I have hooked up with a tank battalion," Hanh said. "We are on the outskirts of Saigon...about to reengage the enemy."

"What of General Le Van?"

"He is lost, General. It is impossible! Once he got through the front lines near Lai Thieu I lost all possibility of finding him before the fall. He dissolved into the madness."

"Damn! Did you not understand the seriousness of the situation, Hanh? I must talk with the general."

There was a pause at the other end.

"Oh, I understand," Hanh said, "and I guarantee you I pursued the general with all due intent. He was just one small step ahead. Under his uniform he wore civilian clothes. I have his uniform."

The revelation shocked Minh. What did this mean? Was he indeed defecting? Or maybe trying to save his spy from the calamity?

"Anyway," Hanh continued, "once he breached the front lines he vanished with most of the civilians retreating into Saigon. The city must be bursting with people. There is nothing I can do now but wait for the fall, then locate him. There will be nowhere for him to hide.

"Have charges been filed against General Le Van?" Hanh continued. "Have you issued a general order for his arrest?"

"No," Minh said after a lengthy pause. "I want to restate that the general is only *suspected* of misconduct at this time."

"I do not remember you using the word *suspected* before," Hanh replied. "You asked that I arrest the general...that it was a matter of national security..."

"I know what I said!" Minh barked into the phone. "New information...is coming to light. It may all be a misunderstanding. But until we have the general, there is no telling what to make of it. I can tell you nothing more at this time...except you must find him and return him to Hanoi as soon as possible."

Hanh paused on the other end. *This is very unusual,* he thought. *What was going on? I must talk to Mother.*

"General," Hanh said. "I just attempted to reach Mother and she was not available. Do you know where she is?"

"Gao Jinh?" Minh said. "Uh...I have no idea, Hanh. Everyone here is busy. It's...unsettled. And...I do not want you talking with anyone about this matter, including your mother."

"What?" Hanh shouted. "That is absurd, General. Do you know what you are saying? Mother is the highest level of authority and...you do not want me telling *her*? Ridiculous!"

"Now, we do not want to start...uh, confusion in Hanoi with this. It is not..."

"No! This has gone far enough, General. I do not know what game you are playing with me, but I will get to the bottom of this when I get hold of Mother."

"You must listen to me," Minh said, but there was a click and the line went dead.

With dread and foreboding, the general slowly replaced the handset in its cradle. Minh could feel the situation moving further out of hand, spreading insidiously like some terminal disease. This story would not end to his liking. There was no possibility he could keep this from becoming a scandal. Even a fabulous tale would bring with it hard questions. Among them: Minh's lifelong support of the perpetrator; or he would have to deal with Hanh and the matriarch—become their puppet. It was a thought that was unacceptable to the general. *My career is over,* he realized. *It is now merely a matter of time.*

Saigon, South Vietnam
April 30, 1975

The Fourth Day

Hanh rode outside the turret as the tank roared through Saigon streets. They came to the gutted US Embassy and rolled quickly past the looters without even slowing. As they proceeded toward Independence Palace, Hanh observed a quiet dread among the silent spectators with only an occasional cheer going up at the sight of the People's Army. As they neared the palace, Hanh could see the lead tank level the gate and enter the courtyard. The tanks fanned out, setting up defensive positions. As his tank came to a stop, Hanh jumped down and staggered sideways into the tank. He had been suffering dizzy spells since his injury, and his balance was unsteady.

He looked around, somewhat amazed. What an incredible sensation! He was standing in the courtyard of the South's presidential palace. The war was obviously, emphatically over! Along behind the tanks came a soldier waving a huge Liberation Star flag. The bearer was grinning ear to ear as he approached the palace. Hanh stepped in front of him.

"Give me the banner," he said to the boy.

"Yes, sir," the boy said, coming to a stop.

Hanh carried the flag up the palace steps, stopped and turned, and began waving the huge banner back and forth. As he could plainly see, the event was being filmed by several foreign news cameras. One reporter and his cameraman came running up to the colonel.

"What is your name?" the reporter asked him in French.

"I am Colonel Boa Hanh of the People's Army of Vietnam. My father fought alongside Ho in our long struggle. It is a tremendous honor to claim the palace and declare victory for my country," he said, in perfect French.

One by one the foreign news correspondents came and interviewed the colonel. Seeing one such filmed report days later, Gao Jinh would say, "He was so like his father there, proud and brave. A hero. A shining example of the best our country has produced. I was humbled by him."

Trucks and tanks loaded with *Bo Doi*, as the young People's Army soldiers were called in the North, rolled into Saigon in ceaseless waves. They seemed tightly disciplined and wide-eyed curious to a Southern population that viewed the now-silent invasion with awe and astonishment.

By late afternoon the city had filled with soldiers, tanks, and equipment. Like Hanh, they were surprised to find stores and markets glutted with supplies and sundries. Looking into stereo shops, furniture stores, motorcycle dealerships, restaurants, and all manner of capitalist ventures, they were amazed by the abundance and prosperity of the nation they had conquered. Were these the downtrodden, suffering brethren they had been told about? The exploited Southerners who were desperate for rescue from the North? From the puzzled looks on the faces of many soldiers, it was evident some misunderstanding had occurred.

Later that evening, Hanh found himself at a roadside food vendor's stand where many *Bo Doi* were queued up waiting to order a newfound delicacy: the American hot dog. With a few low but audible comments, Hanh was recognized and a path to the counter opened for him. He placed his order with the restaurateur and, upon delivery, examined his tubular dinner. But before he could take a bite the stand operator stopped him.

"No, sir. You need to put mustard on first. It is the way it is eaten."

The man showed him how to manipulate the squeeze bottle, then dabbed a little relish on as well. With his first bite, Hanh broke into a broad grin as the soldiers around him laughed and clapped.

"Delicious!" Hanh pronounced to the small crowd.

After ordering two more, he promptly stuffed the rest of it in his mouth.

Later, emerging from the crowd with two hot dogs, Hanh walked to the edge of the busy Bien Hoa Highway, taking alternate bites from each hand. The number of vehicles, motorbikes, buses, trucks, cars, and taxis passing by was amazing! *Such a busy, industrious city,* he thought. *Now that the war has ended, perhaps Hanoi will again be busy.*

Across the street, a large crowd of *Bo Doi* surrounded an ice cream stand. He would have to try some of that next. He continued to eat his tubular delights while casually watching people on the street and the vehicles zipping by. It had been an unbelievable day. *Maybe I will write a book about it one day,* he thought. *I must find a communications hut and call Mother. She will be most interested.*

There!

As he had been surveying the crowd across the street, a man had quickly looked away as Hanh's gaze fell on him. The man was walking swiftly away, moving south down the road. He wore a light green shirt and black pants. Now walking the same direction down his own side of the street, Hanh looked harder at the man who was weaving his way between crowds of oncoming people, seemingly anxious to get away. Could it be? Yes, it might very well be. Hanh picked up the pace, repeatedly stumbling as his head continued to swim from his injury.

"Stop!" Hanh shouted, stepping onto the roadway.

The man turned to look but was obscured by the crowd and traffic.

"Stop that man!" Hanh yelled, running into the street as soldiers and citizens looked up in interest.

A motorcyclist hit Hanh with a glancing blow, spinning the colonel sideways into a troop transport that crushed and rolled the colonel under its wheels before screeching to a halt.

As people screamed and women turned their children away, the young man in the green shirt continued down the street, already late for dinner and seemingly unaware of the carnage behind him.

In the street, the cyclist who had hit Hanh managed to keep his bike upright while sliding to a halt. He looked back at the mangled body with seeming disinterest. In his pocket was a small fortune in dong that would one day help him become the wealthiest man in Vietnam. At his feet were the remains of a half-eaten hot dog.

Bozeman, Montana

Katy, Tim, and I were sitting around the breakfast table. Corn Chex and Wheaties were in the box and the bowls and scattered around the tabletop. We were a little slow this particular morning, having enjoyed shots and beer at the Molly Brown until closing and then gravy-doused midrats at Manny's. So the insistent, loud, and unwelcome rap on the door both startled and annoyed us.

"Okay, okay," I said, on my way to the door as the pounding continued. This had better be good.

"Turn on the TV," Clark said, nearly rolling over me as the door opened. "Channel Eight. Turn it on now!"

I turned to a smiling Heather and gave her a "what the fuck?" kind of look. She just shrugged.

"C'mon, Cameron. Get your ass over here. You've gotta see this shit!"

Clark had the TV on and we crowded around him as the black and white portable slowly came to life, revealing a reporter with a microphone stuck in his face standing in front of a big iron fence.

"...as you already know, by prearrangement with the South Vietnamese government...the tanks and forces of the People's Army began moving into Saigon just before noon. Not a single shot was fired. The lead tank battalion rolled on through Saigon...to the presidential palace, here behind me, without even slowing. Our cameras caught the lead tank smashing the gate at the palace...and the waving of the Liberation Star flag of North Vietnam, now the national flag of all Vietnam, on the steps of the South Vietnamese White House."

"It's over," Clark said, simple and quiet. "Can you fuckin' believe it?"

"Heavy," Tim said.

"In the streets," the reporter continued with backup footage, "there was stunned silence at the unbelievable sight of this war, nearly thirty years old now, ending in such a quick and merciful way. Even to seasoned reporters, the sight of truck after truck of Northern soldiers rolling through the streets was absolutely shocking."

We had known things were looking bad for the South, but the sudden end had caught us unaware. The first sensation I felt was relief. Not shame or anger or regret, or sympathy, or hatred. It was like a tooth that stops hurting; a headache that goes away. I was relieved it had finally come to an end and we wouldn't have to deal with war news any longer. We knew we had lost Vietnam, but we had lost it long ago. Now, maybe we could really begin the recovery.

"Why couldn't this have happened in '70? Or '67?" Clark said, fuming. "The government pissed around for years with everyone crying for a pullout...while thousands died. In the end...with all the dead now...the lost feet, legs, arms, faces...what was it worth? For us, the poor sons-a-bitches who fought...what was it worth? And now that it's all said and done...who will give a damn?"

It was a repeat of Clark, circa 1970. I didn't like it.

"Don't be backslidin' on me, Clark," I said. "Only time will tell."

"Doncha feel some anger, Mark? Look at you. You'll never be whole again...inside or out. Where's the emotion, man? What do you feel, goddamn it?!"

"Oh, I haven't forgotten those little bastards, Clark...and what they're capable of," I said. "But I'm not goin' back to 1970. I like the life I have now. Let's be glad it's over and we're still above ground. That's the good thing. Nobody else will die in this war...or be maimed. I know there are people in Saigon right now who, even in defeat, feel the same way. They're glad it's over, too...and they're ready to move on and start a new life without war. God bless 'em... and us."

Saigon, South Vietnam
April 29, 1975

9:22 a.m. – The Third Day

Before Dat was within thirty meters of the embassy gate, he ran into the human wall that fronted it. No polite excuse-mes or sorry-'bout-thats would get him through the throng. It was time for pushing, elbowing, and wedging. With the teeming mass teetering on a jagged edge, Dat slowly made his way forward while ducking blows and curses thrown his way. When he was within ten meters he could hear the young woman who had climbed to the top of the gate bantering with a guard inside.

"I know ambassador's secretary," the woman was saying. "Get her and see. She no leave me behind."

"Nobody gets in," Dat heard the Marine say. "Get off the gate."

"You lie," the woman said, insistent. "You just let man in!"

"He was an American journalist. Different thing."

"You have let many Vietnamese inside, too. Look at them!" she said, pointing. "I know secretary. Please, for her sake, you find her. I no joke."

"Get off the gate, ma'am. Don't cause trouble."

This is not the way, Dat reasoned. I will not get past the gate. But what else could be done? He looked up and down the wall searching for inspiration, some weakness in the fortification. Doing so, he noticed several men on a steel grid-like power pole just to the right of the gate. They were attempting to get into the embassy compound by stepping off the pole onto the barbed wire that topped the fence. Of course, American Marines were right there turning them back. However, Dat thought, that would be a better vantage point to survey things. From there you could see into the compound. He began working his way toward it.

It took Dat half an hour to cover the twenty meters and reach the girder. Looking up, there were perhaps six or seven men already clinging to the pole. He began climbing. It was not hard to work his way up and into a position where he could now see the thousand or so Vietnamese standing in the street and the embassy grounds inside. There was much activity in the compound as Vietnamese with their luggage were being shuffled back and forth. A company or so of US Marines stood guard at the wall and at various intervals throughout the embassy grounds.

As the helicopters continued their monotonous whirlwind of arrival and departure, Dat searched the faces of the lucky Vietnamese inside who were queuing in line or following escorts, but did not see anyone resembling Nu Chi.

Below him now and to his left, the stubborn woman who had been straddling the top of the gate had been joined by another woman and two men. Dat could sense the guard's growing agitation. As the opposing forces shouted at one another, the young Marine raised his rifle, again requesting the Vietnamese to get off the gate. The tension increased sharply and the crowd, sensing this new development, surged forward. The American servicemen standing guard gave each other anxious looks as an officer strode forward into the confrontation.

Dat was paying scant attention as he continued searching the faces in the compound. In an instant, like looking through a scope and suddenly finding your target fully in vision, there she was! Dat gasped at the clear, undeniable sight of Nu Chi and nearly lost his hold. Looking composed and intent, she was walking calmly along the drive toward the main entrance with a tall, thin-haired American. They were perhaps only twenty meters from the main door of the embassy.

Dat began screaming and waving his arm, but his cries were drowned in the rising heat of the confrontation below him: the Vietnamese and Americans now shouting loudly at one another with the general voice of the crowd rising as well. This caught Nu Chi's attention and she looked toward the main gate, seemingly right at Dat. As he waved wildly and screamed her name, Dat's voice and actions were lost in the commotion. Nu Chi continued toward the entrance and was now at the steps leading to the door.

"No!" Dat screamed in frantic, helpless rage. "Nu Chi! Nu Chi!"

It was at that moment the Marine lieutenant fired off his pistol three times just over the heads of the fence-sitting Vietnamese. Everyone in the compound and outside was momentarily stunned as they caught their breath at the sudden burst of gunfire.

In the blink of quiet that followed, Dat, who ignored the gunshots as if they had never happened, continued screaming her name.

"Nu Chi! Nu Chi!"

The Vietnamese outside, and the American guard inside, turned as one to look at him.

"Nu Chi!" he screamed again, madly waving like the broken arm of a windmill.

Shocked at hearing her name shouted in the lull, Nu Chi searched the scene and located him. It took just an instant for her to recognize Dat, and now she was running to the gate.

They fell into each other's arms, sobbing insanely. Dat pulled back, but upon seeing her face collapsed at her feet. The Marine lieutenant and the tall American stood impatiently to one side.

"Umm, Nu Chi," the tall American began. "If you don't mind, who is this man? I thought everyone you knew had left the country."

"Brian...," Nu Chi said in English, "this is my uncle..."

She stopped midsentence, turned to Dat and said in Vietnamese, "You still have your papers? You are my uncle?"

Dat nodded.

"Uncle...," Nu Chi said, "this is Brian Ochs. I work with him at the Treasury."

"Yes," Dat said. Then in his best attempt at pigeon English. "It is pleasure to meet."

"Do you have some ID? You know, *Can Couics*," the lieutenant broke in.

"Yes. Yes," Dat said, producing his papers and smiling.

"My uncle lives on a remote farm," Nu Chi quickly added. "He has never liked government bureaucracy..."

"Oh, come on!" the lieutenant protested. "These are *six years old*! You expect us to buy this?"

"Brian," Nu Chi said, ignoring the lieutenant, "as you can tell, seeing my uncle is quite unexpected. He is a recluse. I did not think I would ever see him again. Now...I cannot just leave him behind. He must come with me."

"This guy could be anyone," the lieutenant said.

"Lieutenant," Brian Ochs announced, looking somewhat skeptical himself, "Luang Nu Chi has worked closely and competently with the US government for many years. Her father is a highly regarded financial wizard who literally kept the South more or less solvent for over twenty years. I am personally responsible for Nu Chi's safety and evacuation. And now...I suppose her uncle's as well. There's nothing else to be done."

Nu Chi and Dat beamed at one another.

"So...with that we will just take our leave," Ochs said, grabbing Dat's *Can Couics* from the lieutenant and guiding the pair toward the embassy, leaving the lieutenant shaking his head.

"We'll have to work on getting you some new identification papers once we're on the carrier," Brian added as they walked up the embassy steps.

As the sun set on the Republic of South Vietnam, Dat and Nu Chi sat to the side of the main deck of the USS *Blue Ridge* among the teeming refugees and amid the constant chop of arriving and departing helicopters. It was not a beautiful or brilliant sunset, but a dreary muting of a dishwater sky. The ecstatic euphoria and joy of their unlikely reunion inevitably evolved from bursts of laughter to warm smiles, loving looks, and thoughtful glances. Among the constant activity on deck, their musing turned to serious reflection and the profound questions that each faced; questions that could not be avoided.

Looking out at the small armada of American ships, Dat realized his traitorous actions were now irreversible. His future was with the very people he had always considered the enemy and bound to a woman, he admitted to himself, he hardly knew. How had it come to this? What insanity had driven him from a country he had fought so hard for and a position he had labored decades to obtain? In the bargain, he had deserted his only friend and champion, the first woman he had ever loved, his career, and his very country. What were his ancestors thinking now? Traitor! Yes, he thought glumly, the word suited him well.

Nu Chi was wondering just what they would do next? How would they deal with the government?... Her parents?... Each other? She was aiding and abetting a man she loved but with whom she had spent only a few precious hours. To say he was an enemy of her country as well as the United States was a laughable understatement; if found out, she was sure she could be sent to prison for a long time.

More, though, her thoughts centered on her family. How in

the world would she explain this man? The truth? Who would believe it?

They did not look at one another as their reflective moods overtook them. From the rear of the ship came a clamoring and much shouting. Both looked aft as sailors from the ship pushed a helicopter to the edge of the deck.

"What are they doing?" Nu Chi said.

"Making way for more helicopters," a man to her right said. "So many have come from the mainland that there is no room to land."

Watching, Dat saw the helicopter slide off the deck and quickly sink into the ocean. It was not unlike his old life; pushed off a precipice and gone forever. He had made his choices.

Lee Nah had been left behind, and Dat found this harder to bear than he thought it would be. Somewhere inside him, his love for her remained. It would never go away. The hurt and disappointment he knew she would feel would haunt him the rest of his days. The thought added to his misery.

But then another came to him in his strange new surroundings: My actions have not been unreasonable! Had he ever been truly happy? Communism did not suit him and he could not abide Lee Nah's zealous obsession with it. Could he have successfully hidden his disdain for the system and lived a lie the rest of his life? He was a nationalist...not a Communist! He had warred only for his country's liberation, and it had come to pass. For Vietnam, he felt communism was better than tyranny. But it was not for him. What, really, had his journey these last few days been about?

He looked at Nu Chi, who caught his eye and returned a hesitant smile. Time had not been kind to his feelings for her. Absence had not made his heart grow fonder. Instead, his heart had been deceived and their love for one another muted by years of lonely desperation and the impossibility of it all. Gazing at that lovely face and seeing the strength within, his heart warmed in a way it never had with Lee Nah.

"I have missed you...terribly," Dat said, at last. "It was as if I were in prison all those years...and now, I am free. Yes...*free!*"

"I am sorry to say...but I lost faith at the end," Nu Chi said, lowering her eyes. "Even your promises failed to inspire me. I lost all hope...in my country and in you. I thought I had thrown all those years away...that I should have looked forward and left with my family. But, once more...you amazed me, Le Van Dat. How did you do it?... You amazing man!"

His heart soared. In that moment he was struck with exactly what he had seen in Nu Chi all those years ago; something Lee Nah had worked hard to erase. *This* was his soul mate. This was the woman God had put on earth for him to be with. Their meeting and unusual relationship was not by accident, and yet he had nearly thrown it away! Some otherworldly instinct had made him act, had driven him to this regardless of the unreasonableness of it all. His head swam in the awareness that this might be what his ancestors desired all along. This woman, this union, would be the foundation of his life; to be cherished for all time. For just the second time, he took her in his arms and they kissed.

Hanoi, Vietnam

May 2, 1975

General Cho Trang poked his head in the door.

"Minh," he said.

General Tran Van Minh slowly raised his head from where it had rested in his arms. He hadn't slept much now for days. He looked and felt utterly exhausted.

"May I enter?" General Trang asked. "Can we talk?"

"Of course," Minh said, indicating a chair with a wan wave of the hand.

"You look terrible," Trang said. "You must have heard the news of Boa Hanh."

"Yes," Minh said without emotion. "Most unfortunate."

"Indeed," added the general, looking somber. "They say Gao Jinh was devastated by the news."

Minh nodded. He hadn't been sure how to accept the news when told. Personally, he thought Boa Hanh a snake who certainly would not be missed. But he wasn't sure where this put him. He had no idea yet if Gao Jinh, or any of those who had been in contact with Hanh, knew of Dat's treachery. So far, nothing had been said.

"There is more news," Trang said edgily. "Your close and dear friend...General Le Van Dat...is missing."

At the mention of the name, Minh steeled himself. He made no outward show of emotion and said nothing in return. After an awkward moment, Trang continued.

"The last to see him was a young lieutenant somewhere near the front lines. He said the general was most insistent on getting to the front...that he had to be in the action. No one has seen or heard from him since."

"No one?" Minh asked.

"No. They say Lee Nah has gone into seclusion. Heartbroken, no doubt."

"Vanished? No trace?" Minh said.

"None," the general replied. "No body and no reports from him, or about him from any source. I am so sorry, Minh. I know you were close to the general. He was an honorable soldier. But is it not just like Dat to fight to the end?"

"Yes," Minh said, perking up. "He was a true warrior. The best...the bravest...I ever knew."

"We will have to wait and hope something turns up yet...a few more days, eh? He may surface. Perhaps he is grievously wounded and somewhere in a hospital. Talk of a memorial service is circulating. The little general had many friends it seems."

With that, the general rose and made his goodbyes. Once he had gone, the first smile in many days worked its way to Minh's lips.

"He was also the luckiest man I have ever known."

August 1998

Chico, California

I have always been a good husband and father, good athlete, good businessman, good around the house. There is a saying: jack of all trades; master of none. At midlife I have done a half-century checkup and believe I fit that description perfectly, with one notable exception: I was a very good warrior. I had the *opportunity* as a young man to test battle and know I exceeded most men in this exercise. Once enmeshed in the war, I killed men with the efficiency and temperament of a terrorist.

It goes without saying I would rather have great artistic or creative talent, terrific math skills, a photographic memory. I would prefer to have not discovered this one, undeniable talent. Certainly, to not have killed. To not have been immersed in the terrible cruelty, debauchery, ruin, evil, and senselessness. But at midlife, under close scrutiny, it is undeniable: I was better at war than anything else I have ever tried. What, then, do I do with this? How do I face the rest of my days knowing *that* is the best I will be?

With the inevitable movement of time, my hatred for the Vietnamese ebbed through the years until, one day, I realized it had left me. That day, I felt as if a heavy burden had been lifted from my shoulders. All I feel toward my former enemies now is empathy. It is as if I have something in common with the Vietnamese. We share the war's awful experience. Their horror was as great as mine; their losses greater. More than twenty years have passed and the Vietnamese are a long way from being *over* their war, while at home I wonder if we are already forgetting the hard lessons it taught us.

I rarely think of JT's body on that pole anymore, and we can talk of Stan in an easy way now. I won't deny that the pain, loss, and occasional dreams are still with me, but it is blessedly muted with each passing year, and only time knows if they will one day vanish from my thoughts altogether. Aging does some funny things. In my dotage, I even regret the passing of the Georgia boy, Bubba Binks. I know someone, somewhere, loved him and still misses him to this day. I can relate to such emotions.

It is odd, this buffing and chaffing of time on feelings and memories. Youth, high school, the war, and college now seem so long ago; my adolescent peculiarities so alien that the thoughts and images of that time are like nothing more than an old, scratched movie I can't get out of my head. I find at nearly fifty, the disconnect with my youth is complete.

Except for a call one weekend, out of the blue, my age-old reflections of that youth might have been safely preserved.

"I gotta tell ya, man," Bird said, hunched over his lemonade, "I'm a little insecure about where we're goin' with this thing."

"Yeah, me too," I said.

The Birdman and I were on the deck at the back of my home attending to burgers and sausages as they sizzled and spit on the barbie. While I was more interested in the activity of my twelve-year-old daughter and her friends on the trampoline, Bird kept bringing me back to business.

"Life's risky, Bird. We're in a business that seems to be changing by the hour. If we don't move our business to the internet, we'll get run over. In fact, we're already late for that bus."

"Couldn't we ease into it? Maybe just a simple, informative website? Heck, I've heard you say it yourself...there's nothing like the personal approach to selling."

"We've been over this. Today, our customers are more and more going directly to websites, making decisions and purchases without ever talking to another human being. There is nothing like a personal sales pitch...if you get the chance. I have a feeling that's going by the wayside and that the opportunity for better growth exists on the internet. We are doing this, Bird."

"And, I like the idea of spending more time in town. My three kids are still at home, but Stan graduates next year. Yikes!"

"All right, okay," Bird sighed. "I get it, man. Maybe I'm just getting old."

"Yeah, I know what you mean...the world's really changed. Look at these kids," I said, gesturing to my daughter's friends. "I'm not sure where they all live. Katy knows. My point is they're not from this neighborhood. My daughter met them at school. She doesn't even know all the kids on our block. There are just so many choices for socializing and entertaining yourself nowadays. And we cart them all over town. When I think of what my old man would have said if I'd asked him to take me across town to a friend's house...," and I laughed. I wouldn't have dared.

"Honey," Katy called from the house. "There's a phone call for you. Sez he's an old friend."

"Be right there," I replied. "Okay, Birdman. The grill is yours. Make sure you burn my kielbasa. I like 'em that way."

"Well-done will not be a problem," Bird replied.

I slid through the sliding doors and grabbed the phone from Katy.

"Hello."

"It's been a long time, man," the voice said. "Do ya recognize an old friend?"

There *was* something familiar. Put on the spot, though, I couldn't come up with anything.

"Sorry. I guess not. Who is this?"

"It's Buddy, man. Bud Brody. Surely you haven't *totally* forgotten me."

"Oh my God. Buddy!"

From across the room, Katy looked at me with raised eyebrows.

"Ha, found you on the internet, man. Wasn't hard. A lot harder makin' the call, if you know what I mean."

"Yeah, I think I do," I said, sitting down on a stool at the kitchen counter.

There was a pause in which we both thought of the years that had passed; the wall built between us long ago; a wall that still existed.

"Anyway," Buddy continued, "I know we disagreed on a lot of stuff in high school...and we went our separate ways and all...but we're old friends, man...the oldest."

I was glad to let Buddy talk while I collected myself. He was certainly an old friend, all right. But sometimes it's better to move on and let sleeping dogs lie.

"So, how'd you end up in Chico, California?"

"After I graduated there was an opening at a radio station here for a copy writer. It was the only job I could find."

A pregnant pause ensued. We hadn't talked for decades and yet we were still having a hard time drumming up a conversation.

"Was that Katy who answered the phone?"

"Yeah."

"I can't imagine what that's like. You've known each other all your lives. Then again, maybe that's what works. I've been married three times. It just doesn't seem a good idea for me. You got any kids?"

"Three. Look...Buddy. It's been thirty years since we talked. Why now? Why'd you call? What's this about? Somethin' happen?"

"Naw...I don't really know, man. Just...you know. I guess I feel a little guilty...giving you all the shit in high school. I was kind of an asshole...and I feel bad about that. When you're young everything seems so black and white. It was the whole Vietnam thing, man. That fucking war consumed me."

"Yeah, I was a little consumed by it, too. You were right, Bud. Everything you said was true. You got it. I don't know how...but as a teenager you understood it all. The political bullshit and our country's misguided policies...you nailed it. Me?... I was ignorant and patriotic, just like most kids. I went off to that fucking war and it sucked. You have no idea how much, Buddy. The war was a fucking mess. Some good people...better people than you and me...died in Nam. Stanley...JT Johnson, the best friend I ever had...and Joe Wills just disappeared. I have no idea what happened to him, but I'm pretty sure the war fucked him up, too. But you...well; you went off to Canada because you always were one smart son of a bitch. Lucky for you. The rest of us...we just got our asses kicked."

"Whoa. Hold on, Mark. I'm tryin' to make amends here, bro. I'm not that fuckin' smart. I was a cocky kid, that's all. I feel bad... you gotta believe that. Maybe I saw it correctly...but life's choices aren't so clear, are they? I'm sorry...okay.... That's why I called."

"Yeah," I said, cooling down. "Okay, I'm sorry, too. Those were some tough years for me."

"But, Joe Wills, Mark...maybe you lost touch but he sure isn't dead. I found him on the internet, just like I found you. He only lives a little ways from you in Sacramento. I'm surprised you two haven't gotten together."

"Sacramento?"

"Yeah. Hell, he's in the phone book."

"I'll be damned."

"We were so young, man," Bud said. "My choices weren't easy

ones either, ya know. I was exiled from my own country for almost ten years."

What the fuck?

"You're fuckin' kiddin' me, man," I stammered, now royally pissed off. "Canada was tough?! I returned from Nam totally fucked up...to a country that hated veterans. I was treated like shit for all the sacrifices I made. Canada was *tough*! What a loada shit."

"Okay, okay," Buddy cut in. "Fuck it. I really didn't call to upset you...to argue like we used to. I can tell thirty years later you're not over the war yet. Okay, I get it. We'll just leave it at that. Tell you what; I'll call in another ten years. Maybe we can talk then."

The line went dead.

As always, Bud Brody was right. Time had helped, but I wasn't over the war. Another ten years might not do it, either. It was frustrating how time moved along and I didn't think of Nam for ages... then! Katy sat down on a stool and looked at me.

"He was reaching out, Mark; must have been really tough for him to do that. It could have helped both of you. I think you should consider that. Get his phone number and call him back."

So I thought about it. I was surprised at how quickly I had gotten angry with Buddy. Evidently there remained some lingering hostility. I had long said those who had protested were right to do so. They were the smart ones with convictions who followed their conscience, which is a noble and difficult exercise at times. I had agreed with Jimmy Carter, too, when he granted amnesty to those who had fled the country to avoid being drafted. The amnesty was an essential part of the healing process; of moving the country beyond the war. Carter recognized that and acted correctly. So, what the hell was it between me and Buddy? I guess inside those who served resides a resentment of those who fled, or protested, and it can't be easily wiped clean with the sponge of reason, understanding, and maturity. The acts of serving and fleeing were of opposing commitments, but often made with the same passion and conviction.

So, I called Buddy back several days later and our conversation was quite civil, though similarly strained. We would never renew our friendship, and I had no desire to ever speak with him again. The chasm between us was unbridgeable, and that was A-OK with me.

Joe Wills, though; that was another matter.

I rummaged through old memorabilia to come up with Joe's Hula Girls postcard with its odd message: *Have a nice life.* Looking at the scratched writing, I was filled anew with wonder at its intent. What had happened to make Joe write such a life-altering message? It wouldn't be hard to get hold of him and ask. But like Bud Brody's call, would one from me to Joe be likewise received? Looking at the postcard it seemed to be saying *leave me the fuck alone.*

"I think you should do it," Katy said over tea one night. "This whole midlife crisis thing of yours...perhaps a talk with Joe would help clear up some unfinished business...like I think your talks with Buddy might have. At this point, I don't know how you can avoid it."

"Some things in life need to be left alone," I said.

"Some things in life need to be exorcised. Well...it's your call," Katy said.

These kinds of things are easier for women; I'm pretty sure of that. Male curiosity is a few notches lower than the fairer sex's. But it was more than just a social reconnection. We were Vietnam vets. Joe's postcard was from a time filled with emotion and anxieties I knew a lot about; he didn't own the market on that! He didn't pen his postcard haphazardly. There was a mystery and intrigue to the thing that said, *Danger, leave this alone.* My recent conversations with Buddy had dredged up some long-absent hostilities and emotions that weren't welcome back! Did I really need another dose?

I had pinned Joe's postcard up next to my desk at the office and would, on occasion, find myself pulling it down, turning it over, and wondering. Should I call? Without that physical evidence, I could have left Joe alone and gone on with life. But, having the postcard in my hand was like holding the last piece of a puzzle. The thought of completing the puzzle was irresistible.

Finally, I could stand it no longer. I snatched up the phone and dialed his number quickly, before I could change my mind.

"Hello?... Shut up, Marky.... Hello?" a young voice demanded.

"Uh, hello. Is your dad...is Joe there?"

"No, he's workin'. Is this a telemarketer?"

"No. This is just...look, I'll call back later."

"I gotta take a message if you're not a telemarketer. Dad would be real angry if I didn't."

"Okay," I sighed. "Tell him...Mark Cameron..."

"With a K?"

"Yeah...Mark with a K; Cameron with a C. Tell your dad I called and...I'll call another time."

I really hated to leave my name. Who knew how Joe would react when he saw a name from the past he had willfully said good-bye to? I wished he had been there. Or that I hadn't called at all.

The weekend came and I ruined Saturday morning obsessing over whether to call again, or not. After lunch, I grabbed the phone with resolve and again dialed the number quickly. This time Joe himself answered. There was no mistaking the big guy's voice.

"Uh, hello, Joe. It's me...Mark."

"Hello, Mark," Joe responded.

The first two words out of Joe's mouth had a tone of resignation about them, like a man called on to respond but has no desire to do so. Maybe Joe heard the same thing.

"Hey...uh, I've been expecting your call," he added in a more cordial tone.

"I know this must be a surprise...," I started.

"Yeah, for sure...but, uh...my little Stan gave me the message. I had time to think about it. How've you been?" he said. "Shit, that sounded stupid. Where do we start, Mark?"

"How about telling me about your family, Joe? You obviously have kids," I said.

"Oh, so I have to go first."

"Yeah, sorry, it's my dime." Shit, bad humor?

There was a pause that made me feel like an idiot. At that moment I was wishing very hard that Bud had never mentioned Joe Wills and Joe and I had just gone on with our lives. Too late for that now.

"I married Ginger kinda late in life," Joe started. "Let's see...it was 1985. I was working in Palo Alto...living in Mountain View. I'm a finish carpenter, much like your dad...probably not near as good. Worked for another Vietnam vet there; a guy who was in-country early...like '64. Sorry, I'm rambling. Ginger and I got married and had two kids...Stan and Mark. No, don't say it! Well... the Bay Area just got way too expensive for us in the late '80s, so we moved to Sac...I think in 1990. I like it here, I guess. Okay, enough about me. You talk for a while."

"Stan and Mark, huh," I said, in a light tone, trying desperately for lightness. "I live right up the highway from you in Chico. How about that for a coincidence? I finished MSU after I got out of the Nav. I have a B.S. in Film and Television. Tyrone Sparrow...a guy I served with...and I have a marketing and advertising business. Uh...Katy and I have three kids...and, yeah, my oldest is named Stanley...so there you go. Hell...I'll bet you didn't know I married Katy Wicks?... Stan's younger sister. We got married right after I graduated. I'll bet that's a surprise, huh?"

There was a long pause on the other end. Now what? Damn, this was not going well.

"Joe?"

"Yeah," came his sudden reply. "You married Stan's little sister, then?" It was announced more as a statement than a question.

"That's right," I said. "Her first husband...not sure you knew about him...died in a car wreck. We ended up together. I'm a happily married man, Joe. I think I've always loved Katy."

"Mark," Joe said suddenly, after another long pause. "I need to see you."

"Okay," I said, "how about some weekend soon?"

"No," Joe said. "What're you doin' today? It's Saturday...can we get together today?"

"Uh...I don't think so, Joe," I said, surprised. "We have some friends..."

"Tomorrow?"

"Whoa...what is this about?"

"I, uh, I've got something that's on my chest I need to get out. It's important to me...and you, too. But I can't do it over the phone; no way. Can you come to Sacramento tomorrow?"

"Well...sure, I guess. I'll see if Katy wants to..."

"No, Mark. Don't bring Katy...you'll understand when I see you. You'll have to come here. My son's in the Little League All-Star Game tomorrow, so I can't come up there. You come here and we'll go to his game...and we'll talk. Would you do that?"

August 16, 1998

Sacramento, California

The short conversation with Joe Wills ran through my head as I rolled down Highway 99 to the state capital. From uncomfortable first impressions and labored conversation, Joe had zoomed past many of the customary steps in reacquaintance to an immediate meeting. It was a *Seinfeld* moment. Our brief chat on the phone was puzzling and ominous at the same time. The most obvious question: Why was it so darned important we meet immediately? Inside me, his request fired a familiar emotion that had been missing many years. I was not looking forward to this reunion. I felt like the guy who can see an accident about to happen but cannot resist watching.

I would connect with I-5 at Sacramento, get off on Seamas, and turn north on Freeport, per Joe's instructions. The whole trip would take less than two hours. Before noon this Sunday, I would be at Joe's front door. I was growing more nervous and uncomfortable the closer I got.

The house, a single-level rambling ranch with bikes and trampoline in the front yard, sat in the middle of the block. An older Ford pickup was in the driveway, with a still older Toyota in the garage. It looked as if Joe needed new shingles; the sidewalk was cracked and uneven. I walked up and knocked on an old aluminum storm door that banged in the frame as I did so.

The door opened immediately, and in the shadow behind the screen I could make out the large frame of Joe Wills. He spoke first.

"Well, hey...look who's at my front door."

Seeing his silhouette, I could tell he wasn't as muscled or thick as he'd once been. He pushed open the storm door.

"Thanks for asking me down, Joe. It's great to see you again," I said, grabbing the offered hand.

His appearance shocked me. His face was pocked and pitted like someone who'd had a disfiguring case of acne as a teenager, though I knew he hadn't. His left eye was clouded and lazy in the socket like a blind man's. The smile he flashed, though, was the old Joe Wills.

"I appreciate your comin'. I realize how bizarre this must seem. Katy probably thinks I'm a real nutcase. How is she, by the way?"

"Great. She's always great. And, you know, regardless of how long it's been, I think we still qualify as old friends. You'd never ask such a thing if it weren't important to you. Though, you've sure got me wondering."

"Yeah, well, we'll get to that. Did you go to Stan's funeral?" he asked. "What was that like?"

"No...it wasn't a good time for me to be around people at a funeral. I did go to the graveyard for the burial."

Joe just nodded. We were joined in the living room by whom I guessed to be his wife, tugging along a young boy in a baseball uniform.

"Mark, this is my wife, Ginger...and my oldest son, Stan."

"Hello. That's quite a coincidence. My oldest son is Stan, too," I said.

"I'm very happy to meet you," Ginger said. "Joe just hardly ever talks about his past. You're the first old friend of his I've ever met. Thank you for calling and coming down on such short notice."

"It's no problem, really."

"Well," Joe said, hastily, "we'd better get goin'. The game starts at one, but they have warmups. I'll get our little Mark and we'll head out."

I rode with Joe in his truck. Stan sat between us. The ballpark wasn't far, and we spent the time catching up on personal trivia. As Little League parks go, this one was very nice with a well-manicured infield and grass, lights, and a grandstand instead of bleachers.

"Beats the old dirt and rock fields with chicken-wire backstops we had growing up, huh?" Joe said.

I bought hot dogs for everyone at the refreshment stand. As we entered the stands, lots of folks called out to Joe and Ginger. Joe led me up to the top and across to the end of the stands. Ginger and ten-year-old Mark grabbed a seat behind the dugout with other families, far from us.

"I told Ginger we needed some space," Joe said, as we took a seat. "She's a great, great gal, Mark. I was so lucky to find her. She saved my life," he said, with a gravity that underscored the compliment.

"Stan's one hell of a player," Joe continued, lighting up a ciga-rette. "He's big for his age and just owns this league. Pitches, too, though that'll change. He hits the ball too well. Might have a shot at the pros someday, but ya never know. Life does take some funny turns.

"I need to explain a few things," he sighed. "I know my appear-ance caught you by surprise. You couldn't have known my face was disfigured in an explosion my last day in the bush over there. I lost the sight in my left eye. I can see light and shadows, but nothing more. I'm not supposed to drive...couldn't get a license if I wanted to. But, hell, I drive anyway...just who I am, I guess.

"I noticed you shake with your left hand," Joe continued. "Guess I understand that."

"It's easier with people I'm not, uh, comfortable with yet," I responded, truthfully. "You're not the only one with scars. How'd it happen?"

"We'll get to that," he said, quietly. "My mother sent me a small article about your winning the Navy Cross. It was out of the Denver paper. I wasn't too surprised. You always were a tough little son of a gun."

"Not that tough. You know how it was," I responded. "Like the Bronze Star you won...it was more a reaction than anything else. There were too many medals awarded in Vietnam."

"I told *you* about the Bronze Star?" Joe said. "I don't remember that conversation."

I laughed. "No, in the condition you were in I doubt you do."

Joe's son came to the plate. He sent a 2-1 fastball over the left-center fence. We both stood and cheered. Some of the fans knew where Joe was sitting and called out to him. Joe nodded and tipped his cap.

We sat quietly and watched the game a while. I finished the hot dog and licked the spicy mustard off my fingers. Joe lit another cigarette with the one he'd been smoking.

"Ever wonder why us?" Joe said, between innings. "Why our generation? It was the most unpopular war in US history, and it fell right into our laps."

"Just luck?" I said with obvious sarcasm.

"Man...the emotions that came out of the whole thing. The mil-itary brass and politicians seemed to hate us. Our folks thought we were dishonorable and blamed themselves for how they'd raised us. How'd that make you feel, Cam? And our peers? They condemned us for propagating the war. Talk about the shit end of the stick."

"I've had the same thoughts myself," I said. "It was an awful time."

Joe paused, looking intently at me now. A storm brewed behind those sky blue eyes. He had turned the yellowing pages of life's book and glimpsed the injustice of it all, once again, dusting off the anger that had been delegated to the attic of his mind like relics in a duffle bag.

"The World War II generation never appreciated what we did in Nam. They saw all the negative stories on the news and applied it...not only to all us grunts...but our entire generation. The futility of the damn thing...the huge political mistakes and misguided policy that took away our will to win...that cheapened and invalidated Vietnam...they didn't spend five minutes on that. No...it was *our* fault. We didn't fight hard enough. We didn't support the government of the people...didn't know the meaning of sacrifice... like they did in doubya, doubya two."

He looked out over the ball field, a tight squint in the midday sun adding depth to the crow's feet that ran like tributaries from the corners of his eyes. He took a long drag on his cigarette.

"We were braver in the field than our fathers ever were in World War II," he said, exhaling the smoke through his nose like an angry dragon and turning to look at me. Scanning my face, he must have seen the skepticism there. "You don't agree, do you?"

"Oh, c'mon, Joe. Braver?! This is a useless argument you're making. All soldiers are the same in every war...goin' way back in time. Some are brave. Some are cowards. All just wanna live to see a girlfriend or mother again. Who was braver in which war? Who had the nobler cause? It's a moot point...and the soldiers would tell you so. I'm telling you so."

"No, Cam...I'm right about Vietnam and World War II," he said, pointing the two fingers holding his cigarette at me like darts. "You'd better have a damn good reason to ask a man to put his life on the line 'cause there's no greater sacrifice he can make. Our fathers had Hitler, Mussolini, Tojo to fight...some of the biggest evil the world has ever known. They really *were* fighting for freedom and our way of life. Losing wasn't an option.

"What did we have?... Huh? What the fuck did we have to fight for? Not a goddamn thing! We went because we were Americans...because we were asked by our country to go...young men always have been. So we went...and we died. That's bravery and sacrifice above and beyond the call, my friend. Dyin' for nothin'... that's a hell of a thing to ask of a man.

"Well, I'm proud of what I did," Joe continued. "It was the honorable thing...and what I saw was everybody puttin' up a good fight. We did what we could. But the cost was...shit, we're still payin'.

"I went to the Vietnam Memorial. Ever go there?"

"No," I said. "I've never been."

"I went with a couple buddies I served with. I thought, you know, the memorial would be a chance for us to reflect...that we'd stand there and reminisce...the three of us. But as soon as we hit the place, I found myself...indescribably alone. It was damn personal. There was a little kid on a guy's shoulders and he said, 'So, this is Grandpa?' And there was an older couple holding on to one another. What is it about that place?

"I eventually broke down and cried like a baby. Fell to my knees and wept against that black bitch of granite...and didn't feel a bit embarrassed doing it. The power of those names! Stanley, Ray J., and the others...they're all there. It's a beautiful, solemn place. Looking at it...you'd guess the nation must place exceptional value on those named. Hell, someone who didn't know better might mistake it for a victory shrine. Funny, huh?"

"Well...I think in retrospect the nation respects what we did... our sacrifices," I said.

"I'm not so sure. Oh, I hear the homage now and then. You notice that? It's nothing more than guilt. Like the war in the desert... if you can call it that. Desert Storm lasted...what?...a couple days?! I think there were more friendly-fire deaths than enemy KIA. It was held in a flat, stinking desert. No vegetation. No monsoon. No guerrillas. No angry populace to deal with. A much weaker foe than the military or Bush claimed. Man, that must've been rough goin' for those grunts."

He took a long drag on his cigarette. His son finished striking out the side. We both stood and cheered.

"So, what did they get for their weekend war?... Ticker tape parades, yellow ribbons 'round the old oak tree, the collective thanks of a nation. Fuck! It was so obvious...the whole thing. It was a collective guilt trip over how they'd treated us, that's all. Like an adolescent who's trying to right a wrong, the country totally overreacted to Desert Storm. It was embarrassing and pissed me off all over again."

"Okay, you might be right about that," I said. "But I'm glad for the soldiers of Desert Storm. Put your life on the line and that's what you should get."

"Don't talk down to me, Cam," Joe said, looking through smoke that curled menacingly around the marked face. "I'm not disrespecting those soldiers. I would never do that. You *know* what I mean."

"Why labor on it? This isn't going to change anything. Nam happened. It was a long, long time ago. Forget it and move on."

Joe's son came to bat again. This time he hit the first pitch off the center field fence and ended up on third. We stood and cheered.

"Is that what you've done, Cam?" Joe asked as we sat down. "Put it behind you?"

"No," I said, quietly. "Not really. Not yet."

"Didn't think so," Joe said with a raspy chuckle. "Me neither. But I'm not doin' too bad...except for every mornin'."

"Morning?" I said. "What happens in the morning?"

Joe sighed and was quiet while the wheels ground in his head. "There are no mirrors hung in my house...except the one in the bathroom. See...with this," he said, circling his face with his hand, "I can't really grow a beard. Man, I tried...but there are a lot of places where hair doesn't grow anymore. So, I have to shave every morning...you know, to look respectable. To do that, I've gotta look in the mirror because it's like trying to shave lava."

"Hey, it's not too bad. Don't be so vain," I said.

Immediately, I knew I'd said the wrong thing.

"Aw, fuck," I said. "That was a stupid thing to say. I'm really sorry."

There ensued a long quiet stretch where Joe did little but watch the field and suck on his cigarette some more. I felt low. I hadn't felt as low about a misplaced comment in a long time. Meanwhile, Joe's son came to bat again and this time stroked a line drive hard to the third baseman, who couldn't handle it. He reached first and was given a hit by the scorekeeper.

"Tell ya what," Joe said at long last. "Let's just watch the game. You go home and tell Katy I'm just fine. We'll get the families together some weekend for a picnic and, who knows, maybe we can rekindle our old friendship. Whaddya say?"

I didn't say anything but gave Joe a look that said *we've passed that point.* Joe had something serious on his mind, and now I needed to know what it was.

"You shouldn't have called, Mark," Joe said, quietly. "No, no... that's not fair, or right. I sent you the postcard...yeah, I remember doin' it...and you need some answers...and I've got some you can hardly be expecting. But I need to resolve this for Stanley. It's gotta be said.

"I was stationed up by the DMZ...both times in Nam," he began. "Well, it might sound strange, but Stan's outfit ended up in the same area as ours. I saw him once in the back of a transport."

"I remember that!" I said. "Stan wrote about it in a letter."

"Yeah...well, I ran into him again...only up close and personal. It was at another one of those endless battles we fought over there. It was hill 810, or 910...hell, I don't remember. Doesn't matter; it was the same bullshit. The NVA dug in, and some commander wanted to go hit 'em. Drive 'em off that hill. So the Marines attacked...Stan's outfit. The NVA countered. Lots of ordnance was sent in, of course. Didn't seem to touch 'em.

"The unit I was attached to was sent in to give support...a full mechanized company. Sixteen APCs and four tanks. By the time we got there, though, the fighting was essentially over. Those fights always ended that way. The enemy pulled out and disappeared before we could coordinate an attack. Sounds like the whole fucking war, doesn't it?

"We were driving through the bush, mopping up, sorting things out. Hit a clearing and there he was, just standing there. I wasn't as surprised the second time I saw him.

"He was all grown up. I mean he looked like a man, not like the kid I'd last seen. He was real excited to see me...excited to see him, too. He was head honcho of that outfit...lead sergeant. Hell, he was probably still a teenager, but he looked and acted older than that. I knew right away he was a guy I'd have followed into a fight.

"We talked about the war, home, how long we had left in-country...usual bullshit. He was a different kid in Nam."

"Yeah, that's what Katy says, too."

"He mentioned you, as I recall. How the three of us had been in-country at the same time. Stan was proud of that.

"Later, we got bogged down with the APCs and the tanks couldn't go anymore, so we parked 'em in a defensive perimeter at the base of this...hill. Stan's outfit had just come down off the thing, so I went out to talk to him again."

Joe paused. His mouth opened as if to speak, but no words came out. I could see moisture in his eyes, though no tears fell. He collected himself and continued in a barely audible whisper. His eyes looked like they were searching for something far away. I strained to hear him.

"We were, uh...just standing there...the two of us. I don't remember what we were talking about. I don't remember what happened next. I was told this later."

At this point I didn't want to hear what was coming. Like a father of a military son who opens the door to an officer and a priest, I knew that nothing good would follow. But likewise, I also knew there was no other choice but to listen to what had to be said.

"A kid...a young Vietnamese...maybe twelve...had been hiding in a hole, covered up. He rose up from his hiding place...I guess lots of guys saw him. But before anybody could do anything he detonated a satchel charge."

The crowd roared as Joe's son hit another monster shot out of the park. Joe and I sat like statues. Joe glanced at me quickly, then away.

"Stan was between me and the blast," he continued, his voice wavering now. "The blast nearly killed me. I was riddled with shrapnel...but mostly...by pieces of Stan. I was hours on an operating table while they pulled bone fragments and metal out of me. I'm sure I still carry some of Stan with me. It's hard to look in that mirror in the morning."

My head was in my hands. JT's head was on the spike again and the smell was back.

"Fucked up?... Made my experience with Ray J. seem like a picnic," Joe continued. "I'm not sure, but maybe now you understand why I didn't come home. Why I never wanted to see anyone from the neighborhood again.

"Then...you called...and I heard you were married to Katy. Ahhh...I just made up my mind that you needed to know. I can't explain it, but your call made me anxious to get this off my chest... to share it with someone. I dunno if Katy or her family should ever know about this. I'll leave that up to you."

There ensued an immeasurable amount of time when neither of us spoke. Thoughts and visions long buried spun in my head; the war and its cruelty again dominated my thoughts. The old demons never seemed to fully wash away, and now new ones had been added.

"You okay?" Joe said at last.

I looked at him again, this time with a new appreciation. He had carried this secret and curse a long, long time. He was bitter... and who could not understand that? For many, like Joe and Clark, Vietnam was something they suffered every single day.

"Fucking Nam. Fucking, fucking Nam. Yeah, I'm going to be all right," I said. "I'll be damned if I'll let the war drag me back to those days again. I refuse to go there, Joe. I can handle this...it's you I'm worried about. What about Ginger? How much of this does she know?"

"She doesn't. I told her it was a grenade."

"You should tell her this story, too."

He thought on that.

"Why expose her?" Joe said. "Why bring our war...our horror to the uninitiated? She doesn't deserve it. And if I told her, how would she react every time she looked at me? Better to not."

"I don't know that I agree," I said. "Katy and I share everything and it helps...a lot. She's really responsible for me getting back on track. She was my therapist. I think it would really help."

"Now you sound like a doctor," he said. "But you might be right. My Ginger cares. That's the beautiful thing about a good marriage. I don't know, though. I just don't know." He sighed.

"I think you should...and that's all I'll say. Thanks, Joe. Thanks for telling me, and I mean that. I appreciate knowing...and I appreciate your respect and consideration for me, my wife...and the friendship we had growing up. I won't forget this.

"You know, we both knew Stanley well...and I'm sure you'd agree...he'd want you to get past this. He wouldn't want such a thing to ruin your life."

"Hmmm. I didn't think you'd take this so well. No one needs to hear something like this."

"Easier to hear...than live it," I said.

Joe just nodded.

The game ended. The crowd rose and slowly sifted out of the park. We joined Ginger and the boys and all of us went out for pizza. In the brief time I had been with them, I was fond of Joe's family. They seemed healthy and secure. There were smiles and laughter from Joe, too. In this group, he was at peace with himself.

Joe walked me to my car. We faced one another and briefly hugged, as old friends will.

"Say hi to Katy for me. Take care of those kids. And...I hope you'll stay in touch. I promise to do my part from now on."

"I wish you'd have called, Joe," I said. "We could have had this talk twenty-five years ago."

"No, Cam," he said. "We couldn't have. Have a good drive home."

As I pulled away from the curb, I realized I was leaving something behind I had come with: my midlife crisis. Like the day I woke up in the Saigon hospital and the agony of JT's death was gone, my maudlin depression over turning fifty was gone. Before I reached the end of the street, I was laughing at myself. What craziness! Fifty?... Hell, I was happy to be fifty.

I was backtracking to I-5, driving down Seamas, when I noticed the car was getting low on fuel. I started looking for a convenience store. At the I-5 junction there were three stores with gas islands. The choice was an easy one for me...Van's Thriftway.

As an advertising man, I know most consumers don't pay close attention to marketing details, especially in a convenience store. Quick in and out and don't look around much seems to be the idea. But having traveled thousands of miles, I felt I was an expert on convenience stores.

Van's Thriftway is a Shell franchise that is always clean, well-organized, and friendly. It seems a safer choice, too: well-lit, ATMs inside the store, caring employees. It is the antithesis of convenience stores and always my personal choice. As I pulled into the lot, my preference was reinforced, from the clean gas islands to the recently resurfaced blacktop.

This Van's had just installed new credit card pumps, but I made the choice to pay inside, figuring to pick up a pop before my two-hour drive and pay for both at the counter.

Inside, I opened the cooler door to grab a Diet Pepsi and was startled to find the elderly face of a little Asian man looking at me from behind the cans. Something clicked and I flashed on Nam. It was like seeing a VC through the jungle. I'm sure it had something to do with the kind of day I was having. But the thought quickly vanished and all that remained was a smiling face.

"Hello," he said. "Hope I didn't surprise you. I'm just stocking shelves back here."

"You gave me a start," I said. "I thought the soft drink companies were putting salesmen in coolers now."

"Ha, let's hope it never comes to that," he said.

I grabbed my soda and headed for the checkout counter. As sometimes happens, I found myself at the end of a long line of people waiting to pay. The little Asian I'd seen stocking shelves inside the cooler came out of the back room. I was surprised to see he was dressed in an expensive suit with a boutonniere in the lapel.

"I can help someone at this register," he said.

I moved with the two people in front of me to the second register. I had an opportunity to observe the man while he processed the retiree and young lady who were in line ahead of me. I thought this clerk very strange. The man was dressed to the nines, yet cheerfully greeting and quickly processing customers as if it were his great honor to be doing so.

"So...you have gas, too," he said as I approached the counter. "The new white Beetle is yours, is it not? Pump number 5?"

"Yeah, you noticed."

"Cute cars," he said. "I like the way they look. Retro."

"Yeah, I had one in college. Guess I fell right into their marketing scheme."

"Will there be anything else? Smokes?"

"No. I don't smoke."

"Me neither. It's bad for your health. Fourteen seventy-nine, please."

I gave him my credit card.

"I've always liked Vans," I said, "but since when are clerks dressing up in nine-hundred dollar suits?"

"No, not nine hundred. On sale for six ninety-five at Brooks Brothers," he said. "Thank you for the compliment, but I am not a clerk...usually. I am Luang Lo. My family owns the Van's Thriftway stores. Sometimes I just pop in for a while."

"Oh, well then...it's a pleasure to meet you. Like I said, I've always liked your stores."

"Thank you. It is nice to hear," he said, smiling. "Do you live here?"

"No. Up the road in Chico."

"I'm sure you know we have three stores there; seventy-two altogether in California."

The other customers had cleared out. It was just the little old guy and me as his clerk hurried off to dust shelves.

"Why the suit?" I asked.

"It is a special day for me," he said, smiling broadly. "Sign here, please."

While I signed, he continued.

"Today I am becoming an American citizen. It's Citizenship Day at the state capitol. Me and a couple dozen folks are taking the oath of citizenship this afternoon."

"Congratulations," I said. "As well as you speak English I thought you were born here."

"Thank you, again," he replied. "Isn't it a fantastic country? I own all this and I am not even a citizen."

"So, why now?" I said.

"Between you and me...I don't like the direction America is moving," he said, leaning on the counter. "The progressive initiative this country had when my wife and I first arrived in '75 has disappeared. There is less tolerance now...and idealism, too. We've stopped dreaming...or believing we can make things better. The impetus to get that back has to come from individual Americans... like you and me.

"You know, where I come from, everyone is poor. In a country as great and rich as this one, can we afford to let the poor down?... Leave people behind? It is our responsibility to help to...at least level the playing field some. Each vote counts...and now I will have one."

"Wow. You sound like a college kid from the '60s," I said.

"Where are they now?... These college kids?" he challenged, looking at me in a way that seemed oddly familiar.

"They're still here," I said. "But...it's not the same anymore. I know what you're talking about...I remember that idealism, those dreams. They got lost and left behind...somewhere in time. Maybe it was Watergate, the end of the draft...Reagan and the rise of conservatism. I don't know...." I trailed off.

"Sounds to me like you'll make a good citizen," I said, brightening. "That's good to see. Ya know, as it turns out, it's a big day for me, too."

"How so?"

"I'm fifty years old today. Half a century. I'm on my way home. My wife is having a surprise party for me."

"But no surprise," he said.

"No. My wife knows I don't like surprises."

"You are a lucky man to reach fifty, you agree?"

"Yeah, I guess so. I'd rather be twenty again."

"But alive and fifty is okay. Hmmm...August 16, 1948," he said. "That date sticks in my mind for some reason. It was an important day. Let me think."

He scratched his chin a few times and rolled his eyes, attempting to locate a memory. Finally, his face lit up.

"Now I remember! I saw it in the paper today," he said. "August 16, 1948 was the day Babe Ruth died. Fifty years ago today."

"No kidding? I had no idea."

"Yes, the Big Bambino. The Sultan of Swat. You must be his reincarnation."

"Not the way I played baseball."

"My wife and I have become huge baseball fans," he continued. "We love the A's...catch four or five games a year."

The door opened and a middle-aged woman with two beautiful twenty-something daughters filed in, looking expectantly at the man.

"Well, thanks for the talk. It was nice to meet the guy behind Vans."

"Thank you for your business...and the chat," he said. "It was most enjoyable."

As Mark walked to his car, Nu Chi fussed with the boutonniere.

"Who was that?" she said.

"Just another satisfied customer."

As a shimmering sun sank between silhouetted peaks, the delta sky radiated a luminous gold, painting the jungle in a brilliant green that was being quickly consumed by long, ebony shadows.

JT and Mark stood facing the orb like young gods willing their sun to sit and remain on the horizon. Both were lean, bronzed, and naked from the waist up. Beer bottles were easily held by the neck with two fingers. They looked upon their world through aviator sunglasses ringed in gold frames set ablaze by the fiery bath. Their smiles were lopsided with the swagger of youth and its invincibility.

JT looked to Mark, who slowly shifted his gaze to his friend. Mutual smiles widened in appreciation of the moment.

"You know," JT said. "Someday...years from now...this war'll be long over. We'll be like fifty years old...our kids will be grown. I see a resort on that beach over there and we're on the patio next to the pool...our wives on either side. See it? We have a drink in one hand and a doobie in the other. As we watch the sun go down in this beautiful place, just like now...we'll remember this moment... when we were the young lions. Man...won't that be sweet."

Author's Note

Thank you for joining me in telling the story of the Vietnam Generation. As a work of historical fiction this novel graphically illustrated, through its characters, how the world's greatest superpower lost a war to a third world country.

The faces of war are different depending on your vantage point. Who wins and who loses may not be right, or virtuous, but those who fight are always on the losing side.

If you liked the book and have a minute to spare, I would appreciate a short comment on the page or site where you bought the book. You can even leave a comment on sites like Amazon, even if you purchased the book elsewhere.

Reviews from readers like you make a huge difference to helping new readers find stories similar to *NAM, The Story of a Generation*.

- NamTheNovel.com
- Amazon
- Barnes & Noble
- Goodreads
- iBooks

Your help in spreading the word will allow others to learn about our story, The Story of the Vietnam Generation.

Thank you!

Mel Smith

Acknowledgments

I made a genuine effort to provide an accurate history of the Vietnam War in *NAM: The Story of a Generation*. My goal was to provide an engaging narrative offering the war's and the era's rich past. The thirty years of the war had a significant impact on my generation. I would like other generations to know the backstory: what we faced and how we faced it.

Amongst all the references I used were the recollections and stories of countless veterans I've met through the years. Although I do not remember the vast majority of these guys, there are snapshot memories of a conversation in a bar or a gathering, but not a face or a name. These conversations provided me with a better understanding of the personal impact of the war on the war's veterans. Those who were there will never forget. God Bless you all.

But there was one special individual who shared his most vivid memories of being in the bush in Nam: Mike Uphus of Whitehall, Montana. Mike had the office next door to my advertising agency while I was writing the book. He had been in-country from October 1969 to October 1970 with the Army's 5th Infantry of the 1st Battalion, 61st Mechanized. Stationed out of Quang Tri, he spent most of his time near the DMZ at Firebases C2 and A4. He saw and was involved in many firefights, earned a purple heart, and was a private a few times though he ended up E-4.

Mike's stories were graphic: the real misery of monsoon, the first reactions of being shot at or mortared, the fear of sentry duty in the bush in the black of night, coming home and so much more. His recollections were much appreciated and helped write the book. My everlasting thanks to you, Mike.

For the hardcore history of the Vietnam War, my main source for all things historical was *The History 1946-1975 Vietnam at War* by Lt. Gen. Phillip B. Davidson, USA (Ret.) published by Presidio Press copyright 1988.

Lt. Gen. Davidson was a professional soldier, intelligence specialist, and historian who was actively engaged in the Vietnam War from 1967-1969 as Chief Military Intelligence Officer in country

(J-2 MACV) and knows whereof he speaks (from the jacket of the book). He passed away at the age of eighty in 1996.

But like so many novels, there is more than a little autobiography in *NAM*. The neighborhood and era of Mark Cameron's youth were my own in Helena, MT. So, I know whereof I speak. My childhood memories and experiences, and the kids I knew growing up were background fodder for the Vietnam Generation's story. And, of course, there were my own military experiences with the Navy in and around Vietnam from 1968 – 1970 which established for me the mentality, perspective and daily life of servicemen in that environment.

Many authors thank their agent or publisher and I think that is good use of the space. My publisher, Suzanne Fyhrie Parrott of First Steps Publishing, is a friend and collaborator from many years back. I first got to know Suz when she was freelancing design work out of Helena, MT. For years she designed ads, brochures, logos, etc. for my advertising agency. After moving to the Oregon coast she acquired an interest in publishing. By then I was well underway with my book. That was maybe 20 years ago now and finally, here we are. At times I gave up on the book. Agents and publishers were not interested. But it is a new era for authors, Suzanne has made my book a reality. Many thanks Suz.

Also, one late addition is David Aretha who edited the book. David did an excellent job and caught all the weak parts in the story. Way to go David! Much thanks.

I would be remiss if I did not thank my wonderful life partner; my soulmate, the mother of my children, my best friend and companion, the very love of my life, my wife Alane. Thank you for all those evenings and weekends I spent at the computer or at the library while you dealt with our three children.

Speaking of which, I must also thank them: Tyler, Brian and Janna. Thank you for all the time you gave me while I was buried in either the book or my business and not paying more attention to you.

The people close to you pay a price and, therefore, own a piece of any project that consumes so much your time. Thank you, family, for your contribution.

Mel Smith
Author

Mel Smith was born August 15, 1948, in Helena, Montana. He grew up in a blue-collar neighborhood very similar to the one described in *NAM, The Story of a Generation*, on the edge of town, with dirt streets, no sewer service, and one street light on the corner.

He joined the Naval Reserves in the fall of 1966 and started his active duty in July, 1968. He was assigned to the destroyer U.S.S. *Taylor DD-468* out of Pearl Harbor, just after it was deployed on a six month West Pacific tour. On his tour with the Taylor, he was a member of the deck force, the tough ship maintenance division. He transferred to the U.S.S. *DeHaven DD-727* out of Long Beach, California, which left two months later on its own West Pacific tour. On the *DeHaven,* he had the position of Postal Clerk and took over the ship's post office, the best enlisted duty on the ship. Like all servicemen, he was given an early out in April of 1970, as Nixon was winding down Vietnam.

Smith returned to Montana State University and completed a B.S. in Film and Television, graduating in June 1973.

Mel Smith currently lives in Arizona with his wife, Alane. He has three children and three grandchildren. He still operates his own advertising ageny, AdSmith, and writes in his free time.

NamTheNovel.com

Made in the USA
San Bernardino, CA
30 June 2018